THE 13th HOUR

By Alan Zacher

DEDICATION

To Veronica Porter

I love watching old horror movies, like "The Werewolf", "Dracula", and so on. On Saturday nights, on station METV, on a show called *Svengoolie*, these old horror classics are played. This show, *Svengoolie*, even has a website. I belong to it, and it was there that I met Veronica. Not only has she purchased everything I have written, she believes I'm a 'great' writer. Thank you!

THE 13th HOUR
ALAN ZACHER

Chapter One

"Look at you, Uncle Jim," Amanda chided him, looking down at the old man who was now sitting up on the long, old, black leather couch that was positioned by the office door to the place. The top-half of the wooden-framed door was glass, and in black, block letters it read: **JAMES HURTS, PRIVATE INVESTIGATOR**. "You're a mess … Why, you even have on the same clothes you had on last week when I was here," she continued, handing him the cup of Starbucks coffee that she had brought him. "And you're drinking again," she snapped at him, grabbing the empty whisky bottle off the wooden floor and sitting it on top of the old wooden dining-room table that was close to the north wall.

As she walked back to him, Hurts ran his large right hand over the top of his head, feeling the short stubs of his grey hair, and then he wiped his sagging face with the same hand, this time feeing the long, jagged scar on the left side of his face and the stubs from five days without shaving.

"So what," he said. "I'm old and I'm blind." After taking a big drink of coffee, he reached down and got his pack of cigarettes and lighter from the floor, which were next to the ashtray and his much-needed polished black dress shoes and lit a cigarette.

"You're not blind yet," Amanda replied. "That's why I'm making an appointment for you to see Dr. Blinder."

"What's this guy's name again?" Hurts said, taking a long drag from his cigarette.

"Blinder," she replied.

"And he's an eye doctor," Hurts gasped, "and his name is 'Blinder'?"

"Yes," she replied, and then added, "and he's done extensive research on Macular Degeneration—and he's from New York."

"Oh well, now, New York," Hurts stated sarcastically, smashing out his cigarette in the ashtray on the floor. "That changes everything … Honey," Hurts then said, looking up at her. "I don't want to go to any more doctors. I'm done with them."

"Well, what are you going to do with the rest of your life?" Amanda snapped at him. "You're just going to rot?!"

After giving her a cocky smile, Hurts stated, "I have a pla—"

"Yeah, yeah, I know," she said, and then mocking him, she continued, "'A good detective always has a plan.' So what's this 'plan' of yours?"

"I don't have to answer to you," Hurts snapped at her. "Go put the coffee on," he then stated, pointing the north wall. "I need more coffee." Then he waved the now empty paper Starbucks coffee cup at her.

Amanda did as she was told and walked over to the long, old cedar dresser that was butted-up against the north wall, next to an old, wooden door to the closet-sized bathroom. Squeezing herself in between the long, old wooden dining room table that ran parallel with the dresser, Amanda turned on the coffee pot that was on top of the dresser and which was next to Hurts' hotplate and next to the sitting-upright Raggedy Ann doll that Amanda had given him as a Christmas present.

Hurts watched as Amanda picked up the doll and began staring at it and then began stroking its red, curly yarn hair. She was doing this so lovingly. Hurts wondered why she was doing that, and he wondered about what she could be thinking. He looked around the room. First to his right, to his big, old wooden desk, by the south wall, with his old computer and holstered .9mm semi-automatic pistol on top of it. Then, he looked straight ahead, directly across the room, at his ex-partner's, Tom Mayor's, big, old wooden desk with the TV on top of it. Then, he looked beyond that and gazed out the tall, narrow four windows that faced east and the street below the long-shuttered dentist office. Seven years, Hurts thought. Seven years has passed since I first met Amanda, and nothing in this place has changed—except Amanda, me, and the outside world.

He looked over again at Amanda. She was still staring at the doll and stroking its hair. More and more, Hurts mused, she was getting to look just like her mother. Beautiful. And Hurts was right. Amanda, today wearing blue jeans and a white blouse, was five feet, six inches tall, slender, with shoulder-length dark brown hair that matched the color of her eyes and eyebrows. Hurts then thought about the day when he had first met Amanda. Thinking of that day brought a smile to his face. On that day, Amanda had found him the same as she had found him today—sleeping on that couch, dressed in the same clothes he had had on for days, and an empty whiskey bottle dead on the floor next to him. This was in 2011. Four days before Christmas.

She was such a tiny thing back then—couldn't have been over three feet tall, Hurts thought silently. He smiled again, thinking of hearing that tiny voice as he lay hungover and half asleep on that couch and thought she was a leprechaun coming after him again. He and his ex-partner had had a battle with leprechauns a few years before. They thought that he and his ex-partner had stolen their pot of gold. They had not.

No, Hurts wasn't Amanda's uncle. He remembered how on that day when he had first met her, he had yelled at her to stop knocking on the door and to go away, that he was closed. But she kept knocking, and then opened the door and kept asking him if he was James Hurts, the private investigator, like the words said on the four windows. Amanda had seen those words from the street, and she desperately needed his help: her mother had been arrested the day before for stealing twenty million dollars from her place of employment, and Amanda wanted to hire Hurts to prove that she didn't do it. Without lifting his head from the couch, he told her, fine, that he got $300.00 a day, plus expenses. When she replied that she only had twelve dollars and sixty-seven cents, Hurts told her not to let the door hit her in the butt leaving, and added, "Sorry about your mom, kid. The police don't make mistakes."

Amanda exploded. She began pounding the arm of the couch with her tiny fist, screaming, "Yes, they are! My mother didn't do it—and I want her out of jail!"

Hurts finally sat up. After wiping his unshaven face with his right hand, he said, "Kid, you see that coffee pot over there," pointing to the top of the cedar dresser. "Go turn it on. I need coffee."

Hurts did take her case—and, obviously, it wasn't for the twelve dollars and sixty-seven cents. He took the case because he admired Amanda's grit. He admired her guts; her strong will; her determination. He found her to be the most "aggravating" little girl he had ever met—she kept using jaw-breaker big words, like *behooves*; her father had died of colon cancer when she was nine, and she was going to be a doctor when she grew-up, and doctors had to have a large vocabulary—but he admired her. She reminded him of—of, well, him: James Hurts. NOT TO BESTED BY ANY MAN! Yes.

Yes, he took her case, and he solved it, too. Amanda's mother, Jennifer Warner, was a clerk in the Accounting Department of International Investments, Inc., a large brokerage firm in downtown St. Louis. On the day she had been accused and arrested for stealing that twenty million, Amanda was at school, in the sixth grade at St. Mary's Elementary. At noon that day, her mother called Amanda on her cell phone and told her what had happened. She told her not to worry, that it was all just a terrible mistake and she was sure that it would all be straightened out quickly. She also told Amanda that someone from Family Services was coming to get Amanda and that she would be taken care of until this situation was resolved.

Well, Amanda being Amanda was not about to stay with something called "Family Services" with her mother being in jail. She ran home, packed some clothes and such into her backpack, took some money from the cookie jar, and ran away. She roamed the cold, winter streets, trying to figure out how she could help her mother. She kept roaming and roaming the streets until the next morning, she looked up and saw the words written across those four windows: JAMES HURTS, PRIVATE INVESIGATOR.

After interviewing Amanda's mother, her immediate supervisor, and the senior board member of the company, Mr. Theodore Williams—and there were six board members to the company—Hurts was convinced that Amanda's mother was innocent. He had caught both her supervisor and Mr. Williams telling lies, and it was like he always told Amanda: "Sure, a good detective goes by facts and motive, but he also listens to his gut." Yes, the facts and motive did point to Amanda's mother's guilt, but Hurts' gut was screaming at him that that woman didn't steal no twenty million dollars. No way. She was too straight-forward, too honest. Hurts couldn't figure it out, but he knew that something else was going on in that company. Then, one of the other six board members tried to kill Hurts— and he was a vampire. Amanda saved Hurts' life that night. She knew the man; she'd meet him before, like at the company's Christmas gatherings— and the guy just couldn't find it within himself to kill Hurts in front of her.

That was the first encounter Hurts had ever had with vampires. Of course, Hurts knew all about vampires. His ex-partner, Tom, had had battles with vampires and told him all about them. For example, vampires don't sleep in a coffin by day; they're not as strong during the day as they are at night, but they can withstand indirect light and be out in the day; they can't fly, but they can jump to incredible heights and descend them, too; and on and on. Tom told him a lot about vampires. He also told Hurts about "The Community." There are chapters of The Community all over the world. The Community is run by elders. These elders are the oldest and most powerful of their kind. When a human is turned—becomes a vampire—it is The Community that sees to his/her transition, giving that person a new life, a new identity, a new job, and blood so that they don't kill, and on and on. The number one priority of the elders of The Community is to guard the secret of their existence.

Hurts, now armed with this knowledge, and believing that if that guy who had tried to kill him was a board member of that company and a vampire, then maybe that Mr. Williams was also a vampire and maybe that was what this was all about. Hurts was determined to find out.

The next day, Hurts made another appointment to see Mr. Williams again. There, in his plush office, and with Mr. Williams sitting behind his glass-top desk, Hurts put his back to the door, faced Mr. Williams, unbuttoned his wrinkled old topcoat, withdrew his .9mm revolver, and stated, "Now I don't claim to have all the facts, but here's what I think. Mrs. Warner didn't steal no twenty million dollars. Something else is going on here, and you're a vampire and an elder of The Community. You have to the count of three to confess to all of this, or I'm gonna shoot you right between the eyes."

Mr. Williams sat there quietly until Hurts reached the number three and was just about to pull the trigger. Then, zoom. Instantly, Mr. Williams was on top of Hurts and disarmed him.

After sitting back down behind his desk, and with Hurts now sitting in one of the two modern chairs in front of the desk, Mr. Williams told Hurts everything, calling him a very intelligent man.

No, Mr. Williams stated, Mrs. Warner hadn't stolen any money from the company and tried to hide it in Swiss bank accounts. That was all a ruse, perpetrated by three of the six board members to force Mr. Williams to comply with their demands. For the past year, they had complained that the company was becoming too involved in the "affairs of humans"—charities and such. All of it was threatening to expose their secret. They wanted him to stop immediately. Mr. Williams disagreed. Now, they demanded war—one-on-one combat to the death. They had already killed two of the board members who had sided with Mr. Williams, and now they were coming after him.

Mr. Williams looked hopeless and defeated.

After mulling all of this over in his mind, Hurts came up with a plan.

Now, liking Mr. Williams, because he now felt equal to him, and even superior to him, Hurts slapped his right hand down hard on the top of the desk and stated, "Listen, Williams, do you know what your problem is? You live by too many rules. You need to hire me. I get three hundred dollars a day, plus expenses—and if I get you out of this mess, I want you to get Mrs. Warner out of jail—and I want one hell of a cash bonus. Here's my plan …"

Hurts' plan worked beautifully. He stalked the other three vampires and saved Mr. Williams' and Amanda's lives.

The next day, Christmas day, Mr. Williams held a televised news conference in which he stated that Mrs. Warner had not stolen money from the company; that that had been done by board members who had fled the country and were at large. He then demanded the immediate release of Mrs. Warner from jail.

Hurts and Amanda went and picked her up.

Hurts drove them home. Mrs. Warner invited Hurts inside to spend Christmas with them. He declined. She then told Hurts to send her his charges; that it would be one bill she wouldn't mind paying. Hurts told her to forget about it—that Williams had paid. He told her to consider it his Christmas present to her and Amanda. Amanda, hearing this, shouted, "Christmas present! … C'mon, Mom! C'mon!" Dragging her mother out of the car, and telling Hurts not to leave until she returned, she and her mother ran into the house.

About seven minutes later, Amanda came running out of the house, carrying a package wrapped in Christmas paper and a red bow, in both hands.

After getting back into the car, Amanda said, "I had to tell Mom that I had sneaked-a-peek, again, at my three Christmas presents—my medical dictionary and my new laptop—and that I wanted to give you this one," she continued, holding the present up. "I don't know what she was thinking. She said you wouldn't like it. My thought is that I hope when you look at it, you will think of me." With that said, she gave the package to Hurts, and then got up, threw her arms and hands around Hurts' neck, kissed him on the cheek, and then whispered in his ear, "I love you, Mr. Hurts, and I'll never forget you." Then she dashed out of the car and was gone.

Chapter Two

"Amanda," Hurts stated from the couch, still staring at Amanda, who was still staring at the doll and still stroking its hair. "The coffee's done." When she didn't answer, Hurts repeated, "Amanda, the coffee's done … Amanda?!"

"What?" she replied absentmindedly. Then, coming out of deep-thought, and after gazing at the coffeepot, she said, "Coffee. Yes."

"You don't have to get a mug or cup," Hurts said, waving the empty Starbucks cup in his right hand. "Just fill this up."

She walked over and got the cup and then walked back to the coffeepot.

Hurts watched her as she walked back to the coffeepot and thought: *Only seven years has passed since she came into my life. Only seven years. She was just a stubborn, aggravating, snot-nosed kid then, with glasses. Now look at her. Beautiful; eighteen-years-old; coming into her prime; fulfilling her dreams—no, Amanda's too level-headed, too determined, to have just dreams. She has goals. And now she's making one of her goals a reality; she's a first-year student, pre-med at St. Louis University. And you,* Hurts continued thinking. *What about you?*

After that Christmas Day seven years ago, Hurts thought that he would never see Amanda again. Well, why would he? But a week after New Year, she called Hurts and begged him to come to a music recital she was in at her school. He hadn't wanted to go, but she was so persistent that he finally agreed and went. Then, she kept pestering him to attend other events: her soccer games, softball games, and on and on. Their relationship developed and deepened. There were birthdays, Christmases, going to Cardinals baseball games, fishing trips, karate lessons, and somewhere in the midst of all of this, Amanda began calling Hurts "Uncle Jim," and Hurts began thinking of her as his daughter.

Of course, she was not his daughter. Hurts did have two actual daughters, but they had nothing to do with him. Hurts had married right after he had gotten back from Vietnam and had joined the police force. Along with not being the most "honest" of cops, Hurts was not a good husband or father. It was *not* a good marriage. After eight years of tolerating his drinking, gaming, whoring, hardly being home at nights, and slapping her at times during a heated argument, Barb, his ex, finally got fed-up with it all and divorced him. He'd always blamed his ex for his two daughters having nothing to do with him. Even years later, after Hurts had killed that Thesulac demon on the last case he had worked on as a homicide detective, and had found religion, somewhat, and had tried to reconcile with his two daughters, they would still have nothing to do with Hurts.

So, Amanda was his daughter—his unofficial, adopted daughter.

"Thanks," Hurts said as Amanda handed him back the Starbucks paper cup, which was now filled with coffee from his coffeepot.

Standing in front of him and looking down at him, Amanda stated, "So, what about Emily, Uncle Jim?"

After blowing on the coffee and taking a sip, Hurts sighed, and then said, "It's shocking. Just shocking, Amanda … Kidnapped—from her own bed. Poor kid."

"That's why I need your help," Amanda said.

"Honey," Hurts replied, shaking his head, "I haven't had a case in—in months. I'm worn out … I have no energy."

"OH," Amanda snapped at him. "But you have the energy to walk to the gas station at the end of the block for whiskey and cigarettes."

"That's because you won't buy them for me," Hurts snapped back at her.

"In the first place," Amanda began, "I'm not old enough to purchase alcohol—and, no, you don't need whiskey and cigarettes … Now, what about Emily, Uncle Jim?"

"Amanda," Hurts replied, shaking his head again, "you said the police are involved; the FBI; there's an Amber Alert … What can I do?"

"What can YOU do?" she repeated. "What can you do? … Uncle Jim, you have always been here for me … You have always been my Knight-in-Shining-Armor … I need your help. If it was just a kidnapping… But it's not … Vampires … Vampires!"

That bit about his being her 'Knight-in-Shining-Armor' always got to Hurts. He liked her believing that about him, even if he didn't believe it—which he didn't.

"Okay," he replied, setting down the coffee cup on the floor and then getting a cigarette and lighting it. After picking up the coffee cup again, and after taking a long drag off the cigarette, Hurts leaned back on the couch and said, "I'm waking up now. So, give it to me again … The birthday; that disco—and why you think that guy was a vampire."

"Woo-hoo!" she shouted triumphantly, her hands and arms raised above her head.

"Stop that!" Hurts barked. "You haven't done that since you were a kid."

"Well, like I said," Amanda began, "Wednesday is Emily's birthday, Halloween; she'll be thirteen years old. There's a new club in town, in Soulard—a Teen club; no smoking or alcohol permitted; just music and dancing. This being October and Halloween, the theme of the place this month is Goth—black dress and such. For her birthday, two of Emily's girlfriends from school wanted to take her there last night. They're both thirteen, and since Emily's thirteenth birthday falls within this month, the place agreed to permit her entrance. But her parents said she couldn't go unless one of them, or both, went along. Well, Emily didn't want that. So, she asked them, if I agreed to take them, could she go. They said yes, and I took them. I didn't mind. I mean, my God, I've watched Emily grow up from a baby. You know that I think more of her than just a neighbor who lives across the street from me. She's—she's like my baby-sister. I—"

Hurts had met her and her parents, Bob and Marge, several times. Hurts liked them, and he thought Emily was a most beautiful little girl: blonde hair and the most beautiful blue eyes that Hurts had ever seen before.

Crushing out the now smoked cigarette in the ashtray on the floor, and getting impatient, Hurts barked, "So, get to what happened, Amanda— what about that guy?"

"Well, Uncle Jim," she continued, "he was WEIRD ... Well, for one, he was gay. He—"

"Wait a minute, Amanda," Hurts said, interrupting her. "I know that to your generation the word 'gay' means more than just being happy. What do you mean by—"

"That he was homosexual—more girl than boy, with flowing blond hair down to his waist, and long fingernails."

"Oh, you mean queer," Hurts said.

"Don't use THAT word, Uncle Jim," Amanda chided him. "It's terrible. I have a friend who's gay, and she's the best—"

"Okay, okay," Hurts replied. "Get on with what happened."

"Well, we got there about six—and we were having a great time, dressed in black and dancing. Then *they* came in. He was with a bunch of other guys. They were all about the same age, about sixteen or seventeen, and they were all dressed alike—full-length, thin leather black coats ... And they were loud and rough, Uncle Jim. They pushed some people from a table so that they could shove two tables together and all sit together.

They sat down, and then that guy begins sniffing the air, and *then* he looks directly at Emily—he doesn't take his eyes off her. He just keeps staring at her and sniffing."

"Maybe he had a cold," Hurts interjected.

"No," she retorted, "he didn't have a cold. Then, as if hypnotized—or being compelled by some force or power greater than him, he comes straight over to our table. Not taking his eyes off Emily for a second— blue eyes that had a fiery rage of anger and hate within them—he just stands there at the edge of the table, in total silence, staring down at Emily.

"Emily and I were sitting to the back of the table, and Mary and Megan, Emily's two girlfriends, were sitting to the front of the table, and there was an empty chair in front of where he stood.

"Well, I got damn tired and angry at this, and I said, shouting above the music, 'What's your problem, pal?' Not paying any attention to me, he sits down. He leans across the table and says in a most girlish lisp, 'I'm Todd. What's your name?' Well, Emily's scared of him, shaking even. She says, weakly, 'Emily.' So, I say, 'Look. We don't know you; we didn't invite you over; go away.' 'Yeah,' Mary adds. 'We're celebrating Emily's birthday.' 'It's your birthday?' he says, very interested and excited. 'How old are you?' 'Well, actually, like, I'm thirteen, but actually, like, my birthday isn't, actually, like, until Wednesday.' 'Halloween?!' he shouts. 'Halloween! … Oooooh, you are the Chosen One.'

"Then, then, he leans in across the table as if he's going to grab her! Well, I put my hand on his face and shoved him back, hard. He shot up out of that chair—and that's when it happened, Uncle Jim. Yes, it was dark in there. Yes, the multiple spot reflections from the many rotating mirrored balls hanging from the ceiling caused illusions—but in that moment, he changed. His face got bigger; more prominent; harsher, and fangs. 'You bitch!' he screamed angrily at me. I think he would have attacked me right there if it hadn't been for one of the bouncers rushing over and stopping him and warning him that if he and his buddies didn't behave themselves, he'd toss them out as he had the other night. He left our table, but not before saying to Emily, 'Be seeing you real soon.' We left there soon after that."

"You then went home," Hurts said.

"Well, no," Amanda stated. "We went to the Dairy Queen a few blocks from home. Mary and Megan had arranged for us and her parents to have an ice-cream cake."

"Were you followed?"

"I don't think so," Amanda replied, weakly. "The whole time we were there, I kept looking out the windows. I never saw anyone—but the whole time that we were there, even after I got back home and was getting ready for bed, I felt his presence."

"And she was found missing this morning?" he asked.

"Yes," Amanda replied. "She went to bed about nine o'clock. This morning, at six-thirty, after repeatedly calling her to get up and come to breakfast, Marge went into her bedroom and found her gone. About eight o'clock—and Mom had already left for work by this time—Marge called me; she was-was devastated. The police and FBI were already there, and they wanted to interview me about last night. I went over there, and I told them everything—except for my belief about that Todd guy being a vampire."

"What did the police and FBI say? —Any fingerprints? Anything missing? Clothes? Any windows or doors busted?"

"Well, no to all of that," Amanda replied. "Bob is quite sure that he forgot to lock the deadbolt to the kitchen door last night, and you have told me many times how easy it is to open a door with something as simple as a credit card."

"Yes, that's true."

"One thing, though," Amanda then said. "On the wall above the head of Emily's bed hung a large, ornate cross with Jesus on it. It was found this morning on the floor on the opposite side of the room. There's a hole in the wall by where the cross was found. It's as if someone angrily ripped it off the wall and threw it hard."

After setting the now empty coffee cup down on the floor, Hurts wiped his face with his hand. Then he said, "Okay. I've heard enough." Rising slowly from the couch, stretching, he said, "I'll get washed, shaved, dressed, and we'll go."

"Woo—" Amanda began to shout, with raised arms and hands, but then stopped. "That's great, Uncle Jim." As Hurts was walking to the door of the bathroom, Amanda said, "Are we going to begin at The Source? —Interview Emily's parents?"

Hurts turned around, smiled, and said, "Well, at least now you're thinking like a detective. Yes, typically we would begin at The Source, the beginning, which would be at Emily's. But in this case, because you say vampires are involved, I think we better first check with someone who knows vampires, is an elder over them, and of The Community: Williams."

Chapter Three

Shortly after Hurts had entered the closet-sized bathroom and had shut the door, Amanda walked to it and said through the door, "Uncle Jim, you haven't had anything to eat. How about some eggs and bacon?"

"Yeah," she heard Hurts reply. "I am kind of hungry."

So, while Hurts bathed and shaved at the sink in there—no bathtub—Amanda cooked the eggs and bacon on the hotplate that was on top of the dresser. Amanda ALWAYS made sure that the mini refrigerator was always stocked with food. For all the years that Amanda had now known Hurts, she still couldn't believe that he lived there. After his partner, Tom Mayors, quit, he decided to sell his small brick house, pocket the money and move in there.

About thirty minutes later, Hurts came out of the bathroom—looking a lot more presentable than when he had entered it. He was shoeless and wearing the pants of his wrinkled dark blue suit. He had on a white dress shirt, with a tie that matched the color of the suit. The coat of the suit, he had draped across his right arm. He hung it on the back of one of the chairs and sat down to eat.

Now bathed, fed and fully dressed—now wearing his shoes, suit coat and his pistol holstered under his left shoulder—Hurts filled that Starbucks coffee cup with a half-cup of more coffee, and Amanda grabbed her purse, which Hurts had always felt looked like a small black duffle bag with a long cord at the top, and they left the office.

They descended the steps from the second floor to the first floor and exited the old building and onto the sidewalk.

The sun was bright, and there was a slight chill in the crisp air. It was a beautiful autumnal day, and Hurts felt good to be outside.

Hurts' car, a 1997 Nissan Pathfinder, was parked in the street in front of the building. Amanda's car was parked behind Hurts. As they passed Hurts' car, he wondered if it would start. Well, he hadn't started it in three months.

Amanda pressed the door unlock button on her keychain and they got in. Hurts hated her car—it was a VERY sore subject with him. Last year, on her birthday, Williams had bought and given her that car, a white 2017 Ford Taurus. Hurts, not to be bested by ANY man, had a one-sided, ongoing feud with Williams about all the things he had done for Amanda and had given her—like helping her get into St. Louis University, always giving her Christmas and birthday presents, VIP Cardinals baseball tickets, (Hurts loved baseball about as much as he loved trout fishing. He'd always go, but he'd grumble and say, "I don't see nothing so hot about these seats.") and on and on about other things Williams gave to Amanda.

As Hurts got settled in the front seat, Amanda started the car, and the automatic shoulder seatbelt came down across his chest and he almost spilled that cup of coffee in his right hand.

"This damn car," Hurts griped, using his left hand to wipe the lapel of his suit where a drop of coffee had spilled onto it. "There's too many damn gadgets in it—and is that damn lady gonna speak to us?" he continued, pointing to the GPS built into the middle of the dashboard.

Looking at him, Amanda replied, "It's just a recording, Uncle Jim, and no, 'she's' not going to talk with us. I know how to get to Uncle Williams."

That was another sore spot with Hurts—her calling Williams *Uncle Williams*. She began doing that about the same time she began calling Hurts *Uncle Jim*. In this life, Williams was using the name Theodore Williams, and Amanda felt that calling him Theodore sounded too stuffy, and that to call him Teddy, for a man of his breeding and culture, sounded too causal. So, she chose Uncle Williams.

"Well, it's unnatural for that thing to talk to us," Hurts griped. "It's just like that—that Stupid-phone of yours." Hurts acted like he was holding a cellphone in his left hand, brought it up to his mouth and said, "Okay, Google, what is bah, bah, bah. It's all dumb."

"Oh, Uncle Jim," Amanda sighed.

Hurts then pressed the button on the door panel. The window came down, and he tossed the now empty paper Starbucks coffee cup out the window.

"Hey!" Amanda yelled at him. "That's against the law!"

"Well," Hurts began, "some—"

"Yeah, yeah," Amanda snapped at him. "I know: 'Some laws just beg to be broken.' Well, then you pay for the ticket."

"I don't see any cops around here … Do you?"

"Good," Amanda replied, and pulled away from the curb.

***

The Wainwright Building is a twenty-story, modernistic skyscraper of tinted glass and light-brown granite. It is in the heart of downtown St. Louis, by Market Street and 7th Street. International Investments, Inc. consumes the top three floors. Amanda's mother works in the accounting department on the 17th floor, and Williams' plush office, along with the offices of the other five board members, is on the top floor.

Chapter Four

After Hurts and Amanda had ridden the elevator up to the twentieth floor and had entered the outer office of Williams' office, they walked across the thick white carpet to the reception desk. There behind a large, ornate wooden desk—white, it was, like everything else in that outer office: the metal cabinets behind her, the couch, the walls, the black-and-white prints on the walls of scenes of St. Louis, like the Arch—sat Lorraine, Williams' personal secretary. Hurts loved to tease her and flirt with her. She was about five feet, six inches tall; an average-looking body, which was a bit stocky, with an angular-shaped face and shoulder-length light-brown hair that had no style to it at all. She always wore dresses—nice dresses, but plain-looking, which seemed to match the look of her face and her demeanor. She looked to be in her early thirties. Hurts found her to be so prim-and-proper, and for some reason, he found that to be sexy. Oh, yes, one more thing about her—she was a vampire.

"Well, how are you this morning, good-lookin'?" Hurts said to her jovially.

Looking at him with a noncommittal expression, she replied, "It's ten-after- one, James. Shouldn't that be, 'Well, how are you this *afternoon,* good-looking?'" It had taken Hurts a few years of coaxing her to call him 'James' instead of 'Mr. Hurts' before she would.

Hurts laughed and said, "I love you—I'm gonna take you to dinner and buy you a steak. Now, that's s-t-e-a-k; not s-t-a-k-e."

"Thank you," she replied, expressionless.

"Well," Hurts continued, "is it possible to speak with the boss for a few minutes?"

She looked down to the right of her desk, at the multi-plex phone that sat on top of the desk—or more specifically at the buttons at the bottom of the phone which lit up. She picked up the receiver and pressed one of the buttons. A few seconds later, Hurts heard her say, formally and plainly, "Mr. Hurts and Amanda are here, and they would like to speak with you."

After hanging up the receiver, she pointed to the long, deeply upholstered, white couch directly behind them, saying, "Mr. Williams shall be with you momentarily."

That 'momentarily' turned into twenty minutes, and Hurts was getting pissed about it; he did not like being kept waiting—especially by some BIGSHOT!

The wooden, Grecian-style door to his office finally opened wide, and there stood Mr. Theodore Williams. Williams was about five feet, six inches tall with a slender build, and had a most distinguished arura about him of breeding, culture and sophistication. His well-groomed hair was almost white, sparse, and always combed straight back, and complemented the pencil-thin mustache under his thin, straight nose. Although his looks hadn't changed a bit in the eleven years that Hurts had known Williams, he looked to be in his mid-fifties. Hurts knew that he was WAY older than that. He had once heard Amanda say that Williams had told her that he had been a high-ranking official—something called a Centurio—in the Roman army. He was always impeccably dressed. Hurts always felt that he could be a poster-boy for Brooks Brothers Clothing. Today, he was wearing a dark blue pinstripe suit, with a matching tie and a white dress shirt.

"Well, how are two of my favorite people?" he said in that pleasant-sounding voice of his, which had a slight British accent to it. He waved them to come forward.

"We're fine, Williams," Hurts said enthusiastically as they came abreast of him. "Just fine." He then extended his right hand and wanted Williams to shake it. Williams did, and Hurts shook it firmly and warmly, saying, "You look as dapper as ever."

"Thank you, Hurts," Williams replied, a bit confused. He looked to Amanda with an expression that seemed to say: *What's with him?*

Amanda just shrugged her shoulders, as if stating: *Beats me.*

"Well, come in." he said, and he stepped to the side for them to pass through.

The only things that were white in his office were the carpet, the plasterboard walls and the two ornate chairs that were positioned in front of a glass-top desk that stood on a silver, tube-shaped metal frame. The two chairs looked very modern: two wooden-framed chairs with rounded backs that descended into the well-padded seats of the chairs, which was of a white cloth with a bamboo print. Many pictures from sites in places in Europe—like Big Ben, the Eiffel Tower, and such—lined the walls.

"No school today, Amanda?" Williams asked as Hurts and Amanda sat down in the two chairs in front of the desk, and as he went behind his desk and sat down in a deep-upholstered, black leather chair on a moveable metal swivel. The desk and chair faced east, and directly behind them was a floor-to-ceiling, wall-to-wall window with white mini-blinds. Usually the blinds were drawn close, but this day they weren't, and there was a beautiful view of the Arch and of the Mississippi River and the Illinois horizon in the far distance.

"No, I don't have any classes on a Monday," Amanda replied, and she sat her purse down on the floor to the left of chair, because Hurts was sitting to her right.

"How is school going?" he then asked her.

"Great," she said. Williams looked tired to Amanda.

He interlaced his fingers and placed his elbows on the edge of the desk and said, "I apologize for making you both wait so long. For the past three months, I have had a 'situation' here that's demanded most of my—well, what brings you both here to see me?"

Hurts looked at Amanda and then motioned for her to begin.

"Uncle Williams," she began, "do you know a young man with long blond hair by the name of Todd? I think he—"

"He's gay, Williams," Hurts interjected, "and that doesn't mean he's happy; it means he's que—homosexual."

"Yes," Amanda continued. "Do you know him—and is he a vampire?"

Williams removed his elbows from the desk and sat back heavily in the chair. After a few seconds of silence, he said, "Unfortunately, I do know of him—and, yes, he is a vampire. It's sad. He was turned about five months ago by an elderly vampire who owned a bookstore on Broadway Boulevard near Arsenal Street. He dealt, mostly, with books on the Occult. How or where Todd met him, I don't know. We have dealt with the man who turned Todd, but Todd himself has alluded us, so far."

"Why are you after him?" Hurts asked.

"For one, from the time he was turned until now, he has murdered several people, including his own father, who was a poor, uneducated, alcoholic man. He was very abusive with Todd. We were able to clean up and hide his killing of his father, as we were able to clean up and hide the two teachers and three fellow students he murdered at his high school, Roosevelt High. Fortunately, there is a teacher there who is one of us, and he has been most helpful with this—"

"Yes," Amanda interrupted. "I saw on the news about the two teachers and the students missing."

"Yes," Williams replied, and then continued, "Todd's mother died when he was ten … Have you ever wondered, Hurts, why you have never heard or seen a child or teenage vampire?"

"No, not really," Hurts replied. "Why?"

"We, my kind have laws, rules, which we must obey," Williams stated. "It is a cardinal breach of law for any vampire to turn any child or teenager into a vampire—the punishment for doing so is death, immediate death for both. A child or teenager who is turned becomes too much of a threat to our existence to permit to live. They can't control this new power of being a vampire. They become vicious, animalistic, killing creatures … What does all of this have to do with Todd—Todd Sinclair?"

Hurts and Amanda exchanged glances, and then Hurts again motioned for her to speak.

Amanda told him everything. He sat there, through the telling of it all, quiet and intent, and when she had finished speaking, he lowered his head. For the first time since Hurts had first met Williams eleven years ago, he felt that Williams suddenly looked old—and scared.

With his head still lowered, and both hands clutched together, and as if speaking to himself, Williams said, "Could there be more students missing from Roosevelt? … Why didn't he inform us of that? … Perhaps he has—I've been so preoccupied with this other situation that I—" He raised his head, and looking at Amanda, he said, "Amanda, you said that at that club, Todd was with a bunch of other guys. Could that number have been twelve?"

"I don't know, Uncle Williams," she replied. "It's possible. Why?"

Williams lowered his head again and was silent once more—and then he exploded with anger. With a look of unbridled rage upon his usually composed, controlled face, Williams raised his arm above his head. He made a clenched fist, and then he brought it down hard. Hurts had no doubts; with his strength of being a vampire, Hurts knew that his glass-top desk was about to become nothing more than shards of glass. But just before the palm of his fist touched the top of his desk, Williams suddenly stopped. For a few seconds, he held his fist there, like a plane waiting for instructions to land. Then, he removed his hovering hand from above the desk. He sat back in his chair, and with his eyes closed, he began feeling his forehead with his now controlled hand.

Hurts had never seen Williams 'lose it' before. But he enjoyed what he had just witnessed—it made Hurts feel superior to him.

"I cannot believe that old man told Todd about The Ritual," Williams said, with his eyes still closed and still feeling his forehead.

"What the hell is this all about, Williams?" Hurts barked. "Speak to us."

A few seconds later, Williams removed his hand from his forehead, opened his eyes, looked at Hurts, and said reflectively, "The word 'hell' is a most correct choice of words, Hurts … It's about hell; it's about heaven; it's about mocking Christ and Christianity; it's about The Chosen One; it's about The Thirteenth Hour; it's about The Power of Thirteen-fold, it's about—"

Hurts looked at Amanda and barked, "There he goes again, speaking in riddles. You talk to him, Amanda. Maybe you can get him to talk straight."

Amanda gave a nod to Hurts, and then she looked at Williams and said, "Uncle Williams, is Emily dead?"

"No, child," he responded, solemnly. "I'm most certain of this … They have taken her to a place that is secluded—a place in which she can scream and cry for help all she wants, and no one will hear her cries. Doing this to make the blood sweeter. But they shall not harm her until the first stroke of The Thirteenth Hour on the thirty-first of this month, Halloween. Three days of suffering—to mock Christ's crucifixion and resurrection. She shall be bound, probably with rope, and stretched-out, also as with Christ on the cross. She shall be naked. For she, poor child, is The Chosen One."

"But why is Emily The Chosen One, Uncle Williams?" Amanda asked, a look of deep concern bathing her face. "Why are they doing this? —and what will happen to Emily on the first stroke of The Thirteenth Hour?"

"Sadly," Williams began, "Emily meets all of requirements of The Chosen One. You said that when Todd first entered the club that he kept sniffing the air. A vampire can smell when a woman is having her period. Emily has come of age, fertility. Not only that, the mistake was made of informing Todd that not only is this coming Wednesday her birthday—but her thirteenth birthday. The number thirteen is symbolic of transformation. Twelve followers and one savior, ascending from one level of consciousness to a higher level of consciousness or being, or power."

"And what about The Thirteenth Hour?" Amanda asked, a trace of fear escaping from her voice.

"Just before the first stoke of the first second of The Thirteenth Hour," Williams continued, "The Ritual shall begin. They will surround Emily and begin chanting The Lord's Prayer in Latin backwards. With the first stroke of the second, Todd shall be the first to feed upon her. Then, with the second stroke of the second second, they shall all begin feeding on her, and by the thirteenth stroke of the second hand, there shall not be anything left of Emily but bones.”

“Oh, my God,” Amanda gasped, horrified.

“Again, Williams,” Hurts stated. “What’s this all about?”

“Power, Hurts,” Williams replied. “Power. If Todd and his followers succeed in doing this, and if Satan or one of Satan’s chief minions is pleased, he shall appear to them and grant Todd the Power of Thirteen-fold. The power Todd now possesses as a vampire shall be increased thirteen times. His followers, who shall now be disciples, shall also have increased power, but not as much as Todd.”

“How much power are we talkin’ about here, Williams?” Hurts asked.

“I, along with my five fellow board members here, are elders of this chapter of The Community because we are the oldest and the most powerful of our kind. But even with our combined powers, we would still woefully lack the powers of Todd and his followers.”

“How bad could this get?”

Williams leaned back in his chair again. He closed his eyes and began rubbing them again. A few seconds later, he said, “How is your memory of history, Hurts?”

Hurts gave a glance at Amanda, saying, “There he goes again! Talkin’ in riddles.” Looking back at Williams, he said, “Okay, Williams. What about history?”

Williams stopped rubbing his eyes, opened them, and looking straight into Hurts’ face, stated, “Have you ever heard of The Black Plague?”

“Oh, my God!” Amanda gasped again, so horrified at hearing this that she couldn’t completely grasp the full magnitude of it.

“It has been said that the Plague killed 200 million humans,” Williams continued speaking. “I was one of the chief architects in hushing-up the true origins or true cause of the Plague. Its true origins, or true cause, was the after-effects of the mass killing and mass spread of disease by a vampire and his followers who had achieved what Todd is now attempting to achieve.” Williams stopped speaking and was silent, deep in thought. The silence filled the room. It was heavy, suffocating, and there seemed to be no relief from it. Suddenly, Williams exploded again with anger. Looking at Amanda, he stated, quickly and most vehemently, “Amanda, you should not be involved in this. It’s too dangerous. I’m ordering the immediate transfer of your mother to our branch office in London. You shall accompany her—and you shall go too, Hurts.”

"Now, hold on there, partner," Hurts retorted. Leaning forward and placing his elbows on the edge of the top of Williams' desk, he made a T-sign with his hands and said, "I ain't never run from a fight, and I ain't about to start now. I ain't going nowhere."

"I'm sorry, Uncle Williams," Amanda added. "I'm not going anywhere either. Emily is like a sister to me—and I'm going to find her."

Williams calmed down again and was silent. Then he said, "Very well, then." He rose from his chair, and Amanda and Hurts rose from their chairs as well.

"I shall place every available person here that I can on this," Williams said. "Todd must be found and stopped at all costs."

Hurts placed his hand on his chin and began rubbing it, feigning to be thinking. He said, "So this 'at all costs'—Does that mean you want to hire me? Say, at three-hundred dollars a day, plus expenses?"

A half-grin suddenly appeared on Williams' thin lips. "Agreed," he said. Raising his right hand and extending it out across the desk, Williams offered his hand to Hurts. Hurts took it and began shaking it heartily. "James," Williams began. This was the first time that Williams had ever called Hurts by his first name. Hurts was a bit shocked at this and didn't know if he liked it or not. "Be careful—and protect Amanda as you have never protected her before."

"You got it, old friend," Hurts said, most heartily. "And you know that my middle name is *Careful*."

"I thought you said that your middle name is Herman?" Amanda quipped. This brought a much needed, and thankful, laugh from both Amanda and Williams. Hurts just gave her a mean glance.

Chapter Five

Once Hurts and Amanda had stepped out of Williams' office, he shut the door, and as Hurts and Amanda passed Lorraine's desk, without even stopping, Hurts looked down at Lorraine and said, "Now, you remember about our dinner date, and me buying you that *steak*."

"I will, James," she replied expressionlessly, as she stacked manila envelopes, which were all stuffed with typed papers, in a pile on top of her desk. "Have a pleasant afternoon."

At the door to the outer office, Hurts opened it, stepped to the side and made a motion with his arm for Amanda to pass through. As she did, she said, confused, "What was that all about?"

"What?" Hurts retorted. "Can't a guy flirt with a girl?"

"No, no," Amanda replied, "I mean back there in Uncle Williams' office. You-you were so—so *nice*."

Hurts closed the door and said, "Oooooh, I'm always nice."

"No, you're not," she retorted. "—especially to Uncle Williams."

"That's just all in your head, kid," he said. "Come on, let's go."

At the elevator, Amanda suddenly said, "Say, Uncle Jim. I better go down and see Mom. I think I'll tell her that I stopped by to see you and that you're ill. I'm worried about you, and that I think that I should stay with you for a day or two. Can I meet you in the lobby?"

"Sure," Hurts replied. "That sounds like a good plan."

Amanda's mother works in the accounting department, which was on the seventeenth floor, three floors down from the floor they were on. When the elevator came, Amanda got off at the seventeenth floor and Hurts went down to the lobby to wait for her.

There is a smoke shop on the bottom floor of the building two buildings to the left of the Wainwright Building. In fact, this smoke shop is called just that: The Smoke Shop, selling tobacco products, alcohol and such. After about ten minutes of Hurts waiting for Amanda, he decided to dash over to it. He purchased a pack of cigarettes and a half-pint bottle of whiskey. The pack of cigarettes he placed in the right pocket of his suit coat, and the bottle of whiskey, he placed in the inner-pocket of his suit coat—both to be a secret and out of sight of Amanda: He-he-he!

About a half-hour later, Amanda stepped out of one of the four elevators and onto the high-polished marble floor of the cavernous lobby.

"Well, how did it go?" Hurts asked as Amanda came abreast of him.

"Great," she replied. "If she doesn't hear from me, she'll call tonight to see how you're doing ... Well, where do we start? — The Source?"

"I want to begin this by interviewing the principal of Roosevelt High. The principal might know some information about that Todd guy and his buddies that even that guy of Williams' doesn't know ... But first, I want to stop by my old police station and get a copy of the report of the missing students."

Amanda drove east up Market Street, passing the many skyscrapers of downtown St. Louis. The traffic was light. At Tucker Boulevard, she turned left and a half-block later, she pulled the car into the open-gated, high chain-linked fence of the police station parking lot. The old police station is a long, yes, old building, constructed of cement and wood-framed, long, narrow windows.

Getting out of the car, Hurts told Amanda to wait for him. Amanda didn't like being there. It brought back too many bad memories of when her mother had been falsely accused and arrested for stealing all that money from her place of employment. She tried to block it all out of her mind, especially of the day Hurts first brought her here to interview her mother. She had thought that the police were surely going to arrest her for running away from Family Services. But they didn't. Hurts made sure that no one in there knew that it was she. He told everyone that he was babysitting, that she was his granddaughter. "Damn lucky kid," most of them said. "She don't look a damn thing like you, Hurts."

Yes, she didn't like being in that parking lot again. Although, as much as she tried to block that experience out of her mind, there was one incident that happened there that did, now remembering it, bring a smile to her face. As they were leaving the police station, a policewoman—plain-looking, stocky—came up to them, looked down at Amanda, and exclaimed, "Oh, you are just the most precious-looking little girl! What's your name?" Amanda, frightened and clinging to Hurts, tugged on one of the legs of his pants and motioned for him to come down to her. He did, and she whispered in his ear, "What's my name?" Hurts stood up, looked at the woman and said, "Well, Sally, ain't that just like a kid? Too bashful to tell you her name. It's Shirley. Her mom and dad named her that because she's so sweet, like Shirley Temple." Amanda gave Hurts a double look of both shock and surprise. Throughout the entire case, Hurts was forever telling her that she was the most "aggravatin' brat" he had ever met.

About ten minutes later, Hurts returned, carrying two sheets of white paper. He got back into the car and said, "Let's get to Roosevelt."

Amanda got back onto Market Street and began driving east once again. As she drove, Hurts viewed the two sheets of white paper. "Damn," he griped. "I got so many wavy lines dancing in front of my eyes that I can't read."

"Let me make that appointment for you with Dr. Blinder," Amanda stated, chastising him.

Looking at her, he barked, "No, I ain't doing it. It's a waste of time. I'm done with doctors—especially with a guy named Blinder." Looking straight ahead, he said, "Hello. How are you today? I'm Blinder, the eye doctor, and I'll make you see again."

"He's good," Amanda replied, firmly. "You should read his credentials. They are quite impressive."

"Well, he can 'quite' kiss my ass."

"Fine, then," Amanda replied, shaking her head and getting angry. "Go blind."

"Fine, then," Hurts retorted. "I will." And to prove to her that he was his own MAN, Hurts set the two pages down on his lap, reached into the inner pocket of his suit coat, removed that bottle of whiskey from it, screwed off the cap, took a long gulp from it, and said, "Ahhhhh."

Amanda hearing that, and then looking at him, exploded with anger and exclaimed, "Where in the hell did you get that damn whiskey?!"

"I got my ways," Hurts replied, waving the bottle at her.

"You're a mess," she sighed, surrendering. "A real mess." Then she laughed.

After returning that bottle of whiskey to the inner pocket of his suit coat, Hurts picked up the two sheets of paper from his lap and began viewing them again. A few moments later, he looked up and said, "That's strange."

"What's strange, Uncle Jim?"

"Well, this is," he replied, looking at her and waving the two sheets of paper at her. "It don't add up."

"How so?" she asked.

"Well," he began, "Williams told us that Todd and his pals had murdered three of the missing students."

"Yeah," she said.

"Well, this," he continued, shaking the two pages at her, "states that there are ten students missing from Roosevelt—and in the last two months, four boys from Sumner High have gone missing."

"What's your point?" she said, confused.

"My point is," Hurts continued, "is that seven and four is eleven. Where's the twelfth missing student? —the twelfth follower?"

"Oh, I see," Amanda exclaimed. After a second or two of thinking about it, she stated, "Maybe Uncle Williams got the numbers of missing students wrong or something."

"Yeah, maybe," Hurts replied, still thinking about it. "Maybe."

Chapter Six

Roosevelt High School is southwest of downtown St. Louis on Hartford Street. It's a block-long, fortress-like old building of red brick, and tall, narrow, wooden-framed windows. It opened in 1925. As the years passed, and as the neighborhood and neighborhoods surrounding the school deteriorated, and whites fled and blacks moved in, Roosevelt High became known as the "Black School." Then, in the early '80's, people of Bosnian descent were brought to St. Louis by religious and government organizations. They settled into neighborhoods around the school. Today, Roosevelt High has a robust student body of blacks, Bosnians, and a minority of white students.

Hurts was steaming pissed after he and Amanda passed through the metal-detector at the entrance of the school. He had to leave his holstered weapon and that bottle of whiskey with Security. Hurts had warned the guard—a well-built, clean-and-pressed uniformed, young black man—that he had better get both of them back when they left or he'd strangle him with his bare hands—*and don't think that I don't know how much whiskey is in that bottle*. The guard politely reassured him that both would be safe.

They were instructed that the principal's office was on the first floor at the end of the hall, walking north.

As they walked upon the old, in much need of waxing and buffing, black-and-white tiled floor of the wide-and-high hall, the three o'clock dismissal bell rang, making both Amanda and Hurts flinch at the most agitating sound. The hall that just seconds ago was so wide and empty, was suddenly now sardine-crowded with noisy students all vying to get out of the building as fast as they could. Hurts and Amanda managed to squeeze their way through to the Administration Office, in which the principal's office was within.

Printed upon the upper glass section of an old wooden door, stenciled in bold, black, block letters was: ADMINISTRATION OFFICE. Hurts grabbed the old, round, brass doorknob of the door, opened the door, and stepped to the side so that Amanda could walk through. Once inside, their eyes gazed upon the controlled chaos of what a school is like, trying to run a high school on an insufficient government federal and state budget.

The room was large, but crowed, stuffed with three large, old wooden desks placed here and there; three large blackboards with thin wooden frames and tan-coloring caulking hung from three walls by nails. There wasn't a single empty spot on any of the three blackboards; each was stuffed with page after page of school schedules, the announcements of meetings and school activities; both federal and state programs offered; flyers of help for drug abuse, alcohol abuse, school and family violence, unwanted pregnancies, and on and on. A smell of oldness, of mustiness, filled the air of the room, as did a sense of decline—of being past its prime.

Three black women of various ages and four black teenagers rushed about the room. What they were doing, Hurts had no idea. Hurts and Amanda just stood there inside the entrance of the room, next to a line of metal folding chairs that were in front of a waist-high wooden parapet that was to the right of Hurts and jutted-out about five feet from the door.

Finally, one of the three women stopped in front of Hurts and Amanda and said quickly, "Can I help you?" She looked to be in her early fifties, Hurts thought. She had salt-and-pepper grey hair, cut in short style. She was wearing black dress pants and a pullover red sweater.

"Yes," Hurts stated. "We would like to see the principal."

The woman looked to her left, to the south wall of the room. Hurts and Amanda both looked in that direction as well. There was another room there. The door to the room was open. The man, in his mid-thirties, Hurts thought, was so large and obese that he consumed the chair to the point of the almost disappearance of the chair. He was on the phone, speaking, and he sat in front of a much cluttered large, old wooden desk that faced east. The man had shoulder-length black dreadlocks, which matched the dreadlocks of his beard and mustache. He was dressed in a purple suit, a white dress shirt and purple tie. Hurts thought: *What an odd lookin' duck.*

"Do you have an appointment?" the woman asked Hurts.

"No," he replied. "But this is official police business."

"Oh," she said. "Have a seat," she continued, pointing to the folding chairs, "and I'll see if Dr. Washington can see you."

"Thank you," Hurts replied, and he and Amanda both sat down in those most uncomfortable chairs. Hurts then looked to his left at the sun shining through the bank of tall, narrow, wooden-framed windows against the west wall. After a moment or two of doing this, he leaned towards Amanda and whispered, "Did she say that that guy is a doctor?"

"Yes, she did," Amanda said. "But he's not that type of a doctor. He's a doctor of—"

"Dr. Washington will see you now," the woman said, interrupting Amanda. They both rose from the chairs, and walking upon the dark-colored, wooden floor of the room, which was in much need of sanding and waxing, they followed the woman into the office of Dr. Washington.

Because of his extreme size and weight, Dr. Washington had some difficulty rising from the chair he was sitting in to greet Hurts and Amanda when they entered. When they came abreast of the front of the desk, he extended his long, right arm across the top of his desk and shook hands with Hurts. Hurts' hand disappeared into the largeness of Dr. Washington's hand. Hurts had to raise his head up to look into the wide face of the man. As they shook hands, he stated in a most deep, but pleasant-sounding voice, "I'm Dr. Washington … Mary, bring two chairs in so these two people may sit." A moment later, that woman carried in two of those folding chairs, opened them in front of the desk, and after motioning for Hurts and Amanda to be seated, she left the room. "Please be seated," Dr. Washington continued. They all sat down, and Dr. Washington then stated, "Now, you are? —And how may I help you? I'm told that this is a police matter."

"Yes," Hurts replied. He reached into the left pocket of his suit coat and removed one of his business cards. He extended his hand across the top of the desk and gave it to Dr. Washington. Settling back in the chair, Hurts continued, "I'm James Hurts and this is my associate, Miss Amanda Warner." Dr. Washington nodded his head to her in salutation. "We have been hired by the City Police of St. Louis to assist them in trying to find these missing students … Oh, one thing before we get started," Hurts interjected. He reached into the right-side pocket of his suit coat and removed from it the now folded two sheets of paper listing the names and addresses of the missing students. Viewing it for a second, Hurts then looked back at Dr. Washington and said, "This list states that there are ten students missing from Roosevelt High—and are you aware that in the past two months four students have gone missing from Sumner High School, which is about only seven miles from here … That's my old high school. I graduated from there years and years ago—with Paul Revere." This brought a big belly laugh from Dr. Washington. "Anyway," Hurts continued, "Is the list correct?"

"Yes," Dr. Washington replied. "May I add, though, that we have two teachers who are missing from Roosevelt High as well."

"Yes, of course," Hurts stated. "This is being investigated too. What do you make of all of this?"

After thinking for a moment, he shook his large head and said, "Frankly, Mr. Hurts, I'm at a loss. I don't know."

"What we're trying to establish here, Dr. Washington," Hurts continued, "is a common thread—something that connects all of these students together. Were they all friends? What were their likes and dislikes? Did they hang out together, and if so, where? A place away from the school—a place secluded, where they could be themselves … Here," Hurts stated, "Let's take the first missing student. That would be—" Hurts looked down at the two sheets of paper in his hands, pretending that he didn't know the answer to his own question.

"That would be Todd Sinclair," Dr. Washington interjected.

"Yes," Hurts stated, and then he looked up at Dr. Washington. "That's right. What was he like? Were any of the other missing students his friends? Did they all hang out together? —and if so, where?"

Dr. Washington replied: "For starters, because of Todd's sexual orientation, he—"

"He's q—gay," Hurts said, interrupting him.

"Yes," he said. "Because of this alone, Todd didn't have any friends. In fact, three of the missing students bullied him relentlessly—beat him up several times because of his sexual orientation. Oh, he interacted with the other missing students, of course, but friends with any of them, no."

"Now, remember, Dr. Washington," Hurts then stated. "We're trying to find a common thread here that connects all of these missing students to each other."

Dr. Washington leaned back in his chair and began stroking the dreadlocks under his large chin with the sausage-size fingers of his right hand. "That's very interesting, Mr. Hurts," he replied, still stroking the dreadlocks under his chin and thinking about it. "A common thread, or common denominator, if you will, that connects together all of these missing students … Well, Mr. Hurts, this is a poverty-stricken district. These students all come from poor, uneducated families, who are often as not given to drug addiction, alcohol abuse, domestic violence and such. These students are all loners, anti-social, given to drugs, alcohol abuse, crime, violence, gangs. As to where they all may hang out together after school, I don't know. I'm sorry that I can't be of more help to you."

"No, no, Dr. Washington," Hurts jumped in. "You have given us some good food-for-thought here."

Because of his extreme weight, Dr. Washington had trouble again rising from his chair. After he did, he said, "If there is nothing more, I'll say good-day."

Both Hurts and Amanda rose too. Dr. Washington extended his hand across the top of the desk and Hurts shook it, saying, "Thank you for seeing us, Dr. Washington … Now I have to stop by Security and get my .9mm semiautomatic pistol and my bottle of whiskey. Security confiscated them from me when we came in."

"Yes, I'm sorry," Dr. Washington said. "We do have rules here, and they must be obeyed."

"Well, now, Dr. Washington," Hurts began. "Some rules just—"

Suddenly, Amanda began coughing, hard. Hurts looked at her. Turning her face to Hurts, and placing the side of her left hand up to her right temple, shading that side of her eyes from view, she shot Hurts a murderous look that said: "If you so much as say, 'But some rules just beg to be broken.' I'll slap you silly!"

Hurts continued, "—beg to be obeyed."

Chapter Seven

Hurts and Amanda walked to her car, which was parked in the narrow parking-lot of Roosevelt High on the south side of the building—and, yes, Hurts retrieved his weapon and whiskey, and, yes, the bottle of whiskey had not been touched.

They got back into the car and Hurts said, "I'm hungry." Knowing Amanda's adamant dislike of processed foods or fast-food restaurants, he said: "I guess that a hamburger at Burger King is out, right?"

Amanda looked at the wristwatch on her right arm—a silver-colored Citizen watch given to her last Christmas by Williams: Another sore subject with Hurts. "Well, look, Uncle Jim," she began. "It's three-thirty now. I'd like to get back home before Mom gets back home from work, and get a bedroll, pack some clothes and such in a suitcase if I'm going to stay with you for a few days. Where did you want to go now?"

"I was thinkin' that we'd go to that Teen Club and speak to that bouncer about Todd and his buddies. He might know somethin.'"

"The club's closed," she said. "It's only open five to eight p.m., Wednesdays through Sundays."

"Oh," he replied. "Well, then, let's head over to your place—but what about something to eat? I'm hungry."

Three blocks from Roosevelt High School, traveling south, on the left side of the street are four businesses—all huddled together in a one-story, run-down, old building complex with a flat roof and each with a glass edifice for a front wall. To the south-end is a dinky neighborhood bar; next to it is a self-servicing laundromat; next to that is a shop that sells clocks; and last is an agent's office who sells State Farm Insurance.

As Amanda and Hurts came near this complex, Hurts saw that there were four patrol cars of the City police there. Two of the patrol cars were parked in front of the shop that sold clocks. The window of that place was shattered; most of it was lying in large shards on the narrow parking lot of the place. So narrow was this parking lot that two of the patrol cars were forced to park on the street. A police officer stood on the passenger's side of the second patrol car parked on the street, at the curb. Using the top of the patrol car as a table, he looked to be writing something.

"Pull over behind that patrol car," Hurts stated.

Amanda did.

Looking at the officer, squinting his face and straining his eyes to ascertain if he knew the guy, Hurts finally recognized him. He pushed the button on the passenger's side of the door to roll down the window. After leaning his head out of the window, Hurts yelled, "Hey, Pete! Pete Gross!"

The officer set down the pen he was holding, turned his stocky-built body towards Hurts, bent down a bit, looked through the windshield at Hurts, recognized him and shouted, "Hurts! James Hurts!" He quickly walked over to the car, and when he came abreast of Hurts, he bent over and said, "I thought you had died years ago, son. I was lookin' forward to goin' to the funeral—because I knew I'd be the only one there. You were always so well liked, Hurts. How you doin', son?"

"I'm still kickin'," Hurts replied. "I thought that you'd be retired by now. You were old when I retired."

He held up his arms and hands to stop Hurts. "I got five more months," he said, "and then, Elvis has left the building."

"What are you gonna do then?" Hurts asked.

"Get drunk every day; fish," he replied. "I got seven grandkids."

"Wow," Hurts stated. "That's a lot of kids … What's goin' on over there?" Hurts asked, pointing with his left hand to the shop that sold clocks.

"Oh, it was probably just kids," he said. "You know how the kids are in this neighborhood. They didn't even take any money. They just took a miniature grandfather clock."

"Is that right?" Hurts said. "When did this happen?"

"Early this morning—about, maybe, four a.m.," he replied. "Well, I better get back to filling out my report," he said. Before he turned and left, he looked beyond Hurts at Amanda. "Your taste in women has improved, Hurts." He laughed, and then left.

"Strange," Hurts said, thinking.

"What's strange, Uncle Jim?" Amanda asked.

"Those kids," Hurts said. "They break into the place and all they take is a clock?"

"Why do I have the feeling that you think that Todd and his followers did this?"

Hurts looked at her, and admonishing her lightly, he said, "I taught you better than that."

Amanda took offence at this but said nothing. A few moments later, she said, "Yes, I know: 'Don't ever assume anything. What looks to be unrelated, can BE related.'" She thought on this for a moment longer, and then said, "Oh, I know. They stole the clock to keep track of The Thirteenth Hour."

Hurts shot her with the thumb and index-finger of his right hand. "Bingo," he said, smiling. "Always use your brain, kid … Say," Hurts then said. "You never did say something about food. I'm starved. Let's get a hamburger and f—"

"No," she retorted firmly. "Before I left the house this morning, I removed four packages of skinless chicken from the freezer and placed them in the refrigerator to thaw. After I get my sleeping bag, clothes, makeup, and such, I'll grab one of the packs of chicken breasts, grab a head of lettuce and such for a salad, take two potatoes, a can of green beans; and Sunday, Mom baked two blueberry cobblers. I'll grab one of those too."

"Wouldn't it just be easier to stop and get a hamburger?" Hurts moaned.

"No, it wouldn't," Amanda snapped at him. "You're having a nutritious, well-balanced, homecooked supper. Period."

"Oh, well, I just can't wait!" Hurts cried, feigning excited anticipation. To prove his dislike of the whole homecooked supper, Hurts removed that bottle of whiskey from the inner pocket of his suit coat, unscrewed the cap, took a big, long gulp from the bottle and said, "Ahhhhhhhhhhhh."

Amanda, hearing him, looked at him and stated, "You're a mess, Uncle Jim. A real mess."

"That's my name, and don't wear it out," he said. "Say," he continued, "why don't we stop at Starbucks and buy a cup of coffee."

"What?" Amanda barked. "So that you can throw the empty cup out the window when you're done drinking it—and I get a ticket?"

"You won't get a ticket," Hurts reproached her.

"Says you!"

"Okay, okay, Amanda," Hurts said. "I won't throw the cup out the window. I promise. Just buy me a…"

Chapter Eight

While Amanda was in the house, Hurts sat in her car with the window rolled down, smoking and drinking his, yes, Starbucks cup of coffee. There is an unattached garage to the house at the end of their small backyard which faces the alley. It's a one-car garage. Amanda's mother parks her car in it, so Amanda always parks her car on the street at the curb, directly in front of their small, two-story, red brick house. Amanda's mother's home isn't any different from the rest of the homes on the block. They all look the same—even Emily's mom and dad's home, directly across the narrow street from Amanda's, looks the same. While he sat there, he looked over at their house several times. He felt horrible for them. They were such good people.

It was a beautiful day—a bright, sunny, warm day. Hurts loved that neighborhood. He loved the look of all the houses on the block; he loved the look of the narrow street, with its curbs and sidewalks; he loved the look of the old lampposts that lined both sides of the sidewalks, as did the tall, old maple trees—which were now in full autumnal glory: red, yellow, orange, and a mixture of all three of these colors and more. Yes, he loved it all. He didn't care much for the County of St. Louis—the houses of the County were too new and spread-out too far from each other, and no sidewalks or curbs, and no street activity. No, it was the City life for Hurts. He was a City boy, born and bred.

As Hurts sat there in the car, enjoying all of this—and really enjoying his coffee, which was now spiked with whiskey from what remained of it in that bottle. When Amanda had gotten out of the car and had gone inside the house, Hurts had hurried up and removed the white, plastic lid from the cup of coffee, threw it out the window and quickly poured what was left in that bottle into the cup, and returned the now empty bottle to the inner pocket of his suit coat. He suddenly had an overwhelming urge to go fishing. Hurts owned an acre-lot of property right along the banks of the Meramec River in the township of St. James, Missouri, which is about a hundred miles south of St. Louis. Hurts loves it there—fishing, camping and sleeping in a bedroll in his tent; cooking on his propane stove; sitting at night in a lawn chair in front of an open fire, drinking coffee or beer or whiskey. And Amanda loves it too. Over the years, she and Hurts have gone dozens of times.

She loves fishing and camping, and Hurts didn't mind it at all last summer when she asked him if Tom could join them one weekend and go fishing with them. No, Hurts didn't mind that. He liked Tom. He found Tom to be a very polite guy—not very good-looking: tall, lanky, pencil-thin body, with one heck of an acne problem, but Amanda liked him. He was, like Amanda, a first-year student at Rolla University, which is about a hundred miles southeast from St. Louis. He's studying to be an engineer. Amanda and he dated; it's casual dating, not serious. They just liked each other's company. She drove down to see him at Rolla one weekend last month. No, Hurts hadn't minded. He liked Tom, but Tom was awful at fishing. He kept having trouble casting; he found the baiting and the removing the hook from the mouth of a fish disgusting; he was no help at all with pitching the tent or with cleaning the fish or with making a campfire—but, boy, that boy sure could eat. So, no, Hurts hadn't mind it at all when Amanda had asked him if Tom could go fishing with them—but he DID mind it when Amanda was fifteen and asked him if Uncle Williams could come fishing with them!

Absolutely not! He would not even hear of it—of Williams going fishing with them. She kept asking why, and he kept telling her because he said no. She kept it up, though. She kept asking him, begging him, and he finally said yes, adding, "Tell him that he better be ready at six o'clock in the morning Saturday when we pick him up, sharp!" It was awful. Just awful. When they picked him up that Saturday morning, at six a.m., at the street-level of the lobby of the Chase Plaza Hotel—oh, so fancy!—in which Williams rented a penthouse on the top floor of the building, Williams was not only ready and waiting, he was as dapper as ever—wearing the latest, and most fashionable, and most expensive of fishing clothes. Hurts told himself that now, not only could he be a poster-boy for Brooks Brothers Clothing, but for any edition of Field and Stream Magazine. And worse: he had the latest, and most expensive of fishing gear. And worse: he was a fly-fisherman. Hurts hated fly-fishermen—always standing in the water up to their waists; always thrashing the water with the long, thin fishing line of their rods, and on and on. And worse: he caught the most fish of the three of them that weekend, and he was perfect at everything he did—setting up the tent; gleaning wood for the open fire; building the open fire and starting it; cleaning and cooking the fish caught—and he didn't eat a darn bit either. Oh, he made Hurts SO mad. And if all of that wasn't bad enough, that night, as the three of them sat in lawn chairs in front of the campfire, he just had to regale Amanda with stories of his past lives. Now, to be fair, Amanda kept begging him to do this, and he, at first, didn't want to, but finally he did—and that just angered Hurts more.

Yes, he just had to tell Amanda stories of his past lives. She loved them. She hung onto his every word—as if she were hypnotized. Well, why wouldn't she have been? She was only a fifteen-year-old kid. Hurts, yes, not to be BESTED by any man, was just beside himself with boiling anger, seeing and listening to all of Williams' tall tales of garbage! Yes, but one of the stories Williams told Amanda, Hurts had to admit to himself, even as much as every fiber of his being didn't want to, that evening, Williams had whipped Hurts good.

The story was this: In his lofty position in the Roman army, Williams had witnessed the crucifixion and the death of Jesus Christ. In fact, when Jesus was hanging on the cross—His face so swollen, black and blue; blood dripping into His soulful brown eyes from the many piercings on His forehead from His crown of thorns—crying out for water, it was Williams who ordered a foot-soldier to give Him a drink of water. It was only after he saw Jesus choking that he realized that the foot-soldier had first dipped the large sponge in vinegar before placing it on the tip of a spear and jamming it against Jesus's swollen, bruised lips. Enraged by this, Williams threw the foot-soldier to the ground, drew his sword, and was about to fatally stab the man, when Jesus spoke: "Vampire," He said, looking down at Williams. "Do not strike that man." Williams turned around and looked up at Jesus. "Your sins are many, vampire," He continued. "Your soul belongs to Satan, but your heart belongs to the Father. Upon your death, I shall accompany you to hell and restore your soul to you. Go, and sin no more." But Williams didn't leave. He stayed until Jesus took His last breath and died. Williams would not speak of that in detail, but he said because of that day, his life was forever changed.

Yes, that evening, at that campfire, Williams had bested Hurts good: the no-good, stinking vampire!

"Sorry, I kept you waiting so long, Uncle Jim," Amanda said as she came abreast of Hurts. On her right shoulder, beside the long, string-strap of her purse, she had on the black strap of the black bag that contained a sleeping bag. Her left hand, which was at her side, held the black handle of a black suitcase with wheels. Perched on top of the suitcase was a smaller, light-blue suitcase, and on top of that was a white plastic grocery bag, stuffed with most of the food for their supper tonight. Amanda stopped for a moment, looked down to the sidewalk and then proceeded to the rear of the car. There, she pressed a button on her keychain and the trunk popped open. After placing all that she had in the trunk, she closed the trunk and got back into the car.

"Look, Amanda," Hurts said to her, waving the now empty Starbucks cup of coffee at her. "I kept my promise. I didn't throw the cup out the window. See?"

"Well, I'm just so proud of you, Uncle Jim," she stated as she started the car and as the automatic shoulder-belt came down across her chest. "Where's the lid, though?"

"What lid?!" he cried. "Oh," he continued, looking around, "it must have fallen under the seat. I took it—"

"No," she interrupted him. "It's right where you threw it—on the sidewalk."

"Boy, you're an agitatin' brat!" he barked, angry at getting caught. "I wish I had put my plan into—" Hurts stopped speaking.

"What plan?" she asked.

"Just never you mind," Hurts chided her. "I have my ways."

"Yeah. Right," she replied, and dropped the car into Drive and drove away.

Chapter Nine

Back at Hurts' office, while Amanda prepared their supper on the hotplate on top of the old cedar dresser, Hurts went to his large wooden desk, in which the front of it faces the room, and removed his suit coat, tossed it on top of the desk, then removed his shoulder holster and set that down, with his pistol inside of it, down on top of the desk too. Then, picking up his suit coat, he walked to the bathroom to change into the clothes that he would wear to bed. About twenty minutes later, he came out wearing a white T-shirt and grey-colored sweatpants. He was shoeless, but still had his black socks on. He had removed them when they had first come in and had set them at the foot of the couch, next to ashtray.

After asking Amanda if supper was ready, and she telling him that it would be a bit longer, he went straight to his old computer which sat in the middle on the top of his desk. Hurts sat down in his uncomfortable old wooden chair, turned on the computer and went directly to the City of St. Louis Police Crime website. Hurts wanted to see if there were any crimes committed in the last few months that he could link to Todd and his followers. He was slow and methodical in his search—and it paid off. Two crimes, both committed in the past two months, jumped out at him.

The first crime was at a downtown retail store that sold candles. No money was taken, just candles—two dozen boxes of candles. Hurts told himself that maybe where they had taken Emily hadn't any electricity. They were vampires, yes, but they still had to see in the dark. The second crime committed was of an elderly homeless man whose body had washed ashore on the banks of the Mississippi River in Arnold, Missouri. Arnold, Missouri, is about ten miles south of St. Louis. The report stated that it was believed that the man had been killed in downtown St. Louis; his body then thrown into the river, and the body floated downstream to Arnold. The report went on to further state that because of the body being in water for so long a time, at least a month, it was difficult to ascertain the true cause of death. But the body was absent of any blood.

Hurts then sat back in the chair and turned his mind to the direction in which Todd and his followers traveled. *Now, let's see,* he mused. *The shop that sells clocks is near Roosevelt High. The candle store robbery and that homeless guy who was killed both happened downtown. Williams said that they would take Emily to somewhere secluded—somewhere where she could scream and cry all she wanted to, and no one would hear her. Could they be in an old abandoned building? There are sure plenty of them north of downtown—but where? There are probably a hundred buildings like that, if not more. Where are you, guys?* he said, silently. *Give me something more—something that will narrow the search. Come on. Where are you, Emily?*

"Supper's ready, Uncle Jim," Amanda called.

"I'm coming," Hurts replied, and turned off his computer.

The room smelt of the mouthwatering aromas of Amanda's fine cooking, and it was a nutritious, well-balanced, home-cooked meal. Delicious! Amanda had cooked chicken breasts in peanut oil; sliced-up two potatoes and cooked them in peanut oil as well; fresh green beans; a salad; and for dessert, a large chunk of that blueberry cobbler that Amanda's mother had baked, with a dab of whipped cream—and coffee, cup after cup of coffee. Hurts enjoyed it immensely. Although, he did tell Amanda that the blueberry cobbler would taste better warm. He told her that he wished he had a microwave.

"Well," Amanda replied, "now I wish that Mom and I had gotten you that for your birthday instead of that DVD collection of John Wayne movies." Hurts' birthday was October 7th.

"I take it back," Hurts stated quickly. "I take it all back. The cobbler was great! I don't need no stupid microwave. I love my John Wayne movies, pilgrim." He flipped the thumb of his left hand towards the direction of his ex-partner's desk, to the top of it, on which a 19" color TV stood in the middle of it, right next to the box of DVD movies of John Wayne.

"Great," Amanda said. "Now I know what Mom and I can get you for Christmas."

"No," Hurts pouted like little boy. "Don't get me a stupid microwave. Get me more John Wayne movies— 'I die with my boots on, pilgrim.'"

"I think John Wayne died in a hospital from lung cancer—he was a heavy smoker, like you."

"No one likes a smarty-pants," Hurts chided her.

Amanda stuck her tongue out at Hurts. It was blue from having just eaten some of that blueberry cobbler.

"Your tongue's bluc!" Hurts cried, and then started laughing. "You look like one of those little guys on TV—a Snarth, or somthin' like that."

Hurts, now stuffed and feeling good, got up heavily from the table and walked over to the couch and plopped down onto it. He then got the ashtray from the floor, and he then reached into the pocket of his sweatpants and removed from it a pack of cigarettes and his lighter. Sitting back on the couch, with the ashtray on his knees, he began smoking a cigarette. As he smoked, he watched as Amanda traveled back and forth from the table area to the bathroom, carrying pots, pans, dishes, and on and on. She took them in there to wash them in the small sink in the bathroom. She made four trips altogether.

At one point, Hurts said to her, "When are you going to call Williams or your mother?"

"When I'm finished," she replied. Then, she said, "On second thought, I think I'll call them after I wash and change into my pajamas."

"Okay," he said, suddenly remembering that he had forgotten to take his cell phone with him when they had left this morning. He forced himself to get up off the couch and walked over to his desk. He plopped down hard into the chair, and then reached over and pulled the top right drawer open. He withdrew from it his cell phone, flipped it open, turned it on and checked it for messages. There were none. "Hey, Amanda," he called to her.

"Yeah?" she said.

"Remind me to take my cell phone tomorrow," he said. Then, he remembered something else. "And also remind me to take that list of names and addresses of those missing students out of the pocket of the suit that I wore today, and place it in my black pin-stripe suit. I think I'm gonna wear that suit tomorrow."

"Okay," she replied.

After he had taken some of his business cards out of that open drawer, he placed them on the top of the desk next to his cell phone, closed the drawer, returned to the couch, and plopped down upon it again. By this time, Amanda had finished. She came next to the arm of the couch, where she had left her purse on the floor by the door, along with her sleeping bag and suitcases She grabbed the long handle of the suitcase and then headed for the bathroom, saying, "I'm going to wash and change into my pajamas, Uncle Jim."

When Amanda emerged from the bathroom about twenty minutes later, she found Hurts still sitting on the couch, almost asleep. She was washed and wearing white pajamas and white slippers. She grabbed her purse off the floor and walked over to the far end of the dining table, where she had sat during supper, and she sat down there again and called Williams and then her mom. She spoke with Williams for only a few seconds. He had told her that he hadn't any information about Todd. He then apologized and told her that he had "other pressing business to attend to" and said goodbye.

She spoke with her mother much longer, about forty minutes. First Hurts heard her tell her mother that, yes, Hurts seemed better, but that she still thought she should stay with him for at least another day, or two. Then, she and her mother talked about a new dress her mother was thinking about buying at Macy's. "Oh, yes, buy it, Mom," Amanda said. "It looks so good on you." Then, her mother wanted to say goodbye to her, because she wanted to take a shower and get ready for work tomorrow before her favorite TV show came on. A show called "NCIS," with a guy by the name of Mark Harmon. But instead of saying goodbye and hanging up, they just kept talking about that show and how "dreamy" that guy is— old, but "dreamy."

Hurts thought it all was stupid, listening to them ogling over some glamour-boy actor. Hurts didn't watch hardly any TV. Although, he did like watching a channel on Saturdays. The channel is called METV, and every Saturday it plays old westerns from the '50's and '60's—shows like "Gunsmoke," "Dead or Alive" and "Rawhide." Now, those are good shows.

After Amanda had finally said goodbye to her mother and ended their conversation, she walked over to the arm of the couch by the door; heaved the strap of the pouch that contained the sleeping bag onto her right shoulder; turned to the light switch that was midway up the wall by the door and said, "Are you ready for bed, Uncle Jim? Because if you are, I'll turn off the light."

"Sure thing, Amanda," he replied, lying down. "I'm more than ready. I'm tired."

She flipped the switch off and walked to the front of Hurts' ex-partner's big, old wooden desk, which is directly behind the four, narrow, tall, wooden-framed windows: the ones that face the street below and has the writing on them: JAMES HURTS, PRIVATE INVESTIGATOR. She pulled the sleeping roll out of its pouch and spread it out on the wooden floor.

"I'm cold," Hurts said.

"Wait a minute," she replied. She skirted around the dining table and walked to the dresser. At it, she bent down and opened the bottom left-end drawer and removed from it a folded brown wool blanket. She closed the drawer and brought the blanket over to Hurts.

"Here you go," she said, shaking the blanket to full length. Then, she laid it over him and walked back to the sleeping roll. After removing her slippers, she got on her knees, unzipped the sleeping roll and got into it.

Hurts, lying on his back and feeling warm now, and thinking of when Amanda had stayed with him when he had investigated her mom's case (she had slept in a sleeping roll that time too and in the same spot) said, "This is like old times, ain't it, kid?"

Amanda, also lying on her back, and seeing and feeling the light from the full moon shining in on her through the windows, replied, "Yes, it does feel like that, somewhat." She was silent for a moment and then said, "I'm so worried about Emily. I can't image what she must be going through—what they are doing to her."

"Well," Hurts began, "Williams said that they wouldn't hurt her until The Thirteenth Hour."

"Yes, I know," Amanda replied. "But, she's all alone, Uncle Jim. She must be feeling so desperate, so hopeless, so scared—terrified ... I remember when Mom was arrested, and I ran away so Family Services wouldn't get me. I roamed the streets—feeling so lost and hopeless. I didn't know what to do or where to go. I just kept walking the streets. It was awful—I had never felt so alone and scared in my life. And then I found you ... I never told you this, Uncle Jim, but from the first moment I met you—lying asleep on that couch, drunk, hung-over and rude—I felt safe and not alone. Something in me—deep within me—told me that everything would be made right now. You would make it all right—and you did ... But what of Emily?"

Lying on that couch in the dark, and hearing Amanda saying those things about him, for a moment—and just for a moment! —Hurts felt a tear well-up in his eyes. He was so proud of hearing her say those things about him. "Well, Amanda," he replied, finally. "Emily's got great parents. I think she'll be fine"

"But what of the scars, Uncle Jim?"

"Scars?" Hurts stated, confused. "What scars?'

"The scars she'll have from going through all of this," Amanda said, empathically.

"Well," Hurts began, "we all have scars, Amanda. That's just a part of life. They either destroy us or make us stronger. But, again, Emily has great parents. They'll send her to doctors or such. They love her so much."

"Yes, they do ... There's such love in that house. You can feel it; smell it. That house is so complete, whole ... Oh, there's love in our home, but our home isn't complete, whole. There's something missing. Something absent."

"Are you talkin' about your father?" Hurts asked.

"Yes," she said, after a moment of silence. "I—I don't remember him anymore, Uncle Jim. I don't. Sometimes, when Mom's not there, I'll go into her bedroom, sit on her bed and just stare at the picture she has of us together on her nightstand. I just stare and stare at him, but I don't remember him. I don't."

"Oh, Amanda," Hurts said. "Give yourself a break. You were only nine-years-old when your father died … He's there, Amanda. He's in you. Death doesn't stop that. I am the way that I am because of my parents—the no-good drunks! I don't remember my parents, which is good, but I know that they're still there; in me … Amanda, you've been given a great gift. Look—look at all the people in the world—in the WHOLE world—who go about their daily lives praying to just have faith that there's a God. You don't have to have 'faith'. You know that there IS a God. You have seen vampires; you know Williams. That's a gift, Amanda."

"Yes. You're right, Uncle Jim."

"God," Hurts then cried. "I wish that I had some whiskey."

"You don't need any damn whiskey!" Amanda barked at him.

"Says you!" Hurts shot back at her.

"Yes, says me," she replied.

"You know," Hurts stated, "You're cussin' way too much. I stopped using cuss words because I didn't want you pickin' it up from me, and here you are cussin'."

"Well, what are you going to do about it? —spank me?"

"Well," he retorted, "if you keep cussin' and sassin' me, I just might."

"Fine," she replied.

"Fine," he repeated.

"Goodnight," she said.

"Goodnight."

The next morning, Amanda woke Hurts up at seven-thirty. She was already washed, dressed, and had the coffee and breakfast made.

When Hurts came to the dining table, still half asleep, scratching his head, and in much need of coffee, he took a good look at Amanda and was shocked. She was wearing a sleeveless black dress with matching high-heel shoes—and she looked stunning, and she smelled good too. Sitting down and yawning, he said, "Why are you so dressed up?"

She had just taken a sip of coffee from one of Hurts' many different types of coffee mugs and replied, "If I'm to be your associate, I should look the part, right?"

"Yeah, you're right," he said, and began drinking the coffee Amanda had already placed on the table, along with his breakfast: oatmeal and a slice of white bread.

"Hurry up and eat your breakfast, so we can get going," she said.

Hurts looked down at the steaming bowl, which had milk in it, and said, "But I don't like oatmeal. I like eggs and bacon and toast."

"Oatmeal is good for you—and you know that the toaster that Mom and I bought for you two Christmases ago is broke."

"Well, I'll eat it—but I won't like it," Hurts said. "Say," he then said, remembering something. "Don't you have school today?"

"Yeah," she replied, "but I'm going to skip it. I'm all caught-up, so I can afford to miss it. It won't hurt me."

"Well, it better not," Hurts warned, placing a spoon of oatmeal in his mouth, and then making a face of disgust.

After having had such a DELICIOUS meal, Hurts washed, shaved, dressed into his black pin-striped suit—and yes, Amanda had reminded him to remove that list of the names and addresses of the missing students from the pocket of the suit that he had worn the day before—put on his full-length, beige topcoat, and was now ready to begin the day.

They descended the stairs of the office and exited the building and onto the sidewalk.

It was a beautiful day, like it had been yesterday, but a bit colder, with a cold wind in the fresh, fall air.

Hurts and Amanda got into the front seat of her car. Amanda said, "Don't you think we should first check out the home that Todd had lived in and that bookstore of the vampire who turned him?"

"No," Hurts answered, shaking his head. "Williams' people have probably gone through those places pretty good."

"Well," she then stated. "What if he returned to one of those places? You always say that people are creatures of habit."

"Yeah, I know," Hurts replied, "but Williams said that Todd guy is smart. I think he is, and that being the case, he's smart enough to know that Williams' people are watching those places like a hawk. No, let's stay with the list, and hope that one of the parents gives us a lead to Todd's whereabouts."

"Okay," she replied. "Which one of the parents first?"

He removed the folded list from the right pocket of his suit coat, unfolded it, and began viewing it, saying, "Let's take the nearest to Roosevelt High and fan-out from there … That would be—What a name! It must be Russian or something. I can't say it … Ahmed Haracic."

"It's Bosnian," Amanda said. "What's the address?"

"36118 Virginia Avenue," Hurts answered. Amanda began typing it into the GPS. "Is that lady gonna start talkin' to us? You don't have to do that, because I know how to get there."

"Yeah, but I'm driving," Amanda replied, "and I don't know how to get there."

"But I don't want that lady talkin' to us!" Hurts protested.

"It's only a recording, Uncle Jim."

"I don't care," he continued to protest. "It's spooky."

"Well, Happy Halloween," she replied.

"Oh, Halloween ain't until tomorrow," Hurts said. "If we gotta hear that da—that stupid woman talk, you could at least buy me a coffee at Starbucks."

"Fine," she said.

"Fine," he replied, as Amanda pulled away from the curb—to the sound of: "Your time of destination is…."

Chapter Eleven

Hurts hadn't been at that part of Virginia Avenue in probably ten years. It had deteriorated much in that time. All the houses on the block, and in the whole neighborhood—mostly two-story, old brick homes with flat roofs—had seen much better days. The street was made of bloodless, red bricks, left there from the 1900s, and very rough on an automobile's underpinnings. The house that Hurts and Amanda wanted was in the middle of the block on the west side of the street.

As Amanda pulled the car to the cracked curb of the street, Hurts set his cup of Starbucks coffee in the cup holder next to Amanda's. He then looked out the side window at the house. From the in-much-need-of-repair, cracked sidewalk, to the three-step, tilting to the north, cement porch, were two wooden old doors painted a bright white. Both doors had their addresses on them with dark, metallic numbers. The house that Hurts and Amanda wanted was the one on the left, or south side.

"Well, let's go," Hurts said, and they both exited the car.

The steps hadn't a rail, and Hurts had some difficulty keeping his balance as he climbed the steps. At the door, Hurts knocked on it with the back of his hand. No answer. So, Hurts knocked again, Then again. Still no answer. Hurts was beginning to get angry at this, when he heard a voice of a man behind him say, "Help you?" Hurts and Amanda both turned around. At the bottom of the steps, stood a middle-aged man of average height and stocky build, with a bald head. He was dressed in a much-faded denim shirt and much worn blue jeans. He had a wide, old belt on, with a leather pouch attached to it with an assortment of tools in it.

"Are you Mr. Haracic?" Hurts asked.

"No, he dead," the man replied in a thick accent. "Me landlord."

"Is Mrs. Haracic here?"

"She works," he said.

"Do you know Ahmed?" Hurts then asked.

"He gone," the man said.

"Yes, he's missing," Hurts stated. "Do you know any of Ahmed's friends? Do you know a Todd Sinclair?"

The man shook his head no.

"Do you know where Ahmed goes after school? —where he goes with friends?"

After scratching his bald head, the man shrugged his shoulders as if he didn't understand the question. "He no-good," the man then said. "He steals—takes drugs. Bad."

"Okay," Hurts said. "Are the people next door here?"

"Work," the man said.

"Okay, thanks," Hurts said to the man. He turned to Amanda and said, "Well, this was a waste of time. Let's get out of here."

The house they went to next wasn't any better—in looks or in help. It was only four blocks away, and it was the home of missing student Fred Brown. The woman who finally answered the door was a thin woman in her mid-forties. She was dressed in a pullover grey sweater and blue jeans. She looked half asleep, or half drunk, or half high on drugs—or half of all three. She was rude, sarcastic and wouldn't permit Hurts and Amanda to enter the house. They had to stand there at the front door the whole time— and, the whole time, she kept blowing smoke in Hurts' face from the cigarettes she kept smoking. Hurts told himself that in younger days, she was probably a hot looking gal, but not now.

"Look," she said rudely. "I told all of this crap to the police."

"Well, can't you at least tell us where you think Fred might be?" Hurts said.

"Do I look like I got a crystal-ball or somethin'?"

Hurts had had enough of her. He angrily said, "Alright, lady. Ain't you even the least bit concerned that your son is missing?"

"I don't even know if the punk is really my kid," she snapped at Hurts and then slammed the door shut in his face.

"Man," Hurts mumbled. "We're batting a thousand. Come on. Let's go."

After they had gotten back into the car, Amanda turned around and looked behind her, and then she turned back around and looked straight ahead. She reached down with her left hand and pressed a button on the door panel. Hurts' window came down. Hurts looked at her, and she said, "Uncle Jim, is your coffee cup empty?"

"Yeah," he replied, doubtfully.

"So is mine," she stated. "Throw them out the window as far as you can—hopefully to that woman's front door."

Try as he did, Hurts fell woefully short of hitting that woman's front door. When Hurts looked back at Amanda, she said, fuming, "Some trashy people just beg to have trash thrown at them."

Laughing, Hurts said, "That's my girl. That's my girl."

Chapter Twelve

They did much better at the next home. The house was in a much better neighborhood and the parents of the missing teen, Vedad Graovac, were both kind and cooperative. They lived on the second floor of a red brick, two-family, old flat on Dewy Avenue. Three cement steps led to three more cement steps that led to a covered porch. A nice, small raised front yard lined both sides of cement sidewalk, the grass of which was now brown. The mother of the missing teen answered the wooden-framed glass door when Hurts rang the doorbell. He handed her one of his businesses cards and told her why they were here. She was very excited to hear that they wanted to find her missing son. She invited them in, saying in a thick accent, "Come upstairs. Please, come."

She was a short, stocky woman in her mid-forties, with long, brown, graying hair that she wore tight in a bundle on the top of her head. She was dressed in a simple dress of floral print and wore a full-length apron over it; the wearing of the apron seemed to be as natural to her as is the wearing of stethoscope to a doctor. Her eyes were brown, warm and inviting. Hurts thought she was a throwback to a woman of the '40's.

The steps were long and narrow—at least twenty-five of them. At the top of the stairs stood a man, also in his mid-forties. He was also short and stocky, with short salt-and-pepper greying hair. He was dressed in a faded, but clean—very clean—light blue work-shirt and matching pants. Although he too had an aura about him of warmth, there was a sternness to his demeanor—a sternness that demanded respect and obedience. When the three of them had reached the small, narrow wooden-floor platform at the top of the stairs, the woman handed him Hurts' business card. He took it, read it and placed it in his shirt pocket. He then extended his right hand for Hurts to shake. Hurts, winded from his journey up the steps, shook it, feeling the strong grip of a much-callused hand of a man who was accustomed to doing hard work. He, also in a thick accent, invited Hurts and Amanda to step beyond the painted white wooden door to their left, and enter their home.

They stepped immediately into a small living room. To Hurts' right was a narrow hallway that led to a bathroom; beyond that, a small kitchen, and beyond that, a sunporch. The living-room was furnished with old furniture, but all the furniture was immaculately clean and well-cared for. The dining room, which was to the far-right side of the house, was furnished with a long, old, wooden dining room table and six wooden ladderback chairs. Beyond the dining room were two small bedrooms.

The home smelt musty and of the heads of cabbage boiling in a large pot on top of the old stove in the kitchen at low heat. It also smelt of much love. Hurts knew that Amanda felt all this too, and he also knew that Amanda immediately liked these two people, and so did he.

"Sit, sit, please," the woman said, pointing to the long cloth couch. Doilies adorned the two arms of the couch. The floors of all the rooms were of wood, except for the bathroom, kitchen and sunroom, which were of black-and-white tile. Most of the floor in the living-room was covered with an immense rug of Arabic design. In front of the couch was a dark-colored, old coffee table. About two feet in front of that were two dark-colored, leather easy-chairs, both of which had an end-table situated next to it. The one end-table, to the right, had a coffee-cup on top of it, and an ashtray with a few smoked butts in it. The other end-table, to the left of the room, and close to the four narrow, tall, wooden-framed windows that faced the street below, had on it reading glasses, a ball of blue yarn and two long knitting-needles.

Hurts and Amanda walked between the couch and coffee-table and sat down. Hurts sat down by the four windows and Amanda sat down by the side of the room which lead to the hallway. The man and the woman sat down too, in the two easy-chairs which faced them—the woman sat directly across from Hurts and the man sat directly across from Amanda.

"Now," Hurts began. "What we're trying to do here, Mr. and Mrs. Gra—"

"Flora," she said, interrupting Hurts. "Flora."

"Omar," the man added.

"Yes, of course," Hurts said. "Thank you. Now, what we're trying to—"

"Coffee?" she then said, interrupting Hurts again. "Cake?"

Hurts looked at Amanda, and then looked back at Flora and said, "Thank you, but no. We're fine … Now, tell me about Vedad—his friends? Where did he go—"

"Wait," Flora said, interrupting Hurts again. "I show you. Wait." She got up from the easy-chair and left the room, quickly. There was silence in the room now, and it felt awkward. Hurts looked to his left at the four windows, at the thick, white parted drapes on both sides of the windows. He then looked back at Omar and smiled, an uncomfortable smile.

"Here," she said, coming back into the room, carrying in her hands the dark-colored, metallic frame of a picture. "Vedad," she continued, handing the frame to Hurts.

Hurts took the frame and looked at it. It was a headshot of a good-looking young man, with shoulder-length, thick, black hair. He looked very much like the father, but only young and with tight, smooth skin. His eyes were brown, like his mother and father—and warm and inviting too. He looked so happy. Around his neck was a small medallion on a thin gold chain. The medallion itself was of gold, and in small print, stated: IN SERVICE OF PEACE.

"He's a fine-lookin' boy," Hurts said, handing the frame back to Flora. She went back to the chair she had been sitting in and sat back down. For a moment or two, she held the frame against her sagging breasts, but then she lowered it and let it rest on her lap.

"What's that around his neck?" Hurts asked.

"It's medallion of Bosnia Peace," the father said.

Almost in tears, Flora said, "Vedad never see Bosnia. Want to go."

"Oh," Hurts replied. "Now," he started again. "As to Vedad's friends. Do you know a Todd Sinclair?"

They both shook their heads no.

"Did Vedad go out a lot at night?"

They both shook their heads yes.

"Do you know where he went?"

The father replied, "Walking. Street."

"But where?" Hurts persisted. "Where would he go at nights? —To be with friends?"

"I don't know," the father stated, sadly.

"How long has your son been missing?" Hurts then asked.

"Two months," the father replied.

"Two months," Hurts repeated, "and you ain't seen him since then?"

The father said no, but this got rise out of Flora—and Hurts clearly saw it. She looked at her husband and then back at Hurts. She wanted to tell Hurts something, but not in front of her husband.

Hurts said, "I see the ashtray there," he said, pointing to the ashtray on the end-table by Omar. "I hope you don't mind, but I need a smoke." He reached into the right-side pocket of his topcoat and removed his pack of cigarettes and lighter, saying, "Pass me that ashtray, will ya?"

Omar picked up the ashtray, then, he leaned forward, extending out his hand.

Quickly, very quickly, Hurts scooted up to the edge of the couch: he did not want Omar's extended hand to reach the coffee-table. He met Omar's hand as it was just coming to the edge of the coffee-table. Taking the ashtray from Omar with his left hand, Hurts said thanks, and the ashtray dropped to the rug below.

Hurts thrust the pack of cigarettes and lighter back into the pocket of his topcoat, shot up from the couch, and skirted around the coffee-table. By this time, Flora and her husband were both standing up, the picture frame now lying on the end-table next to her reading glasses. Hurts grabbed Flora by her arms and said: "Oh, I'm so sorry. I feel so awful. Your so, so clean house. I have—"

"Accident," she said. "Accident. I get pan and broom." She started to move, but Hurts tightened the grip he had on her and prevented her from moving—not even an inch.

"I'm just so sorry. What a clumsy guy I am. Can you—"

"Accident," she repeated. "I get pan and broom."

"But I'm so sorry, my dear, dear, dear woman," Hurts keep saying.

"I get pan and broom," Omar finally said, and turned and headed down the hallway towards the kitchen. When he was out of sight, Hurts shook Flora and said, quickly and emphatically, "You saw Vedad, yes?"

She shook her head yes.

"When?" Hurts asked. "Tell me, now."

She looked towards the kitchen and then back at Hurts. "Four," she replied. "Four."

"Four days ago?" he said, urgently.

She looked again towards the kitchen and then back at Hurts and shook her head no. "Night," she said.

"You saw Vedad four nights ago, is that right?"

She nodded her head yes.

"Where?!" Hurts pressed her. "Where?!"

She pointed to the middle window. Hurts looked in that direction, hearing her say, "He say, 'Mommy, let me in. Mommy, let me—"

"Flora! No talk!" yelled Omar, standing there beside them with a dustpan and the wooden handle of a broom in his hands. "No talk!" he demanded.

Hurts immediately released her, turned and walked swiftly to the windows. He looked at the outer brick ledge of the windows. He looked at the ground below, and then out into the street.

When he turned back around, he saw both Flora and her husband squatted down; she was holding the dustpan in her hands at the rug where the butts and ashes were, and Omar was holding, and working, the broom.

Hurts walked over and stood by Flora, looking down at her. He said, "Well, I apologize again for having done that. I want to thank you for all your kindness. We must leave now," Hurts said, motioning for Amanda to get up. "We have other appointments." Hurts met Amanda at the edge of the couch, and they began walking to the door of the stairs. They were almost at the door when Hurts heard Flora saying, "Wait. Wait. Please, wait." Hurts turned around, and Flora took Hurts' hands in hers, kissed his right hand, and with tears running down her face, she looked into Hurts' eyes and said, "Find Vedad … Find my Vedad, please."

Before the words left his mouth, Hurts heard himself say, "I will. I promise. I'll find him."

She kissed his hand again and then released them. Hurts could not BELIEVE that he had said that to that poor woman. He knew only too well that Williams would hush it all up—that all those missing students, and those two missing teachers, would remain just that—missing, for eternity.

Hurts had to get out of there. He felt so bad. He gave her a quick goodbye, turned and rushed Amanda out the door and down the steps.

As they were stepping down the steps to the sidewalk—and it felt so good to Hurts to be outside—Amanda said, "Do you think you said enough 'dears' in there to convince them that you 'accidentally' dropped that astray?"

"Maybe," Hurts replied, smiling.

"Do you believe her?"

"Absolutely," he stated unequivocally.

Hurts came abreast of Amanda's car. He watched as she stepped off the curb and into the street, passing in front of her car. She said, "Why didn't Omar want her to tell us about seeing Vedad?"

"Well," Hurts began, shaking his head, "he probably didn't want anybody to think she was nuts."

Amanda now stood before the door of her car, with the keychain to it in her right hand. But instead of pressing the button on it to unlock the doors, she placed her arms and hands on the top of the hood of the car and said, "Why didn't Flora let Vedad in?"

"I don't have the answer to that one," Hurts said. "Although, I do think that Omar came in and chased Vedad away. Good thing too. Vedad, probably, would have had no other choice than to kill them."

"Sad," Amanda mused. "It's all just too—" She suddenly stopped talking. Hurts saw her looking up at Flora and Omar's apartment, at those four windows. Hurts turned around and looked up in that direction too. There, in the same window where Flora said she'd seen Vedad, now stood Flora, staring down at them—so sadly; so hopelessly.

Hurts hated seeing her. He felt so helpless—and he LOATHED that feeling.

"Sad," Amanda repeated. "Say," she then stated, Hurts turning around and looking at her. "Did you smell that cabbage cooking?"

"Yes," he replied, frowning. "It smelt disgustin'."

"Cabbage is good for you—healthy," she stated.

"I'd rather be dead than eat that crap," Hurts replied.

"Gosh," Amanda suddenly stated. "Now I'm hungry. Do you want to eat?"

After looking at the face of his cheap, old Casio wristwatch, he said, "It's only ten-after-two. Let's knock out one more from the list, and then we'll talk about gettin' something to eat."

They then left—and Hurts knew, he just knew, that Flora's eyes were still upon them as they drove away. He also knew that even when they had driven far enough away to be out of her sight of them, her eyes would always be upon them now—and Hurts hated that.

Chapter Thirteen

They should have eaten when Amanda had wanted to, because the next home of another missing student that they visited turned out to be just another complete waste of time. This missing student, Tim Rogan, was from Sumner High School—and, boy, was that home and neighborhood BAD. The mother whom they spoke with was nice and cooperative, but she just didn't have anything new or of importance to tell them. They walked away from there feeling tired, hungry and depressed.

In the car, before Amanda started it, Hurts said, "Now I know that you won't eat a hamburger, but would you be willin' to eat at Zia's?"

"Yeah," she replied, enthusiastically. "I'll always eat at Zia's."

"Do you know how to get to there from here?" he asked.

"I'm not sure how to get to anywhere from here," she said. "But wherever we go, let's just get out of here."

"Do you want me to give you directions or do you want to look it up on your Stupid-phone—I mean, your Smartphone?"

"Do you know the address?" she asked.

"Yes," he replied. "It's 5256 Wilson Avenue."

She typed the address into the GPS, started the car and drove quickly away.

Zia's is on what in St. Louis is known as "The Hill" or "Little Italy." It is a section of a neighborhood southwest of Kingshighway Boulevard that is nationally, even internationally, known for its Italian restaurants and fine dining. Zia's is at the corner of the block. In a single-story, red brick building, with a green awning that traverses the whole front edifice. On good-weather days, there is both indoor and outdoor dining. As with most of the businesses there, Zia's is family-owned and run. Although it possesses an elegance—and is quite pricey—it still has a "family-feel" to it. Whenever Hurts and Amanda dine there, they always sit at a booth to the back of the place. Hurts likes to smell the many, mouthwatering aromas wafting from the kitchen. He just loves the red-and-white checkerboard tablecloths and matching napkins.

Now, sitting in their favorite spot, listening to the din of noise of the patrons, seeing the hustle-and-bustle of the people and of the waiters and waitresses hurrying here and there, and smelling the earthy smells of food cooking, made Hurts feel better.

"Hi, Mike," Hurts said heartily to the young man who came to the booth to give them menus and take their orders. He was a tall guy, thin and agile, with short light-brown hair and a winning personality. Dressed in a white dress shirt, black dress pants, and black tennis shoes, he held an order pad and pen in his hands, ready for action. "Still gonna be a high-school English teacher?"

"Yes, sir, Mr. Hurts," he replied cheerfully. "Thank you for asking. How are you and Amanda today?"

"Fine, Mike," Hurts replied. "Just fine."

"Very good, Mr. Hurts … The usual?" he then asked.

"Yes, yes," Hurts replied. "What else? Your famous spaghetti and meatballs!"

"Very good, Mr. Hurts," he said.

Amanda lowered the menu she was studying, looked at Hurts and stated, "Why do you always get the same thing?"

"Well, what about you? You always get the same thing … 'Oh, Mike,'" Hurts said, pretending to be Amanda, "I'll have Zia's famous salad. Now, Mike, please make sure that the chef gives me plenty of sliced red peppers. I just love red peppers. For the main course, Mike, I'll have chicken parmesan. Now, Mike, make sure that the chef doesn't drown the chicken in tomato sauce. A light coating of sauce will do.'"

"Very funny," Amanda said, sarcastically.

"What will you have, Amanda?" Mike asked.

Slapping down the menu on top of the table, she said, "The usual."

"Very good," he replied. "Drinks?"

"I'll have coffee," Amanda said.

"So will I," Hurts added. Then, he motioned for Mike to come near him. When Mike did, Hurts placed his hand near his mouth and whispered, "I'll also have a glass of beer and a shot of whiskey."

"Very good," he said, and he hurried away.

"You ordered alcohol, didn't you?" she said, angrily.

"So?" he griped. "It's been a long, miserable day. I'm depressed."

"Well, alcohol won't made you happy," she said. "Alcohol is a depress—"

Just then, Hurts' cell phone began ringing in the right pocket of his topcoat. He took it out, flipped it open, brought it to his ear and said, "Hurts."

"Yes, yes," Amanda heard Hurts say excitedly. "No, no. I'm glad you called." Looking at Amanda, he said, "Dr. Washington." Amanda now listened with excited and hopeful anticipation. "Really?" he said. "This is interesting … Yes … Oh, wow … Yes … Yes … Dr. Washington," she then heard Hurts say. "Do you have an address of John Banks? … Yes, yes. I'll wait." Hurts then put his left hand over the phone and said to Amanda, "He's getting on his computer—Do you have a pen and a piece of paper?" Amanda reached to the right-side of her and placed her purse on the table. She hurriedly searched through her purse until she found a pen and pocket-notebook. "… Yes, yes. I'm still here," she heard him say. "Excellent … The address is 22541 Itasca Street." Amanda quickly wrote it on a page from that notebook. Her hand was visibly shaking as she did so. "Thank you so much for this, Dr. Washington. If you get any more information, please call … Yes sir. Again, thank you."

Placing his cell phone back into the pocket of his topcoat, Hurts almost shouted, "We got a tip—a big one!" As he was saying this to Amanda, Mike returned, carrying a black tray which had on it two mugs of coffee, a glass of beer and a shot of whiskey. Mike didn't even have a chance of setting down that shot of whiskey. Hurts grabbed it from him and gulped it down in one swallow, saying to Mike, "I'll have three more of these—and hurry … We must eat fast and get out of here … Let me tell you what Dr. Washington just told me … Now, he said …"

Chapter Fifteen

It was one of Amanda's diehard convictions never to eat food too fast. Doing this was bad for the digestive system and—well, food was to be enjoyed. But, under the present circumstances, she, like Hurts, wolfed the food down—not in the least bit getting any nutrition from it or enjoying it. As she ate, she listened intensely as Hurts informed her of what Dr. Washington had said, which was this:

About ten minutes after the dismissal bell rang at three o'clock today, John Banks stood at the open door to Dr. Washington's office. He said that he felt troubled and wanted to know if Dr. Washington would speak with him. Well, Dr. Washington had told Hurts, John Banks was one of the toughest, if not 'the' toughest, students in the school, and if he felt 'troubled' and wanted to speak with Dr. Washington, Dr. Washington felt it incumbent to listen to him. John is a tall, slender young man with long, unruly red hair. He's street-tough, and has been arrested a few times for drugs—mostly marijuana—stealing, and gang violence. His mother and father are both on disability; the mother has had two operations on her back, and the father is dying from lung cancer. Together, they had owned and ran a neighborhood corner bar a few blocks from their apartment. Because of their deteriorating health, the bar has been closed for the past year. John and his buddies, his 'gang', Dr. Washington had said, hang out there at night, sometimes—only to, you know, John had said, just to 'hang-out.' What was troubling John so much was that about three weeks ago, he and his buddies were hanging out there, when in walks Danin Mujic, one of the ten missing students. John said he acted so strange—he kept his hand over his mouth, and he kept sniffing the air. He told John that he was with Todd and some of the other missing students, and that Todd was their Savior and that they were his Followers. He then told John that Todd needed one more follower, and Danin had been granted permission from Todd to offer this to John, because John was his friend. John blew-up and screamed at Danin, yelling, "I don't 'follow' nobody! If that fairy sticks his nose in my business, I'll cut him up. Now, go tell him." Danin turned around and started to walk away, but stopped, saying, "You're my friend, John. This is a one-time offer—to refuse Todd is a mistake. He has power now—real power." "Hey," John yelled, "I have power—look at all my boys here." Danin then left.

It was a little after six o'clock when Amanda pulled the car to the curb in front of the red brick, two-story family flat that John Banks' parents lived in and rented. The sun was just beginning to set, and the dark, thick clouds blanketing the evening sky forewarned of rain.

After Hurts had knocked on the windowless, sun-bleached, weathered wooden front door, he and Amanda were escorted into the apartment, and then into the small kitchen, by John's mother. She, like the rest of the mothers of the missing students, was in her mid-forties. She was thin, and to Hurts looked sickly. She had long red hair, which was dirty and in need of both washing and cutting—not to mention styling. Her angular face was mapped with age-lines, from both aging and years of heavy smoking. The husband, sitting at the kitchen-table, wearing an oxygen-tube around the back of his neck that came around to the front under his thin nose, blowing air up his nostrils, looked to Hurts to be much more sickly than the wife. He was pencil-thin and emaciated, and the whole time he and Amanda were there, which wasn't long, he kept coughing—and smoking, as the wife did as well.

Hurts came right to the point. He first asked if John was there. The woman, in a gravelly smoker's voice, said that he wasn't. Hurts then told them that Dr. Washington had called him and was worried about John. He wanted Hurts to speak with John. Hurts went on to say that Dr. Washington had told him that John and his friends sometimes hang out at their now closed bar. Did they think that John was there now? Yes, the woman answered. What was the address? She gave it to them, and they left.

It was dark when they stepped back outside, and raining lightly. True to their word, their shuttered bar was only three blocks away, north of their apartment.

It was on the right-hand side of the block, on the corner, facing west. A two-story building of red brick, it looked like the rest of the buildings on the block and in the neighborhood, except for the long picture window on the south-side of the face of the building and for the metallic yawning, painted black, over the wooden-framed glass door of the entrance to the place. John and his parents had lived on the second floor of the building for many years, but as his parents' health worsened to a point in which they could no longer run the business or climb the many stairs to the second floor, they boarded up the place and moved into their present apartment.

Amanda parked her car on the opposite side of the street, directly across from the bar. Because of the sheet of plywood attached to and covering the picture window and the glass of the door to the entrance, Hurts and Amanda couldn't see if anyone was in there or not. Amanda felt anxious. She wanted this very much to lead them to Emily, and so did Hurts.

She reached for the sunken handle of the car door to exit it, but Hurts told her to stop.

"Amanda," he said. "I'm havin' some trouble seein'. "How about takin' my hand and gettin' me to the front door?"

Amanda knew how difficult that must have been for a man like Uncle Jim to ask for help. She would act as if it was nothing.

"Sure, Uncle Jim," she replied ever so casually. "Get out of the car and stand by the door. I want to show you something."

He did as she requested and got out of the car and stood by the door. As he stood there waiting, he heard the trunk of Amanda's car suddenly pop open. She came up to him from behind the car, took his hand in hers and led him to the back of her car. At the trunk, she stepped off the curb and into the street. Facing the open trunk, she motioned for him to look inside of the trunk—with the low-key ceremony of a demonstrator showing a new automobile on the market.

"Well, what do you think?" she said, picking it up in her hands.

Hurts didn't know what to make of it. In her hands, she held a wide leather belt. On the back of it were six notches, which usually would have been for the conveying of bullets, but instead, held six small—about a foot in length and an inch wide—round, highly-glossed, pointed at the bottom-end, wooden stacks. The right side of the belt had a leather holster hanging from it, and in it, Hurts saw the largest water-gun that he had ever seen before. It was translucent-plastic, red-color, with a metallic, small, round container, also of red-color, attached to the bottom of the holster. A small tube ran from the top of it to the butt of the gun.

"What's that thing?" Hurts asked, pointing to the red container.

"It's a booster," Amanda replied, strapping the belt on, and then buckling it. "This baby," she continued, fondly tapping the butt of the water-gun with the palm of her right hand, "can shoot a stream of water seven feet. But, instead of being filled with water, it's filled with holy water. Well, what do you think?"

"I think that my little girl is ready to kick some vampire butt," Hurts said, laughing.

"You got that right, partner," she replied.

"Yeah, but Amanda," Hurts then stated. "More than likely, Todd and his followers ain't in there. We're just here to pump that John kid as much as we can about Todd and where he might be."

"Yeah, I know, Uncle Jim," she replied.

"So, why are you wearin' this?" he asked, and pointed to the belt, the stacks, and the water gun.

"Well," she began, "you always say to be prepared."

"But won't you look silly wearin' that?" Hurts stated, and then added, "And wearin' that over your black dress? … I mean, these are some rough kids."

"Well, I'll just tell them that I'm going to a Halloween party … Come on. Let's go." She stepped back onto the sidewalk, took Hurts in hand, stepped with him back into the street, and started walking across the street, with him saying, "Okay, lead the way, boss."

On the other side of the street, they followed the cracked cement path of the sidewalk to the one-step cement entrance of the bar. At the door, the glass of it covered with a sheet of plywood, Hurts saw a large padlock fastened to the door midway up. Hurts reached into the left pocket of his topcoat and removed from it a mini-flashlight. Clicking it on, he flashed a beam of light on the padlock, saying, "This hasn't been touched in months." He then turned to his left and flashed another beam of light in that direction, keeping the beam of light close to the edifice of the building.

"Give me your hand again," Hurts said, softly, "and let's follow that sidewalk to the back of the house." With Amanda again leading the way, and Hurts flashing another beam of light to the narrow cement sidewalk below, they walked upon the path to the back of the house.

When they reached the back of the house, Hurts shot another beam of light from his mini-flashlight all around. It revealed a small, fallow yard of about fifteen feet long and twelve feet wide. Just beyond it was the alley. To the immediate right of them was a rotting wooden porch, which had another porch on the second-level of the house. On the first-level of the house, the porch had three wooden steps, also rotting, that led to a back door—a plain, windowless door. With Amanda still holding Hurts' hand, they climbed the steps and came to a stop at the door. Hurts clicked off the mini-flashlight and returned it to the pocket of his topcoat. Then, he withdrew his pistol from his shoulder holster under his left shoulder, held the front of it up high and close to his body, grabbed the old, round handle of the door with his left hand, and turned the knob. The door opened.

Amanda's heart was pounding in her chest as Hurts nodded for them to enter.

They stepped into a completely dark room. Hurts had to get his mini-flashlight back out again. He clicked it back on and flashed a beam of light about the room. They had stepped into the old kitchen of the house. The room was filthy, stacked with cardboard boxes everywhere from floor-to-ceiling—empty beer bottles and empty whiskey bottles strewn across the cracking tiled floor like dead toy soldiers, and the place smelled musty.

To the right-hand side of the east wall that faced them were two doors. The one door to the southeast corner of the wall was open and steps ascended to the second-level. The other door, which directly faced them, was closed, but one could see light from the next room emanating from under the door. Hurts motioned with the nod of his head for Amanda to follow him again. Hurts clicked off the mini-flashlight again, returned it to his topcoat pocket, reached for the handle of the door, turned it, and opened the door slightly. After peeping inside the room, he swung the door open wide and entered.

The room was dimly lit by three propane camping-lanterns; ghostly shadows kept bouncing off from them onto the dirty walls and floor. To Hurts' left was a full-length, waist-high bar of dark wood. Backless barstools lined the front of the bar. Behind the bar, also waist-high, also of dark wood, was a counter. A large mirror was positioned in the middle of it, and it was banked on both sides by wooden shelves, long now empty. An assortment of tables and chairs filled the room, and it was much like the previous room had been—filthy. Empty pizza boxes lay about the room, as did empty bags from fast-food restaurants; cigarette butts and empty beer cans, and, oh yes, the dead bodies of John Banks and five of his buddies, or his gang.

Their bodies were spread apart about the room. John Banks' body was closest to Hurts. His young, lean body and face lay spread-eagle across the top of the bar. Hurts knew that it was he. He remembered Dr. Washington describing his unruly, long red hair. His glazed blue eyes were open, and he was staring up at the smoke-stained and dirty tin-ceiling, painted white, long, long ago. His distorted face told the whole story—a look of total surprise; of total shock and of the suffering endured until the end. Still holding his pistol, Hurts moved up to him. He had puncture marks on both sides of his neck. It was the same at the elbows of his arms, wrists and ankles. Hurts touched the left side of his freckled face. Then, Hurts couldn't take it anymore. In a fireball of almost all-consuming, pent-up rage, he exploded in anger.

"I blew it!" he screamed. "I blew it! … They were here. Here! —and I blew it! … They were here less than an hour ago—the body is still warm; the skin still soft … I blew it! … You! Punk!" he screamed at the body of John Banks. "That kid told you not to mess with Todd—but, no, not you! You're tough! Tough! Well, look how 'tough' you are now —you're dead! Dead, dead, dead!"

"Uncle Jim," Amanda pleaded. "Stop." She felt confused, scared and sick to her stomach. She hadn't been this close to a dead body in eleven years, when Hurts had fought and killed those three vampire board members who had tried to frame her mother of stealing money from the company. "No one could have foreseen this—not Uncle Williams, or Dr. Washington, no one."

Hurts spun around and faced her. With pure hate in his eyes, and the want of murder in his heart, he screamed again, "Who's in charge here, Amanda?! Who's in charge here?!"

Quietly, she said, "You are, Uncle Jim."

"That's right," he snapped at her. "That means, I blew it," He then took a few deep breaths and released them. He felt better and, holstering his pistol, then said, "Call Williams and tell him that he has a mess here to clean up … Amanda, let's—let's get out of here."

"Uncle Jim," Hurts heard someone calling him, and shaking him lightly on his left shoulder. "Uncle Jim," he heard Amanda call again. "It's eight o'clock. I have breakfast almost ready. Get up."
Hurts sat up on the couch.

"Here," Amanda said, handing him a mug of steaming coffee. She was dressed in a white, button-down shirt, black dress pants and black leather flats. She didn't look as stunningly dressed as she had the day before, but she looked nice. She turned and walked away.

Hurts' mind felt fuzzy. If he hadn't known better, he would swear that he was hung-over. But he knew that he wasn't. He just couldn't wake up, and he'd had such a restive night of sleep—he kept having nightmares about seeing those dead teenagers, and about not being able to find Amanda. She was lost, and try as he did to always find her, he never did. Yes, his mind felt fuzzy; what happened after they had gotten back to the office was a blur. Well, nothing had happened. They had driven back in silence, and once they had gotten back, feeling depressed, miserable and a bit hopeless, they both went straight to bed—Hurts doesn't even remember changing into his sweatpants, but he must have, because he was wearing them, and he was still wearing his white T-shirt.

He looked down to the floor and spotted his pack of cigarettes and lighter lying next to the ashtray. Next to the ashtray, on the other side of it, were his untied shoes. He reached down for the cigarettes and lighter.

It was a cloudy, sunless day. It looked more like sunset than morning. It was also raining—a light rain, a drizzle, a rain just hard enough to wet the streets, sidewalks and ground. A rain just hard enough to drop the autumn leaves from the trees and splat wet onto the windshield of a passing car.

As Hurts still sat on the couch, drinking his coffee and smoking, and trying to wake up, reality slowly began to creep into his thinking—the cold, hard, not-wanting-to-remember-or-face-it, but one must. It was Wednesday, October 31st. Halloween. Hurts had never given much thought to this holiday—of the joy that this day gives to children; the mystic and the ritual of it; dressing-up as a ghost or witch or former President Nixon; the Halloween decorations; the pumpkins and the stalks of corn; the excited and happy cries of the children: "Trick-or-Treat!"; the gleaning of a bag of candy; all in the name of good, family fun. Hurts regretted that the few times that he had surrendered to his wife's nagging and had unwillingly gone with his wife and two daughters Trick-or-Treating, he had griped the whole time and wanted to be bar-hopping and chasing women. Yes, he now regretted that. He had gone a few times with Amanda and her mother, and all-in-all, found it to be okay.

Yes, today was Wednesday, October 31st. Halloween. And Hurts knew that throughout the day, he would be consistently checking the time on his wristwatch, feeling the continuous urgency of running out of time, of losing hope, and of always seeing in his mind's eye, the eyes of Emily—those crystal-blue eyes of hers. He knew that Amanda would be feeling all of this throughout the day as well. And he also knew that throughout the day both would silently keep saying: *"Where are you, Emily? I must find you before The Thirteenth Hour ... Where are you, Emily? Where are you..."*

"Come and eat your breakfast, Uncle Jim," Amanda said, already sitting at the end of the table.

Hurts got up off the couch and walked over to the middle of the table. After sitting down, he looked down at the steaming bowl in front of him, filled with milk, and said, frowning, "Oatmeal—again?!"

"Oatmeal is good for you," she replied. "It's good for your digestive system. It helps you poop."

"Hey," he barked at her, laughing, "I don't wanna hear that!"

"Well, it does."

"Fine," he replied, still laughing. When he had stopped laughing, he looked at Amanda and said, "Listen, today is a new day. I have hope."

She was glad to hear him say this. It was his way of apologizing for last night, and it was a whole lot better than hearing an empty: "We'll find her. I know we will."

Wearing the same clothes that he had yesterday, his pin-striped black suit, white dress shirt, black tie and topcoat—he just didn't feel like wearing something else—he and Amanda got into her car. He took the folded, two-page list of the names and addresses of the missing students from the right pocket of his topcoat, viewed the second page of it for a moment, looked up and at Amanda, and said, "Right, let's begin." Then added, "Starbucks first?"

"Starbucks first," she replied.

Hurts was sure glad that they had first stopped at Starbucks and had gotten two cups of coffee, because the day turned out to be a total waste of time. They completed interviewing the parents of all the missing students left on the list—and nothing. It was almost a quarter-to-three, and they both felt tired, hungry, frustrated, scared, dejected and running out of hope.

Hurts told Amanda that he had to rest. She had told him that that Teen Town Club didn't open until five p.m., so why didn't they just go back to the office and rest until four o'clock, and then leave for the club? Amanda agreed to this, so they returned to the office.

Hurts, lying on the couch, closed his eyes and placed his arm over his eyes.

"Uncle Jim," he heard Amanda say, "we better eat something. You know what I'd like to have?"

"A hamburger?" Hurts said.

"Noooo," she replied. "I'd like to have tomato soup and a peanut butter-and-jelly sandwich. I'll make it and call you when it's ready."

"Okay," he said.

She made it and they ate. Then, as Amanda washed the pan, bowls and such, Hurts went back to the couch to lie down again. He was soon fast asleep.

"Uncle Jim!" Hurts heard someone screaming at him and shaking him hard on his shoulder. "Uncle Jim! Wake up! It's almost six-thirty! Wake up!"

"What? What?" Hurts mumbled, sitting up. "What time is it?"

"It's almost six-thirty!" Amanda cried. "Oh, Uncle Jim, I fell asleep at the table—I was so tired. Mom called and woke me. I just—"

"Never mind that," Hurts replied, quickly. Rising from the couch, he said, "Let's go."

"Give me five minutes, Uncle Jim," she said, turning. "Just five minutes," she repeated, and ran into the bathroom, slamming the door.

"Well, hurry-up," Hurts said. Then, he added, sitting back down on the couch, "What's wrong? Is that 'oatmeal' startin' to kick-in?"

That 'five minutes' turned out to be eight minutes, and when she came out of the bathroom in a rush, Hurts was shocked at what he saw. Except for her face, she was black. Everything on her was black. Her hair was black, a waist-long black wig. Her fingernails were black, painted on with black lipstick, which she had also used to paint her thin lips. Her tennis-shoes were black, and all the clothes she had on were black: A full-length, thin-leather, black overcoat; black leather pants, and a black dress blouse. And if all of this wasn't bad enough, she had enough black mascara painted around her eyes that would have put any racoon to shame.

"Good Lord, Amanda," Hurts gasped, looking at her. "What is that?"

"It's Goth, Uncle Jim," she said, and placed her hands on her slender hips over her overcoat, and gave a little twist. "How do I look?"

"Beautiful," he replied, mockingly. "Just beautiful. Come on, Let's go."

Chapter Eighteen

Like most neighborhoods in the City of St. Louis, Soulard is old. It was settled in 1790 by Antoine Pierre Soulard, a pioneer Frenchman who first came here as a surveyor for the King of Spain. It is just two miles south of downtown, on Broadway Street, and covers an area of about three miles long and three miles wide. It runs parallel, south and north, of the Mississippi River and Highway 55 to its east, and, of course, there is the block-long plant of Anheuser-Bush and the Lemp mansion surrounding it. Most of its houses and buildings were built in the 1800s—two-story, red brick houses and buildings with flat, Mansard-style roofs. It is best known for The Farmers Market, its many restaurants and bars, and Mardi Gras.

The Teen Town Club is in an old building that, originally, had been an ice-house, a building for just that—storing ice. It is on the corner of 6th Street: a one-story tall building, but long and wide, with many small-pane windows and, of course, made of red brick. It was started by a young man who owns one of the restaurants at Soulard's. He has done quite well there, financially, and he talked two other owners there to go in with him and start the Teen Town Club, a place in which teens can go and have fun, without alcohol or drugs. Their lease at the ice-house is only for a year, but if it becomes popular and financially successful, they'll find a more permeant home for Teen Town Club. From what Hurts could see of the place as he and Amanda entered it, the place was "jumping," as they say.

"Ten dollars!" Hurts bellowed, speaking to the young bouncer at the entrance, who had the build of a gorilla. "You want ten dollars apiece just to get in here?!"

"That's the price, sir," he said, in a rough-sounding voice.

Hurts brushed aside the right-side of his topcoat and suit coat, reached into the back pocket of his pants, and pulled out his wallet.

"Here," he said, handing the young man a twenty. "I'm goin' in with her. I don't want my daughter to be in there alone."

Once inside, Hurts could not only not see—it was so dark in there— he couldn't hear or move around, as well: the music, whatever type of screeching noise that was, was deafening, and the place was so crowded that he kept bumping into people.

"Here, give me your hand, Uncle Jim," Amanda said. They interlocked hands, and Hurts said, "Take me up to the bar." She did.

The bar was to the back of the building, in the middle of it. Directly in front of the bar was the dance floor, cordoned off by a waist-high, gold-colored, horizonal pole. The dance floor took up much of the space of the room. Tables and chairs hugged the four red brick walls.

At the bar, Hurts turned and faced Amanda, and said, "Now, remember, mingle; talk to everyone and anyone. Just keep askin' about Todd. Now, go," he said, shooing her away with his hands. He turned and faced the dance floor. With his back leaning against the bar, he looked out onto the dance floor. It was crowded with kids dancing and having a good time. He'd never seen so many witches, zombies, vampires, and such, in his life. Well, it was Halloween. He turned back around and faced the bar. A young man from behind the bar, dressed as Frankenstein, said, "What will you have, sir?"

Speaking loudly, Hurts said, "You don't serve alcohol here, right?"

"No, sir," he replied, equally as loud. "Just soda, juice or bottled water."

"No," Hurts stated, "I don't want none of that. Say, a question. Do you know Todd Sinclair?"

"Unfortunately, I've met him," the young man stated.

"When was the last time you saw him?"

"Ooooh," he said, thinking, "that would have been Sunday evening."

"Do you know where he or any of his buddies hang out?"

"Not a clue," he replied. Just then, a kid came up and ordered two cokes. He excused himself from Hurts and got that kid his drinks.

Not too long after that, a girl stepped up to the bar, to Hurts' left side. She was wearing a cat's costume, with whiskers, ears and a long tail. Hurts was looking at her, and she turned to him, began looking at him, and then, extending her right hand, made a motion of going to scratch Hurts, and said, "Meow."

"Well, 'meow' to you too," Hurts replied.

That young man from behind the bar came up and said to her, "What will ya have?"

"A bottled water, please," she said.

"Say," Hurts said, speaking to the girl, "you mind if I ask you a question?"

"No, I don't mind," she replied. The young man came back with the girl's bottled water. She was holding four one-dollar bills in her hands, and before the young man or the girl said anything, Hurts said, "Keep your money. This is on me. How much?" he asked the young man.

"Two-seventy-five," he replied.

"For a bottle of water?!" Hurts barked at him.

"Yes, sir," he said.

"Okay," Hurts mumbled, angrily, and reached into his back pants' pocket again and got his wallet. "Here's three dollars," Hurts said, and handed the money to him, saying, "Keep the change." Turning again to the girl, he said, "Now, do you know Todd Sinclair?"

"No," she replied, shaking her head. "Should I know him? I mean, is he, like, a rock-star or something?"

"No," Hurts said. "He's no rock-star—'or somethin'.'

"Well," she then said, "thanks for the water." She turned around, but before she left, she turned to Hurts again, scratched at the air again with her hand, and said, "Meow." She then walked away and disappeared into the crowd.

This was the way it went with all the people who Hurts asked if he or she knew Todd Sinclair. They either said no or they only knew him at the club—and not one of them who knew him there liked him, or his friends, nor wanted anything to do with him.

Amanda finally returned to the bar, looking nervous, sad and dejected.

"Oh, Uncle Jim," she said, moaning. "It was awful, just awful. I got nothing. Nothing … How did you do?" she asked, so hoping to hear great news.

"I got nothin' either," he replied, hating it. "What time is it, Amanda? I can't see my watch in this cave."

She looked at her watch and said with a gasp, "Dear, Lord. It's twenty-to-eight, Uncle Jim … What are we go—?" Suddenly, she stopped speaking. She was looking over in the southeast corner of the room, almost next to the door to the entrance of the place. She seemed to be looking at a young man who was standing by a table talking to the four or five girls who were sitting there.

"Uncle Jim," she said, excitedly. "Do you see that guy over there?" she continued, pointing in the direction of where that young man was standing.

"I can hardly see anything in here, Amanda."

"He's by those girls," she said. "He's wearing a blue suit and a black tie. He has black-framed glasses on now. He wasn't wearing them Sunday. I think he's trying to look like Clark Kent, Superman."

"Well, what about him?" Hurts said, coaxing her to hurry up and tell him.

"He was here Sunday," she replied, quickly. "He was speaking with one of Todd's followers."

"Are you sure, Amanda?" Hurts said.

"Yes, that's him," she replied, still looking at the young man.

Hurts thought for a moment, and then said, "Alright, here's the plan." Amanda turned, faced Hurts, and listened. "Give me ten minutes to get to your car, and then you bring him out to me."

"How am I going to get him to do that?" she asked, protesting. "What would I say to him?"

Hurts looked Amanda straight in the face and said, "Amanda, you're a 'woman'—ain't you?"

"Oh," she said, realizing what he meant. "Okay, I guess … Can you make it to the car?"

"Don't worry about me," Hurts replied. "Just get him out there to me."

Chapter Nineteen

Hurts was glad that he had told Amanda to give him ten minutes to get to her car, because he needed that much time to make it to her car, which was parked on the street a half a block south of that place. Needless-to-say, he had much trouble getting to her car by himself. It was dark, and he couldn't see all that well. But he made it, walking slowly and cautiously. He was also glad that it had stopped raining. It was getting colder, though. A light mist hugged the surface of the street, the sidewalk and the ground.

Within seconds of Hurts reaching Amanda's car, here came Amanda up the sidewalk, walking arm-and-arm with the young man. As they passed by the car, Hurts said, "Hi, Amanda. Who's your friend?"

Amanda, acting surprised to see Hurts, replied, "Oh, hi, Uncle." She was on the other side of the young man, and Hurts was close to him. "Donald," she said to the young man. "This is my uncle. Uncle," she said to Hurts. "This is Donald."

Hurts extended his right hand to shake the young man's hand, but when Donald extended his arm, Hurts, instead of taking his hand, grabbed him by the lapels of his suit coat, spun him around, and pinned him up against the passenger-door of Amanda's car.

Donald screamed, "Hey, what is this, man?! I didn't touch her!"

"Shut up!" Hurts shouted at him. "Shut up!" Holding onto Donald with his left hand, gripping his white shirt at the chest, Hurts withdrew his pistol and pressed the barrel of it against Donald's forehead.

"Don't shoot me, man!" Donald said, pleading with Hurts.

Hurts shook him with his left hand and said, "I don't have no time to mess around here now, Donald. Now, I want some answers from you—and I want them fast!"

"Okay, man," Donald replied, quickly.

"Do you know Todd Sinclair?"

"No, man," he said. "I don't know any Todd Sinclair. I swear, man."

"You were talkin' to one of his buddies Sunday night in the club."

"No, man," he said. "You got me mixed-up with—" He stopped speaking suddenly. Then, he said, "Oh, you mean me talking to Tyler, man. I was talking with Tyler Smith."

"Okay," Hurts said. "What about him? What did you two talk about?"

"Nothing, man. Nothing."

"Come on, Donald," Hurts demanded, getting impatient. "You guys talked about something; now, what was it?"

"It was nothing, man," Donald repeated. "He's changed. It's like he's on PCP or something, man. We went to grade school together, at St. Francis of Assis, in Oakville. But I hadn't seen him since we graduated, man. I go to St. Mary's High, and he goes to Oakville High."

"Donald," Hurts warned, "I'm not gonna tell you again—What did you two talk about?"

"That's what I'm telling you, man," he said. "Nothing, man. I asked if he still lived at home with his mom and dad; he laughed and said: 'Yeah, we all do. We all live under my father's roof, and he doesn't even know it.' Then, all of them started laughing—like hyenas, man. I got away from him, man."

"Okay, Donald," Hurts said, lowering his pistol. "Get out of here." At that, the young man took off, running up the sidewalk as fast as his young legs and feet would carry him.

Hurts turned around and leaned back against the door of the car, thinking.

"Uncle Jim," Amanda said. "I remember now. About three weeks ago, I saw a picture of Tyler."

"What?" Hurts said, still thinking. "Where did you see a picture of him?"

"It was on TV, the evening news," she replied. "His mother and father were being interviewed. They were standing in front of their home, and the mother was holding up a picture of him. They both were crying and pleading for Tyler to come back home. They said that three nights after Tyler disappeared, the motorcycle that they had bought for him two birthdays ago, disappeared. There wasn't a break-in or robbery. It just was gone from the garage. They were sure that Tyler came back and took it."

"None of this makes any sense," Hurts said, wiping his face with his right hand. "There's no Tyler Smith on the list of missing students, and what did Donald mean when he said that Tyler said: 'Yeah, we all do. We all live under my father's roof, and he doesn't even know it.'?"

"I don't know, Uncle Jim," Amanda replied, thinking too.

"Wait a minute here," Hurts then said. "Donald said that he and Tyler went to that—that Catholic grade school in Oakville. That's in the County. Maybe that's why he's not on the list—and what about Tyler telling him that they all lived under his father's roof? Could that be where they all are?"

"It sounds like it," she answered, grabbing on to hope.

"We need an address," Hurts stated quickly. Pointing to the round, pouch-like, brown purse hanging from her right shoulder by its long, thin string, he said, "Can you get an address of Tyler's parents on your cell phone?"

"Let me see," she said quickly, and without even removing the purse from her shoulder, swung it in front of her and pulled the purse open. After removing the cell phone from the purse, she held it in her left hand, and with her right hand began making sweeping motions on the face of the phone with her right index-finger. She then brought the cell phone up to her mouth and said, "Okay, Google. An address of a Smith living in Oakville, Missouri."

A few seconds later, Amanda shouted with joy. "Got it, Uncle Jim! A Mr. Nathen Smith. The address is 122156 Cliff Cave Estates."

"Great," Hurts replied. "Let's go. Get that 'lady' talkin' to us," he said, referring to the GPS. "I don't have a clue where that address is." He turned around to get into the car.

"Uncle Jim," Amanda said, sounding desperate. "We're riding on fumes. We got to stop and get gas."

"Well, let's hurry, then," he said. "We're running out of time."

"Yes," she said, quickly. "But could we stop and get something to eat? I'm starved, Uncle Jim, and I feel weak."

"Amanda," Hurts said, looking at her and shaking his head. "We don't have the time to stop and eat!"

"Well, we got to get gas. Surely, there's a Burger King or something like that near the gas station where we could drive through and get a hamburger and fries."

Hurts was shocked. Shocked! "You, Amanda Warner, would eat a hamburger and fries?!"

"Yes," she replied.

"Well," Hurts said. "Let's do it."

Chapter Twenty

It was a bad break. Just a bad, bad break, and they were doing so well too. Amanda had gotten gas, and, yes, she had gone through the drive-through at a Jack-in-the-Box and got them both hamburgers and fries—and, yes, she liked it. They had eaten them as she drove, and when they had finished eating and Hurts had asked her if she had liked it, she flippantly stated that it was okay. But she had a guilty look of pleasure on her face. The type of look one might have on his or her face at being caught committing a minor sin.

So, they were making good time. They were driving south on Highway 55, and they had just gotten onto Highway 270, travelling east to Telegraph Road, when suddenly, Amanda's car began riding rough from the rear of the car. She pulled the car over, and they both got out to see what the problem was. The rear driver's side tire was flat. Amanda has AAA and wanted to call a tow-truck, but Hurts told her no, that it would take too long. So, he changed the tire himself. He changed it as fast as he could, but it wasn't very fast. It was every bit of ten-thirty when Amanda pulled the car in front of the curb-less sidewalk of Tyler's parents' house.

"This is all wrong," Hurts said, looking out of the window of the car at the beautiful, expensive suburban home of Mr. Nathen Smith, and then viewing all the beautiful, expensive homes around it.

"What's wrong with it, Uncle Jim?" Amanda asked, removing that long, black wig from her head, and then, twisting her upper-body around and tossing the wig onto the back seat.

"Well, this place ain't secluded or anything. It's not a place that thirteen teenage vampires could hide—especially not with a girl screaming. I thought it would be a place like Dracula's castle. This place is for the rich."

Hurts was correct about that. The average price-range for a house there was a little under a half a million. Mr. Nathen Smith's two-story, light-color brick home was the third house on the west side of the street, just past the beginning—or ending, depending on which way you were driving—of the cul-de-sac. Mr. Smith's home was breathtakingly beautiful. The house was constructed of both brick and wood; the wood was painted a high-gloss white. It had two V-pitched roofs of black shingles—the black shingles matched the color of the wooden shutters— with dormers, and a one-step, cement, covered porch, with a waist-high, white-metal railing that ran parallel to the face of the house. The Grecian-style wooden door, painted a high-gloss red, took center stage, with a half-moon-shaped window above the door, and small windows lining both sides of the door. A large, small-paned bay-window was to the north side of the front door. A white dwarfed dogwood tree was to the south-front corner of the house; waist-high evergreen bushes adorned the white railing of the porch, and on the south-end of the house was a two-car wide, cement driveway, the garage of which was to the back of the house.

As Hurts looked at the pristine front yard of Mr. Smith's house, he thought: *Man, these people sure must love Halloween.*

And he was correct. The porch and front yard were festooned with Halloween decorations. On the porch of the house, next to the front door, sat a scarecrow in a rocking-chair, dressed in bib-overalls and a straw-hat. Next to him was a bale of hay, with two carved pumpkins perched on top of it. The yard itself was cornucopia of Halloween heaven. There were white spider webs everywhere; black tombstones made of black foam; bloody heads, arms-and-hands of scary-looking people crawling out of graves; shiny, hard-cardboard signs of witches, ghosts, and vampires attached to wooden stakes that had been driven into the ground; and banking both sides of the cement driveway were solar lamps in the ground, with tiny pumpkins on top and lighting the way to the front porch for all the little Trick-or-Treaters.

Turning to Amanda, Hurts said, "Well, let's go. Take my hand again and guide me to the front door."

They got out of the car, and Hurts waited for Amanda to come and help him. When she came abreast of him, from inside of the house, they suddenly heard the voice of a woman screaming. They both turned towards the house. There was light emanating from the bay-window, and they saw a flash of something zooming back and forth across the window. Withdrawing his pistol from its shoulder-holster, Hurts said, "Get me to that window as fast as you can!"

She grabbed him by his left hand. She led him to the back of her car; they skirted the mailbox made of brick at the south-edge of the driveway and following the solar lights on the left-side of the driveway, moved quickly to the cement sidewalk that led to the one-step cement porch.

When they got onto the porch, they squatted down in front of the bay-window and looked inside. The thin, white drapes were parted, and they were looking into the living-room. Hurts could hear the TV playing. Next to the long, floral print couch, which was up against the west wall of the room, was a wingback chair of the same make of the couch. Sitting on that chair, wearing a white nightgown, slumped over to the side of the chair, as if she were hiding something, lay a woman in her early forties, dead, blood trickling down the side of her neck from two puncture wounds.

To the left side of the room, near the front door, were high-gloss, wooden steps and a rail that ascended to the second-level of the house. On the third step from the top, lay a boy of about ten in age, dressed in blue pajamas, dead with two puncture wounds on his neck as well. At the bottom step, a young man was biting a girl, about eight-years-old, on the neck, hard.

"That's Tyler, Uncle Jim!" Amanda hissed quietly. "I recognize him from the picture … He's killing them, Uncle Jim! We got to stop—"

She started to get up, but Hurts grabbed her by her left arm and whispered, "There's nothin' we can do. We must let it play out. See if he'll lead us to Emily." He released Amanda, and then, holstering his weapon, said, "Come on, let's make a beeline for the car."

They stood up, but instead of following the sidewalk and then the driveway back to the car, they both stepped off the porch and cut across the front yard, Amanda holding Hurts' hand and leading the way. About midway from the porch to the car, Hurts tripped on one of the many hard cardboard posters of a witch or a ghost or of a vampire, knocking it out of the ground. Not wanting to make Amanda fall, Hurts released his hand from hers and fell on the ground, facedown. He fell hard. Somehow, he sustained a cut just above his right eyebrow. As he went down, he yelled, "Damn!"

He rolled over on his back. The fall had knocked the wind out of him. He lay there for a few moments, taking deep breaths. He was just about to try and get up, when—zoom! Tyler was sitting on top of him. He grabbed Hurts by the lapels of his topcoat, leaned over him and said, with blood around his lips and two fangs protruding from his open mouth, "Who are you, old man?"

Hurts looked him straight in the eye and said, "I'm Buffy, The Vampire Killer." Then, he brought up his right arm and struck Tyler on the left side of his face. It was a meaningless punch. It had no effect on Tyler.

"You're dead, is what you are, old man," Tyler replied. With Tyler's left hand, turning and holding Hurts' head to the right, and raising his head high in the night air, his fangs seeming to be growing larger, Tyler began to plunge his upper-body and head down into Hurts' neck. Suddenly, the upper portion of his body went board-stiff. He raised his head high again to the moon, screamed a blood-curdling cry, and then collapsed on top of Hurts.

Hurts immediately felt a stabbing, sharp pain in his chest. He pushed Tyler off him. He rolled over on his stomach and tried to get up. It was difficult, but he finally managed to rise to his hands and knees. Looking at Tyler, he saw one of those hard cardboard postings sticking out from Tyler's back. It was of a ghost, saying: Boo! The wooden stake used to drive it into the ground was now piercing though Tyler's young body.

Standing at the foot of Tyler and Hurts, Amanda said, "I killed him. I took a life. I—" Then she burst into tears.

"You stop that, right now!" Hurts shouted at her, savagely. "You're not a child anymore, Amanda. This is the real world. We do what we must do to survive … Help me up. Help me up."

She did as she was told to do and helped him to his feet. After looking around, and seeing no people or lights being turned on in any of the houses, Hurts said, "Help me drag him inside the house. They both bent over, and Hurts was really feeling pain. Amanda took a hold of Tyler by the dirty jeans of his left ankle, and Hurts did the same with his right. They dragged him up onto the porch and through the open front door and into the living room.

At the bottom of the steps to the second floor, Hurts, exhausted and out of breath, said, "Leave him here." Amanda wasn't too pleased with this, because he was being left next to the little girl, his sister, he had just killed, but she said nothing.

"I got to lie down," Hurts stated, and made a beeline for another, same make and type, high-back wing chair, which was directly across from the chair that the dead woman was sitting in; both chairs faced each other. Before Hurts plopped down hard in that chair, he removed his handkerchief from his back pants' pocket, unfolded it, and placed it over the cut above his right eye. Now sitting in the chair, before Hurts leaned back, raised his head a bit, and closed his eyes, he saw why the woman was bunched over to one side of the chair: There was another little girl, probably about four or five years old, beneath her—as if the woman, the mother, had tried desperately to protect her. She had not.

Passing between the now shattered wooden-framed glass-top coffee table and the couch, Amanda sat down on the couch, feeling tired, confused, physically sick to her stomach and despondent. She looked mindlessly at the candy strewn about the room, all over the plush white carpet, thrown about for some unknown reason, or by whom; all that she could determine was that it had all come from a large, plastic, orange pumpkin with a green handle, which now lay dead on its side on the carpet in the middle of the room. The 19'' color TV, which was positioned on the north-side of the bay-window, against the east wall, was playing a Halloween movie, a comedy titled *Earnest Scared Stupid*. It was almost over. The remote for the TV was on the couch next to Amanda's left hand. She reached for it. She pressed the STOP button.

Amanda looked around the room. It was so beautiful, she thought. The fireplace in the middle of the south wall, with the large mirror above it; the painting above the couch that she was sitting on of sailboats in a seaside harbor; the high-gloss, wooden cornices that ran along the ceilings and the floors; the many lamps and end tables, and the very air of the room—so fresh.

"There was love in this house," Amanda said. Looking at the dead woman in the chair, Amanda continued, shaking her head and feeling sad, "Much, much love." She took a deep breath, let it out, and said, "This house smells complete. Whole ... But something is missing ... Where's the husband? The father?"

Without even opening his eyes, Hurts replied, "Good call. He's probably in one of the other rooms."

"I don't think so," Amanda stated. "I don't feel him."

"Are you getting weird, Amanda?" he said. "Just close your eyes and rest. We'll get up in a minute and look for him."

Amanda was getting impatient. She kept looking at her wristwatch. That moment's rest had turned into fifteen minutes. She said, "Uncle Jim, are you going to get up? It's ten after eleven. Let's go."

"Okay, okay," he replied, taking the bloodstained handkerchief from above his eye and placing it in the pocket of his topcoat. Rising, he said, "Let's check out this place."

"What are we looking for?" she asked. But then she said, "I know; I know — 'anything and everything.'"

"Right," he replied.

They stepped out of the living room, and onto the hardwood floor of the entrance and turned right, walking past the steps that ascended to the second level; they were now in front of the kitchen. To their left, under the stairs, was a hallway. They walked midway down it. On their right, was a white, wooden door. Hurts opened it. It was the bathroom. It had a full-length vanity with a full-length mirror and lights above it; a bathtub; a walk-in shower, and two toilets.

"These people ain't so rich," Hurts said.

"Why do you say that, Uncle Jim?" she asked.

"Well, look at that," he said, pointing to the two toilets. "One of the toilets must be broken and they haven't even removed it."

"The one is not a toilet, actually," she replied. "It's a bidet."

"A what?" Hurts said, dumbfounded.

"A bidet," she replied. "It shoots water up your bottom after going to the bathroom—to clean you."

"How disgustin,'" Hurts said, slamming the door shut.

They turned 180 degrees around and faced two curtained French doors. Hurts swung the doors open. It was the dining room. Beautiful. A crystal chandelier above a long wooden table, with eight wooden ladderback chairs surrounding it. A dark wood China cabinet, the top half of which was of two glass doors, and the bottom of which was of four drawers. Through the glass doors of it, Hurts saw three wooden shelves. The top shelf had crystal glasses of all types. The lower two shelves had plates and cups and saucers of fine Chinaware.

The kitchen was equally as elegant. They stepped onto the shining white linoleum floor of the kitchen. Its surface had the look to it of the face of large boulders. In the southwest corner of the room was a wooden, round kitchen table and matching chairs. By it, against the west wall, was a standing full-length, stainless-steel refrigerator and deep-freezer. Next to this was an electric stove, with a black top and a matching microwave above, built into the white, wooden cabinets that surrounded it. All of this was enclosed, almost, by a waist-high, wooden island with a black marble top. Two more curtained French doors were just beyond the island, against the west wall. At the northeast corner of the kitchen was a white door. Hurts and Amanda walked over to it, and Hurts opened the door. After turning on the light, they saw that it was a three-car garage.

There was one car in it. A 2015 black Hyundai SUV.

"That's strange," Hurts said.

"What's strange, Uncle Jim?" she asked.

"There's only one car here," he replied, pointing to the car, which was straight in front of them. "This is a three-car garage. There should be at least another car here   and that motorcycle parked next to this car doesn't belong where its parked."

"That must be Tyler's motorcycle—the one he had come back for," she said, referring to the 2011 Harley-Davidson that was parked to the south-side of the car. "But why do you say that it shouldn't be parked there?"

"See those four pieces of cardboard on the floor with oil-stains on them in front of the third door to the left?" Hurts said.

Amanda peeked in and looked to the left of the garage.

"Yeah," she replied.

"Well, that's where that motorcycle usually parks."

Hurts turned off the light and shut the door.

Directly behind them was another white wooden door. Hurts then opened that one and turned on that light. It revealed wooden steps that descended to the basement. As they descended the stairs, Amanda asked suddenly, "Why did Tyler kill his family, Uncle Jim?"

"I don't know, Amanda. I don't."

At the bottom step, Hurts and Amanda looked around. It was a full-furnished basement: Hardwood floors; wooden-paneled walls; a drop ceiling; a fireplace to the left of where Hurts and Amanda were standing, against the north wall, in the middle of it; a nearly floor-to-ceiling color TV to the right of the fireplace; a billiard table in the middle of the room, close to the east wall—and, then, there was something that made Hurts' eyes widen and his mouth water with thirst. A full home bar.

It was against the southwest corner of the room, and it looked GRAND to him. Behind the bar where glass shelves, with every type of alcohol a drinker could ever want: a drinkers' paradise.

At the south end of the room was a wooden door, which looked the same as the paneling of the walls. Hurts turned to Amanda and said, "Maybe you better go and check out what's behind that door." He pointed across the room.

"Okay," she said, and did.

It was the laundry room. It wasn't furnished. It had a washer, dryer, and one other thing that caught Amanda's eye. In the southeast corner of the room was what looked to be like a tall, narrow hut made of wood. Amanda opened the narrow door of it. It was a tanning booth. Cool, she thought. Finding nothing else, she opened the door of the room to leave, and when she passed through the door and re-entered the furnished part of the basement, she heard a loud belch and "Boy, I needed that!"

She looked to her left, toward the direction of the sound and voice, only to find Hurts standing behind the bar, smoking a cigarette and gulping down whiskey from a bottle he had obviously removed from behind the bar and had opened.

"That's not yours!" she yelled.

"Who's gonna complain?" he replied flippantly.

Walking to the stairs, she said, "Come on. Let's go."

Hurts kept taking gulps from the bottle.

At the steps, Amanda looked back at him and said, getting quite angry, "Uncle Jim! Are you coming?!"

"Yes, yes," he replied, leaving.

She started up the stairs, saying, "I almost feel like joining you."

"You mean drinkin' whiskey?" he said.

"Yes," she replied, demurely.

"Not until you're twenty-one—and that's an order," he stated firmly.

Chapter Twenty-one

With both of his hands on the ledge of the wooden spiral rail on the second level of the house, gazing down upon the inner-side of the front door and the vestibule of the house, Hurts and Amanda decided to search the north side of the house first. On the north side of the house were five doors made of wood and painted white. Four of the doors were on the west side of the house, and one of the doors was on the east side. All the doors turned out to be doors to bedrooms. The one on the east side of the house was the master bedroom of the mother and father. Beautiful. It had the same carpet as downstairs in the living room; a king-size bed, with a quilt and pillows; end-tables with lamps on them; two dressers, one with a mirror; curtains on the two windows; silver-framed photos of the family, and a half-bathroom, with a vanity, a toilet, a walk-in shower, minus a bidet.

The four doors on the west side of the house were the doors to the children's bedrooms. The one at the far north end of the house probably belonged to the youngest child, the girl that the mother had tried to protect. It was filled with dolls and teddy bears, and on the walls were painted murals of biblical scenes, such as Noah gathering animals onto the Ark. The next bedroom had to be a girl's bedroom, because it too had dolls and teddy bears inside. The next had to be that of a boy, because it was filled with toy cars, soldiers, games and posters of Marvel comic book characters. The last bedroom was, obviously, Tyler's. It, too, had posters that lined the walls, but they were posters of motorcycles, with girl-models wearing bikinis, striking a very provocative pose.

Having searched Tyler's room and finding nothing that would be of any use to them, they walked upon the wooden floor of the second level of the house to the south end of it. At that end of the house were two doors. They were the same as the doors at the opposite end of the house: wooden and painted white. One door was on the west side of the house, and the other one was on the east side of the house, about two feet further south. The door on the west side of the house was the door to another bathroom. It was the same as the one on the first floor, except it, too, was minus a bidet.

Hurts was a bit impressed with what he saw after he had opened the door on the east side of the house and had turned on the light. It was a home office. Very modern looking.

What Hurts spotted immediately was the three shoulder-high, white, metal filing cabinets nestled in the southeast corner of the room. Hurts had always felt that he should get some filing cabinets for his office. His filing method consisted of throwing his case files into the bottom right-side drawer of his desk. When the drawer is full, he gets a cardboard box and dumps it all into the box and tosses it against the southwest corner of the room: he has seven boxes now piled high.

To the west of the filing cabinets was a wooden architecture's drawing desk. There were two windows on the east side of the room. They had white mini-blinds on them. In front of the windows was a modular, L-shaped desk, with a metallic grey frame and an inch-thick black top. On top of the desk was a black multi-plex phone; a metallic black lamp with moveable parts to it; a rolodex; and a computer. Behind the desk, positioned on a sheet of translucent plastic, was a black-padded chair, with arms, wheels and a swivel. The carpet of the room was the same as the carpet in the living-room and bedrooms: white.

In the northeast corner of the room was a tall, thin, standing lamp. About three feet north of the desk was a black leather easy-chair.

Hurts was—exhausted. His body ached, and his mind felt fuzzy. He wanted to sleep. He wanted to make a beeline for that easy-chair and just fall asleep. But something caught his eye; something that seemed familiar to him, and he had to walk over and look at it.

Pinned-up on the west wall of the room were two long scrolls, a little higher than midway up. The scroll on top was an aerial photo of a street-long block of brick buildings and empty lots. The buildings were old, abandoned, many of them boarded-up, and in desperate need of repair. The lots on it were no better, many of them fallow with discarded junk on them. The writing at the top of the scroll read: 14th Street & North Broadway. The scroll below that scroll was beautiful. The writing on the top of that scroll read: LACLEDE'S ESTATES. Below it was more writing. It listed the same address that was on the top scroll: 14th Street & North Broadway. The scroll displayed high-rise, expensive apartments and lofts; office buildings; retail stores; restaurants; bars and nightclubs; a library; a park with a pond; a civic center, and a school for both elementary and high school.

Tapping the aerial photo with the index-finger of his right hand, Hurts said, "I know this place. My younger brother, Paul, and me used to play there when we were kids. We lived only a few blocks away from there. It was a horrible place even back then … I wonder what this Smith does for a livin'?"

"From the business card on the desk here," Amanda said, sitting at the desk, searching it. "It says that he's a realtor developer."

Hurts walked to the easy-chair and plopped down hard in it. He looked at his wristwatch and gasped with horror. "Amanda," he said, feeling awful about it, "it's five-to-twelve … I failed you, Amanda. I failed. We're out of time."

"Don't say that, Uncle Jim!" Amanda replied, releasing a burst of pent-up anger. "It's not too late. I'm going to find Emily."

"Honey," he said, "I did all that I could. I'm just too old—too worn-out."

"Help me, Uncle Jim," she pleaded, frantically opening and closing drawers under the desk. "The answer has got to be here. You always say that the answers are always in front of us—if we just look."

She took a piece of paper from under the phone and read it. "This is a note that Mr. Smith must have written. He had an appointment tonight at six p.m. to show Miss Woo a piece of property that he believes would be an excellent location for a new Chinese restaurant. I wonder if that's the same Miss Woo who owns a Chinese restaurant in Clayton? Good food … There's that number thirteen again! He was supposed to meet her at lot thirteen. I swear, I never want to hear that number again—thirteen! Thirteen! Damn THIRTEEN!"

Hurts was about to answer her—tell her to give it up—when he looked back at that aerial photo. He began studying it.

"Uncle Jim?" she said, looking at him and wondering what he was concentrating on so hard. "Uncle Jim?" she repeated.

Hurts tried to shoot out of the chair, but he fell back into it. He tried again, but the same thing happened. He shouted, "Amanda! Get me out of this chair—now!"

Amanda shot-up out of the chair that she was sitting in, skirted around the front of the desk, went to Hurts, grabbed him under his shoulder, and helped him up. He gently pushed her away and walked as swiftly as he could to the aerial photo.

Standing in front of it, he stared intensely at the middle of it. Then, following the photo with his eyes, he turned his head to his right, north, and followed it to the end. Then, he turned his head in the other direction, to the other end, or beginning, of the photo. Amanda watched anxiously as he did all of this. Then, with the index-finger of his right hand, Hurts began counting the buildings, from left to right. When he got to the middle of the photo again, Amanda saw him clench his right hand into a fist and then strike the photo, hard. He turned and faced the south wall, lowered his head, and said, "Staring at me the whole time. The whole time!" Turning a bit more, he looked at Amanda and said, "What time did you say that that Smith and Woo had an appointment?"

"Six p.m.," she replied.

He turned back again and faced the south wall again. Amanda could see his eyes racing, and she knew that his mind was racing as well.

"Okay, okay," he stated. "Now, let's see. Smith and Woo step into the building. He sees Tyler and shouts, 'Tyler, my son!' and they kill both Smith and Woo … No, think, Hurts. Think! … Okay, they step into the building and see Emily all tied-up—stretched-out, like Jesus on the cross, and they kill them … No, no, no," Hurts chided himself. "Okay, okay," he began again. "They step into the building, and Todd and his followers kill them. But then, Todd gets scared. What if Smith had been watching them in silence? And what if he thinks that Smith may have called his wife on his cell phone? He gets scared that they'll be found out, and he orders Tyler to come back and kill his family. Yes, I like that. That's why he killed them. He didn't want their place of hiding found out … Now, where would that be? A place where thirteen teenage vampires can hide? A place secluded, abandoned—where a girl can scream and yell all she wants, and no one will hear? A place where: 'We all live under my father's roof, and he doesn't even know it?'" Turning and looking again at Amanda, Hurts said, "Where is such a place like that, Amanda?" But before she could even answer, Hurts, raising his right hand, pointed back to the middle of the photo and said, "There. Lot thirteen—building thirteen. That's where they are, Amanda. Building thirteen!"

Throwing her arms above her head, Amanda shouted with joy, "Woo-hoo!" She then rushed over to Hurts, threw her arms and hands around his neck and kissed him on his cheek. Looking at him, she said, excitedly, "You did it, Uncle Jim! You found Emily!"

Hurts grabbed her by the shoulders and gently pushed her at arms-length, saying, "Get on your phone and call Williams. Tell him that he has another mess here to clean up. Tell him that we know where Emily and Todd are; tell him to meet us there—and you don't have to have that 'lady' talkin' to us. I know exactly where it is … Come on, partner, let's go get Emily."

Chapter Twenty-two

Amanda did as Hurts told her to do. She called Williams but got his voicemail. She told him everything.

It was fifteen minutes-to-one a.m.—fifteen minutes until the beginning of The Thirteenth Hour—when Amanda turned onto Broadway at 14th Street. It brought back a lot of memories to Hurts—all of them bad. Hurts told Amanda to drive slowly, so that he could count off the buildings on the west side of the street as they passed by them. There weren't any buildings on the east side of the street. They had all been bulldozed to make way for new construction. The Mississippi River ran parallel with the street, and one, with there not being any buildings on the east side of the street, could easily see the river on this increasingly cold, foggy night.

There were few working streetlamps. Most of the retro-looking lamps had been broken by vandals—I say 'retro', but there is nothing retro about them. They're simply old, from the early 1900s. The street itself is narrow and uneven, and made of red brick.

Hurts didn't need to count off the buildings to the number thirteen, because on the opposite side of the street, about midway up the street, two cars were parked at the curb—far too new and expensive-looking to be left on that abandoned street, or in that 'bad' neighborhood. Amanda pulled her car up behind a new Mercedes convertible sport's car, blue in color. In front of it was a fairly new-looking silver Nissan Altima. Both Hurts and Amanda looked across the street at the building. All the buildings on the block were the same: five-, six-, seven-story, dilapidated old buildings of red brick, with many small-paned windows. All the windows and doors of all the buildings were boarded up with a sheet of plywood.

As Amanda stared at the building, she could feel her heart pounding away in her chest.

"I was hopin' that Williams would be here by now," Hurts said, looking around.

"No," she said, "he's not here yet. But they're all in there."

"How do you know that?" he asked.

She turned her head, looked at him, and said, "I just do."

"Man," he replied, "you better stop gettin' weird on me … Come on, Williams. Where are you?!"

Amanda slid back the sleeve of her black overcoat and looked at the time on her wristwatch. "It's ten minutes until The Thirteenth Hour, Uncle Jim. Shouldn't we be getting in there?"

"Yeah," he said. Then, he remembered something. He remembered the time when he had fought and killed those three vampire board members of the company where Amanda's mother worked. Before the fight had begun, he had ordered Amanda to stay upstairs in a room, where she would be safe. He had slowed the three vampires down with holy water, and he had staked two of them. He felt out-of-breath, so he turned around and leaned up against a table. Unbeknownst to him, the third vampire was sneaking up behind him. From a side door, he suddenly heard Amanda scream, "Look out, Mr. Hurts! Behind you!" Hurts spun around just in time to stake him. He yelled at Amanda for not obeying his orders, saying, "When are you gonna learn to obey orders, Amanda? When?" At this time, Amanda wore black-framed glasses. She had had her head lowered in shame. When Hurts said that to her, she slowly began raising her head until their eyes met. Then she said, so defiantly, "Some orders just beg to be broken."

"Come on, Williams," Hurts said again. "Where are you?! ... Boy, I wish that I had put my plan of action with him into action."

"What 'plan-of-action' with Uncle Williams are you talking about?" she asked, looking at him.

"Well," he began. "I guess that it doesn't matter now. I was gonna ask Williams to turn me."

"Into a vampire?!" she screamed.

"Yeah," he replied.

"Are you insane?!" she stated, still screaming. "He's dead!"

"So?" Hurts replied flatly.

"Again," she stated. "Are you insane?!"

"Why, you like him just as much as you do me?"

"You don't know that!" she snapped at him.

"Okay, okay," he said. "What's your problem?"

"You want to know what my problem is?" she said, looking at him sternly. "I have become you—you, you, you!"

"Oh, don't flatter yourself, kid," he bellowed. "You ain't nothin' like me, and you never will be."

Amanda looked at her wristwatch again. Looking at Hurts, she said, "Now it's eight minutes until The Thirteenth Hour. Are we going to do this?"

"I guess if I asked you to stay here until Williams arrives, you wouldn't do it, would you?"

"No," she replied.

"You're still the most pig-headed, stubborn brat you always were."

"Thank you," she said flatly. Then she said, "So, what's the plan?"

"Plan?" he stated. "I don't have no plan. I'm just gonna go in there shootin' until they take me down … So, are you ready to die?"

"Yes," she stated.

"Well, then," he said, taking a deep breath. "Let's do it … Will you guide me to the front door?"

Twisting the top half of her body around, she placed her purse on the backseat, next to the long, black wig, saying, "Stand by the door again while I get my pistol and belt from the trunk. They got out of the car.

Hurts did as she said and stood on the much-cracked sidewalk by the door of the car and waited for her. As he waited, he heard the trunk of the car pop open. A few seconds later, she came abreast of him, wearing the belt, with the water-pistol, holster and the six stakes in the back of the belt under the long, thin-leather, black overcoat. She took his hand in hers and led him across the street.

At the one-step, cement entrance of the building, Hurts saw that the large padlock that had been attached to the north edge of the sheet of that covered the glass-section of the wooden-framed door had been ripped off from the plywood, and was now lying to the left side of the door. Hurts gingerly grabbed the rusted-out, brass, round handle of the door. He turned the handle. It opened. He let it shut again. He turned to Amanda, nodded, drew his weapon, and so did she, and he opened the door again, wide, and they creeped inside.

They stepped into a narrow, arched-ceiling foyer. The two walls were of red brick, and the floor was concrete. The floor was filthy, dusty. To the north side of the door was an old, wooden chair with arms. In it, and so nicely folded too, were a pair of yellow pajamas. To the south side of the door, sitting up and side-by-side, were the dead bodies of a man and woman. The man had been wearing a dark blue suit. It looked as if it had been ripped off his body. The woman, of Asian descent, had only a bra, panties and red high-heels on. They had puncture marks all over their bodies, on their necks, inner elbows, wrists and ankles. Their eyes were open, and within the dead, glazed, empty stare of them, was the look of total shock and horror.

Hurts motioned to Amanda with his right hand, the hand holding his pistol, to proceed on.

The foyer was about fifteen feet long. At the end of it, Hurts could see light emanating from that direction, and smell, besides the dust, the overwhelming smell of candles burning. This building, in its 'heyday' in the late 1800s, had been a tannery.

The foyer opened into a cavernous, empty space—no walls or ceiling to speak of, just wide-and-long wooden and cement beams mapping the ceiling and standing vertical here and there; candles lying on the dirty, dusty, cement floor, like armies of toy soldiers, lighted the place in dim, spotted, brightness. The many tall, narrow, small-paned windows were boarded-up from the outside with a sheet of plywood. The outer, bloodless, old, red brick walls of the building seemed to be the inner walls of the building. Perhaps, this is why Hurts found it to be so cold in there.

In the center of the space, about ten feet from where Hurts and Amanda were standing, on a foot-high wooden dais—about twelve feet long and twelve feet wide. Bound by ropes at the wrists and ankles—the ropes were tied to four of the vertical cement beams—and stretched-out like Jesus on the cross, stood a naked Emily.

She looked more dead than alive—ghostly pale-white; her waist-long, thick, blonde hair was dirty and matted from not washing, and from being repeatedly touched by filthy and oily hands, and by perspiration. Her face and body were also dirty from being 'man-handled' and repeatedly touched by filthy hands. The dais beneath her feet was wet from urine. Her eyes, her most beautiful blue eyes, were closed, and her head was tilted to one side, as if she were praying for sleep—or death.

They were all gathered around the dais and facing Emily. They were all wearing full-length black overcoats. One of them, who was standing to the south side of the dais and to the other followers, was holding a miniature grandfather's clock. "Three minutes until The Thirteenth Hour, Todd," he said.

There, standing beside and to the left of Emily, stood Todd. His waist-long, blond hair was wild-looking. Beneath his full-length black overcoat, he still had on a white suit. With the long, dirty fingernails of his right hand, he was stroking Emily's neck.

"Not much longer now, my love," he said to her, with a lisp.

Hurts lowered the pistol in his right hand, bringing his left hand up to the butt of the pistol. He took aim at the back of Todd's head. Hurts was in heaven. This was what he lived for. No fears, no regrets; Hurts lived for the fight. He was a man of action. He was in his element here. He felt rejuvenated; he felt young again—he felt GOOD.

"Hey, good-lookin'," Hurts yelled. "Look over here."

With a thunderous growl, and the immediate change from human to vampire, Todd spun around and faced Hurts.

Hurts pulled the trigger of his pistol. Had Todd not been a vampire, or not have the lighting-speed of a vampire, Hurts' bullet would have struck Todd right between the eyes. Sadly, it did not. Todd easily side-stepped it.

And zoom.

Todd was immediately holding Hurts by the lapels of his topcoat and in his face. One of Todd's followers was holding Hurts from behind in a headlock. He had knocked the pistol out of Hurts' hand. Amanda, now standing about three or four feet to Hurts' left, was also being held in a headlock from behind by another one of Todd's followers, while another one, standing in front of her, kept sniffing her as he removed the belt she was wearing. Her oversized water pistol, now empty of holy water, lay on the dirty, dusty, cement floor beside her.

Hurts was so proud of her. Before they were able to capture her and disarm her, Amanda not only sprayed two of them, she staked and killed them too. It was bittersweet, though. Hurts saw that one of the two followers that she had killed had long black hair and was wearing a thin gold chain with a medallion around his neck. Hurts had kept his promise to Flora. Sadly, he had found Vedad. He hoped that Amanda didn't know that she had just killed Vedad. In that moment, Hurts told himself that if by the grace of God, if he got out of this alive, he would beg—Hurts beg?! — Williams to do him a favor. He would return to Flora and her husband's apartment. He would tell them that he had indeed found Vedad but, sadly, Vedad was dead. For government reasons, he was not able to inform them of how their son had died. He would then hand Flora the medallion and tell them that he had planned for Vedad's remains to be flown to Bosnia and buried in an unmarked grave. If they wanted to, Hurts would give them the location of the unmarked grave, and he would even pay for them to visit Vedad's grave. This was all he could do for them.

With fangs protruding from his mouth, Todd hissed in Hurts' face and said, "Now, I know who that one is,"—referring to Amanda— "but who are you, Pops?"

"Why do you people keep askin' me that?" he stated. "I keep tellin' you that I'm Buffy The Vampire Killer." Eyeing that one follower still sniffing Amanda, Hurts said, "Hey, Todd. Tell your little pal there to chill it with Amanda. If you guys touch a single hair on her head, I vow that I'll follow you to the gates of hell and back—and I'll stake you good, boy."

Todd, shaking Hurts hard, said, "You will, will you?!"

"Todd?! Todd?!" the follower holding the clock yelled. "It's a minute until The Thirteenth Hour."

"Shut up!" Todd yelled back at him. Still holding and looking at Hurts, Todd said, "Well, let me make this vow to you, Pops. If you screwed this up for me, I vow that both of you will die a slow and painful death … Hold them," he said to the two followers who had Hurts and Amanda in a headlock. Releasing Hurts, turning and walking back to the dais, Todd said, "Start The Ritual."

Todd stood where he had stood before, on the dais, to the left of Emily, stroking her neck again with his left hand. The others stood at the foot of the dais. Then, Todd stood directly in front of Emily. Facing her, he and the others raised their arms and hands high in the air, and they all began chanting The Lord's Prayer, in Latin, backwards.

Suddenly, the tips of the candles began to flicker, and the whole building began to rumble, as if they were all in the vortex of an earthquake. From the ceiling above Todd and Emily, a white cloud appeared, and then a white face appeared from the middle of the cloud. It was an indeterminate face. Simply a white face with black, fiery eyes.

They finished chanting The Lord's Prayer, and the follower who was holding the clock shouted, "The Thirteenth Hour!"

That's when it happened.

All the pieces of plywood on all the windows came flying off, permitting the light from the moon to shine through. The glass in all the many windows exploded, and, suddenly, the place was crowded with people. They zoomed here and there. Hurts heard cries of agony. Then, he felt released from the headlock that the follower of Todd's had on him. He saw that Amanda was free too. He then heard Williams' voice coming from the direction of the dais. He was speaking Latin and reciting The Lord's Prayer. Hurts looked up at him.

Williams sure looked dapper. He was wearing a camel-colored cloth overcoat. Under that, he was dressed in a dark grey suit with a matching tie. In his right hand, he held a large bejeweled cross with Jesus hanging on it. Smoke was rising from his hand: the cross was burning it, but Williams kept towering it over Todd's head. In his left hand, he held a sword.

Todd dropped to his knees and began crying like a baby, begging for mercy.

From above, came the thunderous roar that filled the entire place and all ears with its demonic voice, "Bad vampire!" it said. "You're no fun at all."

Looking up, Williams raised the cross to him, saying, "In the name of our Lord, Jesus Christ, and by His authority, I say demon, begone!" A beam of white light ascended from the cross and smacked that demon right in the face. The face shriveled and then disappeared, and then the white cloud disappeared too.

A man holding a red cloth in his hands stepped onto the dais and came abreast of Williams. Williams placed the cross gently on the red cloth, and the man wrapped it, turned, and walked off the dais. Another man stepped onto the dais, walked over, and stood behind Emily. With the sword in hand, Williams cut Emily free. She fell into the arms of the man standing behind her. Williams removed his camel-colored overcoat, wrapped Emily in it, and the man handed Emily to Williams. The man then took the sword from Williams and stood guard over Todd.

Hurts took this opportunity to retrieve his pistol and to step over to where Vedad lay. He bent down and stealthily ripped the gold chain and medallion from around his neck, and tucked them into the right pocket of his topcoat.

Carrying Emily in his arms, Williams approached Hurts, saying, "Sorry I'm late, Hurts. I had other pressing business." Handing Emily to Hurts, Williams then said, "Take Amanda and Emily out of here immediately, Hurts … Wait for me. I'll be with you as soon as I can." He turned and walked away.

Out of the corner of his eye, Hurts saw Amanda bend down and pick up her water pistol and belt. Hurts turned around and started walking back to the entrance, saying, "Amanda, lead the way—and don't forget to get Emily's pajamas on that chair."

Chapter Twenty-three

It felt good to be outside again. The cold night air felt crisp and refreshing.

They crossed the street and saw three long white limousines parked behind Amanda's car. When Amanda came abreast of the back, driver-side door, she opened it to permit Hurts to set Emily there. He did. While he stood in the street, with the door to her car open, he leaned in and kept watch over Emily. Amanda moved quickly, maneuvering herself between the trunk of her car and the front of the limousine behind it. She opened the rear passenger-side door, tossed her oversized water pistol and belt onto the floor of the rear seat, brushed the long, black wig onto the floor; placed her purse there too, and scooted in beside Emily, all the while holding in her hands Emily's yellow pajamas.

She removed Williams' camel-colored overcoat from Emily and draped it over the back of the front seat. Then she began trying to dress Emily in her pajamas.

At that moment, Emily, more unconscious than conscious, and with her eyes still closed, began screaming, "I got to escape!" she cried. "I got to get away! … Mommy! Daddy! Help me! … I got to …"

"It's alright, Emily," Amanda kept saying to her as she dressed her. "You're safe now … It's me, honey. Amanda—and Uncle Jim … We found you. You're safe now … Please, stop, honey … "

From behind him, Hurts heard Williams say, "Step to one side, Hurts." Hurts did, and Williams stepped into the backseat of the car, next to Emily.

Emily was still screaming, "Help me, Mom and Dad! … Help me! … I got to …"

Williams took Emily's chin in his left hand, and looking at her, said kindly, but firmly, "Quiet, Emily. Quiet, my precious child … Open your eyes, Emily. Open them." Slowly, she opened her eyes. "That's it, Emily. My, you have such beautiful eyes—so blue and calm … Emily, look into my eyes … Deeper … Deeper … Emily I'm going to count backwards from three to one. When I say the number one, you shall fall into a deep sleep … Three … Two … One." Emily closed her eyes again. "Although you are now asleep, Emily, I know that you can still hear me. Listen to me, Emily. When you awaken, you shall remember none of this. You shall not remember Todd or any of his followers; you shall not remember that they were vampires or what you have had to endure these past three days …

This is what you shall remember and say: At the Teen Club, you met an extremely kind young man. He was dressed in clean bib-overalls and a clean white shirt. He spoke with a country accent. He told you that you were pretty. Outside of the club, the young man's parents were waiting for him in their pickup truck. He told them that you were the one—to be his loving bride. The family was from the back-hills of Tennessee, and they had come to St. Louis for the sole purpose of him selecting a bride. It was wrong of them, but they kidnapped you and brought you to this building. Except for whenever they left the building, and they tied you to a chair with ropes, they were good to you. Earlier this evening, they left, tying you to a chair again, and telling you that they were going shopping for a store-bought wedding dress. Somehow, after they had gone, you managed to free yourself of the ropes. You fled outside. There was an elderly man walking his dog. You pleaded with the man for help. You asked him if he had a cell phone, and, if so, could you use it? He said he did indeed have a cell phone, and he let you use it. You called Amanda and told her where you were. She called Mr. Hurts, and they came and got you. Sleep now, Emily. Sleep."

Williams reached for his overcoat on the back of the front seat and draped it over his right arm. He started to leave, but Amanda brought her mouth to his left ear and whispered something to him. He smiled and nodded his head yes. He, then, existed the car.

Hurts followed him as Williams crossed the street, saying, "Great story, Williams. Just great! You're an intelligent –"

"Save it, Hurts," Williams stated as he stepped up onto the curb on the opposite side of the street. Without stopping or looking at Hurts, he said, "Amanda informed me of your 'plan.' The answer is no. Make that appointment with Dr. Blinder."

"What?!" Hurts cried. Then he exploded with anger. "Why you no-good, stinkin' Va—" Hurts stopped speaking. He thought of Flora and of the favor he wanted from Williams for Flora and her husband. He just stood there, watching Williams walking away. To the cold night wind, he said: "I didn't want to be no stinkin' vampire anyway."

***

Amanda, being the level-headed girl that she is, and not wanting to be speaking on her cell phone while driving, before she had pulled away from the curb on Broadway, had called Emily's parents, Bob and Marge, and told them that she and Uncle Jim had Emily; that she was fine and

98

sleeping, and that they were bringing her home. She would give them all the details when they got there.

It was almost two-thirty a.m. when Amanda pulled her car up to the curb in front of Bob and Marge's house. Marge and Bob were standing at the curb, looking nervous, anxious—and overjoyed. Bob was dressed in the work clothes that he usually wore, even when not working: light blue pants with a matching shirt. The shirt had an emblem written on it above the pocket of the shirt of the company that he worked for: Anheuser-Bush. Bob was a truck-driver there. Marge was dressed in black dress pants and a pullover, green sweater. She was a secretary for some law firm downtown. When they saw Emily, they rushed to open the rear door. Emily woke up, saw them, and shouted, "Mom! Dad!" She looked around and said, "I'm home! I'm home!"

All three of them started crying. They hugged and kissed each other copiously. Bob and Marge then escorted Emily into the house quickly, saying to Hurts and Amanda, "Follow us in! Follow us in!"

In the living room, they sat Emily down on the long brown couch that was positioned against the north wall. Emily sat between Bob and Marge. Hurts and Amanda sat in two wingback chairs that were of the same design as the couch. The chairs were about four feet from each other and faced the couch. A small standing coffee table stood between them.

It was awful. Just awful. When both Bob and Marge weren't hugging and kissing Emily, one of them, in turn, would rise from the couch and begin hugging and kissing Amanda. Then they would do the same thing to Hurts. He hated that!

He had tried several times to tell Bob and Marge the story Williams had fabricated of Emily's kidnapping, but they didn't seem to care about hearing any of it. All that they seemed to care about was that Emily was back home and safe.

Suddenly, Marge exclaimed, "Emily, you smell."

"I know, Mom," she replied, embarrassed. "And I'm starving."

Hurts, believing that this would be a good time to leave—he was exhausted and wanted, needed sleep—rose from the chair and said, "Well, we better get—"

"No, no," Marge protested. Looking at Amanda, she said, "Amanda, will you help me give Emily a bath?"

"Sure," Amanda replied.

"Okay, then," Marge said. Looking at Bob now, she said, "Bob while we help Emily, you cook breakfast."

"You got it," he replied. Standing, he said to Hurts, "Come on, old buddy. I'll put the coffee on, and you can sit in the kitchen with me, drinking coffee while I make breakfast."

Hurts, seeing no way out of this, surrendered and followed Bob into the kitchen.

The coffee did taste good, though—and that breakfast that Bob made was huge and delicious. There were eggs and bacon, toast, cooked ham, pancakes and jam and maple syrup. By the time they were done eating, Hurts was stuffed and wanted nothing more than sleep.

The sun was up when Amanda and Hurts finally left Emily's, but not before more hugging and kissing.

Chapter Twenty-four

The first thing Hurts did when he got back to his office was plopped down hard onto his couch. Amanda went into the bathroom to pack her stuff and leave.

When she came out, about sixteen minutes later, she found Hurts lying on his back on the couch, his head facing the door, fast asleep. His suit coat was slung over the back of his wooden chair at his desk. His pistol, shoulder-holster and tie lay on top of the desk. His shoes were on the wooden floor, next to the plastic, black ashtray, which was next to his pack of cigarettes and lighter.

She stopped at the arm of the couch and looked down at Hurts. She stood up her black suitcase with its long, black handle and small wheels—the smaller blue suitcase on top of the black one. She walked over by Hurts' ex-partner's wooden desk, and after rolling up her sleeping-bag, stuffed it into the black pouch. She slung the strap of the pouch over her right shoulder and walked back to Hurts lying on the couch. Standing near his head, she said, "Uncle Jim? … Uncle Jim?" A few minutes later, he opened his eyes and said, more asleep than awake, "What?"

"I'm leaving now," she said.

"Okay, Amanda," he replied and turned over on his right side, facing the back of the couch. "I'm cold," he said.

Setting down the sleeping bag, Amanda said, "Here, Uncle Jim." She moved to the opposite end of the couch and got the brown blanket that was all bunched up there. She laid it over his body to his neck.

"Thanks, honey," he said. Then, he turned a bit and looked up at Amanda. "Amanda," he said, "make that appointment with that—that Dr. Blinder. I'll go."

"I will, Uncle Jim," she said, smiling and overjoyed.

He turned back over, but then he turned back around again and said, "Before you go, would you make a pot of coffee and turn it on—so, it's ready when I get up later?"

"I will."

"Thanks," he said and turned back over on his right side.

Amanda did as she was asked and made a pot of coffee and turned it on. She walked back to the arm of the couch. She picked up her purse by its long string strap and swung it around her right shoulder. She was about to do the same with the strap of the pouch that contained the sleeping bag, but she didn't. Instead, she turned around and faced the room. She looked around it. Her eyes came to rest on the Raggedy Ann doll sitting on top of the cedar dresser at the north wall of the room. It seemed like centuries had passed since she had given him that doll on that Christmas when he had saved her mother's life and hers. She had told him that day that she loved him, and that she would never forget him.

She looked back down at Hurts and smiled.

She looked about the room again. She said, softly, "There is love in this room." She took a deep breath, released it, and said, "This place smells complete. Whole … I'm complete. Whole." She looked about the room for a third time. This time, though, she looked straight in front of her, at the tall, narrow, wooden-framed, four windows facing east and the street below—or, more specifically, at the writing across the face of the windows. She said it, softly: "James Hurts, Private Investigator." She thought about it a moment, and then said: "Hurts and Warner, Private Investigators." She thought for a few more seconds, and said, "No … Boy, I must be tired."

She turned and, picking up the sleeping bag by its strap, she swung it over her right shoulder. Looking down again at Hurts, she said, "Sleep tight my 'Knight-in-Shining Armor' … See you tomorrow, Dad—or the next day."

With that, she turned and faced the door. With her left hand on the handle of the suitcase with the wheels, she grabbed the round, old, handle of the door with her right hand. She turned the knob, opened the door, and walked through it, shutting and locking the door behind her.

THE 13th HOUR
AGAIN
ALAN ZACHER

Dedication

In the wake of this Coronavirus pandemic, I humbly dedicate this novel to all who have suffered and who have died because of this heinous disease. May God's love and grace be with you all.

Chapter One

Three Sundays ago, on the thirteenth of October, 2019, at exactly thirteen minutes past 1:00 AM, a fiery meteor streaked across the chilly fall night sky in St. Louis, Missouri, hitting and totally destroying the block-long hospital of St. Alexius, or Alexian Brothers Hospital, as it was commonly called by the people of St. Louis.

Alexian Brothers Hospital had been the first hospital in St. Louis, founded and built in 1869 by Alexian Brother Bonaventure Thelen, a brother of a branch of the Franciscan order. The Alexian Brothers of the Alexian Brothers' order dedicated their lives to serving the poor and the ill. As the years passed, and as the population of St. Louis grew, more demand for medical treatment was needed. The hospital grew to its block-long status at 3933 S. Broadway Street, only a few miles south of historic Anheuser-Busch Brewery and still a few more miles south of downtown St. Louis.

Yes, the Alexian Brothers Hospital had a long and noble history with the city and with the people of St. Louis—even an infamous one, which shall be revealed shortly.

It was a most tragic event. 313 people were killed. 212 were employees of the hospital—doctors, nurses, technicians, aides. The rest of the people were patients—men, women and children of all ages and ethnicity: all of them killed, instantly vaporized, gone in a flash by the impact from that flaming Death star. All that remains there now is a deep crater; burned ground of black soot; rocks and boulders; the air for several miles around, thick with a smoldering fog, and an overwhelming stench of sulfur.

The entire city of St. Louis is in mourning, and receiving news coverage, help and condolences from around the world. This horror has affected the lives of many people, and the pain of it shall be felt for many years to come. But life goes on, doesn't it? It has to, regardless of the magnitude of the circumstances or suffering. Life endures, because man endures; and man endures, because life endures. What a topsy-turvy human comedy.

Chapter Two

Five miles west of where Alexian Brothers Hospital once stood, in an old neighborhood, a block of old connecting business buildings built in the late 1930's stood. Above the long-shuttered dentist office that had been on the first floor, printed in large black block letters across the four tall, narrow, wooden-framed windows that faced the street below, read: **HURTS & MAYOR, PRIVATE INVESTIGATORS**.

Crusty, old retired Homicide Police Detective James Hurts was happy with how those words in the window now read. Up until April of this year, only his name had been printed on the windows. But, one day in April, Tom Mayor had called Hurts and wanted to come back and be his partner once more—Hurts was beside himself with joy.

He wouldn't have freely admitted it, but when Tom had quit, Hurts began missing him terribly—and Tom's mother, Lill, too. Hurts, a consummate loner, street smart, and a man who prided himself on not being "bested" by any other man, had always liked Tom because Tom, although educated and having come from a "normal," loving family, was a "down-to-earth" type of guy who had, for most of his adult life, struggled with who and what he was in life. Tom made no bones about telling Hurts that he, Tom, was no P. I. Many times, Hurts had told Tom that he was wrong about that—that Tom WAS a P. I., a good P. I. To Hurts, Tom was intelligent, inquisitive, able to calculate and deduce, and listened to his brain and gut.

In 2007, at Christmastime, Tom had gotten roped into being a P. I. by playing a joke on his mother that had backfired on Tom. One evening, as Tom and his mother were watching a DVD of the movie "The Thin Man," Tom, bored by watching this movie again, and tired of his mother's complaints of Tom haven't worked in years, told Lill that he was thinking of going into the detective business. He told her that he knew he had what it takes to be a detective, like Nick Charles, The Thin Man. To prove this to her, Tom told her that before the movie was over, he would tell her who the killer was, which Tom did. Lill, who at this time was in her mid-eighties and a bit forgetful, was quite impressed with Tom's detective abilities. Tom went on to tell her that the hardest part starting a detective business would be getting his first client; once he did that, the rest would be easy. Tom thought this was funny—until the next morning. Tom was lying on the couch in the living room, still in his pajamas, reading the newspaper, when Lill came rushing in all excited and said, "Tom, the Lord has answered your prayers! Claire wants you to find out who really murdered Tyra!" Tom was shocked and didn't know what to do.

Claire was Tom and Lill's next door neighbor. She was an old, dying widower, and they had known her all of their lives. Tyra had been Claire's great-granddaughter. In 2005, when Tyra was nine years old, her father, John Jones, had come home from work and found Tyra lying in her bed, dead. She had been strangled with the cut cord of a lamp from the living room. The house had not been broken into or anything. Tyra had been what was at that time referred to as "a latchkey kid"—a child who must stay alone in the house. Tyra's mother, Megan, suddenly went missing in 2002, and as the years passed, everyone just assumed that she was dead. John was arrested for Tyra's murder, convicted, and sentenced to be executed in January of 2008. Claire adamantly never believed that John had done it, and she wanted Tom to investigate and reveal who had actually done this most horrific act.

Try as Tom had to extricate himself from this mess, he just couldn't find a way to get himself out. So, he began investigating the case.

After many false starts, and after much frustration, anger, and failure—and after getting shot at by an unknown person, and after someone had murdered Claire—Tom did solve the case. It had been Megan, Tyra's own mother. Unbeknownst to anyone other than the family, Claire and Bud, Claire's dead husband had been worth a few million dollars, and Megan had wanted everyone whose name was on Claire and Bud's will dead so she could return and inherit all the money.

Tom was suddenly a hero—and famous. Their old telephone in the kitchen kept ringing with calls from people who wanted Tom to take their cases. Much to Lill's anger, Tom, for the most part, always refused.

Fame is so fleeting, isn't it? Within three months, the phone stopped ringing. Lill kept nagging Tom to get his detective business up and running. Then, one morning, Tom was reading the newspaper and happened to see a wanted ad for a partner for the private investigator, James Hurts. Wanting to get his mom off his back, Tom called the guy and interviewed for the position.

Hurts wanted a partner, not because he had such a thriving business— which he most-assuredly didn't have—but, yes, he wanted someone to help pay the rent, and it got so boring and lonely at times. Tom instantly realized this and accepted the position.

They spent most of their days killing time—drinking coffee, reading the newspaper, taking naps, or just talking. Tom loved it. Tom did this for about seven months. Then, one day, he suddenly quit: he just didn't want to do it anymore, so he quit.

A few days after Christmas in 2008, Hurts read in the newspaper that Tyra's father, John Jones, had given Tom a check for one million dollars for solving the case. Tom was now set financially for life.

Throughout this whole time, Tom's father had been in an assisted-living facility, and Lill visited him every day at noon. He had Alzheimer's, but in 2014, he died from complications of having Alzheimer's. Tom and Lill were both grief-stricken and devastated by their loss. They went on a worldwide tour—seeing London, Paris, Germany, Belgium, the Netherlands, Italy, and on and on. They did this for almost two years. Then Lill tired of it. She missed being home. So, they came home.

Once there, they quickly settled back into their quiet and boring lives again. Although Lill—white-haired and pudgy—was in her mid-nineties now and moved a bit slower than she had, she was still as feisty as she had ever been. Still devoutly religious, she spent her days attending the many religious groups that she was an active member of and speaking on the phone more with her two daughters, Mary and Eve. Mary lived in Los Angeles and Eve lived in Chicago. And Tom—well, Tom being Tom, didn't do much of anything.

By the end of the passing of three more years, Tom was so bored—and Lill, too—that he called Hurts and asked him if he could be his partner again.

As I have stated, Hurts was overjoyed to have Tom back. They spent the first day of Tom's return eating donuts, drinking coffee, and talking—talk, talk, talk and talk. They reminisced about the "old days," and about their most infamous case—a case in which to this very day no one has ever believed them: No one has ever believed that they fought leprechauns. That's right. You heard me correctly—leprechauns. And they *had* fought them, too. No lie.

It all began on a Thursday evening, about a quarter-to-eight. Hurts and Tom were just about to lock the office and leave, when suddenly the door burst wide open, and a kid came staggering in. He was in his early twenties, wearing a tattered, worn, black T-shirt and tattered, old jeans; the jeans were hanging below his thin hips. He took one step inside and plummeted face down onto the scuffed, dusty, wooden floor.

Hurts asked Tom to help him get the young man over on the old long, black leather couch that was next to the office door. Tom did.

Someone had really given this kid a beating. He was all banged-up. His eyes were swollen shut, his nose was bleeding, and he had long, jagged scratches and tiny bite marks on his arms.

After slapping him a few times to wake him up, Hurts asked him what this was all about.

Half-conscious and in a daze, he—Todd was his name—stated that he was dying of thirst and asked if he could have something to drink—like a cold beer or whiskey. Tom got him a glass of water from the faucet of the sink in the closet-sized bathroom.

The kid gulped it down, and it seemed to revive him some. Then he told Hurts and Tom what had happened.

Three months ago, his grandmother had died and left him an inheritance of stocks and bonds. He cashed them and bought gold—having the pure gold converted into gold coins, each worth about a thousand dollars. Last night, his two F-ing, no-good buddies, who were brothers, kidnapped his girlfriend, Cindy, and threatened to kill her tonight if he didn't give them the gold. Not having a car, and having fifteen gold coins in his pocket, he was walking to their flat—a dive of a run-down, two-family flat, which was only several blocks south from Hurts' and Tom's office—when the brothers jumped him, beat him up, and robbed him of his gold coins as he was passing by their office just now.

Todd begged Hurts and Tom to help him, telling them that Cindy had five gold coins hidden in her purse, and if they would get her back for him, they could have the five coins.

Hurts didn't know if he believed this kid's story or not—but, what the hell? Five coins at a thousand dollars apiece? That's five thousand dollars! Not bad for a few hours of work! Besides, Hurts was bored and was itching for action. Hurts told him they would do it.

Hurts and Tom left Todd lying on the couch, and they got into Hurts' old gray 1997 Nissan Pathfinder and headed south.

Well, Todd had told them the truth. Somewhat. The two brothers had kidnapped the girl. Hurts and Tom rescued her. Well, Hurts did all of the fighting, but Tom helped tie them up with rope. Then they brought her back to the office. Hurts didn't think much of her. He thought of her as being uneducated, low-life white trash. When they freed her from the ropes and kitchen chair around which the two brothers had her bound, she dashed to the refrigerator, drained a bottle of beer in a single gulp, belched, farted, and thought nothing of it. Hurts thought that she had as much class as that of a two-dollar whore—but Tom was infatuated with her, wanted her, lusted for her.

When they got back to the office, and when she saw how badly beaten up her boyfriend was, she hugged him and cried, "Oh, Baby! Who pounded you?! … Did 'em little pricks get the—" Todd quickly began kissing her on the lips.

Seeing this depressed and infuriated Tom, but Hurts, not giving a damn about seeing such affection, stated, "Okay, now, stop … We were promised five gold coins for services rendered." Holding out his hand, Hurts then said, "Pay."

Todd quickly said to Cindy, "I told them about grandma's inheritance, and about changing it to gold coins. I told them if they got you freed from Fred and Tim that they could have the five coins you have."

The expression she had on her narrow, thin, hard-looking face was of anger, but she reluctantly reached into the large, floppy, long-strapped, black handbag. From a hidden compartment deep within the handbag, she removed five gold coins and begrudgingly dropped them flatly into Hurts' waiting hand.

Hurts took one of the coins in his hand, brought it to his mouth, bit it, then inspected it. He gave Tom a wink of approval, and then walked over to his old long wooden desk. He opened the middle drawer and dropped the five coins inside it.

Cindy then said, "Say, Todd and me put the pot—most of the coins in a gym bag and buried it in the yard behind the building of the shitty apartment where we live. If you will help me dig it up, and then help me rent a car so Todd and me can get the hell out of this shitty place, I'll give you—oh, five more gold coins. What do you say?"

"We'll do it!" Tom stated eagerly, leaning against the backside of his desk. "I'll go with you."

"Oh, no you won't," Hurts bellowed. "I'll go."

"No, I said I'd go, so I'll go," Tom insisted.

"No, I'll go," Hurts barked.

"No," Tom began, "I'll go—"

"Look here, Tom," Hurts stated, interrupting him, "you can't go." Raising his left arm and patting his right hand under the armpit of his left shoulder, feeling the holstered .9mm semi-automatic pistol under the wrinkled gray suit he was wearing, he said, "You don't carry a firearm. Granted, we beat up the brothers, tied them up, and I warned them that I'd kill them if they interfered with us again—but they might, and how are you going to protect yourself without a firearm?" This was all a lie, and Tom knew it. Hurts didn't want Tom going because he didn't like it that Tom's mind wasn't on "business," but was on that sleazy girl, Cindy. "No, I'll go. You stay here and protect lover-boy there," he said, pointing to Todd.

After shaking his head angrily, Tom said, "Fine. You go."

Pointing to the narrow wooden door at the northwest corner of the office, Cindy asked, "Is that the bathroom?"

"Yeah," Tom replied.

Cindy rose from the couch and started for the door. Midway, though, she stopped, turned back around and, looking at Hurts, said, "Can we stop at a Walgreens or something? I'm on the rag and I gotta have tampons."

Oooooh, Tom moaned, silently, hungrily. *She's menstruating. Girls get horny when menstruating. Damn. Damn!*

After Hurts and Cindy had left, Todd said, "Man, don't you have any beer or whiskey here?"

"No," Tom replied angrily. It was a lie: Hurts always had a bottle of bourbon in the top right drawer of his desk. "Just lie back down and go to sleep."

Tom walked to the back of his desk and plopped down heavily into his old wooden chair. The chair had arms, and Tom patted them angrily with the palms of his hands for a moment. Then, remembering that he thought that he had broken the heel of his worn, in-much-need-of-a-polish, black dress-shoes at the those two brothers' apartment, Tom removed the shoe and began inspecting it. Yes, the heel was loose and came off in his hand. *Great!* Tom cursed silently. *That's just great!*

Tom removed his other shoe and placed them both at the corner of his desk. Feeling totally enraged and depressed, he leaned his head against the back of the chair and closed his eyes.

"Well, what about pot?" he heard Todd say. "Don't you got—?"

"No!" Tom roared heatedly. "Now, go to sleep!"

Chapter Three

Tom was in sexual bliss. He was in a bed, naked, on top of Cindy's naked body—and he was having "fun" with her. Her legs were spread and high in the air, and she was moving and moaning and groaning in agonizing pleasure. Tom was in heaven. Of course, this was all just a dream, but Tom didn't know this. He was still slumped in his chair at the office. Then, just at the moment of the exquisite release of joy/pain completion, Tom felt a different pain, and in a different place. The pain was on his upper chest—it was heavy and oppressing him. Suddenly, Tom felt hands, many hands, grabbing at his arms and legs, restraining him from moving. He woke with a yelp of unknown fear.

The room was crowded with little men and women—they couldn't have been more than three feet tall. They were all dressed alike, either in all green or red coats, with matching vests and pants and black leather shoes with buckles. They had large, silver-like buckles on their pilgrim-like hats, belts, and shoes, and flaming-red hair and red beards, except for the females, that is.

Tom couldn't believe what he was seeing. He blinked his eyes a few times in shock, trying to wake up. *Leprechauns*! He shouted, silently. *Freakin' leprechauns!*

The pain that he was experiencing to his upper chest was coming from one of the leprechauns straddling his chest. He was smoking a tiny white pipe that had a long, thin handle to it. Tapping the end of it against Tom's wrinkled, fearful forehead, he stated in a thick Irish brogue, "Where's me pot of gold?! Answer me! Where's me pot—" Then he began sniffing the air. He jumped off of Tom and onto the top of Tom's desk. Rejoicing, he did a little jig, shouting, "Me gold! Me gold!" He let out this shriek of laughter, "HeeEEEEE!" spun around, jumped off of Tom's desk, dashed over to Hurts' desk, opened the middle drawer, and cursed, "Damn! Damn!"

He grabbed those five gold coins in his tiny right hand, dashed back to Tom's desk, jumped back on top of it, held out his hand, and demanded angrily, "Where's the rest of me gold?!"

With his mouth dry and pointing with his head toward a sleeping Todd on the couch, Tom said, "That's all they gave us."

"Off with his pants!" the leprechaun shouted, and two of them unbuckled the belt from the pants of the old dark-blue suit that Tom was wearing. They then unfastened Tom's pants and lowered them down to his ankles, revealing his naked legs and Fruit-of-the-Loom underwear. "Now, tape him up!" he continued, and two other leprechauns, duct taped his hands and legs to the arms and front legs of the chair. One of them then shoved a piece of tape over Tom's mouth.

Spotting Tom's shoes on the top of the desk, the leprechaun who had done all the talking began shouting angrily and pointing to Tom's shoes. He cried, "Broken shoes! In need of repair! … One at a time … Damn you … It's nearly dawn … Apron! … One at a time … It's nearly dawn … Tools! … Shoes in need of repair … Polish! … Damn you! … Nearly dawn! … Done!"

After repairing and polishing Tom's shoes until they sparkled like brand new, the leprechaun set them back on top of the desk, jumped down onto the floor, and dashed over to the couch to Todd, who was still sleeping.

"Bring him with us!" he barked.

Ten or twelve of leprechauns lifted Todd from the couch and began carrying him. Todd woke up and began screaming and cursing. "What the hell, man? … Hey, put me down, you little fu—" Bonk! One of them hit Todd on the head with a tiny rubber hammer, knocking him out.

The one who had done all the talking then said, "If you ever want to see him again, bring me me pot of gold to Carondelet Park tomorrow after dark, to the woods at the west end of the park by the pond!"

Then the room was empty. They, including Todd, vanished into thin air.

Chapter Four

Hurts and Cindy returned to the office a little after 7:00 AM. Hurts became furious. After Hurts and Cindy freed Tom from the chair, and after Tom pulled up his pants—and he was a bit embarrassed by Cindy seeing him in his underwear, but he hoped that she felt that he had a big bulge in his Fruit-of-the-Looms—and after Tom told them what had happened, and after Hurts had seen that the five gold coins were gone, he blew-up with boiling anger. He didn't believe Tom at all and wanted to know what he was trying to pull, saying that there was no such thing as "leprechauns" and asked where the gold coins and Todd were.

Out of desperation, Tom turned to Cindy for help. He told her, for Todd's safety and to get him back, that she had better tell them the truth. She didn't want to, but she did. Here's the truth:

She, Todd, and those two brothers would get drunk and high, and piled into the brothers' old car and looked for people to rob. If the night didn't go well, and they didn't find any "easy pigeons" to rob, they would end the night by driving through Carondelet Park, looking for drunken teenagers and homosexuals to rob. Well, two nights ago, they were driving through Carondelet Park. It was raining hard, with lightning and thunder. Suddenly, a lightning bolt struck a tree, shattering it and lighting up the night sky. A rainbow appeared, and one end of it was at that destroyed tree. Todd jumped out of the car and raced over to that tree. He came back carrying in both hands a small black pot filled with gold coins.

Those two brothers wanted Todd to share the gold with them, but Todd told them to "blank" off, that the gold was his. "Well," she ended, "you know the rest—they kidnapped me for a share of the gold, and I guess it was the leprechauns who beat up Todd."

Hurts walked over to his desk and sat down in his wooden chair. He was silent and deep in thought. A few minutes later, he looked up and said with a grin, "I have a plan." That's a "catch-phrase" of Hurts.' "A good detective always has a plan." Rising from his chair and pointing to the top of Tom's desk, he told Tom to get on his laptop and see what he could find out about leprechauns. Then, grabbing the handles of the black gym bag that contained the pot of gold, he told Tom that he and Cindy would be back in about an hour.

They left.

They returned to the office about three hours later. Hurts was carrying the gym bag in one hand and hugging a brown paper grocery bag in his other arm; the bag seemed full and heavy. Cindy had a six-pack of beer in one hand and a fast-food bag of smelly, greasy hamburgers and fries in her other hand. Hurts set the gym bag and the grocery bag down on top of his desk. He told Cindy to do the same.

The grocery bag was stuffed with electrical outlet boxes. Each box had sections all around with quarter-sized disks that could be punched out in order to thread electrical wire through the box.

From the right pocket of his suitcoat, Hurts produced a 10-ounce glass bottle of pure liquid gold. After they had eaten and drank—with Cindy gulping down most of the beers—they spent most of the rest of that day punching out the disks from the electrical boxes, filing the disks, cleaning them, and then painting them with the liquid gold from that bottle.

Using Tom's black cloth laptop case, Hurts dumped all the real gold coins into it. He then set the black pot back into the gym bag. Once the disk-coins were dry, Hurts scooped them up and dropped them into the pot. The stage was now set for the ruse Hurts was about to execute on the leprechauns.

At 7:00 PM, they left the office for Carondelet Park.

Chapter Five

Carondelet Park was only several blocks south of the office. The park has been an historic staple in the City of St. Louis for years, since 1875. Named after Baron Carondelet, it has 180 acres, containing woods, open fields, two man-made lakes, tennis courts, playgrounds, pavilions for picnics and for family get-togethers and for weddings, and is simply a wonderful place to relax.

Hurts knew the park well. Besides having gone there himself as a kid, when his two daughters had been children, he had taken them there several times. That was before his ex-wife got fed-up with his staying out most nights—drinking, gambling, whoring and the occasional slap during a heated argument. Hurts always believed that it was his ex-wife who had turned his daughters against him, wanting nothing to do with him. Never.

Anyway, no pun intended, but Hurts' plan worked like a charm. Cindy led Hurts and Tom to the tree where Todd had found the pot of gold.

The park was deserted. The wind howled through the dry, brown leaves on the trees. Tom found the whole situation to be frightening—well, it was the night before Halloween. Suddenly, the woods were filled with leprechauns. They surrounded Cindy, Hurts and Tom.

The leprechaun who had done all of the talking to Tom, stood in front of them. With pipe in his tiny mouth, and with hands on his hips, he said demandingly, "Do ye have me—" He stopped, sniffed the air, pointed to the gym bag in Hurts' right hand, and cried joyously, "Me gold! Me gold! … Give it to me!"

Hurts bent over and set the gym bag down in front of him on the brown grass. He then unzipped the gym bag, revealing the pot of gold coins—or gold-painted disks, I mean. The leprechaun did a little happy jig in place, and then he reached out for the gold.

"Not so fast, Shorty," Hurts said, stopping him. "Where's Todd?"

Looking up at Hurts, with a deadpan expression upon his impish, reddish face, he shouted demandingly, "Bring him!"

Todd appeared, looking more unconscious than conscious. His hands were bound in front of him at the wrists with duct-tape, and a strip of it covered his mouth. His pants were hugging his ankles and dragging on the ground, which made it difficult for him to walk, and he had fresh scratch marks and bite marks on his arms and legs.

Needless to say, they grabbed Todd and got the hell out of there—fast!

Back at the office, with Todd lying on the couch again, sleeping, Cindy was boiling angry. Hurts had informed her that there was a new deal: Because of what she and Todd had put him and Tom through, and because of what he and Tom had done for them, he and Tom—and Tom had no knowledge of this—wanted half of the gold coins.

Try as she did to negotiate a lesser amount with Hurts, she always failed. Hurts was adamant: He wanted, demanded, half the gold coins. Period.

She begrudgingly, fuming mad, finally surrendered, calling Hurts and Tom no-good, low-down, blankie-blank thieves.

Eyeballing it, Hurts poured what he believed to be half the gold coins from Tom's laptop case into Cindy's large, floppy black purse.

Todd, still half asleep and in a daze, clung to Cindy. She had his left arm around his neck so she could help him down to the car that Hurts had helped her rent so they could flee St. Louis.

When Cindy and Todd reached the door to the office, Tom said self-effacingly, "It was sure nice meeting you, Cindy."

She turned half around with Todd. She shot Tom a murderous stare with her dull brown eyes and stated sardonically, "Get real—Pops!"

Not having a safe, and not wanting the gold stolen, Hurts suggested that they go downtown to the bus station and rent a box there. Then tomorrow morning, they could divide the coins and deposit them into their bank accounts. Tom agreed to this.

They drove to the bus station in their own cars, so they could both drive home after placing Tom's laptop case in the rented box, with the gold coins still inside the laptop.

Before they closed the metallic door of the box and locked it, Hurts, whose palms always itched when it came to money, scooped up ten coins and pocketed them. He told Tom to do the same—you never know when you just might need some extra money for an emergency. Tom took five coins.

They separated and both drove home: Tom to his mom and dad's house in the County, and Hurts to his small red-brick house in the City. A few months after Tom quit, Hurts sold his house and began living at the office.

It was five minutes to 1:30 AM when Tom finally got home, and he was dog-tired. In his upstairs bedroom, after dropping the five gold coins into the middle drawer of his old, large, wooden desk, Tom removed his now much-wrinkled, smelly, light-brown suit and changed into his night clothes for bed: his white sweatpants and white T-shirt. He was so tired that he just dropped onto his bed face up—not even covering himself with a blanket. He went fast to sleep.

He didn't dream of anything. He just slept. Then, as it had been at the office, he suddenly felt a heaviness on his upper chest. He was slapped awake by a sting to the left cheek of his unshaved face.

Leprechauns were in his bed, on both sides of him, holding him down, and that damn leprechaun who had done all of the talking was straddled across his chest again.

Touching Tom's forehead with the long end of his small white pipe, he said, angrily, "Stealing a leprechaun's gold can get ye killed, lad. … Now," he said, placing the end of the pipe in his mouth, and showing Tom the five gold coins in his left hand. "Where's the rest of me gold?! I know that your partner doesn't have it—we got the ten coins that he had—so, where is it?!"

Tom was about to answer him, but before he said a word, he heard his mother scream, "Who are you people?! … Stop! … Put me down! … Where are you taking me?! … Stop! … Lord, Jesus—help me! … Tom! Help me! … Tom! Tom! Tom!"

"Mom!" Tom cried. "Mom! … Please don't take her," Tom stated pleadingly. "Your gold isn't here—but I can get it for you. Please don't take my mom."

"If ye ever want to see her again," he stated angrily and demandingly, "bring me me gold tomorrow night at the park, same as before! … Hammer!" he then shouted, and he hit Tom on the top of his head with it, knocking him out.

Tom awoke with a sharp, stabbing pain at the top of his head, and hearing a ringing sound. He lay there for a few minutes, disoriented. He was bound with duct tape at the wrists and ankles, and his white sweatpants had been pulled down over his ankles. There was also a strip of tape covering his mouth. He didn't know what time it was, but the light shining through the window told him that it must be after dawn. He told himself that the ringing that he was hearing was coming more from the ringing of the phone downstairs than from the ringing between his ears. Then he remembered, and he shouted, "Mom! … They took Mom!"

Chapter Seven

About an hour later, Tom heard footsteps moving quickly up the stairs, and the shouting of, "Tom! … Lill! … Tom! Lill! Tom!" It was Hurts, and Tom was much relieved and happy to hear his crusty, old voice.

Removing a pocketknife from the right-side pocket of the wrinkled, pin-striped gray suit that he was wearing, Hurts said, "So, they got you, too." Cutting the duct tape from Tom's wrists, he continued speaking. "They took my coins, tied me up with duct tape, pulled my pajamas down, and hit me on the head—I'll kill 'em!" Then he cut the duct tape from Tom's ankles.

Tom ripped off that strip of duct tape covering his mouth and cried, with much panic and fear, "Jim, they took Mom! —They took Mom! … He said if I ever want to see Mom again, I was to give him his gold back tonight, at the park!"

Tom sat up as Hurts dropped down heavily onto the edge of the bed.

"Oh, no," Hurts sighed, deeply disturbed. "Oh, no!" He thought for a few moments, and then said, "Okay, here's the plan. We—"

"No, Jim," Tom stated emphatically. "This is Mom we're talking about. No more 'plans' or deals. I want Mom back."

"Okay, Tom," Hurts said. "You're right. We'll get Lill back … Do you have a pla—I mean, what are you going to do?"

"I know exactly what to do," Tom stated resolutely. "You meet me back here at seven—and bring the gold."

Chapter Eight

At exactly 7:00 PM, Hurts pulled up in front of Tom and Lill's house. It was dark by now, so as Tom came out the front door, he turned on the porch light. He was wearing jeans, a plaid shirt, tennis shoes and a light jacket. With the tops of the bags crumpled closed, in both hands Tom was carrying a brown paper grocery-bag.

Wearing the same clothes that he had on earlier in the day, as Tom sat down in the front seat, Hurts asked, "What's in the bags?"

Tom, seeing his laptop case containing the gold coins lying beside Hurts on the seat, replied soberly, "Protection—I hope. Let's go."

With the strap of his laptop case straddling his right shoulder and his hands gripping the closed tops of the two grocery-bags, Tom stood in front of the same tree that he had the night before. Hurts stood to the right side of him.

It was as spooky as it had been the night before, but now, with the knowledge that it was Halloween, it was even scarier.

Suddenly, the leprechauns appeared before them. The one who had done all the talking stood in front of Tom. He sniffed the night air, did a little jig, and then cried joyously, "Me gold! Me gold!"

Tom set the two grocery bags down on both sides of him. Swinging the strap of his laptop case off his shoulder, he then lowered it to the ground in front of him. With a dry mouth and body shaking with fear, Tom unzipped the case, revealing the gold coins, and he said demandingly, "Now, where's my mother?!"

Looking up at Tom, the leprechaun shouted, "Bring her!"

A few seconds later, his mother appeared out of the darkness. Tom was much relieved to see her. Her hands were bound with duct tape at her wrists and she had a strip of tape covering her mouth. Although she looked exhausted and volcanic angry, she didn't have any scratches or bite marks on her. Tom almost laughed, though. The bottom of the white pajamas that she had been wearing were pulled down to her ankles revealing her white underwear, and she had trouble walking.

After looking inside the case at the gold coins, the leprechaun who did all the talking became fuming angry and shouted, "This isn't all me gold! —Where's the rest of it?!"

Picking up the two grocery bags and holding them in both hands, Tom replied, "This is all the gold we have. Cindy and Todd have the rest."

"Not good enough!" he screamed. "Get them!"

A donnybrook then ensued. Leprechauns were all over Tom, and he heard Hurts screaming and cussing the leprechauns. Tom was knocked to the ground. The leprechauns were all over him, scratching him and biting him, and trying to unbuckle his belt and pull his pants off. Through it all, though, Tom held firmly onto the paper grocery bags. He raised the bags over his head, and using his body as a human steamroller, he began rolling to his left. It worked. He rolled the leprechauns off of him. He jumped to his feet, and before any other leprechauns could attack him again, he lowered the bags to his sides and gave a hard jerk with his wrists. The bottoms of both bags ripped open and shoes came cascading from them. Tom had collected every shoe in the house—his Dad's, his Mom's, and his.

"Shoes!" Tom cried. "Shoes in need of repair!"

The fighting stopped, and silence now ruled the night.

"Shoes in need of repair!" said the one who had done all the talking. "Shoes in need of repair … Damn you! … Apron! … Shoes in need of repair … Tools! … Damn you! … One at a time … Shoes in …."

As the leprechauns saw to the repair of the shoes, Tom worked his way over to Hurts. He quickly helped him up off the ground and helped him pull up his pants and the sleeves of his shirt and suit down. Hurts was in a daze. He had bruises to his face and scratches and bites to his arms and legs. He quickly recovered, though—somewhat—and they worked their way over to Lill.

Being exhausted and having gone through the ordeal of being kidnapped and all, and what with her hands being bound at the wrists with duct tape, and what with the bottom of her pajamas encircling her ankles and prohibiting any free movement, Tom and Hurts were forced to drag her to the car—which they did, fast!

Tom drove while Hurts and Tom's mother lay in the back seat "licking-their-wounds" and cussing those leprechauns. Lill said that they were of the devil: "Why, I'm a God-fearing woman, and they pulled my pants down … Why, vampires don't even do that!" (I'll explain what she meant about vampires later.) Hurts vowed to someday return to the park, steal their gold again, and kill as many of those little monsters as he could.

Back home, Tom opened four cans of tomato soup and made three peanut-butter sandwiches, and they ate and drank coffee. After they had eaten, they did feel better. Lill said that she wanted to go to bed. Hurts felt depressed and "damn mad" about having done all of that work and having not made a damn penny from it. He asked Tom to return to the office and just, you know, just talk. Tom did.

Tom and Hurts sat on the old, long, tattered black leather couch, drinking whiskey straight from the bottle that Hurts always kept in one of the drawers of his desk. Hurts, physically hurting, exhausted, depressed, and now drunk, fell asleep quickly—slumped on the couch with his head resting on the back of the couch, his mouth open, and snoring loudly.

Tom, also hurting, exhausted, and drunk, rose heavily from the couch, lumbered over to his desk, popped himself down in his chair, lowered his head on the top of his desk, and settled himself in for much-needed sleep. He was just seconds away from slipping off into a deep sleep, when he heard a constant pounding at the glass of the upper section of the front door to the office. He slowly, reluctantly raised his sleepy, drunken head and looked: It was Cindy and Todd.

They both looked pretty beaten up—bruises to the face, and scratches and bite marks on their arms.

As soon as Tom opened the door, Cindy cried angrily, just fit-to-be-tied mad, "Those little fuckers jumped us and took our gold. They—"

Tom interrupted her and raised his left hand to prevent them from entering. He stated firmly and flatly, "They took our gold, too. We can't help you … You two have been nothing but trouble since the moment we met you. Goodbye!" Having said that, Tom slammed the door shut. But just before he had slammed the door, he spotted something on the floor of the hallway to his left that caught his eye. There, lined up on the floor against the outer wall of the office, was every pair of shoes that Tom had dropped at the park—all looking polished and brand new.

Tom lumbered back to his desk, mumbling, "Who's coming next—The Invisible Man?"

Chapter Nine

Now that I have introduced you to most of the principal characters of our tale, let us return to the main story.

It was a most beautiful fall morning. There was a crisp chill in the air, but the sun was shining brightly—and the citizens of St. Louis needed this, too. They were still feeling the pain of loss and suffering from the meteor striking and totally destroying Alexian Brothers Hospital and killing all of those people. They were all doing the best they could to go on with life. That had happened on a Sunday three weeks ago. Now, it was 10:30, Monday morning, October the twenty-eighth, three days before Halloween.

"But, Jim," Tom cried emphatically. He was sitting at his desk and looking at the screen of his laptop. "Amanda's right. Instagram is a great place to advertise. Everybody goes there."

"Well, why don't we just advertise our services in the Yellow Pages and at bus stops?" Hurts replied from his desk.

Sitting in her well-padded swivel chair, which was positioned next to Tom's chair so that she, too, had access to a desk, Lill said, "I'm with Jim on this. Everybody uses the Yellow Pages."

Lill had become a fixture at the office. Out of sheer boredom with her everyday life, she had started coming to the office with Tom two or three days a week, and Hurts loved it. Besides bringing donuts or cakes that she had baked, she made the place feel more like a home than an office. Because Hurts was bound and determined to live there, she bought him a small gas stove, which was positioned at the east end of the counter against the north wall, a toaster, and a microwave, both of which were on the top of the counter. The Raggedy Ann doll that Amanda had given to Hurts years ago as a Christmas gift sat to the right of the toaster, and the 19-inch old colored TV sat to the left side of the microwave. Why, Lill had even purchased mini-blinds and thin white drapes for the four windows that faced the street below. It was great. Hurts loved having Lill there.

Amanda, sitting on the couch, replied diffidently, "Not to disagree with you, Mrs. Mayor, but hardly anybody uses the paper version of the Yellow Pages anymore. It's all online now. Computers."

Lill thought about it for a moment and then said, "Yes, I suppose you're right, Dear." She rose from the chair, and carrying her coffee mug with her, walked to the counter to fill her mug with more coffee. Grabbing the black handle of the coffeepot, Lill stated, "I guess that I'm just not made for this modern world."

"Oh, I wouldn't say that, Mrs. Mayor," Amanda replied. "I think you're pretty sharp."

"Why, thank you, Sweetie," she said, beaming with joy.

Yes, Hurts was happy, and he loved it that Tom and Lill liked his daughter, Amanda, and that Amanda liked them. Of course, Amanda wasn't his daughter, actually. Although Amanda called Hurts Uncle Jim, Hurts wasn't related to her at all.

When Amanda had been eleven years old, her mother, Jennifer Warner, had been arrested for trying to transfer twenty million dollars into Swiss bank accounts from the accounts of clients of the brokerage firm for which she worked, International Investments, Inc. Amanda's mother worked in the Accounting Department. The transferring of the money had happened in the wee hours of a Sunday night, and when Mrs. Warner went into work the next morning, she was immediately arrested. Amanda was in the sixth grade at St. Mary's Elementary. At noon that day, while Amanda was having lunch in the cafeteria, her cellphone rang. It had been Amanda's mother. She told Amanda what had happened, and that it was all a terrible mistake and would be straightened out soon. Amanda's father had died of colon cancer when Amanda had been nine years old, so there was no one else to take care of Amanda while her mother was in jail. Her mother told her not to worry, though—that someone from Family Services was coming to get her, and that she would stay with Family Services until the situation was resolved. Amanda, being a most strong-willed girl, wasn't going to stand for that. She ran away.

After running back home, she changed into everyday clothes, packed some clothes into her backpack, got her dad's bedroll, and not wanting Family Services or the police to trace her, she left her cellphone on her bed. She took all the money in the cookie jar—$70.00—and left the house.

The first night, Amanda stayed in a cheap hotel near downtown. The second night, not having enough money for another night at that hotel, Amanda spent the night, shivering, in her father's bedroll in the well of the entrance to the St. Louis Public Library.

The next day, tired, lonely, scared, hungry, and out of hope as to what she could do to get her mother out of jail, Amanda mindlessly roamed the city streets.

Then she walked down the cracking, unlevel sidewalk of an old business street. Halfway down the block, she looked up. There, on the second level of an old red-brick building, were four tall, narrow, wooden-framed windows. Written in large black block letters across those windows were the words: **JAMES HURTS, PRIVATE INVESTIGATOR.**

Reading that, a ray of much needed and wanted hope returned to Amanda's heart.

After repeatedly knocking towards the bottom of the wooden-framed door to his office, and not getting a reply, Amanda finally opened the door and stepped inside the office. To the side of the door, was a long black leather couch. With his head resting on the arm of that couch, and with his body lying belly down on the couch, and being fully clothed, except for his suitcoat and shoes, Hurts was dead-drunk hungover—the empty whiskey bottle lying on the wooden floor next to the couch.

In a hungover daze, Hurts told her that he was closed. When she told him why she was there and wanted to hire him, and then told him that she only had eleven dollars, he told her that the police never make mistakes and "don't let the door hit you in the ass going out."

Amanda, outraged by what Hurts had said, pounded the arm of the couch next to his aching head, and screamed angrily, "Yes, they are wrong! My mother didn't do it! I want her out of jail!"

Hurts sat up. After wiping his unshaven face, he looked over toward the wooden counter that was against the wall, spotted the coffeepot on top of it, and said to Amanda, "Do you see that coffeepot over there?" He pointed to it. "Well, turn it on."

As I have said, Amanda was a very strong-willed little girl, and she could be most persuasive. On that day she was with Hurts, he cared nothing for the case or for Amanda's dilemma. Until she said, "You know, Mr. Hurts, some of that twenty million is still missing. Why, I bet if you take the case and solve it, the company will give you a BIG reward—maybe a million!"

Hurts, being a man who always was more than eager to make a buck, was now interested. He agreed to speak with Amanda's mother. Amanda was overjoyed.

Raising her tiny gloved hands above her head, she cried, "Woo-who!"

"Stop that!" Hurts barked at her. He had found Amanda to be a most "aggravating" child. "Just plain, plain aggravating."

At the St. Louis Police Headquarters, the first thing that Hurts did was view video footage of a woman signing in and handing the night security guard of Amanda's mother's place of employment, International Investments, Inc., an employee ID card on the night when all of this had happened. The woman was wearing a floppy black hat that hid most of her face, and she was also wearing a black full-length coat. The employee ID card that she had handed to the guard had identified her to be Mrs. Jennifer Warner, Amanda's mother.

After viewing that video, and after speaking with Mrs. Warner, Hurts was eighty-five percent convinced that Amanda's mother was innocent. Hurts was a man who relied much on his "gut feeling"—and his gut was screaming to him that this woman was no crook.

The next day, Hurts interviewed the person in charge of International Investments, Mr. Theodore Williams, Senior Board Member of the company.

International Investments, Inc. is a worldwide investment brokerage firm, with many branches of the company in many cities. Each branch of the company is run by six board members.

The St. Louis branch of the company is in the Wainwright Building at the corner of 7th Street and Market Street in downtown. It's a twenty-floor skyscraper building of shiny granite and tinted windows. International Investments consumes the top three floors.

Hurts found Mr. Williams to be a dapper man, who wore an expensive suit and matching tie, and seemed to be about fifty-five years of age—and yet, Hurts thought him to be much older than that. There was just something about the guy that made Hurts feel that he belonged to another time: Oh, he was educated, cultured, sophisticated, but, besides the slight British accent Hurts had detected, there was an aura about the guy that said: You're of a time long gone-by.

Hurts had gotten next to nothing from Mr. Williams about Amanda's mother. He had been very evasive, and he was forever stroking the pencil-thin salt-and-pepper moustache below his thin, straight nose—and the guy had no photos or pictures on top of his glass-top desk. Who doesn't have pictures on a desk of family, friends, kids?! Hurts thought that strange. Oh, there were framed photos on the walls of his office. He was most proud to point out the framed photo on one of the walls of him standing in a line—him standing in the middle—with five other old and well-dressed men. These men, he had told Hurts, were his fellow board members.

The next day, Hurts spoke with a Ms. Cogwell. She was Amanda's mother's supervisor at International Investments, head of the Accounting Department. She was a woman in her mid-fifties, Hurts would say—but, she too seemed to be much older. She was thin, with a plain, sourpuss face, and seemed to Hurts to be uptight and protective of herself and of the company. She was of about the same height as Amanda's mother, and Hurts, again, had gotten next to nothing from her—and she, too, had no photos on her desk. Hurts had just found that to be strange.

Hurts was at a loss as to what to do next. Then, everything changed.

As I have stated, Amanda was a most strong-willed little girl, and she was, in Hurts' mind, a "health nut"—besides being, according to Hurts: "Aggravating. Just plain, plain aggravating." She adamantly refused to eat in fast-food restaurants, and she didn't like Hurts smoking so much around her. See, Amanda's father had died of colon cancer when she had been nine years old, and she vowed to become a doctor when she grew up.

After Hurts had spoken to Ms. Cogwell, as he was driving back to his office, Amanda had demanded that they first stop at a grocery store. There, they could buy groceries and, on Hurts' hotplate back at the office, Amanda would prepare for them a well-balanced, nutritious supper. Hurts moaned and groaned about doing it, but he did. They got groceries—just as they had gotten a small Christmas tree, next, for Hurts' "gloomy" office. Amanda just had to have one.

Well, armed now with groceries and that Christmas tree, when Hurts got about six blocks from the office, he looked in the rearview mirror of his car and spotted an expensive, new, shiny black Mercedes about seven cars behind him. Hurts had seen that car before.

The first evening that Amanda had stayed with Hurts, she faked coughing because of the room being so smoky from his chain-smoking. She had been sitting on the couch, reading from the text of a chemistry book that she had packed into her backpack before she ran away from home. Hurts had been at his desk, busy at his old computer trying to find out as much as he could about the company, International Investments.

"Alright," he had barked at Amanda, rising from his wooden chair. "I'll crack a window."

He walked over to one of those four windows that faced the street below and opened it. He looked out of that window, down onto the street. Parked on the street, right below the building, and right behind his car was an expensive, new, black Mercedes. Seeing it, Hurts thought, *What's a car like that, doing in a neighborhood like this?*

Seeing that car again as they drove back to Hurts' office, he knew, he just knew, that that was the same car that he had seen the other night.

Hurts floored the gas pedal, and the car shifted into high speed, scaring Amanda. Hurts told her not to worry or to be scared, saying, "I have a plan—A good detective always has a plan."

Yes, Hurts was driving at a high speed, going in and out of the correct lane and through red stoplights, but he didn't want that car to lose him. He just wanted to get a little distance between that car and him so he could put his plan into action.

He drove down a neighborhood street. The neighborhood was old and dilapidated, housed with many two-story red-brick houses that were abandoned and boarded up. He chose one of them. He told Amanda to hide on the floor of the car and to stay there until he returned.

Using his right shoulder as a battering-ram, he burst the front door of the house open and dashed inside. The house faced east. Hurts was in the bare living room of the house. He placed his back up against the west wall of the room. He removed a mini flashlight from the right pocket of his topcoat, clicked it on, and began flashing it towards the front door. He then removed his .9mm semi-automatic firearm from its holster under his left armpit and waited for whoever was to come.

It wasn't a long wait.

Within minutes, a tall man, who was about a foot taller than Hurts' 5', 7" height, had a slender build, and was immaculately dressed—expensive suit and tie and a full-length camel topcoat—stood at the door of the house. Just like Mr. Williams, the man had an arura about him of sophistication, education, culture, and seemed to be older than he looked. For some reason, Hurts felt that he had seen the guy before, but he didn't know where that could have been.

He stepped inside, looked at Hurts, sniffed the musty air of the room, and in an authoritative voice, stated, "Where's the girl? ... What did Theodore Williams say to you—?"

"Now, hold on there, Pal," Hurts replied, interrupting him and brandishing his firearm at the guy. "I'm the one who's holding the weapon here—so I'll ask the questions."

Zoom!

In a flash, the man had Hurts pinned up against the wall, his right hand pressing against Hurts' chest and his left hand with an iron grip on Hurts' wrist of the hand that held the weapon. With one flick of the guy's powerful hand, the weapon went flying from Hurts' grip.

The guy had changed physically.

He now seemed taller. His chest and shoulders were bigger, and his face was larger with a protruding forehead, and the pupils of his eyes were now two flaming fireballs straight from hell.

He switched hands—now pinning Hurts to the wall with his left hand, and placing his now long fingernailed right hand on top of Hurts' head. He turned Hurts' head a bit to the left, tilted it back a bit, and then, raising his head back and opening his mouth wide, exposing two long, sharp fangs, he brought his head down for the kill.

And that's when it happened. Seeming to come from near the floor, that was when Hurts heard, "Excuse me, Mr. Campball. Mr. Campball?"

It was Amanda.

Out of sheer animal instinct, the man, still holding on to Hurts, turned around, bent down, and hissed and roared in Amanda's face.

She screamed, took a step back and was frozen in place with fear.

Seeing who it was, the man seemed to struggle with himself as to what he should do. A few seconds later, he cried, "No! I can't! —I can't!" He tossed Hurts to the side of the room like a ragdoll and then ran out the door.

Amanda rushed over to Hurts and knelt down by him.

"Oh, my back!" Hurts cried in pain.

"Are you okay, Mr. Hurts?!" she asked.

Between breathing deeply and moaning, Hurts snapped at Amanda, saying, "I thought that I told you to stay in the car."

"But, I didn't think that Mr. Campball would hurt—"

"No, butts, Amanda," Hurts chided her. "When I give you an order, I expect it—" Hurts stopped speaking. Then he said, "What did you just call that guy, Amanda?"

"That's what I'm trying to tell you, Mr. Hurts!" she cried excitedly. "That was Mr. Campball. He works with Mom."

"Of course!" Hurts said, remembering and realizing something. "That's where I had seen that guy before—He was one of the guys in that picture hanging on the wall of Mr. Williams' office. The guy's a board member! ... Now, we're getting somewhere."

Chapter Ten

It took Hurts about an hour of resting and struggling to get back up on his feet before they were able to leave that house and drive back to his office.

Exhausted and in pain, Hurts went straight to the couch and lay down. Amanda got a blanket for Hurts and covered him with it, saying, "You just rest, Mr. Hurts, and I'll get the groceries and the Christmas tree from the car." He barked at her, telling her that she couldn't do all of that—but she did. He was shocked.

True to her word, she brought the groceries up, then she dragged that Christmas tree up, and not only that, she dragged it up on top of Tom's old desk, set it in a stand, fastened the tree to the stand tightly, ran the three sets of multi-colored lights she had also insisted that Hurts buy, and then, standing on a chair, cooked them supper on Hurts' hotplate.

The meal was delicious, and after Hurts had eaten and had several cups of coffee and several cigarettes, he did feel better.

Amanda, like most eleven-year-old kids, was fascinated with the concept of vampires, and now that she knew that vampires truly existed, she kept peppering Hurts with questions about them.

Hurts told her that had been his first encounter with a vampire, but that he did know all about vampires because his partner, his ex-partner, Tom Mayor, had told him all about vampires.

After Tom had solved the murder of his next-door neighbor's great-grand-daughter's murder, he had become famous, and he got flooded with calls to investigate other cases, but Tom always refused: He didn't want to be a P. I. Soon, the "flood" of calls that he had been getting became nothing more than an occasional trickle. Tom had told him that his mother, Lill, was furious with him. Then, one morning, the phone rang. Lill had answered it. It had been a young unwed woman, who had stopped at a grocery store after she had gotten off from work. She had stepped out of her car, onto the parking lot of the grocery store and was heading for the entrance of the store when, from behind, an arm grabbed her around her waist, and another hand appeared at her throat—and that hand had a knife in it. Before she could react or scream, she had heard a "snapping" sound. The arms and hands were suddenly gone. She turned around, looked down, and saw a mean-looking man lying at her feet. The man had that knife in one of his hands—and he was dead. The man had been a hitman for the number one Mafia Family at that time in St. Louis, the Cambino Family.

The poor woman was desperate: Why had a Mafia hit-man tried to kill her?—And who had killed that hit-man? Could-would Mr. Mayor please help her? Lill had told the woman that Tom most definitely would—she would see to it, and she did.

She had given Tom no choice: Either take the case and help this poor woman—or get the hell out of her house.

Tom took the case.

After Tom had met and interviewed the woman, he began following her in his car, spying on her with a pair of binoculars. One evening, parked across the street from her small house, he watched as she exited the front door of the house and began opening the door of the unattached garage that was to the north side of the house. As she began entering the garage, Tom, viewing her with those binoculars, suddenly spotted a man stealthily moving across her front lawn towards the entrance of the garage.

Tom knew that couldn't be good. He didn't know what to do to warn the woman of the danger. He had decided to lay on his horn as fast and as hard as he could. Then, as he was just about to place his hand on the horn—Zoom! From behind that man, Tom saw a flash, and then a man appeared behind that other man. He spun that man around and-and—well, had "lunch" on the man's throat! Biting him good. He wiped blood from his mouth, and then, as if realizing that he was being watched, turned towards Tom. With a bloody, fanged mouth, he now hissed and roared at Tom. Tom, having viewed all of that with binoculars, and now viewing that guy's mouth and teeth—magnified by the binoculars—Tom, so scared, had wet his pants. The guy then zoomed away—and Tom had gotten the hell out of there. He went home.

Back home, Hurts had told Amanda, Lill had kept Tom's supper warm for him. As he was eating, she had asked him how the case was going. Tom, still shaking by what he had witnessed, and pants still wet, had replied, "It's not. I'm quitting."

"What?!" Lill had cried, shocked and angry. "Why?"

"Because I am," Tom had replied flatly.

"But why, Tom?" she had repeated. "Why?"

"Because, because," Tom had begun, upset, frustrated and scared, "because I saw a guy kill another guy just now—and that guy who had done the killing was a vampire!"

"Tom," Lill had said angrily, shaking an index finger at him warningly. "Your father and I have defended you our whole lives—to family, neighbors, friends, and I'm not standing for it another moment. If you don't help that girl, I'm through with you, Tom. There's no such thing as 'vampires' … Who are you?!" Tom then heard his mother cry.

Tom looked in the direction that his mother was looking, towards the entrance of the kitchen. There, standing in the doorless entrance to the kitchen, was a man.

"Mom?! Mom?!" Tom had screamed. "That's him, Mom! That's the vampire!"

Tom grabbed a kitchen-knife that was on the table, shot up out of the chair that he had been sitting in, and—not moving, still standing from where he had risen from the chair—began brandishing the knife at the man.

Zoom!

Within a second, the man was abreast of Tom and had disarmed him of the knife.

He hadn't changed, physically, but Lill, seeing what she had seen—the man's speed—convinced her that Tom, for once in his life, had told the truth: The man was a vampire. Lill dropped to her knees and began supplicating to Jesus to save them from this demon.

"Please, Mr. Mayor—and Mrs. Mayor," the man had said, first to Tom, then to Lill, "I mean you no harm … Please, Mr. Mayor," he repeated, pointing to the chair that Tom had risen from, "be seated." Turning now to Lill, he said, "Please, Mrs. Mayor, get up and take a seat. I need to speak with you both."

Yes, Hurts had told Amanda, the man had informed them that he was indeed a vampire—but he was also the father of the woman of the case that Tom was investigating. He had wanted, needed, their help.

He told them his story.

Twenty years ago, his wife had died from having had a heart attack. He had thought that he would never love again. Then, six years ago, he had met another woman. They fell in love—romantically, happily, totally in love. They had gone away for a weekend of romance at the Lake of the Ozarks. He had gotten drunk and had told her that he loved her and wanted to spend eternity with her. She had taken that literally and "turned" him— meaning transforming him from being human into a vampire.

Hurts then told Amanda that the man told Tom and Lill this: There is a world-wide secret organization that protects the secret of the existence of vampires. This organization is called "The Community," and it has chapters in most major cities. It is run by vampires called "The Elders." The Elders are the oldest and most powerful of their kind. When a human is turned, one must join The Community. You have no choice—you either join The Community or you face death. Once you are turned, and once you joined The Community, they give you a new identity, move you to a different location—maybe to a different state or even a different country— help you obtain employment, supply you with blood, and on and on. Sadly, though, one's previous life is over—one can never go back or have contact with any of the people whom that person had known in that life—this included wife, husband, brothers, sisters, or even one's children.

The man—Paul was his name—had begged The Community to permit him to remain in St. Louis. They had. Over the years, missing his daughter so much, he would furtively watch her from time-to-time, just to see how she was doing. He had just happened to be doing that on the day that the hitman had tried to kill her. It had been he who had killed that hit man.

Not wanting The Community to find out what he was doing—which was trying to protect his daughter—he had begged Tom and Lill to help him find out what this was all about—who, and why, was somebody trying to kill her.

Tom, now feeling truly sorry for the man, and no longer scared of him, had agreed to help him, which had angered Lill. After the man had left, Lill said, "Granted, I'm sad for him—but he's of the devil, Tom! I don't want you involved in this. It's too dangerous—and, again, he's a child of Satan."

Tom couldn't BELIEVE Lill! Here she had hounded him and hounded him to take a case—any case!—and now that he had, and wanted to help, now she was telling him not to do it—to quit.

Tom 'soft-pedaled' it with his mother, and with Paul's help, began investigating the case.

Tom eventually solved the case—and he could have gotten he and his mother killed in the process.

For several reasons, I don't want to reveal the identity of Paul's daughter, but she, like Amanda's mother, had worked at a financial brokerage firm. Of course, the one that she had worked at was privately owned and was much, much smaller than International Investments. The owner of the company, Mr. McCarthy, was in his late fifties, several years divorced, had a passion and obsession for gambling, drinking, womanizing and just living the 'good' life—the 'high' life. He was deeply in debt. He, as they say, had "cooked-the-books". He was certain, with time, that Paul's daughter, who worked for him as secretary, accountant, bookkeeper, and all-around-employee, would eventually discover what he had done and would report him not only to the proper authorities, but to the police. Mr. McCarthy was friends with old Antonio Cambino, Godfather of the Mafia Cambino Family, and had negotiated, for a price, a favor from him—to kill Paul's daughter.

All of this had eventually become known to Tom because of things Tom had done, and had *had* done, during the course of the investigation. Such as having Paul act as a customer at Cambino's restaurant, and with the superpowers of his hearing, listening-in on conversations of the family, and he and Paul breaking into the office one night of Paul's daughter's place of employment and searching for anything they could find that would reveal to them why all of this was happening. It was while they were searching the desk of her boss that Tom had discovered another set of audit reports that were quite different—in sums of money of accounts— from the audit reports in Paul's daughter's desk.

Paul had told Tom that one of the conversations that he had heard from members of the Cambino family was that another hitman had been hired to kill Paul's daughter. This hit-man, they said, was from "out-of-town", and was "very different"—and he would kill her the next evening just before she left the office, and no one would ever see or hear from her again. Paul had also told Tom that they told Mr. McCarthy to be out of the office by a quarter-to-five.

Like Hurts, Tom had come up with a plan to save Paul's daughter.

Hurts told Amanda that Tom being Tom—a guy who likes being "the center of attention"—thought he had come up with a great plan: a plan that would make him look like a hero again, and this 'plan' involved his mother, Lill.

After Tom left Paul, before he had returned home, he had stopped at Wal-Mart and had bought a cheap cellphone. When he got home, he gave Lill the cellphone and told her his plan.

His plan was this:

The next day, at 4:00 PM, Tom would drive Paul and his mother to the Burger King that was directly across the street from Mr. McCarthy's office building. He would park in the parking lot of that Burger King. At 4:30, Tom would exit the car, enter the building, and climb the stairs to Mr. McCarthy's office on the second floor. He would confront Mr. McCarthy, have Paul's daughter hide in Mr. McCarthy's office, wait for the hitman, and save the day, having them all arrested. This is where and how Lill came into the picture. As soon as Paul saw someone who he thought to be a hit-man entering the building, he, with his vampire speed, would dash up to the office, subdue the hit-man, and then leave before the police came. Now, as soon as Paul exited the car, Lill was to get on that cellphone that he had bought for her and call the police.

Lill was not pleased with the plan. "Do you mean to tell me that you expect me to sit in your car—alone!—with that vampire?" she had asked angrily.

"Yes," he had replied.

"Well, I'll do it—but I don't like It! I'd rather sit in the car with a snake—but I'll do it."

And she did. But the next day, as she and Tom were leaving home to pick up Paul, she had gotten a long multi-colored umbrella with a long silver tip from the hall closet.

Seeing her do that, Tom asked, "What are you going to do with that—hit Paul over the head?"

"Maybe," she replied flatly. "Maybe."

It had been a good plan, but it just didn't happen as Tom had planned.

At exactly 4:30, Tom, dressed in suit and tie and wearing a full-length beige overcoat, was at the entrance to Mr. McCarthy's office. Mr. McCarthy was just stepping out of the door.

Earlier on in the investigation, Tom had visited the office and had met Mr. McCarthy. Not wanting Mr. McCarthy to know that Tom was a private investigator, he had told Paul's daughter to say that he was a man wanting to date her.

Seeing Tom, Mr. McCarthy said somewhat sarcastically, "Still trying to get a date?"

With his hand in the pocket of his topcoat, Tom, pretending to have a gun, pointed his pocket at Mr. McCarthy and stated commandingly, "Alright, McCarthy, I know you cooked the books and that you hired Cambino to kill—"

"What are you saying?!" he protested greatly.

"Shut up!" Tom replied angrily. "Just get back in that office. Move—now!"

Once inside the office, Paul's daughter was very startled and confused by what she was seeing.

Tom said quickly, "I don't have time to explain. Another hitman is coming to kill you. Get into McCarthy's office, lock the door, get under his desk—and no matter what you hear, don't come out until I say you can. Go, now!"

She did.

Paul's daughter's desk faced the door to the entrance of the office and was near the outer wall of Mr. McCarthy's office. Tom stood in front of her desk, turned around, and leaned up against the desk. Mr. McCarthy was still standing by the entrance door to the office. Tom, thinking that Mr. McCarthy was thinking about how he could make a fast exit, said, pointing to a sofa that was in the corner of the room, "Park it, McCarthy. We'll just relax and wait for that hit-man." Mr. McCarthy did as Tom demanded and sat down.

That half-hour that Tom waited for that hitman to come seemed like the longest half-hour of his life. Every minute seemed like an hour, but 5:00 PM finally came—and Tom was scared to death.

The door to Mr. McCarthy's office opened and in walked—quietly— a quiet man who looked like an ape wearing a suit and tie that were too small for him—and this guy was hairy, well, like an ape, but quiet. He looked about the room. Then he looked at Tom. Then at Mr. McCarthy, then back at Tom. In a deep-sounding voice, but a quiet voice, he said, "Is this McCarthy's Financial Investments?"

"Yes, it is," Tom had replied, his body shaking now from fear, and still with his right hand in the pocket of his topcoat, still pretending to have a gun.

"Are you Mr. McCarthy?" he had asked quietly.

Mr. McCarthy jumped up from the sofa and shouted, "I'm Mr. McCarthy—and that man is a private investigator and has a gun in his pocket."

"Where's the girl?" he then said. He sniffed the air, looked towards the closed door to Mr. McCarthy's office, and said, "Ah, there she is."

"Now, look here, Pal," Tom had begun, but—Zoom!

The guy was on top of Tom in a second, and he changed, physically, into a vampire. Holding on to Tom by the lapels of his topcoat, and staring down at him, he said yes—quietly, "You may leave now, Mr. McCarthy."

Mr. McCarthy did. He bolted out of there as if he had winged feet.

With a dry mouth and shaking body, Tom said, "Maybe-maybe we could talk this out—you seem like a kind man."

The man tilted back his head and opened his mouth wide, revealing two long, sharp white fangs.

In that moment, Tom wet his pants again, and he knew that he was going to die. Overcome with fear, Tom closed his eyes and cried, "Mommy! … I want my Mommy!"

All was lost, and Tom knew it. Then he felt a sharp, stabbing pain right below his collar bone. He opened his eyes and looked down. There, sticking out of that guy's chest, was the long silver tip of Lill's umbrella.

Paul shoved the now dead guy to the side, and holding on to Tom by his shaking shoulders cried, "Are you okay, Tom?! … Is—" Paul continued. He sniffed the air and said, "Yes, she's safe—and you peed in your pants again!"

In a daze and feeling his chest, Tom moaned, "I'm having a heart attack. I'm dying."

"You're not dying, Tom," Paul had replied. "Sorry I'm late. Your Mom couldn't work that phone—she kept getting a wrong number. I finally took the phone from her and called the police. I told the police that I was you. They'll be here any moment now."

Heaving the body of that dead guy over his right shoulder, Paul said, "I'll get rid of this guy. Remember, you called the police."

Zoom! Paul and that dead guy were gone.

"I'm dying," Tom had repeated. "I'm dying."

Chapter Eleven

Amanda was enthralled with all that Hurts had told her about vampires, and with all he told her about Tom's valiant exploits. Hurts—a man who was not to be "bested" by any other man—wanted to do some bragging about his own bravery and courage.

"Of course, Amanda, I wouldn't have believed Tom about the existence of vampires had it not been for my own battles with the supernatural," Hurts began. "Before I retired from the police force, the last case that I worked on was the killings and suicides of the employees and guests of the re-opening of the Grand Hotel downtown. It turned out to be an invisible demon that whispers your worst fears into your ear. The thing almost got me. I thought that I was going crazy. It kept telling me that my boss knew that while I had been with the Vice Department that I kept stealing money—which was a lie! I never took no money," Hurts stated, lying. "Well, I got on my computer, and I started searching the—" Hurts stopped speaking in mid-sentence. He had an epiphany. He slammed his fist down hard on top of the dining-table.

"This case of your mom has nothing to do with your mom," Hurts said excitedly. "No," he continued, "it has nothing to do with your mom— but it has everything to do with The Community, with The Elders, with vampires. Now, I don't have many of the answers to all of this, but I know who does, and tomorrow, I'm going to get those answers from him."

"Who is that, Mr. Hurts?!" Amanda wanted to know.

"One Mr. Theodore Williams, Senior Board member of International Investments."

The next morning, Hurts, sitting in Mr. Williams' office for the second time, confronted him. Sitting in a modern-looking chair directly across the glass-top desk of Mr. Williams, Hurts stated, "Now, Mr. Williams, you're a man of the world—rich, educated, cultured, well-bred, and I'm just a man of the streets. Oh, now, don't get me wrong, I've been down the block. So, why don't we just put our cards on the table? ... Mrs. Warner didn't steal no money—and you, Sir, are an Elder of The Community and a vampire."

For a second, Mr. Williams was stunned by what Hurts had said, but then he quickly recovered his composure and stated politely and with much dignity, "I don't know what you are talking about, Mr. Hurts. Don't be absurd. I think you should leave, Mr. Hurts. Good-day."

Hurts rose from the chair to leave. He walked to the closed door of Mr. Williams' office. But instead of reaching for the gold handle of the door, he turned around, faced Mr. Williams, withdrew his firearm, pointed it at Mr. Williams, and said, "You got two choices here, Williams. One, you can tell me the truth, or, two, I'm going to count to three—and if you don't come clean by the count of three, I'm going to put a bullet right between your eyes."

Mr. Williams remained seated and silent. He placed his elbows up on top of his desk and interlaced his fingers, and he just stared deadpanned at Hurts.

A few seconds passed.

"Okay," Hurts said, "have it your way. "One…"

No response from Mr. Williams.

"Two…" Hurts continued.

Still, no response from Mr. Williams.

"Okay, Williams," Hurts said. "Last chance."

Still, no response from Mr. Williams.

"Fine," Hurts said. "See you in heaven—or hell. Three."

Then, then, just before Hurts' index finger squeezed the trigger of his weapon—Zoom!

Mr. Williams was abreast of Hurts, his left hand holding Hurts at bay; his right hand raised high in the air, holding the wrist of Hurts' hand that held the weapon.

Mr. Williams released Hurts, turned around, and proceeded to walk back to his desk, saying, "You are an intelligent man, Mr. Hurts."

"Oh, I get the job done," Hurts replied, returning his firearm to the holster under his left armpit.

Before Mr. Williams sat back down in the well-padded black leather swivel chair that was behind his desk, he motioned for Hurts to be seated again. He did.

After a few moments of silence had passed, Hurts said, "So, what's this all about?"

After sighing heavily, Mr. Williams replied, "In a word, Mr. Hurts: War. I'm at war."

He then told Hurts the whole story.

He told Hurts that he was correct about Amanda's mother having not stolen any money. In fact, no money had been stolen. That had been a total ruse to spite Mr. Williams. Why Amanda's mother had been chosen as a victim—well, it had been a random act; it could have been anyone from the accounting department. He then proceeded to tell Hurts that for the past year, a rift had occurred between himself and three of his fellow board members—and, yes, he added, all of the five other board members of the company were Elders of The Community and were like him, a vampire. Board members Mr. Campball, Mr. Kennedy, and Mr. Graves believed that this chapter of International Investments was becoming far too involved in the affairs of humans—with the company's financial support and other activities to the many charities of St. Louis. They wanted this stopped, before it jeopardized the much-guarded secret of their existence— that of being vampires. Mr. Williams disagreed with them and believed that they, as a company, should continue with the work and assistance that they give to the citizens of St. Louis. This had been a serious mistake on Mr. Williams' part. The rift only got worse. The framing of Amanda's mother had been done to illustrate to Mr. Williams how easily one could be exposed. Now these three board members demanded battle—to the death. They had already done battle with the other two board members who had sided with Mr. Williams: Mr. Silvers and Mr. Thomas—and had killed them. Now it was Mr. Williams' turn. He was to do battle with them that evening, and he knew that he could not defeat all three of them—he would be killed.

Hurts, as usual, came up with a plan.

Now, liking Mr. Williams—or at least feeling equal to him, or maybe even better than him—Hurts told Mr. Williams that he needed to hire him, and that if he got him out of this mess, well, he then needed to give Hurts a HUGE bonus.

"Deal?" Hurts said, extending his right hand across the top of the desk.

Mr. Williams thought for a moment, and then replied, "Deal."

Hurts then told him his plan.

It would take too long to tell you everything about this, so I shall be brief.

Hurts had a buddy who owned and operated an old factory north of downtown. The factory produced and sold oil and grease. Hurts gave Mr. Williams the address of that factory and told Mr. Williams to have those three other board members meet him at that address at eight o'clock to do battle.

After Hurts left Mr. Williams' office, he stopped at police headquarters, got two old walkie-talkies from storage; stopped at a grocery store and bought three one-gallon jugs of milk—which he emptied—

stopped at a church and filled those jugs of milk with holy water; then he broke two spindles from the staircase leading to the second level of his office and made stakes out of them.

That night, as he and Amanda were driving to the back of that factory, Hurts told Amanda that place was probably the last place in St. Louis that still got its water from a well. Hurts poured those three jugs of milk, now filled with holy water, into the tank that held the water from the well.

He selected a room from the main floor of the factory, making sure the room had sprinklers and a sewage drain. He placed a rubber mat over the sewage drain.

He clipped the microphone of one of the walkie-talkies to the lapel of Amanda's coat and stuffed the walkie-talkie into a pocket of her coat. He did the same to himself with the other walkie-talkie. With umbrella in hand, he told Amanda to follow him.

He took her to the second floor of the building. There, at the end of a hallway, was a door. It was the door to a closet-sized room. In that room was a black pipe that ran from floor to ceiling. Towards the floor of that pipe was a valve. Handing the umbrella to Amanda, Hurts said, "Now, that's the valve that I told you about. When you hear me shout, 'Now, Amanda! Now!' you turn that valve." He then handed Amanda his cellphone. "After you do that," he continued, "I want you to run out of this building, get into my car, and call the police."

Now the stage was set for battle.

Hurts walked back to that room on the first floor and waited for Mr. Williams to come.

When Mr. Williams came, Hurts was facing the door of that room, leaning up against a long wooden table that was near the northwest wall of the room, just in front of the rubber mat he had placed over that sewage drain. It was fifteen minutes to eight o'clock.

Seeing him, Hurts leaned back further on the table and retrieved a full-length black hooded raincoat that he had brought with him from the office and a pair of latex gloves tucked away in one of the pockets of the raincoat. This would be the third time that he had seen Mr. Williams, and Hurts thought the guy should do advertisement for the Brooks Brothers Clothing chain—the guy was always so dapperly dressed in expensive suits and ties. Hurt had told him to wear old clothes, and here he was wearing a white pullover Polo shirt and a pair of black dress pants.

"Come on over here, Williams," Hurts said, holding the hooded raincoat in his hands, "and try this on for size."

Mr. Williams did. Then Hurts told him to put on the latex gloves.

Now the stage was really set to do battle.

At exactly eight o' clock, Mr. Williams sniffed the air, his body went stiff, and he said, "They're here."

Well dressed and silent, the three of them entered the room—Mr. Campball was in front of the other two, Mr. Kennedy and Mr. Graves.

When Mr. Campball saw Hurts, he said to Mr. Williams angrily, "What's he doing here, Theodore?! He doesn't belong here!"

Cheerfully, Hurts replied, "Well, now, boys. If we're going to battle, you need a referee—that would be me, and I'm Williams' manager. I didn't have time, but I was going to buy a T-shirt and get printing on the back of it that read: 'Campball sucks as a vampire'."

Zoom!

Mr. Campball was on top of Hurts in a flash, and he had physically changed into his massive vampire form.

Holding onto Hurts tightly by the sides of his topcoat, Campball hissed and roared in Hurts' face. With his two long white fangs dripping with saliva, he said, "I should have killed you the other night!"

"Campball," Hurts replied, "you got bad breath." Then Hurts shoved him back. He pressed the button on the side of the microphone and shouted into it, "Now, Amanda! Now!" As Hurts was shouting this, out of the corner of his eye, he saw Mr. Williams throw the hood of his raincoat over his head and then drop down into a fetal position on that rubber mat.

A second later, the sprinklers on the ceiling came on, bathing the entire room with a steady mist of water—now mixed with holy water.

With this, Mr. Kennedy and Mr. Graves now changed, too, into vampire form.

The whole idea of all of this was not to immediately stake the three—and Hurts had four small stakes that he had made from those two spindles under his topcoat and suit, tucked between his belt and pants—but to slow them down first so he would then have the time to stake them.

It worked like a charm.

They moved about the room sporadically, confused, in pain; white sparks bounced off their bodies; they hissed and roared, and they kept smacking their faces and bodies with open palms. Hurts would later say they looked like a guy who was desperately trying to rid himself from a swarm of attacking bees.

Hurts staked all three of them—first Mr. Campball, then Mr. Kennedy, and last, Mr. Graves.

After he had staked Mr. Kennedy, Hurts felt a terrible pain in his chest, and he felt short of breath. He faced the table and placed his hands on top of it. He needed a moment of rest.

And that was when he heard her; her voice came from the direction of the door to the room.

"Look out, Mr. Hurts! Behind you!"

It was Amanda.

But before Hurts could turn around, he felt two hands grabbing him by the shoulders of his topcoat. The hands dragged him to the end of that table and then spun him around. It was Mr. Graves. Before he came in for the kill, though, he suddenly had an odd look on his wet face. He looked down at the stake sticking out of his chest. As he had been dragging Hurts to the end of that table, this had given him enough time to reach and get another stake, and when Mr. Graves had spun Hurts around—Hurts plunged it into his chest.

Exhausted, in pain, and soaking wet, Hurts bent down and placed his wet hands on his knees. He took several deep breaths. Then he looked in the direction of the door.

There stood Amanda, that umbrella above her head.

"Shut it off, Amanda!" Hurts bellowed at her.

She disappeared.

Hurts was helping Mr. Williams remove his hooded raincoat when Amanda returned to the room, and Hurts gave it to her good with both barrels.

"I didn't tell you to go poking your nose in here to see what going on," he barked at her. "No, I told you—I ordered you—to leave the building." In shame, Amanda lowered her head. "When are you going to start obeying orders, Amanda? When?"

Slowly, Amanda began raising her head, and when the pupils of her dark-brown eyes, through the lenses of her black-framed glasses, met Hurts' eyes, she said with deadpan conviction, and quoting one of Hurts' favorite catch-phrases, "Some orders just beg to be broken."

Hurts was shocked.

"Are you sassing me, Amanda?" he bellowed at her. She lowered her head again. "Don't you ever sass me. I'm the—" He stopped speaking. He turned to Mr. Williams, shrugged his wet shoulders, and said, "Kids. What are you going to do with them?"

Mr. Williams turned and faced Amanda. He squatted down so he could almost be eye-to-eye with her. He placed his right hand on her chin and gently raised up her head. Softly and compassionately, he said, "I trust, Amanda, that you shall keep my secret?"

She nodded her head that she would.

Then Mr. Williams continued, "Tomorrow morning, I shall hold a televised press conference. On it, I shall state that the crime committed at International Investments had been done by three of my fellow board members, who have fled the country. I shall also state that you mom is innocent. I shall demand that all charges be dismissed, and that she be immediately released from jail."

What Hurts saw next truly did shock him.

Amanda had her arms wrapped around Mr. Williams' neck, and she was crying uncontrollably like a baby. Hurts was—well, just shocked.

True to his word, the next morning Mr. Williams had that televised press conference—and he stated all that he had told Amanda he would.

Hurts drove Amanda downtown to police headquarters.

Even with all of Mr. Williams' influence, and knowing prominent people of St. Louis—like the mayor!—it was three o'clock before Mrs. Warner was finally released from jail. Well, it was a Saturday—and it was also Christmas Day! So, yeah, it had taken some time.

Hurts parked his car on the street in front of Mrs. Warner's and Amanda's house. It was a small red-brick house, but nice, in a nice, quiet, well-kept neighborhood.

Mrs. Warner said, "Send me your bill, Mr. Hurts—that's one bill I won't mind paying."

"There's no charge, Mrs. Warner," Hurts replied. "Williams is taking care of that … Consider it my Christmas present to you and Amanda."

"Christmas present!" Amanda cried from the back of the car. She dashed out of the back and threw open the front door of the car, saying, "Come on, Mom. Come on … Now, don't you leave, Mr. Hurts. I'll be right back … Come on, Mom. Hurry!"

About ten minutes later, Amanda came running out of the house, carrying a wrapped package in both hands.

After she got back into the car, she scooted across the seat close to Hurts. Handing him the package, she said, "I had to tell Mom that I had peeked at the three presents she bought me. She said that you wouldn't like this gift, Mr. Hurts, and I know you won't. But my thought is—my hope is—that when you look at it, you'll think of me."

Having said that, she jumped up on the seat, threw her arms around his neck, kissed him on the cheek, and then whispered in his ear, "I love you, Mr. Hurts, and I'll never forget you." Then, she quickly opened and closed the door and dashed away.

When Hurts got back to his office, he ripped open the present that Amanda had given him. It was a smiling Raggedy Ann doll, with red yarn hair, wearing a red and white dress.

Gently stroking its hair, Hurts mumbled, "Aggravating. She was just plain, plain aggravating."

Chapter Twelve

Hurts thought he would never see or hear from Amanda again, but he was wrong. The following week, Amanda called him and begged him to come to her school and watch her play in a basketball game. Hurts hadn't wanted to, but Amanda being Amanda—so strong-willed and aggravating—Hurts finally said yes and went, and he loved it. She kept doing it—kept calling him and inviting him to events at her school, and their relationship just snowballed. With hockey tickets, or baseball tickets that Mr. Williams would give her—which angered Hurts: the seats were always "prime" and, again, Hurts was not a man to be "bested" by any other man—they would have a great time at the games. Hurts loved fishing and camping. He owned a half-acre lot on the banks of the Meramec River in St. James, Missouri and sometimes on weekends he began taking Amanda with him. She loved it and became quite adept at fishing and camping.

The years passed, and somewhere along the way, Amanda began calling Hurts "Uncle Jim." Hurts loved it—but he didn't like it that she started calling Mr. Williams "Uncle Williams," and he most definitely didn't like all of the things that Mr. Williams kept doing for Amanda—like buying her a new car, and helping her get into St. Louis University, pre-med, so that she could fulfill her life-long dream of one day becoming a doctor. Her dad had died from colon cancer when Amanda had been nine years old and she had vowed to dedicate her life to the relieving of suffering of others.

Yes, she was Hurts' unofficial adopted daughter, and she had matured into a beautiful young woman—slender build, a symmetrical-shaped face, with dark-colored eyes and eyebrows, and shoulder-length flowing rich dark-brown hair.

Hurts was so proud of her, and last year, he was really proud of her.

In October of last year, three days before Halloween, on the morning of that day, she had come up to his office, desperately wanting and needing his help. Once she had seen him, though, she had become furious with him. As she had the first day that she had met Hurts, she found him lying on that long, tattered black leather couch, fully clothed, more unconscious than conscious, nursing one hell of a hangover, an empty bottle of whiskey lying dead on the dusty wooden floor beside him.

Hurts wasn't doing so well. Besides feeling the pains of old age, and not having had a case in four months, Hurts was going blind from Macular

Degeneration. Amanda kept demanding that he see a doctor that she had found who specialized in the treatment of that disease, but Hurts kept refusing to see him. For one thing, Hurts was fed-up with all the doctors that Amanda had already taken him to, with no improvement, and, secondly, this doctor that she kept persisting that he see had the name "Blinder"—what kind of a name is that for an eye doctor to have? No, he didn't want to go!

Both Amanda and Hurts loved Starbuck's coffee, and it was Amanda's custom to bring them both a cup from there whenever she popped in. That morning had been no different. After he gulped down the coffee she had brought him, and after he had three cups of the coffee that she made from the coffeepot on top of the long cedar dresser along the north wall of the office, and after he had smoked several cigarettes, Hurts now felt more alive than dead, but he still didn't want to help her.

"Well, what can I do?" he said. "That's horrible that Emily was kidnaped last night, but there's nothing that I can do—let the police handle it."

Emily was a twelve-year-old girl with blonde hair and the most beautiful blue eyes. The family, Bob and Marge, lived across the street from Amanda, and Amanda had known Emily ever since her birth—had babysat her—and Emily was like the younger sister that Amanda had never had. Over the years, Hurts had met Emily and her parents several times. He thought they were "good people."

"No, I don't think that the police can do anything with this one, Uncle Jim," Amanda said.

"Why not?" Hurts asked.

"Because-because," she began, terribly upset, "I think she was kidnaped by vampires."

Hurts was a bit shocked by this, was silent for a moment, and then said, "Okay, refill my coffee." He waved the once again empty Starbuck's paper cup at her. "And then tell me all about it."

Amanda did.

Wednesday, Halloween, would be Emily's thirteenth birthday. During the past year, some of the civic leaders and some of the owners of restaurants and bars in the Soulard District wanted to have a venue in which young adults could gather and dance and have fun, free from alcohol and drugs. At the end of that summer, such a place opened in one of the old red-brick buildings off of Broadway Boulevard in the Soulard District. It was named "Teen Town." It was a big hit with young adults.

Two of Emily's classmates from school had wanted to take Emily there Sunday evening. They had both just turned thirteen, and since Emily would be thirteen in a few days she would be permitted in, provided that she was accompanied by an adult. Well, she didn't want THAT to be her parents—what thirteen-year-old would?!—so she asked her parents if Amanda agreed to take her if she could go there with her two classmates. They had both agreed to this, and so had Amanda.

Since it was the month of October, the month of Halloween, the theme of Teen Town for that month was Goth—wearing Goth clothes and such.

Teen Town was open from 5:00 to 8:00 PM, Wednesdays through Sundays.

Dressed in Goth clothes, Goth makeup, and Goth hair and fingernails—everything black—they went: Amanda and Emily wore waist-length black wigs, and Emily's two classmates had dyed their hair black with non-permanent dye.

Amanda, Emily, and Emily's two friends were all having a great time, talking, laughing, dancing, until 'they' came in. They were loud, rowdy, and rude. When these guys entered, they had even pushed three guys out from sitting at one of the tables so that they could bunch-up two tables and could all sit together. There were thirteen of them—all of them about the same age, about sixteen or seventeen—and they were all dressed about the same: everyday shirt and jeans, and all of them were wearing a full-length, thin-leathered black topcoat. Yes, they were mostly the same, except for one of them who seemed to be the leader of them. He was tall, about five-feet seven, slender build, feminine features, and waist-long, flowing blond hair—and he was dressed in a white suit.

He kept looking around the room and sniffing the air.

Then he spotted Emily. His blue eyes—which Amanda told Hurts had anger and evil in them—lit up. He got up from the table, walked arrogantly over to their table, and without even asking to be invited or their permission, sat down directly across from Emily and began staring at her, as if he were trying to hypnotize her.

"My name is Todd," he had finally said arrogantly, with a voice that had a lisp to it. "What's yours?"

Emily was frightened of him. She was silent for a few moments, but then replied quietly and shyly, "Emily."

"Come here often, Emily?" he asked.

He was sitting next to one of Emily's two friends, Mary. Mary spoke up and said, "No. Wednesday is Emily's birthday, and we're celebrating it now."

"Your birthday is Wednesday? Halloween?!" he said, most interested and most emphatically.

Emily nodded yes at him.

"How old will you be?!" he demanded to know.

Mary spoke up again, "She'll be sweet thirteen."

"You are the 'Chosen One,'" he said, and he leaned across the table and breathed in a deep whiff of air.

Amanda had had enough of this. With her right hand on his face, she pushed him back and said, "Look, no one asked you to come over here, so leave. Now!"

Todd became so angry that he shot up from the chair, knocking it over. He screamed at Amanda, "You bitch! I'll kill you!"

A beefy, muscular young bouncer rushed over. He towered over Todd, got in his face, and shouted at him, "I'm giving you only one warning, Todd. Don't start any trouble tonight! If you do, I'll throw you and your buddies out like I did the other night. Got it?!"

With his hands high in the air in a dismissive gesture, he stated, "Okay, okay. No trouble."

The bouncer turned around and walked away. Todd turned back to the table, stared at Emily again, and said, "I'll see you soon, Emily"

He then rejoined his friends at their two tables.

Amanda, Emily, and her two friends left shortly after that—Amanda had initiated their leaving, saying that it was getting late and that she had a bad feeling about what had just happened. So, they had left. What she hadn't told them was that the moment she had touched Todd's face, something within her—something deep within her—told her that Todd was a vampire.

After they left Teen Town, they went to an ice-cream parlor, which was several blocks away from Amanda's and Emily's neighborhood. There, they had been met by Emily's mom and dad, Marge and Bob. They all had a good time there—talking, laughing and eating ice-cream birthday cake. The entire time that they had been there, though, Amanda couldn't shake off the nagging, frightening feeling that they—especially Emily— were being watched.

The next morning, at exactly 7:00 AM, the phone rang. Amanda's mother had already left for work. It was Marge. She was hysterical with fear, worry and grief. Emily was gone. Amanda hung up the phone and rushed over to their house.

By the time she got there, the police had arrived, and this was followed by the FBI arriving.

Nothing in the house had been disturbed—no doors or windows had been tampered with, or as much as the police and the FBI could discern.

Emily had gone to bed around 9:00 PM. Her bed had been slept in, no clothes were missing, and the drawers to her dresser were all closed. The only odd thing in her room was this: Above the headboard of her bed had hung a crucifix, fastened to that wall by a nail. Now that crucifix lay upon the carpeted floor on the opposite side of the room. On the opposite wall, about halfway up, was a small hole. It was as if someone, seeing that cross with Jesus upon it, had become so enraged by it that he or she had ripped it from the wall and threw it across the room.

The police and then the FBI interviewed Amanda. In the course of the interview, Amanda had told the police and the FBI all about Todd and what had happed at Teen Town—well, she had told them everything except for her belief that Todd was a vampire.

When Amanda had finished speaking, Hurts rose from the couch, saying, "Okay, I've heard enough. Let me get washed and change clothes, and we'll begin."

"Woo-who!" Amanda cried, triumphant.

"Stop that!" Hurts barked at her. "You ain't done that since you were a kid."

"Well, where are we going to start, Uncle Jim?" Amanda wanted to know. "At the source?" she then added.

Smiling and nodding his head at her, he said, "Now, you're thinking like a detective. But, this time, no. Not at the source, the beginning. Since you believe that guy's a vampire, I think we had better first speak to the one person in this city who can give us answers about vampires—Mr. Theodore Williams: Your 'Uncle Williams'," Hurts stated mockingly.

Chapter Thirteen

International Investments, Inc. occupied the top three floors of the Wainwright Building at 7th and Market Street in downtown St. Louis. The Wainwright Building was a twenty-story skyscraper of shiny-looking brown granite and tinted windows. Amanda's mother worked in the accounting department on the eighteenth floor and Mr. Williams' plush office, along with the offices of the other five board members, was on the top floor.

Mr. Williams' secretary, Lorraine, was a plain-looking woman in her early thirties, with shoulder-length brown hair, a slender build, and always wore simple, but nice-looking dresses.

Hurts hadn't been interested in her when he had first met her, but after he had come to realize that she, too, was a vampire, well, then he had found an allurement to her. Whenever he saw her now, he would lightly flirt with her, saying to her such things as this: "Now, remember, Lorraine, someday I'm taking you to dinner and buying you a steak—that's S-T-E-A-K, not the other kind of stake."

She would always give him a patronizing smile and nod her head at him dismissively.

Mr. Williams had just come back to his office from a meeting, and although he was in a rush and looking tired, he was glad to see them. He rushed them into his office.

The three of them sat. Mr. Williams was ensconced comfortably in his well-padded chair behind his glass-topped desk, while Hurts and Amanda sat across from him in the two modern-looking, well-padded round-back chairs. Mr. Williams said heartily, "Well, how are two of my favorite people doing today? … How's school, Amanda?"

"Fine, Uncle Williams," Amanda replied.

Hearing her calling him 'Uncle Williams' always felt like a thorn in Hurts' ass.

"That's excellent, Amanda," he said with pride.

After taking a deep breath and then expelling it, Amanda said, "Uncle Williams, I-I need your help. Do you, by chance, know of a young man with long blond hair whose name is Todd?"

As Hurts had often mused, Mr. Williams was always a dapperly dressed man—expensive suits upon his slender body; his salt-and-pepper hair always combed straight back and matching the pin mustache under his thin, Roman nose. He was a man of prowess of his station in life. So, too, was he in his demeanor: His demeanor was always sanguine. A man who was always in control of his emotions and temperament—until that moment.

When he heard Amanda say the word "Todd" his face went blank. He had been visibly startled by her having stated that name. He tried to hide this by replying ever-so causally, "Unfortunately, I do. Why? How do you know that name?"

Amanda told him all about what had taken place at Teen Town Sunday evening; she told him all about what Todd had said and had done; she told him all about touching Todd's face and believing that he was a vampire; she told him all about Todd's friends, and she told him all about Emily being gone from her home that morning—gone; not a trace of her; vanished into the air.

When Amanda stopped speaking, Mr. Williams' face went blank; he was pensive and in deep thought; his mind seemed to be racing, trying desperately to comprehend something. He seemed in a daze, confused, perplexed, and at a loss as to what to do.

"I've been so preoccupied with another situation here that I didn't—" he stated more to himself than to Hurts and to Amanda. He quickly recovered from the trance he was in, and he said to Amanda, "What I'm about to ask you, Amanda, is most important—think before you answer: How many friends were with Todd that evening?"

Amanda did as Mr. Williams had asked and thought about it for a moment, trying to remember the exact number of young men, teenagers, like Todd, that she had seen that evening with him.

In frustration, she finally gave up trying and said, "I don't know, Uncle Williams. It was like I said. In order for them to all sit together, they had butted up two tables together."

"Could the number have been twelve?!" he asked emphatically.

"Yes," she replied. "The number could have definitely been twelve."

Mr. Williams sank back in his chair. He rested his elbows on the arms of the chair, interlaced his fingers together, and brought his hands up to his mouth. In deep contemplation, he stated, "I had heard about other students from Roosevelt High missing, but I just hadn't thought that had—"

"Stop talking in riddles, Williams!" Hurts barked at him. "What's this all about? … Is that Todd guy a vampire or not?"

"Yes, he is a vampire," Mr. Williams replied. "It's a tragic state of affairs. His mother died when had been quite young, and his father had been a low-life alcoholic—and he was extremely abusive to Todd ... Todd is an intelligent lad. He was turned four months ago, and he has managed to elude us so far. He killed his father, and then he killed the vampire who had turned him: An elderly man who had owned and operated a bookstore on the north side of downtown, a bookstore that deals with the Occult, witchcraft, voodoo and vampires—and the man was a pedophile. He had not been in good standing with The Community and had been warned not to associate with children. How or when he had met Todd, I don't know."

"So, why are you looking for him, Williams?" Hurts asked.

"Have you ever wondered, Hurts, why you have never seen or heard of child or teenage vampires?" Mr. Williams asked.

Shaking his head in disgust, Hurts said, "Okay, I'll bite. Why ain't I ever seen or heard of kid vampires?"

"Because they become like beasts. Killing machines," he replied. "No compunction at all. The sudden power is too overwhelming for them. The punishment for any vampire who turns a human child into a vampire is death—for the vampire and for the child who is turned."

Mr. Williams became pensive again. Silent. Deep in thought. Then he exploded in a fit of anger.

"I can't believe that old man told that boy about the Ritual of the Thirteenth Hour. I can't believe it!"

Looking at Amanda, Hurts said, griping, "Here we go again—more riddles ... Okay, Williams. What's the Thirteenth Hour?"

Mr. Williams composed himself, and after taking a deep breath and expelling it, he began speaking again.

"It is an ancient ritual known only to God, Satan, fallen angels, demons and vampires. Throughout the history of our kind it has only been performed three times—and has only succeeded once." Looking at Amanda, he then said, "Sadly, Amanda, your friend Emily is the 'Chosen One'. She is the Chosen One because, one, she is a virgin; two, because she is twelve years old; and three, because she shall turn thirteen on October the thirty-first, Halloween."

With a dry mouth, and with much fear, Amanda asked, "Is she dead, Uncle Williams?"

"No, she's not dead, Amanda," he replied quietly. "They won't harm her until the Thirteenth Hour. They—"

"Again, Williams," Hurts bellowed at him. "What's this all about?!"

"It's about mocking God, Hurts," he replied. "It's about the desire for increased power ... Todd has turned twelve of his fellow students from

Roosevelt High School into vampires. These twelve students are now his disciples. Twelve disciples and one savior—thirteen. The number thirteen in Hebrew numerology is 'transformation'—of ascending from one plane of consciousness, or power, to a higher plane of consciousness, or power."

"Well, now I'm totally lost," Hurts said, throwing up his hands. Turning to Amanda, he said, "Are you getting any of this?"

"Hurts, listen to me," Mr. Williams said to him. "They have kidnaped Emily to make a sacrifice of her to Satan. They shall take her to a place that is hidden, secluded—a place in which she can scream and yell and no one shall hear her. She shall be stripped naked, bound, suspended standing up with her arms stretched out—like Christ hanging on the cross—and for three days they shall taunt her, but, no, they shall not harm her until the Thirteenth Hour of the thirty-first of October, Halloween. Then, at the stroke of the Thirteenth Hour, first Todd shall bite her, then they all shall feed upon her until all the blood is drained from her body and the flesh is ripped from her bones. If Satan, or one of his high-ranking minions is pleased by this, their vampire powers shall be increased thirteen-fold."

"How powerful will they become?" Hurts asked.

Pointing to a recently hung framed picture of the new five board members of International Investments hanging on the south wall of his office, Mr. Williams said, "We are Elders of The Community because we are the oldest and the most powerful of our kind, but even with our combined powers, we could not defeat them."

He fell silent again.

Amanda waited a few moments, and then she said, "How serious is all of this, Uncle Williams?"

Staring straight at her, and with dead-level seriousness, he said, "Amanda, do you know of the Black Plague of the thirteenth century?"

"Oh, my God!" Amanda gasped in total shock and fear.

As if not only stating this, but reliving it, Mr. Williams continued, "It has been said that the Black Plague killed two-hundred million people … Of course, my kind hushed it up, but the true origins of the Black Plague was caused by a vampire who had succeeded in doing what Todd and his disciples are attempting to do. They—" Mr. Williams stopped speaking and he exploded again in raging anger. "This is too dangerous!" he cried. "Amanda, I'm ordering that your mother be immediately, tomorrow, transferred to our branch office in London!—and you shall accompany her." Quickly looking at Hurts, he added, "And you too, Hurts."

"Oh, now, hold on there , partner," Hurts cried indignantly. "I ain't going nowhere."

"I'm not either, Uncle Williams," Amanda spoke up. "Emily's my friend, and I'm going to find her."

As quickly as Mr. Williams had exploded with anger, he just as quickly recovered his composure.

"Alright," he said, rising from his chair. "We must stop Todd and find Emily, at all costs. I'll place every available person that I can on this."

With that said, both Hurts and Amanda stood up.

Before leaving, though, Hurts said to Mr. Williams, "Does this mean that you're hiring me, Williams?"

"Yes, yes," he replied. "Of course."

"Great," Hurts stated, smiling.

"One more thing, Hurts," Mr. Williams said, extending his right hand across the top of the desk. Hurts took his hand, and Mr. Williams said, "Protect Amanda as you have never protected her before."

"That's a given, Williams," Hurts replied. "That's a given."

Chapter Fourteen

And so, the case began, and it did not go well.

They interviewed the principal of Roosevelt High School. Roosevelt High School is an old school in a poor neighborhood west of downtown St. Louis—they got nothing, really, from the principal. They interviewed the parents of all the twelve missing students—they got nothing, really, from any of them.

Hurts and Amanda both agreed that she should stay with him until this case was resolved. Amanda told her mother that Hurts was ill and that she was going to stay with him for a few days.

No, the case wasn't going well, but the next evening, they almost came upon Todd and his twelve disciples.

Hurts and Amanda had been eating dinner at Zio's on the Hill, when Hurts' cellphone rang. It had been the principal from Roosevelt High School, a Dr. Washington. He told Hurts that earlier in the day a very troubled student had come to his office. This student was a friend of one of the missing students, and he had told him that he had seen him the night before and that Todd had wanted him to become one of his followers. Dr. Washington had gone on to tell Hurts that the student had told his friend to tell Todd: "I don't 'follow' nobody!—especially not a fuckin' fairy like Todd." The friend then told him that he would regret this.

Hurts asked Dr. Washington for the name and address of that student's parents. Dr. Washington gave Hurts the information that he had asked for.

Because of Hurts' failing eyesight, Amanda had been doing all of the driving—in the car that Mr. Williams, Uncle Williams, had bought her: a 2017 silver 4-door Ford Taurus.

They drove to the residence of that student's parents.

It was an old red-brick two-story multi-family flat, and it was in not the "best" of neighborhoods. The parents of that student were middle-aged, with little education, and poor. They rented the bottom flat. The boy wasn't there. He was out with his friends. The father of the boy was on disability, heart problems. He had owned and ran a neighborhood bar several blocks north from where they lived. That bar was all boarded up now, he told Hurts and Amanda. He also told Hurts and Amanda that was where his son probably was right now, at that abandoned bar. He knew that his son and his son's friends—four rough teenagers—liked to hang out there and get drunk and high.

Hurts got the address of that bar from the father, and he and Amanda drove there.

It was on the southwest corner of the block, and it was, or had been, a real dump of a place—just a red-brick two-story old house that had been converted into a bar.

Because it was night, and because of Hurts' failing eyesight, Amanda led Hurts by hand to the boarded-up front door of the place. But before she did that, she led Hurts to the back of her car. She wanted to get something from the trunk of the car—and she was most proud of it, too.

After she opened the trunk, she removed a black leather belt. On the right side of the belt was a black holster. In the holster was the largest plastic water-gun that Hurts had ever seen. It had a small tank to it. Amanda told Hurts that it could shoot a stream of water twenty feet, but instead of water, it was filled with holy water. To the back of the belt were notches for bullets, but instead of bullets the notches contained small wooden stakes.

"Well, what do you think of this, Uncle Jim?" she asked, strapping on the belt.

"I think that my little girl is ready to kick some vampire ass," Hurts replied, laughing.

Sadly, though, when they entered that boarded up bar, they found all five of those teenage boys dead, with bite marks to the throat, wrists, and ankles. Hurts was furious. He blamed himself for not having gotten there sooner.

The next day, Halloween, was miserable. Hurts was at a loss as to what to do next to find Todd and his disciples—and, of course, to find Emily and stop Todd from sacrificing her to Satan and have his vampire power increased thirteen-fold.

As a last thought, he told Amanda that maybe they should go to that club, that Teen Town. Maybe they would get lucky and Todd and his disciples would show up—or, at least, they could speak with the bartenders, bouncers, and patrons and see if they could get a lead on Todd.

Hurts wore his old wrinkled dark-blue suit, and Amanda, once again, donned her black Goth clothes and her black wig.

It turned out to be a smart move on Hurts' part. They got lucky.

They got there at 6:00 PM, and they had gotten nothing. It seemed to have been a waste of time. Then, with only a half an hour left until the place closed, at 8:00, in walks a young man.

Amanda and Hurts had been standing by the bar. When Amanda spotted him, she turned to Hurts and said quickly and excitedly, "Uncle Jim! You see that guy over there, talking to those two girls?"

It was so dark in that place that Hurts could hardly see anything.

Squinting his eyes, he said, "Where?"

"Over there by the door," Amanda stated, pointing in that direction. "He's wearing a dark-gray suit and tie. He has glasses on—and he wasn't wearing them Sunday. I think he's trying to look like Clark Kent, Superman."

"Okay," Hurts replied. "What about him?"

"He was speaking with one of Todd's friends—one of his disciples."

Hurts thought for a moment and then said, "Okay, here's the plan. Give me ten minutes to get back to your car and then bring him to me."

"How do I get him to do that?!" Amanda protested.

Hurts looked at her dumbfoundedly and stated sarcastically, "You're a woman, ain't you?"

"Oh, I understand," she replied. "It's dark outside. Can you make it back to the car by yourself?"

"You let me worry about that," Hurts stated. "You just bring him to me."

Amanda had parked her car as close as she could to Teen Town, which had been about a half a block north of the club.

Hurts did make it by himself back to her car. When he got there, he turned around and leaned up against the passenger's side of the car and waited for Amanda and that young man to come.

About twenty minutes later, here came Amanda, walking arm-in-arm with that young man.

When they came abreast of Hurts, he said in a friendly tone, "Why, hello, Amanda. Who's your friend?"

"Oh, hello, Uncle Jim," Amanda replied, acting surprised to see Hurts. "This is my friend Donald."

"Why, hello, Donald," Hurts said, and extended his right hand out to the young man.

The moment Donald took his hand, Hurts spun him around up against Amanda's car, grabbed Donald by his shirt with his left hand, and with his right hand, Hurts withdrew his firearm and placed the barrel of it up against Donald's forehead, saying, "I want some information, and I want it fast, kid. Do you know Todd Sinclair?"

"I don't know what you're talking about, man," Donald replied, his voice trembling with fear. "I don't know anyone by that name."

"You were talking to one of Todd's friends Sunday night," Hurts said.

"Man, Sunday night, I—" Then Donald stopped talking. He thought for a moment and then said, "Oh, I know. I spoke with Tyler—Tyler Smith. We went to grade school together at St. Francis Elementary in Oakville."

"Well, what did you two talk about?" Hurts asked demandingly.

"Not much, man. I hadn't seen him in years. He had changed, man. He was spooky—like he was on PCP or something. I asked him what high school he was going to, and he said, 'I don't go to high school'. Then I asked if he still lives with his mom and dad. He just laughed, man—real spooky, and says, 'Yeah. We all do. We all live under my father's roof and he doesn't even know it.' The guy's wacko, man. I got away from him and his friends, fast."

"Is that all?" Hurts asked.

"Yeah, man. That's all."

Hurts removed his weapon from Donald's forehead, saying, "Okay, Donald. Now, get the hell out of here."

Donald did. He ran down the sidewalk at full speed.

Musing on something, Hurts touched the right pocket of his topcoat and said, "Something ain't right here. There ain't no Tyler Smith on the list of those missing students from Roosevelt High that I had gotten from the police station. Why? ... Wait a minute," Hurts then stated, realizing something. "That list only has twelve names on it. It should have thirteen. That's it!—and the reason that his name ain't on the list might be because that Donald just told us that Tyler grew up in Oakville, which is in the County."

"Yes, and I saw a picture of Tyler, Uncle Jim," Amanda stated excitedly.

"Where did you see a picture of him, Amanda?" Hurts asked.

"It was about three weeks ago, on TV, the news," Amanda replied. "It was of his mom and dad. They were crying, and his mother was holding a picture of him in her hands. They were pleading for Tyler to come home. They had bought him a motorcycle, and three nights after he disappeared, the motorcycle was gone from the garage. They believed that Tyler had come back home and had taken the motorcycle."

"Oh," Hurts replied. Then he started thinking again. A few minutes later, he said, "I keep thinking of what that Donald said: 'We all live under my father's roof and he doesn't even know it.' Could it be? ... Say," Hurts then said, "can you look up an address on your cellphone?"

"Sure I can," Amanda replied. "I'm connected to the internet."

"Do it," Hurts said demandingly. "See if there's an address for a Smith in Oakville."

She removed her large, floppy brown purse from her shoulder, brought the purse to the front of her, and fished around in it until she found her cellphone. She made a few swipes with the index finger of her right hand, thumb-typed on it, and then cried, "Got it! Mr. Nathen Smith. The address is 122156 Cliff Cave Estates."

"This could be it," Hurts stated excitedly and anxiously. "Come on, let's go!"

Chapter Fifteen

It had been a bad, bad break, and they had been making such good time, too. Amanda—that waist-long, black wig that she had been wearing, now lying on the back seat of her car—told Hurts that she was low on gas, so they stopped and got gas. Then, Amanda said she was so hungry, that she felt weak. Much to Hurts' shock and surprise—Amanda always being a health-conscious person—agreed to stop at the take-out widow of a fast-food place, Jack-in-the-Box, and get hamburgers, fries and coffee.

Yes, they had been making good time.

Driving south, they had just gotten off Highway 55 and were heading east on Highway 270 to Telegraph Road when, suddenly, Amanda's car began riding rough from the rear of the car. Amanda pulled over. The rear driver's side tire was flat.

It took Hurts a long time to change it. By the time they got to Tyler's parents' home, it was nearly 10:30. Time was quickly running out for Hurts and Amanda—and, of course, for Emily.

Parked in front of Tyler's parents' home and viewing the beauty of that expensive house and of the homes surrounding it, Hurts stated, "This is all wrong."

"What's wrong with it, Uncle Jim?" Amanda asked.

"Well, just look at this place," Hurts said. "This ain't a place where thirteen teenage vampires can hide—and with a screaming girl. This place is for rich people."

Hurts was correct about that. The houses in that neighborhood were in the average price range of half a million dollars. Tyler's parents' house was a two-story light-colored brick house with two roofs and several dormers. It was at the end of a cul-de-sac.

Looking at the Smiths' well-trimmed and well-maintained front yard, Hurts mused: *These people sure must love Halloween.*

Hurts made that assumption because on the covered front porch of their home, there were fake spider webs, carved, lit pumpkins, and a clothed scarecrow sitting in a rocking chair at the end of the large bay window. The front lawn was festooned with two-feet-long-and-two-feet-wide glossy cardboard signs of witches, ghosts and vampires that were stuck in the ground by wooden stakes.

Turning to Amanda, Hurts said, "Well, we might as well interview these people. We might get something. Guide me to the front door."

They exited the car and Hurts waited for Amanda to come and take his hand. Then suddenly, as Amanda came abreast of him, they heard screams coming from inside the house. Hurts looked that way, and through that bay window, he saw flashes of something zooming back and forth across the room.

Withdrawing his firearm with his right hand and extending his left arm out to Amanda, he said, "Quick, Amanda! Get me to that window!"

Following the concrete path of the sidewalk that was on the side of the double-car-wide driveway, Amanda led Hurts to the covered porch of Tyler's parents' home. At the bay window, Hurts and Amanda knelt down and peeked in the window.

Through the parted thin white drapes, they gazed into the living room of the home. Hurts could hear the TV playing. Next to the long floral-printed couch was a matching winged chair. Slumped in that chair, her body turned to one side of it, as if she had tried desperately to guard or hide something, was a woman in her early forties, dressed in a white nightgown. She was dead. Two puncture marks were on one side of her neck, and blood trickled down onto her nightgown.

To the opposite side of the room, up against the wall, just a few feet from the entrance, were high-gloss wooden steps and a rail that led to the second-level of the house. On the third step from the top step, lay a boy about ten years old, dressed in blue pajamas, also dead with two puncture marks to the throat. At the bottom step, a young man was biting a screaming little girl, dressed in a white nightgown with little bears on it, in the neck, hard.

"That's Tyler, Uncle Jim!" Amanda exclaimed, horrified by what she was seeing. "I recognize him from the picture. He's killing them. We have to—"

Amanda started to rise, but Hurts grabbed her by her left arm and whispered, "There ain't nothing we can do. We have to let it play out. See if he'll lead us to Emily." Hurts holstered his firearm and said, "Come on, let's get back to the car."

They left the porch, but instead of using the sidewalk, they made a beeline for the car, cutting across the front lawn, Amanda leading the way, holding Hurts' hand.

They had gotten about midway across the front lawn, when Hurts tripped on one of those glossy cardboard signs of witches, ghosts and vampires, ripping it from the ground. He fell to the ground, angrily shouting, "Damnit-to-hell!"

The fall knocked the wind out of him, but he quickly turned over on his back, wanting to get up as quickly as he could. No such luck.

Zoom!

Tyler was straddled on top of his chest.

Holding onto Hurts by the lapels of his topcoat, roaring and hissing into the crisp, chilly night air, and with bloody fangs protruding, he growled menacingly, "Who are you, old man?!"

Hurts looked at him straight in the face and whipped calmly and flatly, "Why, I'm Buffy the Vampire Killer." Then with a closed right fist, he gave Tyler a hard punch right across the left side of his face.

This had no true effect on Tyler, except to increase his anger and his desire for more blood.

"You're dead!" he howled.

Grabbing Hurts' head in his hands and turning it to the left, he tilted his head back high in the air. Permitting his two white fangs to extend to their fullest, he came down for the kill.

Then suddenly the upper portion of his body went board-stiff. He roared in agony at the moonlit night, and then he plummeted on top of Hurts.

Hurts felt an immediate sharp, stabbing pain to his chest. He pushed Tyler off of him. He rolled over on his back. In pain, he rose to his hands and knees. He looked to his left at Tyler's lifeless body. A wooden stake from one of those cardboard signs was sticking out of his back. The sign had been of a ghost, saying: "BOO!"

Standing at the foot of Tyler and Hurts, Amanda cried, "I killed him. I killed a human—" and then she burst into tears.

"Stop that!" Hurts chided her. "You stop that right now. You're not a child anymore. We do what we have to do to survive … Help me up."

She did.

"Come on," Hurts said, panting and out of breath. "Help me drag him inside."

Once inside, they dropped Tyler's lifeless body just inside of the ornate Grecian-style, wooden-framed, oval, stained-glass front door.

At the end of the room, near the bay window, was another winged-chair of floral-print upholstery. Hurts lumbered over to it, plopped down in it hard, and closed his eyes.

Amanda walked over to the couch and sat down at the far end of it—not wanting to be near the dead woman. She hadn't wanted to look at her, but she did.

"She has a baby in her arms, Uncle Jim!" Amanda cried, grief-stricken and shocked with outrage. "He killed a baby!"

"Don't look at it, Amanda," Hurts said, with his eyes still closed. "Just rest. Just rest."

Amanda looked about the living room. She gazed upon the dark wooden-framed coffee-table that was directly in front of her, with its glass top, with a red-glass vase of flowers in it and a small bowl filled with an assortment of chocolate candy. She looked at the thick beige carpet; the almost floor-to-ceiling TV; at the lit fireplace, giving inviting warmth; at the many framed pictures of the family, carefully positioned upon the snow-white, painted walls.

"Even with all this death, there was love in this house," Amanda said, sighing heavily. "I feel it."

"Throughout this entire case, Amanda," Hurts stated flatly, his eyes still shut, "you have been saying things like that: 'I feel this. I feel that.' Are you getting weird on me?"

"No," she replied. "I-I just sense things."

Hurts finally opened his eyes. He gazed about the room.

"Oh, yeah?" he said to her flatly. "And what are you 'sensing' about this room?"

"What do you mean?" she replied, puzzled.

"Where's the father?" Hurts asked her. "He's not here. Where is he?"

With his body aching and feeling exhausted, and not wanting to leave the comfort of that chair, Hurts said, "Come on. Let's search the house and see if we can find that guy."

They did.

They searched the entire first floor. They viewed the hallway at the south end of the living room, under the staircase, the bathroom, and the dining room. In the kitchen, on the north side of the house, to the back, was a door that connected the kitchen to the three-car garage. Hurts opened that door, and after turning on the light, they looked inside.

There, before them, was a 2015 black Hyundai SUV, and parked next to it was a 2011 Harley-Davidson motorcycle.

"That's strange," Hurts said.

"What's strange, Uncle Jim?" Amanda asked.

"There's a car missing," Hurts replied. "That motorcycle ain't usually parked where it's at. Do you see those four pieces of cardboard on the floor there by that workbench?"

"Yeah," she replied, looking at the four pieces of cardboard by the wall.

"See the oil stains on the cardboard?" he continued. "Well, that's where that motorcycles usually parked. A car is missing."

After turning off the light and closing the door, they checked the basement. As they descended the carpeted stairs to the refurbished basement, Amanda asked, "Why did Tyler murder his family, Uncle Jim?"

"I have no idea, Amanda," he replied. "None."

Having found nothing on the first floor or downstairs, they then proceeded to the second floor.

They checked the three bedrooms that were on the north side of the house, and then they walked down the hallway to the south side of the house. After checking the bathroom and another bedroom that was on that side, they came to the last door on the second floor. It was on the east side of the house, and the room had curtained windows that faced the front yard and the street. It, at one time, had probably been another bedroom, but now was an office—a very modern-looking office.

Nestled in the corner of the room, was a white metallic filing cabinet. Next to that was an architect drawing desk. In front of the two windows at the east wall was a modular L-shaped desk. On top of the desk was a black multi-plex phone, a black metallic lamp with moveable parts, a rolodex, and a computer. Behind the desk, positioned on a sheet of hard plastic, was a black padded chair with arms and swiveled wheels. About two feet north of the desk was a black leather easy-chair.

His body aching, feeling exhausted, dejected, angry, hopeless, and in need of sleep, Hurts made a beeline for that easy-chair. But instead of sitting down, he walked over to the west wall of the room. Something had caught his attention.

Pinned up on the wall, a little more than midway up, were two long scrolls. The top scroll was an aerial photo of a street-long block of red-brick buildings and of vacant lots. The buildings were old and abandoned; many of them were boarded up and were in desperate need of repair. A business district with buildings that had gone back in time to the late eighteenth century; had seen its day-in-the-sun; dwindled; died, and now was a neglected, forgotten shell of its former days. The lots were no better, many of them fallow with a large amount of thrown-away junk on them. The writing at the top of the scroll read: 14th Street & North Broadway. The scroll below that one was beautiful. The writing on top of that scroll read: LACLEDE'S ESTATES. Below it was more writing. It listed the same address that was on the top scroll: 14th Street & North Broadway. That scroll, in color, displayed fancy high-rise apartments, office buildings, retail stores, restaurants, bars, nightclubs, a library, a park, a pond, and on and on.

Tapping that aerial photo with the back knuckle of his right index finger, Hurts said, "I know this place. My younger brother, Paul, and me grew up around there. It's just north of downtown. Even back then—it was a real shit-place ... I wonder what this Smith guy does for a living?"

Amanda, now sitting at the desk, desperately searching it for something that would tell her something about where Todd and Emily might be, said, "From his business cards, it states that he's a real estate developer."

Hurts walked over to that easy-chair and plopped down into it. He then looked at his wristwatch and gasped with horror. "Amanda," he began, "it's five-to-twelve ... I've failed you, Amanda. We're out of time."

"Don't say that, Uncle Jim!" Amanda replied, releasing a burst of pent-up anger. "It's not too late. I'm going to find Emily."

"Honey," he said, "I did all that I could. I'm just too old—too worn-out."

"Help me, Uncle Jim," she pleaded, frantically opening drawers under the top of the desk. "The answer has got to be here! You always say that the answers are always in front of us—if we just look."

She spotted a piece of paper under the phone, and after having read it, she stated, "This is a note that Mr. Smith must have written. He had an appointment tonight at 6:00 PM to show Miss Woo a piece of property that he believes would be an excellent location for a new Chinese restaurant ... I wonder if that's the same Miss Woo who owns a Chinese restaurant in Clayton? Good food ... There's that damn number thirteen again! He was supposed to meet her at lot thirteen. I swear, I never want to hear that damn number again. Thirteen! Thirteen! Thirteen!"

Hurts had been about to answer her—to tell her to give it up—when he looked again at that aerial photo on the wall. He began staring at it.

"Could it be?!" he shouted.

"Could what be, Uncle Jim?" she asked.

Hurts then tried to get out of that chair, but he kept falling back into it.

"Help me get out of this no-good chair!" he cried. "Hurry!"

Amanda did.

Standing in front of that aerial photo, Hurts began studying it. After a few seconds had passed, he turned his head to the left. Starting at the south end of that aerial photo, Hurts began counting off the buildings in the photo. When he came to the middle of the photo, he stopped. He clenched his right hand into a fist and struck that photo, hard.

"Staring me in the face the whole time. The whole time!" he said.

Hurts turned to Amanda and said, "I know why Tyler came back here and killed his family. The father and that Woo person must have seen them. Todd and his disciples probably killed them, but before they did, they hadn't asked them if they'd called anyone on their cellphones and told them where they were. Todd probably got scared and ordered Tyler to come back here and kill them to prevent them from speaking … Remember what Donald had said: 'Yeah, we all live under my father's roof, and he doesn't even know it'? … Where can thirteen teenage vampires hide, and where can a twelve-year-old girl scream her head off, and no one will hear?"

Before Amanda even had the chance to answer, Hurts pointed to the middle of that aerial photo and said, "There. Lot thirteen—building thirteen. That's where they are! … Get on your cellphone. Call Williams. Tell him that he has another mess here to clean up. Tell him that we have found Todd and Emily. Give him the address. Tell him to meet us there … Come on. Let's go get Emily."

Raising her hands in the air above her head, Amanda cried joyously, "Woo-who!"

Chapter Sixteen

Amanda did what Hurts told her to do. She called Mr. Williams, but she got his voicemail. She told him everything.

By the time Amanda and Hurts got there, it was fifteen minutes until 1:00 AM—fifteen minutes until the Thirteenth Hour.

Hurts told Amanda to pull up behind an expensive-looking light-blue Mercedes convertible sport's car. In front of that car was a fairly new-looking silver Nissan Altima. He was certain that the owners of those two cars parked upon that deserted street were Mr. Smith and Miss Woo, and he had been correct.

Sitting in the front seat of Amanda's car, across the old red-brick street from the boarded-up five-story red-brick building with many tall, narrow small-paned windows, all of which were also boarded-up, Hurts felt disappointed, angry, depressed and just damn mad. *Where is Williams?!* he kept wondering—and kept screaming silently—as he kept looking out the windows of the car for him.

They were quickly running out of time to stop Todd and to save Amanda. Hurts knew this, but he didn't want to confront Todd and his disciples without Mr. Williams.

After looking at his wristwatch—again!—he finally said to Amanda demandingly and flatly, "Call Williams again!"

She did—no luck. She got his voicemail again.

It was now seven minutes until the Thirteenth Hour.

"Well," Hurts finally said, boiling angry, "I guess if I told you to stay in the car, you wouldn't do it, would you?"

"No," she replied flatly.

"I didn't think so," he said, and then added, "Brat!"

"So, what's the plan?"

"'Plan'?!" he barked at her. "Plan?! … I ain't got no plan. I'm just going in there shooting until they kill me. That's the plan!"

Using one of Hurts' often-used phrases, she said, "Come on. Let's go."

They both exited the car. But before Amanda took Hurts' hand and led him across the street to the boarded-up door of the entrance of that building, she first stopped at the trunk of her car and got that belt with the oversized water-pistol and those small stakes.

It was dark in that musty, dirty foyer, but there was just enough light for Amanda and Hurts to see two dead bodies propped up against the south wall of the entrance of the building. The two bodies were of a man, and of a woman of Asian descent.

There was light coming from the open room at the end of the long hallway. Amanda led Hurts towards it.

The room was cavernous, lit by multiple candles.

Towards the back of the room, about thirty feet from where Hurts and Amanda were standing, there upon a foot-high, wooden dais—naked and stretched out like Jesus hanging upon the cross, held there by ropes to her wrists and ankles—was Emily. She looked more dead than alive. Unconscious. By her left side, was Todd, fondling her neck with his right hand and his tongue. His disciples were in front of the dais—one of them was holding in his hands a large wooden clock.

Releasing Amanda's hand, Hurts withdrew his firearm and pointed it at Todd. He took dead aim at Todd's head.

"Hey, good looking!" Hurts yelled.

Todd spun around, roaring and hissing angrily.

Hurts squeezed the trigger. The shot rang out, echoing throughout the room.

Hurts' ability as a marksman and his aim was, as the saying goes, spot on. Had Todd not been a vampire, with the lightning speed of a vampire, Hurts' bullet would have struck Todd right between his eyes. But, sadly, being a vampire, he easily avoided being hit.

Then, zoom!

Instantly, he was abreast of Hurts, in his face, and holding onto him by the collar of Hurts' topcoat.

Amanda was about four feet away from Hurts, to his left side. Three of Todd's disciples were surrounding her, and one of the three was behind Amanda and had her in a headlock grip.

Hurts was so proud of her. Before they had subdued her and disarmed her, Amanda had staked two of them.

Growling and hissing in Hurts' face, fangs dripping with saliva and the lust for blood, Todd lisped, "Now, I know who she is, but who are you, Pops?!"

Staring at him with a deadpan expression on his face, Hurts replied flatly, "Why do you people keep asking me that? I keep telling you that I'm Buffy The Vampire Killer. ... Say, Todd," Hurts continued, "tell your buddy there..." he indicated with his head towards Amanda, "...to be gentle with Amanda—because I vow that if you harm a single hair on her head, I'll hunt you down to hell and back, and I'll stake you good, boy."

"Is that so?!" Todd replied, shaking Hurts hard. "Is that a fact, Pops?! Well, let me make a vow to you. If you have screwed this up for me, I vow that you and she will both die a slow and painful death."

"You got bad breath, Todd," Hurts stated, taunting him.

"Todd!! Todd!" the one holding the clock yelled. "One minute until the Thirteenth Hour!"

Still staring angrily at Hurts and still holding on to him, Todd shouted, "Let the reciting of Satan's Prayer begin! ... Hold him!" Todd demanded.

One of Todd's disciples came up behind Hurts and placed him, too, in a headlock.

Todd returned to the dais and stood in front of her. His disciples stood at the foot of the dais.

In unison, they all began reciting Satan's Prayer, which was reciting The Lord's Prayer backwards.

Suddenly, the candles started flickering, and the entire building began shaking. Then, demonic laughter came from above.

When Hurts looked up towards the ceiling, he saw a white cloud appear above the dais, hovering above Todd and Emily.

From that cloud, a face manifested—a non-descript face with fiery eyes.

The one who held the clock shouted with excitement and joy, "It's the Thirteenth Hour! ... The Thirteenth Hour!"

In that moment, Hurts knew they had lost. Todd had won, and there wasn't anything that he could do about it. All was lost; all would die— Hurts, Amanda and Emily. All was lost and all would die.

Then the entire building shook again; the sheets of plywood that covered every window in that room were ripped off, permitting the light of the moon to shine through; the windows exploded, and the room was suddenly filled with shadows of people—flashes of people who were zooming here and there.

Hurts felt himself released. He looked over at Amanda, and she had been freed, too.

From the dais, Hurts heard more reciting—but that reciting was different and coming from someone else, not from Todd or from one of his disciples.

It was coming from Mr. Williams. Dressed in a three-piece dark-gray suit with matching tie, and a full-length camel topcoat, he stood upon the dais. In his right hand was a bejeweled cross; in his left hand, he had a sword.

Cowering on the floor of that dais, like a naughty dog being punished, knelt Todd, crying and pleading for mercy. Mr. Williams stood commandingly over him, reciting The Lord's Prayer in Latin.

Yes, Mr. Williams had finally come, and he had saved the day—and the lives of Hurts, Amanda and, of course, Emily.

And, yes. After that experience, Hurts finally did see Dr. Blinder, much to Amanda's relief. He had the treatment and it had worked. Most of Hurts' sight was restored.

Chapter Seventeen

Yes, Amanda was Hurts' unofficial adopted daughter, and he loved her and was proud of her. Except for the past six months, she was troubling Hurts. From the moment that he had first met Amanda, she had vowed to become a doctor—this was her life-wish and passion. Now, whenever he would ask her how school was going, she'd just shrug her shoulders and say indifferently, "Oh, it's okay. It's there."

Hurts couldn't understand this—and he didn't like the fact that she was spending so much damn time with that damn prissy college classmate of hers—that, that Missy. Hurts couldn't figure out why Amanda had anything to do with her. They were so different. Amanda was a tomboy. She liked fishing, camping and sports. Well, that damn Missy didn't like any of that! She loved the THEATRE and the SYMPHONY—oh, so, hoity-toity! Hurts couldn't stand the girl—and!—and!—Amanda had cut all her hair off! All of her lovely, shoulder-length, dark-brown hair. Now she looks like—well, like a boy! Hurts hated all of this—and!—and!—and!—if all this wasn't bad enough, well, this was the topper.

From time to time, Hurts would catch Amanda and Tom flirting lightly with each other—and, boy, that really stuck in Hurts' craw. He wouldn't stand for it! No, Sir. If Tom kept it up, he'd pull out his weapon, stick the barrel of it against Tom's forehead, and say, most vehemently, "That's my daughter! What's the matter with you? You're old enough to be her father! Keep your damn roaming eyes, tongue—and hands!—off of her, or I'll put a bullet right between your no-good eyes. Now, Amanda's got a boyfriend, somewhat. His name is Tom, and he's a good kid—goes to college at Rolla University. He'll be back home soon for Thanksgiving break—and I don't want you messing that up. Got it?! Good!"

Yes, Hurts was troubled.

I apologize for having been so long-winded about all of this. I promise not to digress so much from this point on.

Now, back to the main story:

"Well, hey, now," Hurts protested, sitting at his desk. "What about my idea of signs or paintings of you and me, Tom, at bus stops?"

"I think that's a great idea, Jim," Lill said, sitting by Tom at his desk, sipping coffee.

"Yeah, yeah," Hurts replied, thinking. "And listen to this. We could get one of those guys who paints those-those—Oh, what do you call that?

You know—he paints pictures on the sides of buildings. What's that called? It's—"

"Do you mean murals, Uncle Jim?" Amanda said, still sitting on the couch.

"That's it!" Hurts shouted excitedly, pointing to Amanda. "Murals … Tom, we could have a guy paint one of those of us on the back of the bench—with the words: 'Got pests? Call us. We're the exterminators!'"

"That's lovely, Jim," Lill said, nodding her head in agreement.

"Well, now, Lill," Hurts added warningly. "As long as the guy paints the picture of us on the back of the bench and not on the seat of it—I don't want some person's smelly ass sitting on my face!"

This brought gales of laughter from everyone. Everyone except Hurts. He had been serious.

"Stop laughing, you hyenas!" Hurts warned. "I'm not—"

At that moment, Amanda's cellphone began ringing in her purse. Her large, floppy brown purse with its long shoulder strap was on the couch beside her. She fished around deep inside of the purse until she found her cellphone. She answered it, saying, "Hello? … Oh, hi, Uncle Williams," she said cheerfully.

What does that BIGSHOT want? Hurts barked silently.

"… Why, yes, Uncle Williams. I'm at Uncle Jim's office now. I'm with him, Tom and Tom's mother, Lill … What?! …"

Suddenly, Amanda's face changed from pleasantness to concern, then to stunned disbelief. Hurts knew something was wrong.

"… Yes, I'll tell them, Uncle Williams … Yes, immediately."

Amanda hung up and just stared blankly, trying desperately to comprehend something.

"Honey?" Hurts asked. "What is it?"

In a daze, she looked at Hurts and said, with fear in her voice, "Uncle Williams wants all of us in his office—immediately."

"Why?" Hurts asked.

"It could be-be—" She stopped speaking. She looked at Lill, then at Tom, and then back at Hurts.

"—the beginning of the apocalypse."

Chapter Eighteen

They all piled into Hurts' old black 1997 Nissan Pathfinder and he drove straight to the Wainwright Building downtown.

It was a beautiful fall day. The sun was shining brightly. There was a crisp breeze in the air, and the leaves of the trees were turning in all their autumnal glory.

Upon entering the outer office of Mr. Williams' office on the twentieth floor of the building, he was anxiously waiting for them and whisked them swiftly into his plush office—he didn't even give Hurts any time to flirt with his secretary, Lorraine, something Hurts always took pleasure in doing, she being a vampire.

From behind his desk, before he himself sat down, Mr. Williams immediately gestured with his outstretched hand and offered Tom's mother a seat in one of the two well-padded round-back white modular chairs that were directly in front of the desk. Tom sat down in the other one. Before entering his office, Mr. Williams had instructed Lorraine to bring in two more chairs. She brought two wooden folding chairs, which she placed to the north-end of the desk. Amanda sat in the inner one, next to Lill, and Hurts sat in the outer one.

Over the past year, Tom had met Mr. Williams three times. Once, he had given Amanda tickets to a Blue's hockey game, and twice tickets to Cardinals baseball games. Each time, Amanda had invited Hurts and Tom, and Mr. Williams had gone along, too. Hurts had told Tom all about Mr. Williams, and Tom liked him, found him to be a good guy.

Lill had never met him and knew nothing about him, but she was quite impressed with him—with his elegant office, with his elegant dress—on this day, wearing a light-gray suit, matching tie and matching folded handkerchief in the chest pocket of his suitcoat—with his arura of sophistication, breeding and good manners.

After they were all seated, Mr. Williams, looking grave and concerned, took a deep breath, expelled it, and said, "Thank you all for coming here on such short notice." He stopped speaking, took another breath, and continued, "I need your help. I'm in trouble … Amanda, Hurts," he said, looking at Amanda first, and then at Hurts. "What had happened last year with Todd attempting to increase his vampire powers thirteen-fold by performing the Ritual of The Thirteenth Hour on Halloween is taking place in London, Paris, Germany, New York and in

Chicago … I-I hadn't realized that it wasn't random—wasn't happenstance—until it was too late. I have sent most of my men, my soldiers, if you will, to assist with the preventing of this happening—I even sent four of the six board members. I only have eight of my soldiers here. I-I have been deceived. This was all a ruse orchestrated by-by Satan."

"Satan?!" Lill cried incredulously. "You mean, 'The Satan'?!"

"Yes," Mr. Williams replied reluctantly and quietly.

"Why is he doing this, Uncle Williams?" Amanda asked.

"As I informed you on the phone, Amanda," he said, "to begin the apocalypse."

"Dear God," Lill cried, making the sign of the cross. "Help us all."

"Is the Thirteenth Hour going to be done here again, Williams?" Hurts asked.

"Yes and no," Mr. Williams stated.

"What the hell does that mean, Williams?!" Hurts barked.

Mr. Williams bowed his head, was silent for a moment, and then he raised his head and began speaking again. "Three weeks ago, Alexian Brothers Hospital on Broadway was destroyed by a meteor. This, too, was done by Satan … Have any of you ever seen that movie 'The Exorcist'?"

"Oh, yes," Amanda replied. "It was scary."

"I saw it," Tom also replied.

"Are you guys talkin' about the movie with that little girl spinning her head around and vomiting pea soup?"

"Yes, that's the movie, Hurts," Mr. Williams said. "That movie was based on a true event that happened here in St. Louis at Alexian Brothers Hospital in 1947. Only it wasn't a young girl; it was a fourteen-year-old boy. The exorcism was performed at Alexian Brothers Hospital on Good Friday and the three Catholic priests who performed the exorcism were successful in casting Satan out of him on Easter Sunday—or so all were led to believe."

Mr. Williams paused again. He was pensive and uncertain how to begin what he next wanted to say.

He took another deep breath, expelled it, and said, "Satan has taken possession of that boy's body again. The boy is now an elderly man. Satan walks amongst us now, here in St. Louis, in human form."

"Why?!" Amanda and Lill cried, almost in unison.

"It's as I have said," Mr. Williams replied., "To begin the apocalypse. He has attempted this two times before. Of the two times that he has attempted this, and failed, I, with the assistance of others, was able to thwart him from succeeding the second time … Three days from now it shall be Halloween. Unlike the Ritual of the Thirteenth Hour to increase a vampire's power thirteen-fold, Satan shall not torment a child for three days. He may wait until Halloween to kidnap the Chosen One. Like the Thirteenth Hour, the Chosen One shall be a virgin child of twelve-years-of-age, whose birthday is on the thirty-first of October, Halloween. Upon an altar, on the stroke of the thirteenth second of the thirteenth hour of Halloween, he shall impregnate the child. Thus, beginning the Unholy Trinity—the father, Satan; the son, the antichrist; and the false prophet, who shall be an entity of many. His army of demons shall destroy all religions except one: his religion. Satan's religion, which shall be called Nero Caesar, which in Hebrew, adds up to the number 666."

"Excuse me, Mr. Williams," Lill said. "Are these demons you are speaking of, are they vampires or fallen angels?—And in my book, vampires and fallen angels are both Sons of Satan."

There was an awkward silence. Everyone except for Lill and Hurts felt uncomfortable.

Tom placed his hand on his mother's arm and said gingerly, "Mom, Mr. Williams is a vampire."

"What?!" she cried incredulously and looked at Mr. Williams.

Mr. Williams simply smiled at her pleasantly and nodded his head yes.

"He's one of the good guys, Mom," Tom added.

"To answer your question, Mrs. Mayor," Mr. Williams stated. "Demons are neither vampires nor fallen angels. Before God created Adam and Eve, and before the rebellion of Satan, Lucifer was God's most cherished angel. God so loved him that he ordained the earth to Lucifer and gave him rule over the beings who inhabited the earth at this time. When he fell, and a third of the angels followed him, God destroyed these beings who had lived upon the earth. These beings are demons—formless spirits—powers and principalities—who seek to control and possess the minds and bodies of human beings. From these spirits, Satan shall form his army: He has already chosen twelve to be his disciples at the Ritual—in the past three weeks, twelve men have suddenly gone missing in St. Louis.

"Say, Williams," Hurts said. "You said that the kid that Satan possessed was fourteen in 1947. That would make him—what? How old?"

"Eighty-six," Amanda stated.

"Jumping Jesus, Williams!" Hurts exclaimed. Cupping his hand to the side of his mouth so the rest of them wouldn't hear, he whispered, "Can a guy that old even get it up?"

"Satan possesses his body, Hurts," Mr. Williams replied. "Yes, he can."

"Obviously, this child of Satan's, the antichrist, shall be different. For one thing, instead of nine months, he shall be born in three months—and Satan will probably kill the mother shortly after that time. In three years, it shall be as if the boy is thirteen-years-old. Satan, the boy, and the twelve disciples shall then travel to Russia. For the next three years, Satan shall begin increasing his army of demons and ingratiating himself and the boy to the Russian people. At the end of the third year, the boy shall be as if he's twenty-one, and with Satan's help, and with the help of the now sizeable army of demons, the boy shall overthrow the government of Russia and rule. He shall rule for three years, and then he shall start invading and conquering other European countries, and he shall not stop until he invades and conquers Israel. In the next three years, in Jerusalem, he has Solomon's Temple rebuilt, and he shall rule from inside of the temple. This shall—well, I believe you know the rest."

Mr. Williams stopped speaking. He lowered his head, as if in shame.

"Look, Williams," Hurts began. "What is it—?"

"I have been so deceived!" Mr. Williams screamed angrily. He raised his head and screamed it again, "I have been so deceived! For years now, Satan has been one step—no! Many steps ahead of me … I was so certain of the date—the date of this all happening. I knew of its coming. I did! I did!"

He paused again. He composed himself. He looked at Lill and said, "Please forgive my outburst of anger, Mrs. Mayor. I-I—It's as I have told Amanda and Hurts. I was there when Jesus was crucified. I was a high-ranking soldier in the Roman Army. He spoke to me. He cried out for water. A foot-soldier had taken his spear, impaled a large sponge upon the tip of it, dipped it into a bucket filled with a mixture of water and vinegar, and then shoved the sponge to Jesus' lips. Jesus began choking, and that soldier had thought that funny and had begun laughing. I don't know why but seeing this had enraged me. I struck the soldier, knocking him down. I drew my sword, and was about to kill him, when Jesus spoke. He said: 'Vampire, do not strike that man. Your sins are great. Your soul belongs to Satan, but your heart still belongs to the Father. Sin no more. Upon your death, I shall accompany you to hell and restore your soul to you. Go.'

This changed me. It did. I-I was a special consultant to Helena, to St. Helena, Constantine's mother. She commissioned me to find Jesus' cross—which I did. I-I was there when Jerusalem was destroyed, burned. I helped the sect who had written The Dead Sea Scrolls escape from Jerusalem. I helped them hide the scrolls in the caves. I-I—" He stopped speaking. He began thinking. When he began speaking again, it was as if he were reliving it. "I took two of the scrolls—they were from the Book of Enoch. I took them because they spoke of my kind, and because they foretold of this event. But I got the date wrong. The two scrolls were so badly damaged in the fire. They foretold that this would happen in the land of the 'New World Order'; in the land of 1776. Well, I didn't know what this meant until America came into being. They foretold of it happening in the middle of the land, at the 'Gateway to the West', by the bank of the river of muddy water that divides the land. It would be here that the Dragon would return to his origins, desecrate that which first had been good and holy, and amidst his unholy fragrance, upon his stone altar of pure—the rest of that was too badly burnt. But, I believe that the 'origins' is a church, and the first church here in St. Louis is the Old Cathedral, on the grounds of the Gateway Arch—and yesterday, two of my people saw two demons there."

Mr. Williams paused again, became pensive. Then, he spoke again.

"I was so certain of the date. I was so certain that this would happen in the year 2113. It had just seemed logical to me that the year would be 2113. If you add these numbers, in Jewish numerology, you have the number 7. The number 7 is spirit, duality, creation—the menorah has seven branches to it. Yes, I was so sure of the date, but I was wrong. If you take the date 1776 and add up the numbers, you get the number 21 … Well, at least I got the century correct—the Twenty-first Century, and the number 21 is symbolic: It means 'The period of the Great Rebellion'. Then, if you take the symbolism of the menorah representing the Jewish people's forty years of being lost in the wilderness, and then, finally, entering the Promised Land, you take the number 40 and subtract it from the number 21, and you have—"

"The number 19," Amanda said.

"Yes, exactly," Mr. Williams replied. "The number 19. The true date—2019. This year. Now … How could I have been so wrong?"

"Alright, so you got the date," Hurts barked. "Big deal. So, what do you want us to do?"

"Find the girl before he kidnaps her!" Mr. Williams stated emphatically. "Find Satan himself—kill him!—or the person whose body and mind he is possessing! ... I've made a list with his name and address, and I have access to his bank accounts and credit cards. Even though Satan has taken possession of his body and mind, the human part of him shall still have to eat and sleep. If he should use one of the cards or cash a check, I'll know ... I also have a list of the names and addresses of the twelve men who are missing, and a list of all the twelve-year-old girls in St. Louis whose thirteenth birthday shall be on Halloween—of which there are three. From these three girls, he shall choose one to be the Chosen One."

"Say, Williams?" Hurts then said. "Does this mean that you're hiring us?"

"Yes, of course, Hurts," Mr. Williams replied. "You shall be paid."

"Now you're talkin' my language, pilgrim," Hurts stated joyously.

"One moment, please," Mr. Williams said. Then Hurts and Amanda witnessed something that they had never seen Mr. Williams do before— had never even given a thought that this always impeccably dressed person would ever do. They watched as Mr. Williams loosened the knot of his silk tie and lowered it. Then he unbuttoned the top button of his white silk shirt. After he had done that, he removed from around his neck a thin gold chain that had a key on it.

Rising from his chair, he said, "Excuse me."

He walked over to the corner of the room. Facing the wall, he inserted that key into a door that seemed invisible to the naked eye. He opened the door.

From inside of this closet, he removed three full-length black topcoats. He draped these three coats over his left arm. He then removed three more items from the closet. These three items were hand-sized, and each wrapped in a shiny blue cloth.

Returning to Hurts, Tom, and Tom's mother, Mr. Williams said to Lill, as he handed a topcoat and one of the items wrapped in the blue cloth to Tom, "I'm sorry, Mrs. Mayor, but I only have three of these. I believe that it is best that I give them to Hurts, Amanda, and Tom."

This he did.

Amanda was the first of them to unwrap the blue cloth and see what the item was—it was a bejeweled cross.

"Please be most revered with these crosses. Each of them contains a piece of wood from the cross of Christ. On the inside of these coats is a pocket. Place the crosses in these pockets. Carry these crosses with you at all times. Wear these coats. Satan's disciples shall be wearing coats similar to these—you shall know them by the wearing of such coats as these, and by their eyes being totally black, no pupils. During the day, they shall wear sunglasses." Stepping away, Mr. Williams said, "Excuse me again."

He walked again to that closet. This time, he removed from it three sheathed swords.

As he handed them out to Tom, to Amanda, and to Hurts, he said, "These are three swords of St. Michael, the Archangel ... Please, do not ask me how I have come in possession of them: That would be too long of a story to tell. Wear them with you, under these coats, at all times—if you come into contact with Satan or his disciples, you must cut the head off. They, too, shall be carrying swords."

"Why do I suddenly feel like Robin Hood?" Hurts remarked with a laugh.

As Tom, Amanda, and Hurts donned the topcoats and then the swords, Mr. Williams returned behind his desk, but he remained standing. With his hands closed into fists, he placed his knuckles on top of his desk, leaned forward, and stated most earnestly, "Satan is not God, but he is god-like. He can read your thoughts. He now knows that you are in the fight. Say his name as little as possible. Say the name of the person he possesses as little as possible. Say the names of the three girls whom he seeks to kidnap as little as possible—and always remember: Satan is a liar and a master at deceiving. Stay together; do not separate. He shall seek to divide you, both physically and mentally. Be extra tolerant of what you say and do to each other ... What Satan is attempting to do is inevitable—it's in the Bible—he shall succeed. But it doesn't have to be on our watch, our time."

Mr. Williams stopped speaking. He raised his right hand above the desk. He said, "Now rise and place your right hand on mine."

They did.

Mr. Williams resumed speaking, "From this moment on, we pledge to God to stop Satan. With His grace, strength, wisdom and will, we shall prevail ... Do I have an Amen?"

In unison, they all said Amen.

Mr. Williams then said, "Now, as Hurts is always so fond of saying, 'Let's do this!'"

Chapter Nineteen

It was a little after four before they finally got back to the office. Just as they were leaving Mr. Williams' office, Amanda said that she had better go down and tell her mother that she would be staying a few days with Hurts. She said that she would tell her mother that Hurts was ill, and she felt that she should stay with him.

Amanda's mother worked in the Accounting Department on the eighteenth floor. Tom, Lill and Hurts waited for her in the spacious, elegant, busy lobby of the Wainwright Building. As they waited for Amanda, Hurts told Lill and Tom that he thought it was a good idea for Amanda to stay with him.

Lill spoke up, saying, "I'll go one better. Instead of you and Amanda sleeping in that cramped office, why don't you and Amanda stay with us? We've got plenty of room. You can stay in Eve's old room, and Amanda can sleep in Mary's old room."

Hurts thought that was an excellent idea. He had stayed at their house before and loved it there and, besides, Mr. Williams had told them—had warned them!—to stay together.

So, that was settled. They would all stay at Tom and Lill's.

They were all hungry. So before they returned to the office, Hurts pulled in through a drive-through window at Burger King and they all got a Whopper and fries—well, all of them except for Amanda. Amanda being Amanda—a "health nut!" as Hurts sometimes called her—wanted "healthy" food. So Hurts drove to a health food store, and Amanda bought a freshly made roast beef sandwich, a baked potato with butter and sour cream, and an order of green beans.

Finally, before returning to the office, Hurts drove to a Starbuck's, and from the drive-through window, ordered four large cups of coffee.

Now, finally back at the office, they ate, and then they got down to work.

Hurts was sitting at his desk, busily looking at the screen of his old computer, checking out the accounts and the personal history of the man who Satan now possessed. The black topcoat that Mr. Williams had given him draped across the back of his chair, and the sword leaned up against the left side of the desk.

Amanda was sitting on the couch, busy typing information from a sheet of paper that was on the couch to her left into her cellphone. The topcoat that Mr. Williams had given to her was lying on the couch to her right, lying over the sword he had given her. Her large, floppy brown purse was lying on top of both of those items.

Tom and Lill were both seated at Tom's desk. Lill was helping Tom with the two sheets of paper that Mr. Williams had given them of the names and addresses of the twelve missing men, and of the names and addresses of the three twelve-year-old girls whose thirteenth birthday would be on Halloween. Tom was checking all of this out on his laptop. The topcoat that Mr. Williams had given to him was draped across the back of his chair, and the sword was leaning up against one side of his desk.

Hurts asked Amanda, "How are you coming with getting his credit card and checking account entered into your cellphone?"

"I'm done," she said, replacing her cellphone back into her purse. "If he uses his credit card or tries to cash a check, we'll know. I've placed an 'Alert' on it, so my phone will beep when he tries."

"That's great, honey," Hurts said, still staring at the screen on his computer. "Three Wednesdays ago, he withdrew five thousand from his saving's account. He's probably using that for rent and food."

"Where do you think they're at, Uncle Jim?" Amanda asked.

"Well," Hurts said, thinking, "I'd say an unabandoned warehouse or something like that. You got him and twelve demons—and then you're going to have a screaming kid on top of all of that. No, you need someplace that's secluded, private, for that … How are you two doing?" he then said to Lill and Tom.

Still looking into the screen of his laptop, Tom replied, "Nothing is jumping out at me. Nothing strange yet."

Hurts paused and looked over at Lill and Tom.

"You know, this is all just a waste of time, don't you?" Hurts stated flatly.

"Why do you say that, Jim?" Lill said.

"Because Williams told us that that old SOB, Satan," Hurts said, "is reading our thoughts. If that's the case then, if we do find him, he'll know it and just leave before we get there."

"Well, what else would you have us do, Jim?" Tom said.

"Think!" Hurts barked at Tom. "Think outside the box. Come up with a great plan!"

"Do you have one, Uncle Jim?" Amanda asked.

Looking at her sardonically, he replied, "Does a bear poop in the woods? ... Here it is."

Hurts first looked around the room. Then, looking straight ahead, he said, "Okay, Satan. Are you listening to me? ... Say, look. We're tired and want sleep. So, why don't you and your boys give it a rest tonight, and we'll start the game tomorrow? ... The way I see it, there are two things that you want and need. One, is one of those three girls, the Chosen One. Two, the use of that altar at the Old Cathedral Church on Halloween night. Right? ... Now, I've never played chess, but I figure if we can stop you from getting one of the two—then, that's a stalemate. So, here's my plan:

"In a few moments, I'm going to call Williams. I'm going to tell him that tomorrow morning I want him to send us a fancy limousine, and cameras, and all the rest that would make us look like reporters. Tomorrow, we're going to go to the houses of those three girls, pretending to be reporters, doing a featured story on girls born on Halloween. Since your old pal, Williams, is so rich and has that fancy penthouse apartment at the Chase Park Plaza Hotel, I know that it would be no problem for him to get suites for the families, relatives, and friends of the three girls, and all of us to stay there from tomorrow until Friday morning, the day after Halloween. ... Oh, it will be such fun! On Halloween night, we'll have a big fancy costume ball—we'll all be there: Williams, his eight soldiers, me, police, maybe a few priests; but you won't be able to get to those three girls at all.

"Now, should you, by chance, succeed in kidnaping one of those three girls, the 'Chosen One,' then, we—Williams, his soldiers, me, and Tom—shall stop you from entering that church, the Old Cathedral, on Halloween. Either way—that's a stalemate to me. You can't win, and we can't win. ... So, Satie, that's my plan. I'll be watching for your moves."

Hurts stop speaking, looked at them, and said, "Well, what do you think?"

"I think that you've gone senile, Jim," Tom said with a laugh. "But, actually, I think it's a damn good plan. You're right; he needs the girl and the altar of that church. If he doesn't have both, we've stopped him. Strike one up for you."

"I agree, Jim," Lill said. "Good job."

Besides being a man of action, Hurts always took pleasure in having his ego flattered. He looked at Amanda and said, "What do you think of my idea, honey?"

She shrugged her slender shoulders—a little too indifferently for Hurts' liking—and stated noncommittally, "It's good, Uncle Jim. Yeah, it's good."

Turning back to Tom, Hurts said, "Read me the names of those three girls—and where do they live?"

"Hand me that sheet of paper, Mom," Tom said to Lill.

She did.

Tom took the sheet of paper in his hands and, looking at it, said, "Michele Johnston. She lives in Arnold. Next, Eve Taylor. Hey!" Tom exclaimed. "She lives in Mehlville. She attends Mehlville Middle School—my old school."

"Tom?" Lill said. "Did you say her name is Eve?"

Tom looked at her and replied, "Yeah."

"Well, Tom," Lill began, "I gave that name to your sister because it means life—and Eve was the first woman. Now, I don't know about these things like you and—"

"Say!" Hurts exclaimed. "I think that you may have something here, Lill … Yeah," Hurts said, thinking about it. "Satan wants to create life, and her name means life. That girl could be the Chosen One." Turning and looking at Amanda, he said, "What do you think, Amanda?"

Again, she shrugged her shoulders and said noncommittally, "It sounds right, Uncle Jim."

Hurts was getting worried about Amanda. All throughout the first case of The Thirteenth Hour, last year, Amanda was forever saying that she felt this, or that she felt that about something—and she'd been correct each time. But, now she never said anything like that. Now she just seemed so troubled at times and, in Hurts' words, "dead on the inside."

"Are you feeling anything about that name?" Hurts asked, emphasizing the word "feeling."

"No," she replied indifferently.

Turning back to Tom, Hurts said, "What about the third girl?"

Gazing at that sheet of paper again, Tom said, "Phosphorus Reed, and she lives in Holly Hills." Tom looked up and at Hurts. "Doesn't that old man who Satan is possessing live in Holly Hills?"

Hurts seemed to be thinking of something.

"Jim?" Tom said.

"What?" Hurts replied, leaving his train of thought. "Oh, yes. Yes. He does. That's a nice area, too. Beautiful, small red-brick homes. It's only several blocks south of here."

"What did that guy do for a living?"

"He was an office clerk for AT & T at the headquarters downtown. From what I could gather, he lived a quiet, boring life—never married; no kids; never in any trouble; nothing. He drives a 2001 4-door silver Kia."

Hurts was silent. He began thinking again of what he had been thinking of when Tom had interrupted him.

"Damn," he cursed. Not looking at anyone, or saying this to anyone, he said, "I wish I could remember. That name … Where have I heard that name before? I know that I know that name—but I can't remember!"

He searched and searched his memory. No luck. Finally, he gave up, saying, "Look, I'm exhausted. I'll call Williams and tell him my plan, and then let's close this place up and go."

"Sounds good to me," Lill said. Then she added, "This morning, I made a meatloaf. It's all cooked and just has to be warmed. I'll whip-up some mashed potatoes, open a couple cans of string beans, toss a salad, and we'll finish it all off with a big bowl of chocolate ice cream."

"Great," Amanda said. "I'm starving."

"I can eat," Hurts chimed in.

Lill rose from the chair.

As she was walking to the dining room table to get her white purse, Hurts said, "I'll call Williams. I'll only be a moment."

He picked up the receiver of the old black phone that was positioned on top of the desk at the corner of it. He began to dial. That's when Amanda screamed.

Hurts shot a look toward Amanda. He shot another look around the room. The room was packed with leprechauns. Hurts shot up out of the chair.

Lill grabbed her purse off the dining room table. She held it high above her head by its thin white strap, ready to do battle.

Tom shot up out of his chair. For a moment, he thought about grabbing his sword, but then he dismissed that thought.

Standing abreast of Amanda, but facing Hurts, was the leprechaun who had done all of the talking the last encounter Hurts and Tom had had with them. He stood there staring at Hurts, with that tiny white pipe with its long white stem in his tiny, lipless, arrogantly grinning mouth.

Hurts quickly reached into the inside of the dark-blue pin-stripe suitcoat he was wearing, removed his weapon from the shoulder holster under his left armpit, and pointed it at that leprechaun.

Removing the pipe from his mouth and holding up his hands, he said, "Peace, Mr. Hurts. Peace. I mean you no harm."

"Yeah?" Hurts replied arrogantly and doubtfully. "What do you want?"

Pointing the end of the pipe at Hurts, he said, "Your services, my good man. Your services. It's a-hiring you I be."

"Hiring me?!" Hurts cried incredulously. "What for?"

Before he could answer, Tom said, "Don't listen to him, Jim."

"Yeah," Lill said, still holding her purse high in the air, still ready and wanting to do battle. "He's of the devil … You pulled my pants down—and I'm a God-fearing woman!"

"Yeah," Tom said, and then added, "And I still have the scars on my legs and arms of your bite marks!"

"Please. Please. A thousand pardons," he said, first looking at Lill, and then at Tom. "But let's let bygones be bygones. That's in the past. Now is today … There's riches to be made here."

"Riches?" Hurts said, now interested.

Looking back at Hurts, he smiled and said, "Ah, a man after me own heart. Yes, Mr. Hurts—riches!"

"What do I—we—have to do?"

His reddish face became fiery red with heated anger that matched the redness of his red beard. He shouted most angrily, "Find me pot of gold!"

"Do you mean to tell me that your pot of gold has been stolen again?!" Hurts said.

"Aye," he replied. "By the very person you be seeking."

"Who?" Hurts said.

"Satan!"

"Why on earth would Satan steal your pot of gold?" Hurts asked.

"That be a mystery now, Mr. Hurts—but find it and be rewarded beyond your wildest dreams!"

"Okay," Hurts replied, re-holstering his weapon. "If I find it, I want half of it."

"No, no, no, Mr. Hurts," he said, shaking his head from side to side. "Me gold is me gold—private. Can't bargain with it."

"Well, then, what do I get out of it?—Where's these 'riches' you said?!" Hurts barked at him.

"Would you be liking women now, Mr. Hurts?" he asked.

"Yeah, I like women."

"Would you be wanting ten, twenty, a thousand?" he said.

"Wait a minute, wait a minute," Hurts said, holding up his hands. "I don't—Say, what's your name, anyway?"

"The name be too long and too difficult for you to say," he replied. He thought for a moment and said, "Call me—oh, I know. Call me O'Malley. Yes, that be fine."

"Okay, O'Malley," Hurts replied. "Look, let's cut to the chase here. I don't want women—I want money."

"I'm disappointed in you, Mr. Hurts," he sighed. "What I have to offer is worth far more than money."

"So, what are you offering?" Hurts said arrogantly.

O'Malley nodded, touched the brim of the green pilgrim-like hat he had on, saluted Hurts, and said, "Find me gold, and I be granting you three wishes."

"And I can wish for anything?" Hurts asked cautiously and doubtfully.

"Aye. Anything," he said. "You can wish to be the richest man in the world."

"I'll take it!" Hurts cried emphatically and eagerly.

"So, we have a bargain, Mr. Hurts?"

"Well, yeah," Hurts replied. "We have a—Hey, how do I know that you'll keep your end of the deal?"

"Stretch out your right hand, Mr. Hurts," O'Malley stated.

Hurts did.

A second later, Hurts yelled with pain. He looked down at his hand. There, on the palm of his right hand, by his thumb, was the green outline of a lucky charm.

Angrily, looking back up at O'Malley, Hurts barked, "What is this?!"

"That be me contract, Mr. Hurts—signed, sealed and delivered … Now, find me gold!"

"I will," Hurts replied. Hurts then thought of something and said, "Say, O'Malley, are you still living in the woods of Carondelet Park? How do I contact you?"

"Just say me name three times, fast, and I be here," he replied.

"Got it," Hurts replied.

"So, good doing business with—"

"Mr. O'Malley?" Amanda said, rising from the couch.

He turned to her, looked up at her, and said, "Aye, lass?"

"Mr. O'Malley, Uncle Jim has told me how adept of a shoemaker you are."

"Aye, lass," he repeated.

"Last week," Amanda began, pointing to the knee-high black books she was wearing over her jeans, "I bought these boots, and they're too tight. Can you make them feel more comfortable?"

"I, I can, lass … Apron!" he shouted. "Shoes in need of repair."

"Well," Lill said, "the left heel of my comfort shoes is loose. Will you fix that?"

"Tools!" O'Malley shouted. "One shoe at a time … Shoes in need of repair … one shoe at—"

"My shoes," Tom chimed in, "most assuredly need a good polishing."

"Shoes in need of repair," O'Malley kept repeating. "One shoe at a—"

"What's going on here, people?!" Hurts bellowed. "We have work to—"

Hurts stopped speaking. He spotted a leprechaun opening the door to the bathroom.

"Hey!" Hurts yelled. "You don't go in there. If you got to go to the bathroom, go to the restroom at the gas station down the block."

Two leprechauns were walking on top of the dining room table.

"Hey, you two!" Hurts screamed angrily. "Get off of that damn table!" Then Hurts looked down to the left side of his desk. Standing there, with her tiny hands interlaced together and touching her chin, was a female leprechaun, staring up at Hurts amorously. "What's your problem?" Hurts barked. She began batting her eyes at Hurts.

"O'Malley!" Hurts yelled, shocked. "O'Malley! … Tell this little girl to …."

Chapter Twenty

As Lill was in the kitchen of her home busily preparing supper, Hurts was in Lill's living room, pacing back and forth—and he was fuming angry. He kept cursing silently: *Where in the hell are they?! What's taking Amanda and Tom so long?! Where are they?!*

After the leprechauns had left—well, had disappeared into thin air, and as the three of them were getting ready to leave the office, Amanda had asked Hurts if he would mind driving Lill home. Amanda had wanted Tom to follow her home in his car. This way, she could pack some clothes to stay at Lill and Tom's home, and then have Tom drive her over to their place so she could leave her car at home.

Tom had agreed to do that, but Hurts had quickly said, "Oh, I'll drive you home, honey."

"No, Uncle Jim," Amanda had replied, "Tom can take me."

Hurts had shot Tom a look that stated: *You just watch your P's-and-Q's, Mister!*

It was nearly seven o'clock when Amanda and Tom had finally stepped through the front door of Lill and Tom's two-story old house in South County, or Mehlville, as it is known.

Amanda's mother, Jennifer Warner, was home from work by the time Tom and Amanda had gotten to Amanda's home, so Tom stayed in his car while Amanda packed some clothes in a suitcase, packed some toiletries in a night bag, said goodbye to her mother, retrieved her oversized water pistol—filled with holy water, and the belt with small wooden stakes in the notches of the belt from the truck of her car—and retuned to Tom's car.

Upon reentering Tom's car, Amanda said, with a troubled tone in her voice, "Tom, can we go somewhere and talk?"

"Sure," Tom said.

They went to Starbuck's on Loughborough Ave, which was just a mile or two south from Amanda's home.

At Starbuck's, Tom bought both of them a cup of coffee, and they sat at one of the small tables at the glass edifice of the front of the building.

Feeling a bit nervous about what she might want to talk about, and being aware of Hurts' dislike of their light flirting, Tom took a deep breath, expelled it, and said, feigning cheerfulness, "Well, Amanda, what did you want to talk about?"

With a look of deep concern upon her troubled face, she took a sip of coffee from her paper cup and said with a sigh, "I feel lost."

"Lost about what, Amanda?" Tom asked.

"About life—about who I am."

"I don't understand," Tom replied. "What do you mean by 'who you are'?"

"All my life, I have wanted to be a doctor—that's all I have ever wanted to be!" she said. "But, now, I-I … I just don't know anymore. It's so hard—the amount of homework, going to classes. It's-it's overwhelming … I want to quit … Oh, I don't know." She was silent for a moment, and then she continued, "And, a year ago, I suddenly started-started sensing things—ESP, or something like that. I could sense things about people and events before the person said something or before something had happened."

"Yes, Jim told me about that," Tom said.

"It used to scare me, and I didn't want it," she replied, shaking her head in anger. "But now, about three weeks ago—nothing. It's gone, and I miss not having it."

"You say that this stopped about three weeks ago?" Tom asked.

"Yes."

"Do you think that—you know… *him*," Tom said, pointing to the high-polished wooden floor, "is preventing you from having premonitions?"

"I never thought of that, Tom," she stated, with a dash of hope. "You may be right. Thank you."

"Always here to help a pretty woman," Tom replied, smiling.

"I only wish that my other problems were so easily explained."

"Such as?" Tom then said.

Amanda took another drink from her cup. She set the cup down on the table, and she began staring into the cup.

Tom could see that she was having an internal fight with herself— should she or should she not tell Tom anymore? This had been what Tom had "sensed" coming from her.

Finally, she looked back up at Tom, inhaled a deep breath, expelled it, and said, "Missy."

"She's nice person," Tom said. He had only met her twice, so he actually didn't know her. He had just said that about her to be kind, and of the two times that he had met her, Tom had felt that she and Amanda seemed awfully friendly together. "What about her?"

Looking at Tom and desperately hoping that he would understand how difficult this was for her, she said, "We have indulged in more than-than a causal relationship."

Tom nodded his head and said, "Are you in love with her?"

Amanda laughed and said, "No. It's not like that. We've just, a few times, have had sex."

"And that bothers you?"

"Yes, it bothers me!" she replied emphatically.

"Why?"

"Why?!" she replied in a whispered scream. "Because—who am I? Am I straight? … Am I gay? … Am I a doctor? … Who am I? … What am I? … I don't know anymore."

Making the T-sign with his hands, Tom said, "Time out, Amanda. Give it a rest … Now, who initiated the sex—you or Missy?"

"Well," Amanda began slowly, "Missy did. Some time ago, Missy told me that she preferred women to men—but I never made anything of it. I didn't care. We were friends. Then, one night, it-it just happened."

"You said 'a few times'. Who initiated the sex the other times?"

"Well, we both did," she replied.

"Have you ever done this before with other girls?" Tom asked.

"No," she stated definitely. "Never."

"What about this Tom guy, Amanda?" Tom asked. "Have you and he been intimate?"

"Yes," she replied. "A few times."

"He'll be back home soon for Thanksgiving break, from Rolla University, right?"

"Yes," Amanda replied.

"Do you plan to see him?

"Well, yeah," she replied. "Why are you asking me all of these questions? … It's all just so confusing … Uncle Jim's going to hate me."

"Amanda," Tom said, "you're young, and young people sometimes experiment with sexuality."

"Did you?" she asked.

"Well, no," Tom replied. "But I might have if circumstances had been different … Look, maybe all of this is just a phase that you're going through. You're troubled; you're, as you said, overwhelmed with school. Maybe all of this will pass." Tom stopped speaking for a moment, and then he continued. "My advice to you, Amanda, is to stay the course. Don't quit school. What are you going to do if you quit? What?"

She shrugged her shoulders and replied, "I don't know."

"Well, until you do know, I wouldn't quit … And as far as Jim is concerned, yes, he doesn't have any formal education, but don't count him short. Jim is one smart cookie, and if I had some feelings that your relationship with Missy was more than causal, which I did—well, you can just bet that Jim has questioned it … Yes, Jim is 'old school', but give him time. He'll come around—and if he doesn't, well, that's his problem. This is your life, Amanda. You have to do what you think is best … He loves you, Amanda. He does, and nothing is going to change that … Bottom line: Go slow with all of it … And anyway, we all might be dead in a few days, so what would any of this matter?"

***

"What took you two so long?!" Hurts bellowed after Tom and Amanda entered through the front door of Lill and Tom's home.

Tom looked at Amanda, and she looked at him, and then she looked at Hurts, raising the suitcase that she was holding by its handle in her right hand. "Packing, Uncle Jim."

"It took you an hour-and-twenty-minutes to pack"?!" he barked.

"Well, I felt like having a coffee, so we stopped at Starbuck's and had one," Amanda said.

"Lill made coffee here," Hurts stated. "So, why would you—?"

"Supper's ready," Lill's voice was heard coming from the kitchen. "Come and get it."

All through supper, Hurts kept giving Tom mean looks.

After supper, they all sat in the living room watching TV and discussing what they were going to do tomorrow. While Hurts had been waiting—angrily and anxiously—for Tom and Amanda to arrive at Lill's home, he had called Mr. Williams and told him of his plan. Mr. Williams liked it, and told him to do it—tomorrow, they would act as reporters for the St. Louis Post-Dispatch Newspaper, pretending that they were doing a featured story on girls born in St. Louis on Halloween. They would offer the three girls, family, and friends lodging and celebrations until the day after Halloween at the glorious Central West-end Chase Park Plaza Hotel—free of charge! The three girls would be safe, and Satan would be thwarted from kidnapping the Chosen one, whichever one that was.

Tired, but anxious about what tomorrow might bring, they all went to bed at nine-thirty.

Dressed in his usual sleeping clothes—a white T-shirt and gray sweatpants—Tom was lying up in bed reading a book. For some years

193

now, Tom had been wanting to read the book *War and Peace*. He felt that any person who wants to consider himself an educated person should read such worthy novels as *War and Peace*. Last year, Tom had finally purchased a paperback copy of it. The novel was long, and the sporadic reading of it that Tom gave to it was going slow, real slow. Tom found the story to be BORING. As many times as Tom had tried to give some real reading to it, he was only on page 92.

He had struggled through a page of the book and—feeling good about having accomplished that—was about to turn the page, when a light knocking came from his door.

Tom hoped that the person knocking upon his door would be Amanda. Ever since Amanda had told Tom about having had sex with Missy, Tom couldn't get the mental picture out of his head of them two in bed, enjoying each other's bodies. The image of this kept making Tom horny. He thought that Amanda might be horny, too.

"Come in," Tom said anxiously.

It wasn't Amanda. It was Hurts.

He had his suitcoat off, and the black leather shoulder-holster—and weapon—under his left armpit showed prominently against the contrast of the white shirt that he was wearing, with the collar of the shirt unbuttoned and the black tie loosened.

With a no nonsense, stern-looking face, he walked up to the side of the bed, pointed the index-finger of his right hand at Tom, and said sternly, "I want to know—right now, and no bullshit!—what you and Amanda were talking about."

Tom lowered the book in his hands and replied, "We said nothing, Jim—nothing of importance. We just talked."

Not satisfied with that reply, Hurts bellowed, "Don't hand me that, Mayor, 'cause I don't believe you … Now, what did you two talk about?"

"Frankly, Jim," Tom stated flatly. "What we discussed is none of your business."

"It is, too, my business, Mayor," Hurts stated angrily. "She's my daughter!—And you're going to tell me or I'm going to—" He stopped speaking, raised his left hand up, and with his right hand, began patting his shoulder-holster.

Tom was shocked. He couldn't believe what he was witnessing.

"I can't believe you!" Tom exclaimed. "I can't believe you! This is just the type of thing that Mr. Williams warned us about—that Satan would try and pit us against each other."

With his fisted hands on his hips, Hurts stated arrogantly, "I don't give a rat's ass what Williams said. I want to know what you two talked about."

"Fine, Jim," Tom replied. "Fine. Amanda's thinking about quitting school, and she's heartbroken at the thought of you being disappointed in her if she does quit."

"Why does she want to quit school?"

"I don't know," Tom replied. "All she said was that it was overwhelming."

"Well, what did you say?"

"I told her not to quit," Tom said. "I also told her that you loved her and would never be disappointed in her … There, Jim," Tom said. "Now you know—Are you happy now? Are you happy?"

"I'm never happy," Hurts stated arrogantly. He turned around and marched out of the room.

Tom brought the book back up to his face, but instead of beginning to read again, he tossed the book over the side of the bed, mumbling, "*War and Peace*. To hell with it."

Chapter Twenty-One

The next morning, Tuesday, October the twenty-eighth, Tom awoke at 6:00 AM. He felt like having a run. He donned his jogging clothes and tennis shoes and left his bedroom.

As he passed the bathroom, he could hear that the shower was on. He wondered who was in there taking a shower. He told himself that it couldn't be his mother—she doesn't rise from bed until about 8:00, and it couldn't be Jim. Jim doesn't take a bath. He always just washes and shaves at the sink. It had to be Amanda. Because of what had happened the night before between him and Jim, Tom tried to block out the image he had in his head of Amanda standing in the bathtub, naked, with hot, soapy water cascading down her slender body.

He quickly descended the stairs and went out the front door.

It was a beautiful fall morning. The sun was shining brightly. There was a light, warm breeze in the crisp air, and the leaves of the trees were coming into their full autumnal beauty.

Tom was gone for almost two hours. He had a most enjoyable run, slow and paced.

When he returned, he found them all in the kitchen. Lill was at the stove cooking, and still dressed in her full-length white nightgown, with her white robe over the nightgown, and in her white slippers. Hurts and Amanda were both sitting at the kitchen table drinking coffee. Hurts was wearing his old wrinkled dark-blue suit, and Amanda—and she looked H-O-T, hot!—was wearing a sleeveless red dress with matching high heeled shoes, and a thin gold chain and cross around her neck with matching dangling earrings.

Plates, cloth napkins, utensils, and glasses of orange juice were on the table.

"Did you have a good run, sweet-cheeks?" Hurts said, friendly enough.

"Yeah, it was good," Tom replied. He picked one of the glasses of orange juice and polished it off. After setting the empty glass back down on the table, Tom said, "You ought to start running, Jim."

Hurts gave a grunt and bellowed, "Any time you ever see me running, you'll know that my laxative has kicked in."

Amanda thought that was hysterical and burst out into laughter. Well, it was pretty funny—for no-humor Hurts to have said that.

"Breakfast is ready," Lill said, carrying two large, steaming plates, one of scrambled eggs and the other plate of bacon. Setting the plates upon the table, Lill said, "I have toast ready. I'll get that plate … Go ahead and start eating." Walking back to the counter by the stove, Lill said, "Tom, Jim and Amanda have agreed to help you get all the Halloween decorations up from the basement—and Charlie."

Charlie was Lill's scarecrow. Her beloved husband, Pat, rest his soul, had made it for her years ago. During Halloween, Charlie sat upon an old rocking-chair on the front porch, ready to greet all of the little Trick-or-Treaters.

The meal was delicious. They had to eat a bit fast, though. Hurts had told them that Mr. Williams was sending the limousine over at nine o'clock.

Rising from her chair, Lill said, "I better get to washing the dishes and skillets. I want to bathe and dress."

"Go ahead and take your bath, Lill," Amanda said. "I'll do the dishes. After eating that big meal, I'm stuffed. I need to work off some of those calories."

"Are you sure, dear?" Lill said. "You don't mind?"

"No, not at all," Amanda replied.

Lill left the kitchen and headed for the stairs to the second level of the house.

At exactly nine o'clock, the front doorbell chimed. Hurts made it a point to beat Tom to the door.

After opening the door, Hurts and Tom—Tom standing behind Hurts—saw an average-sized man with short brown hair, wearing a dark-colored suit and matching tie, and an overcoat the same as Mr. Williams had given them. Tom told himself that this guy must be one of Mr. Williams' "soldiers." In his right hand, he was holding a set of keys and in his left hand—holding it up by the hook of the clothes-hanger—a black chauffer's uniform with a matching cap. Across his chest, suspended there by a black strap from around his neck, was a .35mm camera.

Tom looked beyond this guy, and there, parked on the street in front of the house, was a block-long white limousine. It sparkled in the bright morning sun. Behind the limousine was a dark-blue Ford SUV. There was a man sitting behind the steering-wheel.

"The keys to the limousine, sir," the man said to Hurts, handing him the keys. Then he handed Hurts the clothes-hanger with that chauffer's uniform and cap on it. Lastly, he removed the camera from around his neck.

"Take that, will you, Tom?" Hurts said.

Tom took the camera.

"Thanks, pal," Hurts said to the man. He turned around and walked away.

There was a white folded piece of paper pinned to that chauffer's uniform. Hurts handed Tom the uniform, saying, "Read what that note says, Tom."

Tom did.

Tom was furious—boiling angry! The note read: *This uniform is for Tom Mayor.*

Giving Hurts the "evil-eye," Tom stated through grinding teeth, "This is YOUR doing!"

Smiling, Hurts said ever-so pleasantly, "Oh, now, Tom, would I do something like that?"

"Yes, you would!" Tom replied, snapping at him. "I don't want to be a damn chauffer—I want to be a reporter!"

Shaking his head and throwing his hands in the air, Hurts sighed. "Well, Tom, we all have our crosses to bear—or is that 'bare'?"

"I'm taking a shower!" Tom cried, turned, and stormed up the stairs.

Hurts was pleased.

Chapter Twenty-Two

They were all ready to go. Amanda and Hurts were both wearing the full-length black topcoats that Mr. Williams had given them to wear to hide the sheathed swords. Lill was wearing a pretty white dress of floral print, with an imitation pearl necklace around her neck and matching clip-on earrings.

They were all standing by the front door, waiting for Tom.

Hurts looked impatiently at his cheap Timex wristwatch, walked to the foot of the stairs, looked up, and shouted, "Come on, Tom. It's twenty-to-ten! Let's go."

About six minutes later, a reluctant Tom came down the stairs, wearing his full-length black topcoat over that chauffer's uniform and matching cap.

Upon seeing him, they all burst into laughter.

"Alright," Tom said sardonically. "Yeah, yeah, yeah."

Still laughing, Hurts said, "Here's the keys, Mr. Chauffer."

"Great," Tom mumbled, taking the keys. "Let's go."

The limousine was equally as beautiful on the inside as it was on the outside. The middle of it had two long, well-padded white leather seats that faced each other. The windows were tinted, and a retractable sunroof was above them.

"Open the door for us, Mr. Chauffer," Hurts said as they came abreast of the vehicle.

Tom opened the middle passenger's door and barked, "Just get in!"

Tom found the cab of the limousine quite impressive. The long, well-padded leather seat was also white, and there was a button on the dashboard to warm the seat. The dashboard had a phone and a GPS. The steering wheel was also of white leather and besides all of the other gizmos on it, there was a button that could control the window of tinted glass that divided the cab of the limousine from the passengers' section. Tom pressed it. After the window retracted, Hurts said, "Do you know how to get to Michele Johnston's parents' house?"

"Yeah," Tom said. "I looked up the address on my laptop before coming back downstairs."

"Let's do this," Hurts stated.

At first, Tom had some fears about driving that limousine. It was so long, and he had never done anything like that before—it was like driving a semi. He had to adjust his driving to the length of the vehicle. But he quickly got the hang of it, and then he began enjoying driving it. It was a most 'smooth' riding vehicle, and it began to feel like he was in command of a very high-tech piece of equipment—like flying an airplane or something.

As Tom drove, he listened to how they were going to proceed with this. Mr. Williams had told Hurts that they had better use pseudonyms. Hurts didn't know what that was, and Mr. Williams had replied, "Fake names."

They decided that Amanda would do most of the talking. She would be Reporter Amanda Williams, which had really, silently, ticked-off Hurts: *Why was she using Williams' name? Why not his name? Amanda Hurts.* Lill would be the Senior Feature Editor, Lill Smith. With that .35mm camera hanging from his neck, Hurts would be the photographer, James Jones, and Tom—well, it was decided that he didn't need a fake name, since he wouldn't talk, and with being only a chauffeur.

Tom got on Highway 55, driving south. At the Reavis Barracks exit, he began driving east. One block up Reavis Barracks Road, he turned right onto Lemay Ferry Road and began driving south again. He drove for about five miles, passing the South County Mall and then crossing over the bridge of the Meramec River. The Meramec River is the line of demarcation that separates St. Louis County from the township of Arnold.

Arnold, up until about twenty-five years ago, was still pretty much a rural place—not much there at all.

Michele Johnston's parents lived one mile away from the river—and all of them were a bit shocked when Tom pulled that long, sparkling white, expensive, fancy limousine into that dump of a trailer park.

The three-foot-high and three-foot-wide wooden sign to the south of the entrance of the trailer park read, in black block letters: **ARNOLD ESTATES**. But the sign was so old, sun-bleached, and rotting, that it actually read: **NOLD ES ATE**.

The whole place was a hodge-podge of old, dilapidated, rusting, metal trailers. Some were singles; some were doubles—two singles welded into a larger single. Some had rotting wooden porches attached to them, with rusting tin roofs. One place had a large, deep plastic pool with a green-skim of algae floating on top of still water. Old cars and pick-up trucks dominated the neighborhood—some of them were up on cement blocks in the grassless, fallow front yards—and of the place, poverty screamed out at you.

Michele's parents lived at the end of the block. Next door to their place, a very mean-looking pit-bull was tethered to a dying tree by a chain and kept barking viciously.

Looking out the passenger's window of the limousine at Michele's parents' trailer, Hurts said, "Damn, these people are 'dirt poor' … Let's do it."

They exited the limousine.

As they all began ascending the three-step, rickety wooden porch of the trailer, Lill leaned on the rail for support; it wobbled, and Lill started to fall backwards. Fortunately, Tom was behind her, and when she shot backwards, Tom reached out and grabbed her, holding her up.

Their front porch was furnished with three dingy-white plastic chairs and a matching table. On top of the table were four empty beer bottles and a black plastic ashtray filled with smoked butts. The front door to the trailer was of thin white metal and a screen-door was in front of it—the bottom half of that screen-door was missing its screen.

With Amanda in the middle—Hurts to the left of her, and Lill to her right, and of course Tom trailing behind them all—Hurts opened the creaking screen-door and pounded a few times on the inner door.

Three long minutes passed before the inner door slowly opened.

From behind the screen-door stood a woman in her mid-thirties. She was about five-feet-five-inches-tall, with a stocky build, almost to the point of being fat, with a round, plain-looking face, and waist-long, stringy black hair that matched the color of her eyes and eyebrows—the eyes had a vacantness and fear to them. She was dressed in an old gray sweatshirt and tattered old jeans.

"Yes?" she said softly, with just a trace of caution.

"Mrs. Johnston?" Amanda stated, enthusiastically and cheerfully.

"Yes," she repeated, equally as cautiously.

"Hi, my name is Amanda Williams," Amanda said. "I'm a reporter with the Post-Dispatch Newspaper."

The woman looked beyond them, to her left, and saw the limousine parked upon the uneven, cracking concrete street, and her eyes widened in disbelief.

"You have a daughter by the name of Michele, right?" Amanda continued.

"Yes," she repeated, a look of confusion, concern, and questioning upon her face. She looked like a low-witted person trying to quickly access the situation and decide if she should cuss them and slam the door on them or continue listening.

"She was born on Halloween, the thirty-first of October, right?" Amanda stated.

"Yes, but what—?" she started to say, agitation and anger replacing questioning and fear.

"Well, Mrs. Johnston," Amanda said, interrupting her, "we have something great for you and your daughter. It's spectacular!—like winning the lottery!"

Now, she was interested.

Turning to Lill, Amanda said, "May I introduce Mrs. Lillian Smith. She is the Senior Editor of Featured Stories for the Post-Dispatch."

The woman nodded at Lill, and Lill nodded back at her.

Amanda now turned to Hurts and said, "And this is our photographer, Mr. James Jones … Mrs. Johnston, may we come in for a moment and explain to you what this is all about—and about all we have planned for your daughter and family?"

"Yes," she said anxiously, pushing open the screen-door.

They entered—Tom entering last and feeling very much left out of all of this—being only a chauffeur!

The inside of the place was more pleasant than Hurts would have thought—cramped, but not bad. The ceiling was a white drop-ceiling, and the floor was light-colored wood; in earlier days, the floor had had a high-polished shine to it, but now it was in need of a good waxing. The kitchen was to Hurts' right. Under a small, drape-less window, against the wall of the closet-sized kitchen, was a white Formica-top table with an L-shaped, well-padded, red leather bench. Directly across from that—no more than six feet between—was a stove, a refrigerator, and a white Formica-top counter with a microwave on it and several bottles of assorted whiskey. An ashtray, a pack of cigarettes, and lighter lay beside the whiskey bottles.

The living room was to Hurts' left. The walls were of a cheap imitation wood paneling. Below a window that was larger than the window in the kitchen—which had old white mini-blinds on it and a thin white drape—was a long beige cloth couch that sagged in the middle. In front of the couch was a worn dark-stained coffee-table. At the end of the couch was a wooden end table. On it were a shaded lamp, a coffee cup, an ashtray—filled with smoked butts—and another pack of cigarettes. Directly across from the couch, was a floor-to-ceiling color TV set.

Their home smelled of nicotine, whiskey, and of someone who was struggling to get through daily life.

"Would you like to sit down?" she offered, motioning towards the living room.

"Thank you," Amanda replied, and they all sat on the couch. Having nowhere else to sit, the woman stood in front of them, in front of the coffee table.

"Now, Mrs. Johnston," Amanda began, "we're doing a featured story on children in St. Louis who were born on Halloween. There are three such children, and your daughter is one of them. We are offering to have you and your family, as we are offering this to all three children who were born on Halloween, to be our guests at the Chase Park Plaza Hotel, beginning today and ending Friday. Every night we will sponsor a dance, with prizes to win, and on Halloween, we're having a grand costume ball. Each of the three girls born on Halloween will compose a speech on what it's like to have been born on Halloween, and the one who has the best costume and the best speech will win a cash prize of fifteen-hundred dollars ... Now, Mrs. Johnston," Amanda then said. "Do you think this would be okay with your husband?"

"Oh, yeah," she replied, most eagerly. "He will—he needs a vacation bad. He works real long hours at the gas station up the street—he's the mechanic," she said, emphasizing him being a "mechanic" and looking directly at Tom.

"Great!" Amanda said. "Would there be a problem with getting Michele a three-day leave of absence from school? We would like to pick her up as soon as possible."

"Michele gets school here," she said. "Would you like to talk to her?"

"Yes," Amanda replied. "That would be great."

They all rose from the couch and followed Mrs. Johnston down the narrow hallway.

At the end of the hallway, they all stood in front of a narrow wooden door. A little more than midway up the door was a black cloth tacked and draped across the door. In large, sparkling gold letters were the words: WELCOME TO SLYTHERIN HOUSE.

Hurts said to himself: *What the hell is a Slytherin House?*

Hurts and the rest of them were about to enter a room that all dreams are made of—one of make-believe; one of imagination; one of struggle; one of pain and suffering; one of hope, prayers and love.

They were all a bit taken aback by the room. It was small and crowded—desk and chair, bed, two wooden bookshelves, a wooden dresser, a small TV on top of a wooden stand in the corner of the room, and another smaller wooden dresser with a mirror and chair in front of it. But what truly made the room seem so small and crowded—and magical—was all of the Harry Potter stuff, that character from J. K. Rowling's novels. The walls and even the ceiling were festooned with posters of scenes and characters from the books and movies of Harry Potter. There was a poster of Harry dressed in a black robe, holding a wand in one hand; one of Hermione Granger; one of Ron Weasley, and of Dumbledore, and on and on. On top of the desk and on top of both dressers were tiny figurines of many of the characters. Leaning against the side of one of the dressers was a broomstick, but this broomstick was not for sweeping, but for flying. On the top shelf of one of the bookshelves were seven paperback books, all of the Harry Potter novels written by J. K. Rowling. On the shelf below that were several DVDs, which were the movies of Harry Potter. In the southeast corner of the room stood a full-size poster of Hermione Granger, the young girl in the Harry Potter books and movies.

Yes, the room was quite impressive—and magical.

And there, by the window, was the wheelchair, positioned more for lying down than for sitting upright—and in it was Michele. She was wearing a bright yellow knit pullover sweater/blouse and black jeans. She looked like her mother: same long dark hair and dark eyes and eyebrows. Unlike her mother, though, she was wafer-thin. Her arms, hands and legs seemed twisted, and seemed to move about uncontrollably. Saliva was coming from her mouth.

"Michele," her mother said cheerfully, walking to her. "I have a wonderful surprise for you." She wiped the saliva from Michele's mouth with the sleeve of her left arm, saying, "These people are gonna tell you about it."

Amanda approached Michele, bent over a bit, and said warmly and enthusiastically, "Hi, Michele! … You must be a big Harry Potter fan."

"Yes," her mother said, brushing strands of hair from Michele's face with her hand. "Her dream is to someday go to Orlando Resort, Disneyland, in Florida."

Hurts told himself that whatever other faults this woman might have, that she definitely loved her daughter.

"That would be wonderful," Amanda said. "Well, I have something also …."

As Amanda spoke with Michele, Hurts motioned for her mother to come over to him.

She did.

Hurts quietly asked her what was wrong with her daughter.

"MS," she replied sadly.

Hurts told her that he was sorry and then asked her to have Amanda return to them.

Amanda did, and Hurts, Tom and Amanda exchanged words.

Amanda walked back over to Michele, bent over again in front of her, and said, "I have a change of plans for you, Michele. Because you are so very, very special, we are going to send your mom, dad, and you to Orlando Resort, Disneyland, for two weeks."

Michele began jumping up and down with joy in the wheelchair. In a weak-sounding voice, she cried, "Mom! Mom!"

"Oh, thank you!" her mother said, rejoicing and crying.

Amanda placed her closed hands on her hips, and said brusquely, "Well, we're not muggles, are we, Michele?!"

Hurts said to himself: *What the hell is a muggle?*

Chapter Twenty-Three

All of them were back sitting in the limousine again in front of Mrs. Johnston's trailer. Hurts was sitting in the back seat that faced the cab of the limousine, Amanda and Lill were sitting in the seat that faced Hurts, and Tom, because he was the chauffer, was sitting behind the steering wheel, but with his body turned so he could see Lill, Amanda, and Hurts. They were silent. They all had mixed emotions about what had just happened. On the one hand, they were all happy about what they had done, but on the other hand, they were all sad as well.

Tom finally broke the silence saying, "Yeah, you were right, Jim. Even Satan wouldn't take that girl as the Chosen One."

"Actually," Hurts replied, "I don't think that little girl could even have a baby. Poor kid."

"I'm going to cry," Lill said.

Amanda placed her arm around the back of Lill's neck.

"That was a mighty nice thing you did, Tom," Hurts said.

"Yeah," Tom replied, "I'll call the travel agency I used when Mom and I went to Europe. I'll prepay with twenty thousand dollars. That should cover all of their expenses. I'll tell the guy to make it anonymous—never say where the money came from."

They were all silent again.

Then Hurts said, "Come on, Tom. Let's get the hell out of here. This place is just too damn sad."

"Yeah," Tom replied, turning back to the steering wheel.

"Do you know where you're going, Tom?" Hurts asked.

"Oh, yeah," Tom replied, starting the car. "Eve Taylor lives in my neck of the woods."

Tom crossed over the river again and began driving north on Lemay Ferry Road. When he had come to Reavis Barracks Road again, he turned right. Eve Taylor's parents' house was about a half a block up Reavis Barracks, on the south side of it, at 865 Rainbow in the Southside Estates.

Their home was only several blocks south from Tom and Lill's home. Of course, the homes there were much newer than the homes where Tom and Lill lived. These homes, all of them ranch-style brick houses, had been built in the late '50's.

Hurts hated the County—no curbs; no sidewalks; houses too spread apart; and with people who were all just too damn uppity for Hurts' blood.

Tom parked the limousine at the curb-less street in front of Mr. and Mrs. Taylor's house. It was beautiful—not ostentatious, but nice, middleclass.

The front yard of their house was about a quarter of a half-acre long and wide, and very well maintained. A one-car garage was at the east-end of the house; a pristine cement driveway that had swirls in it lay before them. A cement sidewalk was adjacent to the north side of the driveway. Halfway up the driveway, the sidewalk curved inward to the west, and then curved again north, and came to a stop at the cement covered porch. A three-foot-high and three-foot-wide rock bed flanked both sides of the porch. Although out of season, finely trimmed rose bushes adorned the beds. A dwarf dogwood tree was to the west of the house.

The wooden front door of the house was painted a high-gloss red, with an oval stained-glass window in the middle of it.

Halloween decorations and carved, ominous-looking pumpkins consumed the front porch. Along both sides of the sidewalk, positioned about three feet apart, were solar nightlights stuck in the ground. Each of these had the head of an orange pumpkin.

Seeing these, Lill said, "Oh, those lights look so pretty. I wish we had them for our front yard, Tom."

"I'll make a note of it, Mom," Tom replied noncommittally.

"Okay, people," Hurts stated. "Let's do this."

They exited the limousine and walked up the sidewalk to the front door.

Hurts pressed the button of the doorbell.

They heard it chiming from inside.

There was a glass storm-door in front of the front door. A few seconds later, the front door opened.

Through the glass storm-door, a woman in her late thirties, but who looked much younger, said, "Yes, may I help you?" She was wearing a white blouse and black dress pants. Her hair was light-brown and was cut short, just below her ears. Her face was angular-shaped, with a small, straight nose and thin lips, colored and accented with red lipstick.

Amanda immediately went into her pitch about them, except for Tom, being reporters and about doing a featured story on her daughter, Eve, because of her being born on Halloween.

The woman did not seem to be all that impressed, but she invited them inside to tell her more.

They stepped inside.

They stepped upon the high-gloss wooden floor of the hallway. Directly in front of them, about twelve feet away, was the door-less entrance to the kitchen. They could see an oval-shaped dark wood table with matching ladderback chairs. Beyond the table and chairs, against the wall, were two glass French doors that led to the cement patio and to the back yard, which was about a half-acre long and wide.

To their immediate left was a waist-high dark-wood parapet that extended to half the length of the room: it had four spindles on it that reached the ceiling. Beyond the parapet was the living-room with wall-to-wall plush white carpet. A long elegant-looking white sofa sat against the inner wall, beneath a gold-framed picture of a serene pasture by a lake. A winged-chair of the same design as the sofa sat by the large bay window which was framed by thin white curtains that reached from floor-to-ceiling. A white brick fireplace took up the east wall, with an ornate mirror that hung above it. At the end of the sofa was a dark-wood end table with a shaded light-blue glass-based lamp on it, and a gold-framed picture of Mrs. Taylor, a man, and two girls standing in front of the Eiffel Tower.

Sitting upon the sofa, Mrs. Taylor said, "Will you be seated?"

Amanda and Lill sat on the sofa next to Mrs. Taylor; Hurts took the winged-back chair. Having nowhere else to sit, and Tom had gotten the impression from Mrs. Taylor that the invitation to sit had not applied to him—what with him being only a chauffeur. So, Tom just stood there by the front door.

How rude, Tom thought silently.

Amanda went into her speech about what this was all about, and about wanting her daughter, Eve, and the family to spend the next three days and nights at the luxurious Chase Park Plaza Hotel—and about the costume parties and the fifteen hundred dollars prize money for the best costume and best speech.

Shaking her head, Mrs. Taylor told Amanda that most of what she was asking was out of the question. She was not about to remove her two children from school for three days, and her husband could not just take off work for three days—he was the office manager of the Laclede Gas Company downtown.

"Why, just tonight alone," Mrs. Taylor said, "Eve is on the girls' basketball team at school, and she has a game tonight against the girls' basketball team of Kirkwood Middle School. No, tonight is definitely out. I would like my children to take advantage of all opportunities that come their way, but no. I'll speak with my husband, and perhaps we can come tomorrow evening and Thursday evening."

Holding up the camera that was suspended from the black strap around his neck, Hurts said, "Can we come to the game tonight? I'd like to take some pictures."

"Yes, of course," she replied.

Shortly thereafter, they said goodbye to Mrs. Taylor and left.

As they were walking back to the limousine, Lill said, "Wasn't her living room just gorgeous?"

"I didn't see anything so hot about it," Tom replied flatly.

"Oh, but that fireplace was so white and beautiful," Lill stated.

"Our fireplace is just as nice as hers," Tom snapped at her.

"What's your problem, Tom?" Lill stated angrily.

"Oh, Jim's right. County people are too uppity."

"Well, we live in the County," Lill said. "Are we 'uppity'?"

"I can afford to be 'uppity'," Tom countered. "I have money!"

"Well, when I find O'Malley's gold, I'll be the richest man in the world!" Hurts barked at them arrogantly.

"I-I—Oh, I got nothing," Amanda sighed.

"Don't you worry, Baby-girl," Hurts stated with much hubris. "I'm going to buy the biggest mansion in the world. It will have fifteen bathrooms, and each will have gold toilet paper. We'll be wiping our butts with gold toilet paper. Now, that's rich!"

"Now, that's disgusting," Tom replied.

"Yes," Lill said. "Let's change the subject."

And they did.

Sitting back in the limousine, they discussed how they should proceed.

"Alright, look," Hurts said. "We don't yet know what the parents of that-that Phosphorous gal is—" Hurts stopped speaking. Thinking. Then he said, "Why does the name of that girl bug me so much? Where have I heard that name before?! I can't remember." He thought for a second or two longer, and then he gave up. "Oh, well," he said. "Anyway, I'm afraid that we're going to have to split."

"But, Uncle Jim," Amanda stated, protesting. "Uncle Williams told us to stay together."

"Well, I don't give a damn about what 'Uncle Teddy' said," Hurts replied sardonically. "We have to decide here. Again, if the parents of that Phosphorous girl agree to stay at the Chase, then someone is going to have to stay with that family tonight to make it all look legit—and I think that should be you and Lill. Williams told me that he knows enough residents there who have children, that he can get it together to have a big party. So, Tom and me will go to Eve's basketball game tonight. I'll drive my car, and after the game is over, I'll come back here and watch the house."

"You're going to stay here all night by yourself?!" Tom cried.

"Yeah," Hurts replied.

"I'll leave the limousine at the school and come with you," Tom said.

"You don't have to do that, Tom," Hurts said.

"No, I don't have to do it, Jim," Tom replied. "But you're my partner—so, I'm doing it."

"Okay, if you want to, Tom," Hurts said, feeling an unusual warm feeling of gratitude towards Tom. "Okay, then, let's do this. On to Phosphorous' house."

Chapter Twenty-Four

Tom drove the limousine to the end of the subdivision and turned left onto Reavis Barracks Road again, driving west. A block down, he came to a stop at a red light at the intersection of Reavis Barracks Road and Lemay Ferry Road. The street that Tom was on, Reavis Barracks Road, was two lanes both ways. Tom was in the outer lane.

He was becoming agitated that the red stop light was taking so long to turn green and was about to curse out loud when—Bam!

The car behind the limousine bumped into the rear of the vehicle. Not all that hard, but enough to jolt them all in their seats.

"What the hell!" Tom shouted.

Engine revving and tires screeching, the car sped backwards and then drove up alongside the limousine.

It was a fairly new-looking silver 4-door Kia.

The passenger's side window rolled down and there in the passenger's seat, sat a man with black hair and black sunglasses. He was wearing a black topcoat similar to the ones that Tom, Hurts and Amanda had on.

He stared straight ahead. Then he removed the sunglasses, turned his head, and looked at Tom through the glass of the driver's side window of the limousine. His eyes were totally black.

"He's a demon!" Tom cried.

"Lord, help us!" Lill pleaded, making the sign of the cross.

The light finally turned green.

"Get us out of here, Tom!" Hurts screamed.

Tom's left foot hammered down hard on the gas pedal of the limousine. The vehicle kicked gently into high gear and sped off through the intersection and down Reavis Barracks Road.

Yes, the limousine was a 'smooth' riding vehicle, but it was so long of a vehicle, it was not made for fast speeds. It was simply slow, compared to other cars. The Kia easily kept pace with the limousine.

Hurts saw that, besides a driver and that other guy in the front seat, there were three more men all wearing sunglasses and black topcoats in the rear seat.

Hurts shouted to Tom, "Give a hard left turn to the steering wheel, Tom, and ram those guys!"

"I don't want to do that, Jim!" Tom exclaimed. "This isn't even our car."

About twenty feet ahead was the intersection of Reavis Barracks Road and Union Road. At the corner, on the right side of the road, was a small strip mall—a parking lot, with a family-owned restaurant, an auto supply shop, a pet store, and an antique store.

"Pull into that parking lot, Tom!" Hurts ordered. "If it's a fight that they want, let's give it to them!" Looking at Amanda, he said, "Are you ready for this?"

Brushing the sides of that black topcoat open, she patted the hilt of her sword and said, "I was born ready."

Tom turned into the parking lot and threw the vehicle into Park.

All heads turned left and looked anxiously and nervously out of the windows of the limousine.

The car hadn't followed them into the parking lot—didn't even make any attempt to do that.

They all watched as the car passed through the intersection and entered the entrance of Highway 55 north at Reavis Barracks Road and disappeared.

"Whew!" Tom sighed, much relieved, turning and positioning his body so that he could now look at them in the back seats. "What was that all about?"

At that moment, Hurts' cellphone chimed. It didn't ring, it 'chimed'. From past experience, Hurts knew that a chime meant a text message. The only text messages Hurts ever got were advertisements, so he just ignored them. Well, he couldn't get his fingers to text back anyway. But, for some unknown reason, he wanted to see this text.

He reached into the right pocket of that black topcoat, removed his cellphone, flipped it open, pressed the button for text messages and read it.

He exploded with volcanic anger.

"Why, that no-good, son-of-a-bitch!" he screamed. "That no-good, son—"

"What is it, Uncle Jim?!" Amanda cried, concerned.

Still looking at his cellphone, Hurts said, "It's him! It's Satan … He says: 'You have been warned. Stop now—or else! Your move, Mr. Hurts!'" Looking up at Amanda, Hurts screamed, "Why, that no-good, dirty—"

"Calm down, Jim," Tom said. "Calm down. He's taunting you—trying to get your goat."

"Well, he's got it!" Hurts barked angrily at Tom.

"You know, Jim," Tom began, "I think we just struck a nerve with him. Perhaps, the house that we just left is the house of, you know, the Chosen One."

"I think you're right, Tom," Hurts agreed.

"What do we do now, Uncle Jim?" Amanda asked.

"We stay the course," Hurts replied adamantly. "We keep with the plan. That's what we do." Hurts looked towards the floorboard of the limousine and said, "Okay, you SOB. You know our plan, so you know our next move. So, why don't you meet us there? At Phosphorus'. I dare you! … Okay, Tom, on to Phosphorus'

Chapter Twenty-Five

As the demons had done, Tom, too, crossed the intersection and got on Highway 55 at the Reavis Barracks entrance and headed north, back into the city. He crossed over River De Peres' bridge and exited the highway at Loughborough Avenue. Then he drove west on it.

The Holly Hills neighborhood runs east and west from Highway 55 at Loughborough to Morganford Road. The distance of it is about three miles long and about five miles wide, encompassing several streets and the historic Carondelet Park.

Most of the homes in Holly Hills were built after the year 1927.

Loughborough runs parallel with Carondelet Park, and the homes of the street on the north side of the park are all two-or three-story Tudor-style brick mansions, all worth about half-a-million. The houses on the south side of the park are nice, but not nearly worth that much.

Phosphorus Reed's parents' house was on a short, one-sided block at the west-end of the park. All the houses on the block looked pretty much the same—red-brick two-story homes with a three-widow dormer in the middle of the second roof, and both roofs being half-mooned-shaped, orange clay tiles. The windows of the houses were long and narrow with wooden frames, often painted white. The supports of the covered cement porches, were of two large, wide columns at both ends of the porches, made of a mixture of cement and white boulders. Nice houses—especially beautiful at this time of the year, with all of the tall maple trees that lined both sides of the curbed sidewalk and street.

The cement sidewalks to the houses were in the middle of the front yards. The front yards were short and two-tiered. The first tier was four steps high, grass, now brown in color, on both sides of the sidewalk. This leveled off for about five feet—more grass—then the second four-step tier began. It leveled off again for about another five feet, and the sidewalks stopped abruptly at the cement three-step porches.

All the houses were set close together, and all faced the park that was directly across the street. There were eight houses to the block, and all of them faced east. The old man whose mind and body Satan now possessed again lived five blocks south of there. Mr. and Mrs. Reed lived in the last of the eight houses on the block.

The detached garages for each house were set at the end of the back yards and faced the alley.

Tom parked the long limousine on the street in front of Mr. and Mrs. Reed's house.

They exited the limousine and began climbing the steps.

Hurts was very winded and out-of-breath by the time they had reached the front door of the Reeds' house.

There was a white metal-framed glass storm door in front of a heavy-looking wooden-paneled front door, which had four small windows at the top of the door.

Hurts pressed the button of the doorbell. No reply. He waited a few minutes and pressed the button again. Still, no reply. He then opened the storm door and pounded on the front door a few times with the closed palm of his right hand. Still, no reply.

Giving up, Hurts said, "Well, I guess they're not home."

"What do we do now, Uncle Jim?" Amanda asked.

Feeling tired, hungry and disgusted, Hurts turned around, saying, "I don't know."

He looked across the street into the park. From the height of standing on the porch, Hurts could see one of the two manmade lakes of the park. An old man with a boy were fishing at the far end of the lake, and a line of Canadian geese were swimming peacefully across the south end of the lake.

With regret, Hurts thought of the few times that he had brought his two daughters to the park when they had been very young to play on the swings. He had always moaned and groaned about having to do it.

"It's beautiful, isn't it?" Lill said, standing next to him and looking toward the park.

"Yes," he replied mindlessly, still thinking about his daughters, about what he had lost with them.

Looking at the bank of woods at the northeast side of the park, Hurts now thought of O'Malley.

"Say, Lill," Hurts said, turning to Lill and pointing to the woods. "When O'Malley and the other leprechauns kidnapped you that night to get their gold back, is that where they kept you?"

"Yes!" she replied angrily.

"All day?!" he asked.

"Yes!" she stated with equal anger.

"And no one saw you?"

"No," she replied, and began shaking the fist of her right hand at the woods. "And those damn-damn little devils had me tied to a tree with a piece of tape over my mouth—and they had pulled the bottom of my pajamas down!”

Hurts laughed, remembering that.

“Well, what now, Jim?” Tom said.

Hurts thought for a moment and then said, “Well, again, I think we’re going have to split—you, Amanda, and Lill coming back here tonight and seeing if you can get that girl and her mom and dad to agree to go to the Chase, and I’ll cover that basketball game at Eve’s school.”

“But, Uncle Jim,” Amanda began to object. “Uncle Williams said—”

“Enough, Amanda!” Hurts replied, snapping at her. “I don’t want to hear it.” Turning to Tom, he said, “What does this guy,” pointing to the front door, “do for a living, anyway?”

“He owns his own small computer company, Reed’s Electronics, in Fenton.”

Hurts now turned to Amanda, who was not at all pleased with Hurts for having snapped at her and said, “Amanda, get on your cellphone and see if you can get this guy’s work number—please.”

Leaving the purse on her right shoulder by its long brown strap, Amanda swung her floppy brown purse to the front of her and fished out her cellphone. She did a few strokes on the face of the phone, and then she thumbed-typed on it. A few seconds later, she said, “Got it.”

“Okay, now call him and see if you guys can come back here tonight—and give your all, honey. You know what to do.”

Amanda dialed the number.

After Amanda had spoken with Mr. Reed’s secretary, she spoke with him. First, she identified herself, and then she went into her speech. She told him everything—and she really piled it on deep, too. Hurts was so proud of her: *What a great liar she is! A chip off the old block.*

During their conversation, they heard Amanda say: “Oh, I’m sorry to hear that … At Barnes-Jewish Hospital? … Oh, good … Well, this would be such a wonderful opportunity for your daughter—and fun … Well, what if I and my two associates stop by your home tomorrow? Would that be possible? … At two? … Oh, that’s wonderful, Mr. Reed … Yes, see you tomorrow.”

“What’s the story?” Hurts asked.

“Phosphorus is in the hospital,” Amanda stated. “Last week, she had her tonsils removed. She’s being released tomorrow. He seemed excited about everything I said. We can see them tomorrow.”

Nodding his head, Hurts said, "Okay, that sounds good." He thought for a moment and continued speaking, "She should be safe tonight—being in a hospital. So, we'll all go to that basketball game tonight. It's at seven tonight, right?"

"Yeah," Tom said.

"I'm hungry," Amanda said.

"You know, Amanda," Tom said, smiling. "For someone who eats as much as you do—how do you kept that sexy, slender shape of yours?"

Hurts shot Tom a mean, deadly look.

Placing her right hand behind her head, placing her left hand on her left hip, and taking a flirtatious pose, Amanda replied, "Because I eat nutritiously, and I work out."

"Yeah, yeah, yeah," Hurts interjected sardonically. "Well, I am hungry, too—and I don't work out."

"Well, now," Lill said. "I got chicken wings and chicken legs in the refrigerator." Looking at Amanda, she said, "Because you're so health conscious, Amanda, I'll cook some of them in peanut oil, and I'll deep fry the rest. We'll have baked potatoes, green beans, and, oh, I have that chocolate cake I bought last week at the store."

"It sounds good to me, Lill," Amanda said.

"Okay," Hurts said. "Let's go."

"Well, I'm not wearing this damn monkey suit," Tom stated resolutely, pinching the chest of the chauffeur uniform, "to that basketball game tonight. No way."

"You have to," Hurts stated arrogantly.

"Why?" Tom demanded to know.

Wanting to be mean to Tom, Hurt replied rudely, "Because you ain't nothing more than a chauffeur!"

Chapter Twenty-Six

The supper was delicious. They all enjoyed it immensely. Amanda helped Lill prepare and serve it. Lill, wanting to be formal, wanted to serve the meal in their dining room, but Tom, Amanda, and Hurts, especially Hurts, wanted to eat in the kitchen—it's more friendly and homey. So, they had eaten in the kitchen, at the kitchen table, talking and at times even laughing.

Hurts and Amanda started talking about the unexpected and phenomenal success of the St. Louis Blues winning the Stanley Cup. Mr. Williams always gave them tickets to front row seats of every hometown game played. Although they had enjoyed that, their favorite team sport was baseball. Baseball, to them, was the only team sport with individuality to it: one-on-one, pitcher against batter. Hurts and Amanda loved all sports, but they both had a passion for boxing—one-on-one, alone, two people duking it out, may the best man win.

Knowing that Tom and Lill didn't care for sports and feeling that she and Hurts were leaving them out of the conversation, she said, to Lil, "When I have some free time, I'm going to travel like you and Tom have—to Europe. I bet that was great."

"Oh, Paris was so beautiful," Lill said emphatically, cherishing the sweet memory of it.

"Yes, it was," Tom replied.

"Where would you like to travel to, Uncle Jim?" Amanda asked.

"Nowhere," Hurts replied flatly. "I've done my traveling—to Vietnam. Nothing but damn jungles, rain, getting shot at, and having to wipe your ass with leaves. No thanks."

"Here we go again about toilet paper," Tom said, rolling his eyes. "You know, Jim. I'm going to go to Costco and buy you a semi-truck full of toilet paper—gold toilet paper."

"And I'd take it, too!" Hurts bellowed.

They all laughed.

At 6:15, they all stood at the hall closet, next to the front door. All of them were wearing the same clothes that they had been wearing throughout the day: Hurts was wearing his dark-blue suit, Amanda was wearing that red dress, Lill was wearing that white dress of floral design, and Tom—well, Tom was wearing that chauffeur's uniform with matching cap.

From the closet, Tom first handed Hurts and Amanda their swords; then he handed them their full-length black topcoat. After putting on his sword and topcoat, they left.

Once more, Tom got on Highway 55, driving south; and once more, he exited the highway at Reavis Barracks Road, driving east. At Lemay Ferry Road, he turned right, driving south again.

He drove on Lemay Ferry Road for three miles, passing Mehlville High School on his left. A mile later, he made a left, turning onto Buckley Road. Mehlville Middle School was one mile up on the left.

Mehlville Middle School, on Buckley, was one of three middle schools in the Mehlville School District. It was a fairly new building—a block long, one-story, red-brick, half-an-H-shaped building. It ran north and south and had a student body of three hundred kids. The school's small gymnasium comprised the whole south-end of the outer leg of the building.

Because of the limousine's length, Tom knew that he couldn't park it in one of the regular parking spots, so he parked it parallel to the curb near the circular-roof entrance to the building.

It was almost dark. There was a chill in the crisp, windy night air—and something else. The air seemed electrified. It was eerie. It was as if this was a defining moment. This eeriness was felt by all four of them as they entered the main entrance of the building.

Feeling like an outsider, or an uninvited guest to a party, they walked down the long hallway to the entrance of the gymnasium, passing the seemingly endless line of lockers on both sides, and then the boys' and the girls' locker-rooms.

They passed through the three open metallic-framed doors of the gymnasium and stepped into the high-polished, light-colored wooden floor. The gymnasium ran east and west. The retractable wooden bleachers paralleled each other and consumed the north and south walls. A row of tinted small-paned windows outlined the upper walls of the room. Suspended from the metallic-beamed roof of the gymnasium were two thick glass basketball backboards with baskets, that faced each other at opposite ends of the court. The electronic scoreboard was high up against the west wall.

The place was packed with people—the majority of them were loud, energetic, if not just plain rowdy. There were students from both schools, parents, a few teachers, two young, no-nonsense-looking female coaches in their early twenties, and two adult females of stocky build and who both were wearing referee's garb—vertical black-and-white striped shirts and beige pants.

Lill spotted Mrs. Taylor standing over by the south bleachers. They all walked over to her.

She was standing there with a man and two young girls. She introduced them to Amanda, Hurts and Lill (but not Tom—what with he being only a chauffeur, which made Tom boiling angry).

The man, Jerry, was her husband. He was a quite handsome man, and one could easily tell by his assertive demeanor and speech that he was a man of authority and education. He was about as tall as Tom, five-feet-seven-inches, and he had raven-black hair, matching eyebrows and eyes. His face was perfectly symmetrical, and he had a captivating smile and presence that said: *Yes, I know I'm handsome.* He was wearing a pair of gray dress pants, a white dress shirt, and a pullover black sweatshirt with writing on it, in white letters: MEHLVILLE MIDDLE SCHOOL—GO PANTHERS!

Although one could tell that the two young girls were the children of these two people, they looked more like the mother than the father—light-brown hair and an angular-shaped face. The smaller girl, and younger one, was named Tereasa. She was wearing white jeans and a pullover light-pink blouse, and she had a pink ribbon in her hair.

Then there was Eve.

Eve, like most children her age, was in her own world—a world dominated by "Look at me. I'm all that matters. Me. Me. Me."

She was about three inches less than five feet tall, slender, and at that awkward age of not being at all comfortable with all of the fast-coming changes to her body and emotions and with not being beautiful just yet, but that day would definitely come, soon.

She was dressed in the school's basketball team's wear—a loose-fitting T-shirt, shorts, knee-high white socks, and white tennis shoes. The T-shirt and shorts were gold with a black stripe on both sides of the clothes. Above the chest area of the T-shirt, written in white letters, was: PANTHERS. Under that, and also on the back, was a large numeral 1, also written in white.

Several times, as Amanda was speaking with Mr. and Mrs. Taylor, she tried to motion to Hurts to take pictures of them, but he seemed to be oblivious to this. Finally, Amanda said, feigning good humor, "Well, Mr. Photographer. How about some pictures?"

"What?" Hurts replied, confused. "Oh, yes," he quickly stated. He raised the camera hanging from his neck by the strap, pointed it at the family, and said, "Smile!"

The game began exactly at 7:00. It was a six-on-six game. Both girls who were playing Center for their respective teams—both being the tallest girls on both teams—took center court, squared off anxiously, and impatiently waited—bodies tense and ready for action—for the coach to toss the basketball in the air and blow the whistle hanging from a cloth strap from around her neck.

The opposing team, Kirkwood Middle School, got the ball.

The people all watched as the two teams went back and forth across the court, to the sounds of tennis shoes screeching, whistle blowing, cheering and booing, parents-turned-coach screaming approval and disapproval, the roar of the crowd—the excitement, the joy, all in the name of teaching patriotism, teamwork, sportsmanship, character-building, and how to have good, clean fun.

When the game first started, Amanda leaned into Hurts and whispered, "Uncle Jim. Have you noticed that Eve's number is One? Maybe the Chosen One?—And, she's playing Small Forward, which is Three. Could that be the Unholy Trinity?—Satan, Anti-Christ and the False Prophet?"

Rubbing his chin with his hand, Hurts replied, "I don't know, Amanda. That could all be just coincidence."

By first quarter, Mehlville Middle School was losing, eight to four.

Eve was not very skilled at playing basketball. She was too timid; not aggressive enough; too awkward at dribbling, passing, defending, and keeping the ball moving.

In the second quarter, though, she got a big break. Eve intercepted the ball and began moving and dribbling towards the home hoop. She was almost there when another teammate, guarding her, lost her balance, tripped, and fell on top of Eve, knocking her down to the floor.

The game was stopped.

Eve's left knee hurt. The manager of the team told her that she was done for the night.

Before she left the gymnasium, she stopped by to tell her mom and dad that she was okay.

Limping, she left the gymnasium and headed for the girls' locker room to shower and change her clothes.

Hurts placed his right hand on Amanda's left arm and said, "We had better leave and make sure that Eve is safe."

He said this to Tom and Lill, too. They both, not liking sports, were very glad.

Rising from the bench, Amanda said goodbye to Mr. and Mrs. Taylor and told them that she would call them tomorrow about making arrangements to take them to the Chase Hotel tomorrow night for the costume party, and for the grand Halloween ball on Thursday evening.

For a few minutes, all four of them just stood outside the girls' locker room, not knowing what to do. Then Amanda said that she and Lill would enter, pretending to want to say goodbye to Eve. Both Hurts and Tom thought that was a good idea.

Amanda opened the door, permitting Lill to go in first, and then Amanda entered, and the door closed behind her.

Thinking about that game he had just watched, Tom said, "I know that you love sports, Jim, but, damn, I find sports to—"

Tom's speaking was interrupted by the sound of his mother screaming, "Lord, Jesus! Save us!"

Tom threw the door open, and they both rushed inside.

It was a bit dark in there, except for a beam of light coming from the southeast corner of the room.

The room was small and crowded, with lockers and long wooden benches in front of the lockers. A wall divided this room from another room, which held the stalls of showers.

The room felt damp and hot.

The room was also crowded with men—thirteen men to be exact. They were all wearing full-length black topcoats and, although it was semi-dark in the room, sunglasses.

Hurts saw the men; he saw a man standing next to Eve, who was staring straight ahead and who looked like she was in some type of hypnotic trance, and he saw Amanda lying on the floor, with her drawn sword in her right hand. Hurts gasped with horror. He didn't know if she were alive or dead.

Before Hurts or Tom could respond, they were both hit in the head from behind and knocked unconscious.

The man who had attacked and knocked Hurts out drew his sword. He was about to fatally strike Hurts when the man standing next to Eve, raised his left arm and hand and commanded, "Stop! … Leave, all of you."

The twelve men left.

The man took off his sunglasses, stepped over Amanda, and walked over to Lill.

Lill was enshrouded in a beam of sparkling, pure light.

The man stood in front of Lill, staring at her, and she stared back at him.

To Lill, this guy looked so average—average height, average weight, average build, average looks. A guy, if you passed him on the street, you wouldn't give a second thought to. He seemed to her to just look like an average-looking, old man.

His hair was spare and white, and combed to the right side of his head. His face was a map of wrinkles, and his shoulders were a bit hunched over from age. Upon his face, sagging neck, and to the backs of his hands, were age-spots.

He was smartly, but casually dressed in a gray Herringbone sports-jacket, a white dress shirt, with gray tie, and black dress pants and black leather, tie-up dress shoes.

Yes, to Lill, he just looked so average—except for the pupils of his eyes: They were two flaming fireballs from hell.

With his left hand, he flicked the beam of light that was surrounding Lill with his middle finger. A white spark jumped from the beam when he did so.

In a pleasant-enough sounding voice, old, but pleasant-sounding, he said, "The Armor of God. I'm impressed, Mrs. Mayor."

"Thank you, Mr. Satan," she replied.

He sniffed the air, and then, waving his left hand in front of his face, said, "My, my, my. Is that you, Mrs. Mayor?"

Looking embarrassed, Lill replied, "Forgive my-my indiscretion. I'm old and scared … Is my son and Amanda dead?"

"No," he replied. "None of them are dead—yet."

"Oh, thank you, Mr. Satan … Please don't harm that little girl, Mr. Satan. Why do this? You know that in the end, you will lose. So, why do this?"

He thought for a moment, and then said, "Have you ever heard this phrase, Mrs. Mayor: 'Better to rule in hell than to serve in heaven'?"

"No, I can't say that I have ever heard that before, Mr. Satan—but what an awful price to pay just for the want of power."

"You are wise, Mrs. Mayor," he said. "Why not join me?"

"Me?!" Lill cried, shocked.

"Yes," he replied. Then, he spoke again, but when he did, it was the voice of Lill's dead husband, Pat: "Lill," it said, "Lill. I miss you so much. Join Satan, and we shall be together again—forever."

"Oh, Pat!" Lill cried joyously. "I've missed you, too. I-I—" She stopped speaking. She composed herself and said, "Thank you, Mr. Satan."

"My pleasure, Mrs. Mayor," he said.

"No, not for permitting me to speak with my husband," Lill countered. "You know as well as I, Mr. Satan, that the dead are dead, and they will not awaken until Christ returns. No, thank you for showing me how evil you truly are."

He nodded his head and said, "This is my last warning, Mrs. Mayor. Tell your friends and that damn vampire, Mr. Williams, to stay out of my business—for when we meet again, you all shall die … Come, Eve!" he commanded.

Eve followed him, and they left, and the Armor of God surrounding Lill disappeared.

Chapter Twenty-Seven

They all went to bed early, by nine o'clock—Lill and Tom in their own bedrooms and Hurts and Amanda in their assigned bedrooms in Lill and Tom's home. They all felt exhausted. Tom, Hurts and Amanda were not only in physical pain, but also disgusted and ashamed. Satan had most assuredly won that round, and they were ashamed, so ashamed, that they had failed to prevent Satan from kidnapping the Chosen One, Eve.

After Satan had left, Hurts had been the first of them to regain consciousness. He had helped Lill awaken Tom.

Amanda had sustained the most serious physical damage—a long, jagged cut to the right side of her forehead, right below the hairline.

When Hurts had gone to her, lying on the floor, unconscious, he had held her so tenderly in his arms, and with tears in his eyes, he kept saying, pleading, "Come on, Baby. Wake up … Come on, Amanda … Don't leave. God! Don't leave me! … Come on, Baby. Wake…."

She did.

Hurts had removed the white handkerchief from his back pants pocket, placed it over the bleeding cut on her forehead, and Lill, Tom and Hurts had helped her get up, and they left that locker-room and that school as fast as they could.

Hurts had wanted to take Amanda to the hospital, but she had adamantly refused. At the kitchen table, Lill had administrated disinfectant to the wound with cotton-swabs and had bandaged it with four butterfly-bandages.

Before they had left the kitchen for bed, Hurts, with a sudden, all-consuming burst of volcanic rage screamed, "If it's the last thing that I do in life, I'm going kill that son-of-a-bitch!—Do you hear me, Satan?!"

***

It was a little after 10:00 PM. Amanda was sitting up in the single-sized bed, with two pillows propping up her back and head. She was wearing yellow pajamas with tiny brown bears on them, and she had the multi-colored quilt pulled up to her waist. With a thick book in hand, she reluctantly turned the page. She had a splitting headache, but she had so much homework to do—and she had that big chemistry test next week. So she was forcing herself to get some of that homework done.

The book that she was holding in her hands was a chemistry textbook. Reading it was complex and slow-going. It was causing her eyes to blur—

that and that damn headache that she had—and she was about to take a rest, when there came a light knocking on the door.

A few seconds later, Hurts peeked his head though the door and said, "Mind if I come in for a moment?"

Setting the book down on her lap, she replied, "No, come on in, Uncle Jim."

Hurts entered the room, wearing a white T-shirt, gray sweatpants, and white socks.

He walked over and sat down on the edge of the bed.

Looking at her, and especially at that wound on her forehead, he said, feigning cheerfulness, "How's my favorite girl doing?

"I'm okay, Uncle Jim," she replied truthfully.

Reaching out and touching the bandaged wound ever-so-gently with the tips of his large fingers, he said, "Well, I still wish you would have let me take you to the hospital. You could have a concussion."

"No, I'm fine, Uncle Jim," she replied. "I don't have a concussion— well, at least not a chronic one."

"How do you know?" he asked.

Flabbergasted, she replied somewhat arrogantly, "Well, I *am* studying to be a doctor."

"Yes, of course," Hurts conceded diffidently. He paused, and then said, this time feigning enthusiasm, "I'm going to be so proud when you become—" He stopped. When he resumed speaking, he said, "I'll be so proud at whatever you decide to become."

Amanda was stunned, simply stunned.

Rising from the bed, Hurts said, "We got a busy day tomorrow. Get some rest."

"I will, Uncle Jim," she replied, for some reason feeling sad.

At the door to the bedroom, Hurts paused. He stood there indecisively for a moment and then said, "How's Missy doing?"

"I haven't spoken with her since last week," Amanda replied. "Why do you ask?"

Rubbing his hands together, Hurts replied, "Oh, I was just wondering … Why don't you give her a call and see how she's doing?"

Amanda was about to tell Hurts how much she loved him, but he quickly left the room.

Although he was gone, his presence still dominated the room.

Amanda tossed off the quilt and got out of the bed. She walked over to the wooden desk that was against the wall and opened her purse that she had tossed on top of the desk. She fished around in it for her cellphone. Finding it, she returned to the bed with it.

Placing it down in the bed beside her, she fluffed up the pillows, pulled that quilt back up to her waist, picked up her cellphone again, leaned back on the pillows, and brought up her cellphone in front of her. She then swiped the face of it a few times with the index finger of her right hand. She pressed a number on her speed-dial. The number began ringing.

"Well, how are you?" she said enthusiastically and cheerfully. "... Yes, I've missed you, too ... Listen, I'm sorry I cut you off last week when you called ... No, no. It's just that school's been a real bitch, Tom ... I know!" she screeched into the phone. "Me, too! ... This has been my hardest semester ... Well, the toughest has been ...."

Chapter Twenty-Eight

The next morning, Wednesday, October 30th, Tom awoke at 7:30 AM. Although his muscles and bones ached a bit and felt tight, and his head hurt from the hit to the back of his head, he felt like taking a run. So, he donned his jogging clothes, descended the stairs, and left the house.

As far as Tom could tell, no one except for him had gotten up yet.

It was a beautiful fall day. The air smelt crisp and refreshing, and the sun shone brightly. A great day for a nice slow run.

Tom jogged for a little more than an hour. Before entering the house, he got the newspaper lying on the sidewalk of the front yard.

Once inside the house, he found Hurts sitting on the couch, watching the local news on TV and drinking a cup of coffee. He was dressed in his old wrinkled black pin-striped suit, with a black tie.

As Tom approached the stairs, Lill came dragging herself down the stairs, wearing her white nightgown, white robe, and white slippers, mumbling, "Coffee. I need coffee."

From inside the kitchen, Amanda said, "The coffee's ready, Lill."

When Tom came abreast of Hurts, he began unfolding the newspaper to read it.

"Don't bother," Hurts said, referring to the newspaper. "It's all over the news," he stated, pointing to the TV. "An Amber Alert has been issued for that Eve girl—and her parents have singled us out. The Post-Dispatch has already informed them that they never heard of us. Good thing we gave them false names … I talked to Williams a little while ago. He's frustrated. He's going to put all of his eggs in one basket and see if he can stop Satan from getting to the altar of that church, the Old Cathedral … Oh, and he's sending someone by to get that limousine."

"Well," Tom said, "that's one good thing. I won't have to wear that monkey suit anymore."

"Say, Tom?" Hurts said. "Do you have that list of names and addresses of the twelve men who are missing?"

"Yeah," Tom replied. "It's up in my bedroom on my desk. Why?"

"Well, I was thinking that we might interview the families of those missing men. Maybe we'll get lucky and get a lead as to where they all might be."

"Yeah, that sounds good," Tom said.

"Come on, you guys," Amanda said from the kitchen. "I got breakfast ready."

Amanda, dressed in jeans and a light-green knit pullover blouse, had made oatmeal. Because of Hurts' adamant dislike—hatred—of oatmeal, she had fried some bacon too.

After eating and after drinking three or four cups of coffee, they all felt a lot better.

Hurts was just about to rise from the table to step outside and smoke when his cellphone began ringing. He reached into the right-side pocket of his suitcoat, got his cellphone, flipped it open, and said, "Hello?"

It was Mr. Williams. From what the others could gather from listening to what Hurts was saying and replying, they all knew that it wasn't good.

As Hurts was replacing his cellphone back into the same pocket of his suitcoat, Tom said, "Well, what's going on, Jim?"

Hurts sighed, shook his head, and said, "Williams told me that Satan just texted him. Williams had four of his soldiers guarding the Old Cathedral, and sometime early this morning Satan's boys ambushed Williams' guys and killed them."

"Oh, my Lord!" Lill cried.

"Now, Williams only has four soldiers left," Hurts said.

"Wow!" Tom said. "That's bad—for us."

"It gets worse," Hurts then stated. "Williams also told me that twelve more men are missing in St. Louis."

"What?!" Tom and Amanda said, almost in unison. "Why, Jim? Did Mr. Williams say why Satan would want twelve more demons?"

"He doesn't know, Tom," Hurts said. "He can't figure it out."

Just then, Hurts' cellphone chimed in the pocket of his suitcoat.

Hurts looked at each of them, and they were all looking at the pocket of his suitcoat that held his cellphone. They all knew who it was.

"Don't answer it, Uncle Jim," Amanda warned.

"Yeah, Jim," Tom agreed. "Don't."

Hurts, being Hurts, waved at them dismissively and retrieved his cellphone again from the pocket of his suitcoat. He flipped the cellphone open and read.

"Why, that no-good son-of-a-bitch!" Hurts cursed.

"What does he say, Uncle Jim?!" Amanda cried.

Closing his cellphone and then returning it to that same pocket, Hurts said, "He says: 'Check, Mr. Hurts. Your move!'"

Chapter Twenty-Nine

Hurts was boiling mad about that text message that Satan sent him. He pounded the table with the bottom of his clenched fist, saying, "Before I cut that son-of-a-bitch's head off, I'm gonna pull down his pants, shove my pistol up his ass, and pull the trigger!"

The mental image of Hurts doing that produced gales of laughter from Tom, Amanda and Lill.

Hurts took offense at this and called them all laughing hyenas. He told Tom and Lill to get dressed so they could go interview the families of the twelve missing men who were now possessed by a demon.

As Hurts waited for Tom and Lill, one of Mr. Williams' soldiers came and got the limousine.

About forty minutes later, Tom and Lill descended the stairs. Tom, believing that he should look presentable, being Hurts' partner, and with having to wear that damn chauffer's uniform yesterday, was now dressed in black dress pants, a plaid shirt with a dark tie, and a brown sports jacket. Lill was wearing light-blue stretch pants and a pullover beige blouse. Her white purse was hanging from her right shoulder by the thin white strap.

At the hall closet, Tom handed Hurts and Amanda their swords and their topcoats. Dressed now, they left. They all piled into Hurts' car, his 1997 black Nissan Pathfinder.

***

It turned out to be a miserable day—just simply miserable.

They interviewed the wives, former wives, girlfriends, mothers, and fathers of those twelve missing men—and got nothing! It had been a total waste of time.

Four of the men's wives had been divorced for years, and they had no idea about where they could be—and didn't care. Another four of the men's wives had all stated that their husbands were alcoholics, dope takers and dope pushers, womanizers, low-lives, gone for days at a time, didn't pay the bills or child support; so, frankly, they didn't give a shit where they could be. One of the twelve missing men was a registered sex offender, and on and on it went. It was frustrating!—and time consuming.

Most of the twelve missing men lived on the north side of downtown St. Louis: very poor and bad areas. One lived in Kirkwood; another lived in Fenton.

Yes, it had been a most miserable and worthless day.

230

By five o'clock, Hurts, Tom, Amanda and Lill were all tired, fed-up, disgusted, depressed, and hungry.

The last person that they had spoken with lived in a cheap, rundown apartment on Kingshighway Boulevard, on the South Side of St. Louis.

They were so close to Zio's Restaurant, and Tom knowing of Hurts' and Amanda's love of Zio's said, "Yeah, guys, why don't we take a break and go to Zio's?"

They all agreed to this—whole-heartedly.

***

Zio's is an institution in St. Louis. The restaurant has been around for thirty-two years and is still owned and run by the family who started it. It's at the corner of Wilson and Edwards Street, on what's affectionally known as "The Hill." The entire section there is Italian bars and Italian restaurants, a legacy of the early Italians who migrated to and settled in that part of St. Louis.

Zio's is in an old red-brick two-story building, with a bright green awning that surrounds the entire front of the building and half of the south side of the building. The south side of the building is a patio section for outside dining, with white plastic tables and chairs, and the tables have large orange umbrellas in the center of them.

Old Fat Tony, the patriarch of the family, and his ninety-year-old wife still live on the second level of the building.

The place looks much larger from the outside than it truly is on the inside.

Once you pass through the heavy dark-stained wooden ornate door with two stripes of tinted-colored glass on it, the place is small and crowded with tables and chairs.

Old Fat Tony, always the bigshot maître de, met them as they came through the door.

Standing behind a waist-high wooden podium, dressed in black dress pants, a white dress shirt, and red suspenders standing guard on both sides of his protruding belly, he greeted them warmly in his thick Italian accent. "Mr. Hurts! My best customer. Welcome. Welcome."

He stepped from behind the podium and with open arms, went up to Hurts and hugged him.

"If you try to kiss me, Tony," Hurts stated warningly, "I told you before that I'll knock you on your fat ass."

Fat Tony stepped back, and with the palms of his stubby, sausage-fat fingers waving up and down, he laughed and replied, "Always with the

231

jokes. Fat Tony loves you. Best customer." He then turned to Amanda and said, acting shocked, "Amanda, you cut off your hair! Your beautiful, beautiful hair!" But, then he quickly added, "You're still beautiful—beautiful!"

"Stop with the talk, Tony," Hurts barked at Fat Tony, "I'm hungry."

Fat Tony turned around and looked about the room. He turned back around and made a motion with his left arm to two couples who were sitting on the long black wooden bench that was against the south wall of the foyer. The two couples rose from the bench and followed Fat Tony back to the podium. From underneath the podium, Fat Tony removed four menus. He handed each a menu, snapped the index finger and the thumb of his right hand, and a female waitress miraculously appeared.

Fat Tony stepped back to Hurts and said, "A small wait, my good friend. A small wait."

"I don't mind 'a small wait', Tony," Hurts said, "but I want my favorite table—and I see Mike over there, and I want him, too."

Fat Tony turned around and faced towards the direction that Hurts had pointed to, which was the southwest section of the waist-high, light-colored wood-paneled room. In that area, there were three tables that were larger and spread farther apart than were the rest of the tables and chairs. All the tables and chairs were of dark-colored wood, with matching ladderback chairs with red padded seats, but one of the three tables that Hurts wanted was round and was near the two metallic swinging doors to the kitchen: Hurts loved to smell the mouth-watering aromas wafting from behind those doors. Mike was a tall, slender college-kid who was studying to become a high school English teacher. Hurts liked him and thought of him as the best waiter there.

Fat Tony raised his voice, saying, "Michael! Michael!"

Michael, or Mike, as he liked to be called, was standing to the back of one of those three large tables that Hurts had requested—the one in the middle. With pen and pad in hand, he had been taking the orders of the people who were sitting at that table when he heard Fat Tony call his name. He looked up.

"That a-table is-a next for Mr. Hurts!" he stated.

Mike gave him a thumb's-up sign.

Turning back to Hurts, Fat Tony said, with arms and hands out, "There! Anything for my best customer … There! Sit!" he said, making a motion toward the now empty bench. "Sit!" he repeated. He turned back around and turned his attention to the bar at the corner of the room: A row of barstools in front of the high-gloss wooden bar, with customers sitting on them.

"Liberto!" he yelled to one of the two middle-aged men who were both busy working behind the bar, and who were both Fat Tony's sons.

Liberto looked to his father.

"A round of free drinks for my best customer, Mr. Hurts!"

Liberto nodded yes.

"Well, now you're talkin', Tony," Hurts cried joyously. Hurts turned to Amanda, Tom, and Lill and said, "What do you all want?"

"I'll have a glass of red wine," Tom said.

"Me, too," Lill joined in.

"A coke," stated Amanda.

Hurts turned back to Liberto and yelled, "Two red wines, a coke, and a glass of beer."

That 'small wait' tuned out to be forty minutes, but the food and the service are so good at Zio's that they didn't care all that much about the wait.

Now, sitting at that large middle table, with their menus in hand, and with Mike standing by Hurts with his pen and pad, Hurts said, slapping his menu down on top of the table, "I don't have to look at no damn menu, you know what I want, Mike."

"Fettuccini Alfredo, Mr. Hurts?" Mike asked, but he already knew what the answer would be.

"You know it, Mike," Hurts replied. "The usual—and make sure you give me the famous Zio's salad. Why, you can't go to Zio's without getting the salad."

"Excellent choice, Mr. Hurts," Mike said as he wrote the order down on the pad in his left hand.

"Oh, that does sound delicious," Lill said hungrily. "I'll have that, too."

Mike nodded and wrote her order down.

Turning to Amanda, Mike said with a smile, "The 'usual' for you, Amanda?"

"Well, I should say no, to be different," Amanda said, also with a smile, "but I love my steak. So, yes, I'll have my 'usual' … Give me my steak cooked medium-rare, with a baked potato, extra butter and sour cream, and green beans—and, yes, I must have the Zio's salad, too."

"Another excellent choice," Mike stated, writing that down.

"You know," Tom said, "that steak does sound good." Looking up at Mike, he said, "I'll have the steak, too—with salad."

"All excellent choices," Mike said, then asked, "Drinks?

"I'll have coffee, Mike," Amanda said.

"I'll have coffee, too," Tom said, but then added, "And a glass of red wine."

"I'll have that, too," Lill said.

"I want coffee, too, Mike," Hurts said. "And, Mike, I want a glass of beer—and four shots of bourbon lined up right here," he continued, tapping the top of the table with the index finger of his right hand, "in front of me."

"Very good, Mr. Hurts," Mike said. "I'll get you your drinks."

Before Mike left, a server placed three red plastic baskets down in the middle of the table. The baskets contained warm garlic breadsticks. The baskets were all covered with a green and white checkered cloth.

All of them—Hurts, Amanda, Tom, and Lill—dove into those breadsticks hungrily.

About seven minutes later, Mike returned, with another server helping him, with their drinks.

Hurts immediately took an extended gulp of his glass of beer. He followed this by picking up one of the four shots of bourbon that were in front of him, brought the shot-glass to his lips, tilted his head back, and swallowed the entire contents of that shot-glass in one quick gulp.

After Mike and that server had left, Amanda who was sitting to Hurts' left side, turned to him and in a low voice said, "Uncle Jim, may I have one of your shots of whiskey?"

"What?!" Hurts bellowed at her, shocked. "You want to drink whiskey?!"

"Well, I'd just like to try it," she replied gingerly.

"Oh, I don't think—"

"Oh, let her try one, Jim," Tom said, interrupting Hurts. "One can't hurt her."

"Well, I don't know about this, Amanda," Hurts said. He thought for a few minutes and then said reluctantly, "Okay." He grabbed the lower part of the third shot-glass that was nearest to his left with the index finger and thumb of his left hand and slid the glass over to her.

She stared down at it for a moment, then began studying it for another moment. Like Hurts had done, she picked it up, brought it to her open mouth, tilted her head back, and downed it in one gulp. She slammed the empty glass back down on top of the table, looked straight ahead, shook the upper-portion of her body and head, and then she began breathing heavily, coughing and choking uncontrollably.

"What's wrong here?!" Mike cried, dashing back to the table.

"Aaaah, nothing is wrong here, Mike," Hurts replied quickly. "She's alright. Amanda just choked some on a breadstick. That's all."

"I'm fine, Mike," she said, recovering. "Thank you for caring."

Mike saw the empty shot-glass on the table in front of her. He looked down at Amanda, smiled, and said, laughing, "The next time you do that, Amanda, try it with water or soda."

"There ain't gonna be a next time," Hurts barked, staring angrily at Amanda.

The food was delicious—simply delicious.

By the time they had eaten and had dessert—a square, fluffy, crusty banana cream cake—and several more cups of coffee, it was ten-to-eight when they finally piled, stuffed now, back into Hurts' car.

Amanda was sitting in the front seat with Hurts, and Tom and his mom were in the back seat. All of them were feeling pretty good now—especially Hurts: When Mike had come back with the food, Hurts had ordered another glass of beer and four more shots of bourbon—and, this time, he drank them all himself!

He had just inserted the key of the car into the ignition switch, when his cellphone began ringing. Instead of starting the car, Hurts reached into the right-side pocket of that black topcoat, brought out his cell, opened it, raised it to his right ear, and said, "Hello?"

Amanda, Tom and Lill all heard Hurts scream into the phone, "What?!" They listened intently, and even nervously. "Why, Williams?! Why would he do that? He's got the Chosen One … Well, okay. Keep me posted … Bye."

Looking confused, dejected, and boiling angry, Hurts lowered the cellphone to his lap.

"What's wrong, Uncle Jim?" Amanda asked, concerned. "What did Uncle Williams say?"

Hurts really didn't know what to say, so he just blurted it out angrily, "Earlier tonight, that damn Satan and his buddies kidnapped that other girl—that Phosphorus."

"Oh, my Lord!" Lill cried and made the sign of the cross.

"Why, Jim?" Tom asked, completely taken aback by this news.

Shaking his head, Hurts replied, "Williams doesn't know. He can't figure it out."

At that moment, Hurts' cellphone chimed—and they all knew who it was.

Hurts looked down at the phone still in his right hand.

"Don't-don't answer it, Uncle Jim," Amanda said with a trace of pleading in her voice.

Hurts raised the phone up a bit, flipped it open, pressed the text message button with his thumb, and began reading. The light from his cellphone shone on his grim-looking face in the dark car.

Squeezing the cellphone hard in his right hand, as if his hands were choking the very life out of someone, Hurts screamed at it viciously, "I'll show you that I'm 'man' enough! I'll show you—I'll cut your damn head off!"

"Jim, what did he say?!" Tom demanded to know.

"Yes, tell us, Uncle Jim," Amanda said.

"He said: 'We're at 10666 Grand Street … Come and get us—if you're man enough, Mr. Hurts.'"

Hurts returned his cellphone to the right-side pocket of that topcoat, then he yelled, "Everybody get out of the car. I'm going."

"Are you insane?!" Tom yelled. "That's just what he wants! It's a trap."

"Tom's right, Uncle Jim," Amanda cried, worried.

"I don't give a shit if it's a trap!" Hurts yelled. "I'm fed-up with playing this damn cat-and-mouse game. I'm going. Now, all of you, get out of my car!"

"Well, you're damn right you're going alone!" Tom cursed. "You and your damn stubborn pride—Who in the hell do you think you are?! … Well, you're not getting me killed—or my mother."

"Good! Go!" Hurts screamed.

Flipping the handle of the door open, Tom started to get out of the car. Then, he stopped suddenly. He wrestled with himself, and then he dropped back in the seat and slammed the door shut.

"I'm going," he said.

"What?!" Lill cried, shocked.

"No, Tom," Amanda said. "Don't—"

"I don't want you going, Tom!" Hurts barked at him. "Why would you go when you know that it's a trap?!"

"Because you're my partner!" Tom screamed at him. Then he added, "You fool!"

"But, I don't want you—"

Looking at Lill, Tom said, "Mom and Amanda, get out of the car."

"I said, I don't—"

"No, Tom," Amanda stated adamantly. "I'm—"

"I said that I want all of you to get the hell—"

"Mom," Tom stated flatly. "Get out of the—"

"Now, you listen here, Tom," Lill countered angrily. "I have had just about enough of this foolishness—and you don't sass me, Jim—or you either, Tom! I'm old enough to be your mother! … Well, I am your mother—so, don't tell me what to do. I'm going!"

"Look!" Hurts said. "Nobody is—"

"Start the car, Uncle Jim," Amanda demanded.

"How many times do I have to—?"

Amanda placed the tips of her two index fingers in her ears and began saying, "Blah, blah, blah, Uncle Jim. I can't hear you. Start the car."

Tom thought that was funny, so he placed his two index fingers in his ears and said, "Blah, blah, blah. I can't hear you, Jim. Start the car."

Lill followed suit and placed her two index fingers in her ears and said, "Blah, blah, blah. I can't hear that well anyway, but with my fingers in my ears, I really can't hear. Start the car, Jim."

"Enough!" Hurts yelled, with a grin and a laugh.

Starting the car, he said, "You're all nuts!"

As Hurts was driving the car out of Zio's parking lot, Tom said, "Boy, I wish I could speak Klingon. If I could, I'd say…" Tom lowered his voice a few octaves, and in a deep, aggressive voice, stated, "Today is a good day to die!"

Hurts bellowed, "What the hell is a Klingon?!"

Chapter Thirty

That address, 10666 Grand Street, was only eight minutes away from Zio's. It was only twelve blocks northwest from the office. Hurts knew the area well. It was a combination of businesses, houses and apartments—all set close together and all old, rundown buildings.

Grand Street ran north and south, and that address, 10666 Grand, was at the corner of Grand and Ohio Street, on the west side of the street.

Hurts parked his car at the curb in front of that address.

It was an old two-story red-brick building. The first-story's edifice of the building was glass; even the door to it was glass, with a metallic frame. The second-story of the building was red-brick, with tall, narrow, wooden-framed, curtained windows. The lights were on at both levels.

With the lights being on, and with the edifice of that place being glass, even though there wasn't a sign, it was easy to discern that the place was a self-service laundromat—because on both sides of the south and north wall, from floor-to-midway up, were washers and dryers. The place was eerily empty.

"Well," Hurts said doubtfully, looking around Amanda and gazing out of the passenger's side window of the car at the inside of the place, "something ain't right here. The joint is a ghost town."

"Yeah," Lill agreed.

"Well, maybe it was just a lie," Tom said. "Maybe he just wanted to goad you—to get you to go on another wild goose chase."

"Yeah, you might be right, Tom," Hurts replied, with some doubt escaping from his voice. "But he-he—Oh, never mind."

"Well, we're here," Tom said. "We might as well take a look around."

They all exited the car.

They walked upon the cracking, unlevel pavement of the cement sidewalk that led to the glass door.

Now standing in front of the glass door, which was in the middle of the face of the building, Hurts brought his hands up to the sides of his face, leaned up against the glass door, and looked inside.

Besides the washers and dryers, the place had a white drop-ceiling with long fluorescent lights. The floor was cement—just plain cement. The room was about three-hundred-feet long, then it narrowed to an arched hallway. This hallway was very short in length and width. Just beyond the arched doorway, on the south side, was a cement step. Above the step was a plain-looking door, painted a dull white. Directly across from that door was another door, also painted a dull white, with a sign midway up to the side of the door which read in metallic letters: RESTROOM. On the back wall of the room was nothing more than a heavy metal door with a horizontal bar across it midway up. That bar was for opening and closing the door. Above the door was a tin box attached to the wall. It had a pimply plastic red cover to it, with letters that would have shone the word EXIT, but the light bulb inside the box was burned out.

Hurts grabbed the handle of the door and opened it.

They all entered.

Once inside, they all looked around.

Looking at the door past that archway, Hurts said, "Come on."

They followed him.

At that door, Hurts grabbed the old round brass handle and gave it a turn. It was locked.

Lill turned around and opened the door that was directly opposite to that other door. That room was indeed a restroom—a closet-sized restroom that was in pretty bad shape.

"Good Lord," Lill cried, fanning her right hand in front of her face. "It stinks in there." She let the door shut quickly.

Looking at Tom, Hurts said, "Well, there's nothing here. Let's get out—"

Amanda had stayed behind by the entrance to the place. Suddenly she yelled, "Demons!"

Hurts, Tom and Lill looked towards the glass edifice and towards the glass door of the place.

Parked directly behind Hurts' car was a fairly new-looking 4-door silver Kia. Men dressed in topcoats like the ones Hurts, Tom and Amanda were wearing, and wearing sunglasses, were piling out of that car.

On the right side of that glass door, midway up, and above the handle to the door, was a knob-lock.

"Quick, Amanda!" Hurts yelled. "Lock the door!"

She did.

Hurts, Tom and Lill ran towards the door.

There were six demons in all, and when they came abreast of the door and found it to be locked, the three of them who were in front of the other three, began pounding on the glass with the bottom of their clenched fists.

Watching them doing this, Hurts said, "Williams told me that demons aren't as strong or as fast as vampires are."

"Yeah, but if they keep pounding on the glass like that," Tom cried, "it'll shatter!"

They watched as one of the demons who was in front, turned around and said something to one of the other demons. That demon then left, dashing north, keeping close to the building.

"He's going around to the back!" Tom yelled.

"That door in the back is solid metal," Hurts said. "It's an exit door. He can't get in here that way."

"Well, what are we going to do, Jim?!" Tom cried, panicking. "We're trapped in here!"

Brushing his topcoat aside to reveal his sword, Hurts said determinedly, "We're going to fight—that's what we're going to do!"

"Oh, Jim," Tom sighed. "I don't want to fight here! I got Mom to think of. We're out—"

From behind them, they heard a man's rough-sounding voice say, in a thick Bosnian accent, "Who you?! … Who them, hitting door?! … I closing. Go way!"

They all turned around and looked in that direction.

Standing before them, near the door on the south-side of the room which was now open, was an heavy man of average height who appeared to be in his early forties. His old, wash-worn clothes were too tight on him—a long-sleeved denim shirt and a pair of jeans—and he had a shock of black hair that needed combing.

"I closing. Go way," he repeated.

Hurts moved towards him, fast. The others followed.

When Hurts came up to the man, he turned his head and looked towards that door. It was a narrow passageway with stairs leading to the second-level of the building.

After withdrawing his weapon and pointing it at the man, Hurts said tersely, "Get back up those stairs."

"No rob! No rob!" the man pleaded, holding up his hands. "Got no money!"

"I said to get up those steps, fatso!" Hurts demanded. "Now move! Now!"

The man turned and began lumbering up the stairs. There was a small, round wooden rail on one side of the wall, but the passageway was so narrow that the man just extended his arms and hands and used the two walls to support him going up the steps.

Following that man, Hurts said, "The last person through the door— close it and lock it!"

"Okay," Amanda said.

As they ascended the stairs, Hurts said, "What's that awful smell?"

"Cabbage," Lill replied. "Oh, I just love cabbage."

At the top of the stairs, they stepped immediately onto the wooden floor of the kitchen. To the right of them was an old gas stove, and next to it was an old refrigerator. A wooden waist-high counter ran against the wall. At the end of the counter was a wooden-framed door. The top half of it was glass.

The room was poorly lit, and it was semi-dark in there.

To the side of the room, against the wall, right there in the room, was a wooden picnic table with a bench attached to both sides of it. On top of the bench were white paper plates, plastic forks, knifes and spoons, and plastic cups, and on the middle of the table was a huge ceramic black bowl with cabbage steaming from it. Sitting on the benches were children ranging from the ages of three to fifteen years old.

A heavy-set woman in her early forties, with long dark-brown hair that was tied in a bun on the top of her head, and who was dressed in a plain-looking beige dress with a full-length apron on, jumped up when they all entered the room.

She had been sitting at the rear of the bench.

She screamed, terribly frightened.

"Shut up!" Hurts barked at her.

"Oh, that cabbage smells divine," Lill said to that woman. "Do you cook it with bacon?"

"Lill?!" Hurts screamed. "This ain't no time to be swapping recipes!" Spotting that door by the counter, Hurts then said to that woman, "Quick, momma!" He pointed to that door. "Is that the back door?!"

The woman nodded yes.

"Quick, everyone," Hurts yelled, holstering his weapon. "Let's go!"

They all bolted towards that door. Hurts unlocked the door, turned the knob, and he threw the door open. They all passed through the door.

They stepped out onto an eight-foot-wide and twelve-foot-long unpainted wooden porch, with a waist-high wooden parapet to it. On the south side of the porch, stretched across the end post of the porch to the post at the start of the steps, was a clothesline made of rope. On this clothesline, pinned to it with clothes-pins, were shirts, pants, T-shirts and underwear of different sizes and styles.

The stairs to the porch had a waist-high wooden railing on both sides. The stairs were deep, and they seemed endless and dangerous. They ended at the ground-level of a small, unkept, fenceless backyard.

Hurts and Amanda had already begun descending the steps, but before Tom had started down the steps, he had first ripped from that clothesline a long-sleeved plaid cotton shirt. Then he took hold of Lill's left hand and aided her down the steps.

When Hurts had almost reached the last step, he heard Tom say, "Hey, Jim! Do you have your pocketknife and your lighter?!"

"Yeah," he yelled back to Tom.

"Well, give them to me when we get to your car."

"Okay," he replied.

Once reaching the bottom of the steps, Hurts spun around and looked towards the back of the building—looking for that demon who they thought had come around to that back door. Hurts saw no one.

When they were all off the stairs, they walked swiftly to the sidewalk, and then they walked east, following that side of the building to the front of it.

At the corner edge of the building, Hurts held up his right hand.

They all stopped.

Hurts peeked around the corner of the building.

There was one demon standing in front of the glass door to that building. He was facing the building, looking inside it. He was also standing on shards of glass from that front door having been shattered by those other demons.

Hurts just assumed that he must have been the one who had come around to that back door.

After brushing back his topcoat, Hurts drew his sword. He turned around and whispered, "Stay here. Wait for my signal. When you see it—run for my car."

Hurts crept up behind that demon. He looked over his left shoulder at the inside of that place. It was empty, but that door on the south side of the room was now lying in pieces on the cement floor.

With his left hand, Hurts tapped that demon on his right shoulder.

Hurts already had the sword raised horizontally to the side of that demon's neck. When he turned around, Hurts swung the blade from one side of his neck to the other side, severing his head.

Hurts quickly re-sheathed his sword, and then he waved his arms at Tom, Amanda and Lill.

Amanda and Lill made a beeline for Hurts' car, but Tom, still holding that shirt in his hands, moved to the rear of the car that had brought those demons. Standing in the street, on the driver's side of that car in front if the gas tank, Tom motioned for Hurts to join him.

Hurts did.

As Hurts approached Tom, Tom said quickly, "Give me your pocketknife and lighter."

Hurts had his pocketknife and lighter in the right pocket of his suitcoat. He first brought out the pocketknife. He opened the blade and then he handed the knife to Tom. Then he removed the lighter from his pocket and handed it to Tom, saying, "I know what you're doing. Smart, Tom. Real smart."

"Thanks," Tom replied. "Just keep an eye out for me. Let me know if those demons start coming."

"You got it, partner," Hurts said, turning his attention towards the building.

Tom bent over a bit and slipped the tip of the blade of the pocketknife in between the body of the car and the cover of the gas tank. When he had slipped the blade of the knife halfway in, he gave a sharp twist of his right wrist. The cover popped open. Tom closed the blade of the pocketknife and handed it back to Hurts. Tom unscrewed the gas cap, tossed it over his right shoulder and began stuffing that shirt down the gas tank. When he had stuffed as much of that shirt down the into the gas as he thought he could, Tom took the lighter and set that shirt on fire.

Looking towards that corner of the building that Hurts, Tom, Amanda and Lill had come from, Hurts yelled, "Here they come, Tom! Let's go!"

Hurts and Tom turned and started running for Hurts' car.

Hurts and Tom made it to the car. They got inside. Amanda was, again, in the front seat, and Lill was, again, in the back seat.

Hurts quickly started the car.

"They're at the car, Uncle Jim!" Amanda yelled.

One of the demons threw open the rear passenger door.

"They're getting in, Uncle Jim!" Amanda yelled again.

Hurts threw the car into Drive and slammed his foot onto the gas petal.

The engine revved, the back wheels screeched, and the car sped away—but it was too late.

That one demon who had thrown open the back door had jumped inside before Hurts had driven away.

He was punching at Tom. To prevent this from continuing, Tom was holding onto that demon by his wrists. They wrestled each other down to the floor of the rear of the car. That demon was on top of Tom. They continued wrestling, and Lill kept hitting that demon in the head with her purse.

As dangerous and as frightening as this was, what happened next made Tom laugh out loud.

Tom could only surmise that Lill had gotten the idea to do what she did from Tom's years of watching *The Three Stooges* on TV. Tom watched as his mother removed the sunglasses from the face of that demon and then gave him two fingers to his black eyes.

The demon reared-up his body a bit. Tom took advantage of this and raised his knees up. Then he worked to get his legs and feet in front of the demon. The door was still open. With the heels of his shoes now parallel with the chest of the demon, Tom shouted, "Jim! Make a sharp left and a sharp right!"

Hurts did.

It worked like a charm.

The quick jerking movement of the car caused the demon to lose his balance. Tom thrust his legs and heels forward, hard, kicking that demon in the chest. He went flying backwards, out of the car.

Lill helped Tom scramble back up onto the back seat.

"Slow down, Jim," Tom said. "I have to shut the door."

Hurts did.

The car slowed down to a crawl.

Tom reached over and shut the door—and that's when it happened: BOOM!

Tom turned around and looked out the rear windshield. He saw the demons all standing in the middle of the street. Behind them was their car—it was now nothing more than a fireball of flames.

Smiling, Tom said, "I sure hope those boys like walking."

Chapter Thirty-One

It was 9:00 PM when they returned to Lill and Tom's house. They were sitting in the kitchen at the table. They were exhausted and in a daze.

Suddenly, Amanda broke the silence by saying, "I'm hungry."

"You're always hungry," Hurts replied flatly.

"Well, now," Lill began. "There's chicken left in the refrigerator—and there's more coleslaw, and potato salad, and we still have some of that cake left."

"That sounds great, Lill," Amanda said.

"Who else is hungry?" Lill asked.

"I could eat," Tom said.

"Yeah, I guess I could eat, too," Hurts added.

"Right," Lill said. "Now, Amanda, you get the plates, utensils, and cups, and I'll start warming the food and making a pot of coffee."

Lill and Amanda got up and left the table.

Hurts began strumming the top of the table with the fingers of his right hand. He looked at Tom. Tom saw him looking at him. To Tom, Hurts seemed to be struggling with himself. Then, he finally said, "I'm sorry, Tom. You were right. My damn pride almost got you guys killed tonight."

Knowing how difficult it was for Hurts to apologize—about anything!—Tom really appreciated hearing that from Hurts.

"Oh, that's okay, Jim," Tom replied. "To be honest with you," Tom continued, "that was damn FUN!"

Hurts' face lit up, and he exclaimed cheerfully, "It was, wasn't it?!"

"Boy, Jim," Tom said excitedly. "You should have seen the look on that demon's face when I booted him out of the car. His arms and hands were flying everywhere." Tom threw his arms and hands up above his shoulders and started moving them wildly. "It was a sight!"

They both started laughing—then, in the right pocket of Hurts' suitcoat, his cellphone chimed.

The laughing came to an immediate halt. Everyone stopped what they were doing. You could feel the tension in the air. All eyes were on Hurts. They all knew who it was.

As Hurts removed his cellphone from the pocket of his suitcoat, he said to Tom without looking at him, "You didn't give me my lighter back."

"I dropped it when that demon attacked me," Tom replied. "It's in the back of the car somewhere."

Hurts flipped open the phone, pressed the text button, and then read.

After he had read the text message, he closed the phone, shook his head, and said flatly, "Asshole."

"What did he say, Uncle Jim?!" Hurts heard Amanda ask.

Displaying no emotions, Hurts replied, "He said, 'Very lucky, Mr. Hurts. The game's still on. Your move.'"

Still holding his cellphone in his right hand, Hurts raised his hand high and straight out in front of him. He turned his hand upside down. Then he opened his fingers. The cellphone crashed to the kitchen floor. Hurts raised his right leg up, bent his knee over the cellphone, and then he brought his leg down hard—smashing that cellphone to pieces.

Looking straight ahead, Hurts said, "There! That's my move, Satan!"

Chapter Thirty-Two

The next morning, Thursday, October, Thirty-first, Tom awoke at twenty minutes-to-eight AM. He felt tired and he didn't feel like getting out of bed. In fact, he didn't feel like doing anything—not even taking a run.

The mere thought of having to get out of bed and begin the day was appalling to him. He just didn't want to face the day—or to even bring to mind what day it actually was, but he finally did: It was Halloween.

Halloween, yes. Halloween. A day that every kid waking up would long for, yearn for evening to come. The anticipation of it; the excitement of it; the thrill of it; the fun of it. Dressing up in a costume and pretending to be something you're not. Something magical—a witch, a ghost, a vampire, a doctor, and on and on; of stepping into the homes of neighbors and of strangers and being welcomed, and then rewarded with sweets. All in the name of good, wholesome family fun.

Yes, the children would wait anxiously for evening to come, but not Tom or anyone else in that household. For them, the coming of that evening meant danger, uncertainty, fear, a donnybrook, death, and the unthinkable possibility of the beginning of the end—the apocalypse. Armageddon.

* * *

When Tom stepped into the kitchen, still wearing his nightclothes— his white T-shirt, sweatpants and brown leather slippers—he found Hurts sitting at the kitchen table drinking a cup of coffee. He was washed and clean-shaven, wearing his old dark-blue suit again. Tom smelt the welcome aroma of eggs and bacon being cooked. Lill, still wearing her white nightgown, white robe, and white slippers, was busy at the stove. Amanda was standing at the corner of the counter. Her back was to Tom. She was standing in front of the toaster that was on top of the counter, spreading butter onto toast as it came out of the toaster. She looked stunning. She was wearing a lavender blouse, black jeans, and those knee-high black leather boots that she had told O'Malley were too tight on her and asked if he could make them more comfortable to wear, which he had.

"You look more dead than alive, son." Hurts whipped as Tom entered the kitchen.

"Coffee," Tom said as he dragged his still sleepy body across the room. "I need coffee."

"Oh, Uncle Jim," Amanda stated suddenly. "I forgot. Uncle Williams called early this morning—he wanted to know why you weren't answering your cellphone. I told him that you accidentally dropped it and had, accidentally, stepped on it … Anyway, he told me that he has gotten permission from the pastor of the Old Cathedral for us to be there tonight. He wants us there at midnight."

"Sounds good," Hurts replied flatly.

As Tom was pouring himself a cup of coffee, Lill said, "And, Tom, you never did get the Halloween decorations up from downstairs."

Replacing the coffeepot back in the coffeemaker, Tom said, "I'll do it after breakfast."

"Oh, good," she replied. "And don't forget to bring up Charlie"—the scarecrow—"and the rocking-chair for him to sit on, on the porch."

"Got it," Tom said, now moving towards the kitchen table.

Carrying two steaming platters, one in each hand, Lill said cheerfully, "Okay, let's eat."

The breakfast was hearty and delicious.

At one point, as they ate, Lill said, "I need to get to the grocery-store. I think I'll buy three or four big bags of candy for the little Trick-or-Treaters tonight … I feel like making a meatloaf tonight for supper. Does that sound good to you all?"

Hurts and Tom both nodded their heads yes.

Amanda said, "I've never made a meatloaf, Lill. Is that difficult to make?"

"Oh, no, dear," Lill replied. "I'll show you. I have my recipe for it in my recipe-box, in the third drawer of the counter."

"I'll take a look at it and help you," Amanda said.

"Great," Lill replied, then added, "And, I think I'll get some ears of corn—doesn't that sound …"

***

After they finished eating breakfast, Lill went back upstairs, bathed, and dressed—into a pair of beige stretch pants, a white blouse, and a pair of beige leather flat shoes—she came back downstairs and left for the grocery store. Before leaving, though, she said she was going to buy three or four pumpkins for the front porch. She wouldn't carve them; that would take too long to do and would be too messy.

Tom went down into the basement and brought up the Halloween decorations—and, of course, the rocking chair and Charlie.

Hurts and Amanda helped Tom put up the decorations, which didn't take long to do at all. There wasn't much—not like at Christmas. Now, Christmas was, indeed, a chore to do! Christmas had always been Tom's mom and dad's favorite holiday, and they had the Christmas stuff to prove it: Seven large cardboard boxes of Christmas cheer. It would take Tom a full week, working on it four hours a day, to put up all of that Christmas stuff that his parents had, both inside and outside.

But, no, for Halloween there were few decorations: A string of lights for the picture window in the living room. The lights were tiny orange plastic pumpkins. There was a full-length cardboard image of a skeleton that was hung on the front door and, of course, there was the rocking-chair and, of course, there was Charlie.

Tom couldn't remember when, where, or why his father had gotten Charlie. Charlie had become as much a natural figure to their front porch at Halloween as the Christmas tree did in the living room at Christmas.

Charlie was the figure of a full-sized male mannequin. Tom's dad had dressed it in bib-overalls, a denim shirt, a red bandana for around its neck, a white pillow over its head—two large orange buttons for eyes, and six large orange buttons for a mouth—and a straw hat.

Satisfied with having gotten all of the Halloween decorations done, Amanda sat down at the kitchen table with Tom's mother's recipe box, Hurts went outside to his car to look for his lighter, and Tom went upstairs to take a shower and then dress.

Wearing just his white robe and white slippers, Tom shut the bathroom door, removed the robe, hung it up on a peg on the inner side of the door, shook off his slippers, and approached the drawn shower curtain circling the upper section of the bathtub. He drew it back, and then he jumped back, letting out a startled gasp of "Oh!"

Standing there in all her natural loveliness was Amanda—totally naked. She raised her arms out to Tom.

"Make love to me, Tom," she said.

Feeling confused and embarrassed, Tom turned his head to one side and closed his eyes.

"Amanda, have you lost your mind? We can't—" Tom stopped speaking. He thought of something. *Wait a minute*, he thought. *Amanda was downstairs in the kitchen. How did she get up here so fast? How did she get—Oh, no! T*om screamed, silently. He opened his eyes again, turned his head, and looked again at Amanda.

"Take me, Tom," Amanda said seductively, fondling her grapefruit-sized breasts with the tips of her fingers. "You know you want me. Join me."

Slowly, Tom raised his right hand. Leveling it off, and pointing his index finger at Amanda, Tom commanded, "In the name of Our Lord, Jesus Christ, and by His authority, I say, Satan, be gone!"

Amanda disappeared.

Shaking, Tom dragged himself over to the toilet. He closed the lid of it, turned around, plopped down heavily onto it, lowered his head, and buried his face in his hands.

***

Showered, shaved, and wearing his jeans, a light-brown shirt and white tennis shoes, Tom descended the stairs.

He found Amanda sitting on the couch in the living room, watching a game show on TV.

He approached her gingerly, trying to block out the image of seeing her naked. He unconsciously began staring down at her.

She looked up at him, saw him staring at her, and did a double-take.

"Why are you looking at me like that?" she asked, a bit disturbed.

"Oh, sorry, Amanda," Tom quickly replied, embarrassed. "I-I-well, I—"

"You, too?" she stated.

"What do you mean?" Tom said, confused.

"I've been seeing-seeing DELUSIONS all morning," she replied. "I've seen Missy, Uncle Jim and you—all of you were naked, and all of you wanted to have sex with me."

"Wow!" Tom said. "I thought that I was going nuts."

"He's a deceiver, he is," Amanda replied, shaking her head.

"Yes, he is," Tom said. He was silent for a moment, and then he said, "Say, Amanda. How-how-how did I—Well," he continued, with a nervous laugh. "How did I look, you know, naked?"

Amanda extended her hand over the arm of the couch. With the thumb and the index finger of her hand only a quarter-of-an-inch apart, she said, "Small."

"What?!" Tom cried.

Amanda burst out laughing.

Tom, feigning anger, stated, "Amanda, that's not funny. Don't ever joke about that with …."

***

Hurts was standing on the porch, looking out onto the street. He was leaning up against the top of the black waist-high iron rail, finishing his third cigarette. He leaned forward and flicked the smoked cigarette over the line of trimmed evergreen bushes that lined the front of the porch. He turned around and looked at Charlie, sitting on the rocking chair.

"You got the good-life, Charlie," he said.

Charlie's arms and hands raised up.

"Join me, Mr. Hurts," Charlie said. "Join me and I shall grant you unlimited power."

Hurts reared back, startled. He was only startled for a moment—for only a moment, then he got boiling angry. He drew his weapon and dashed over to Charlie. He bent down. With his left hand, he grabbed Charlie by its bib-overalls, at the chest area. He took his weapon, and he shoved the barrel of it against Charlie's forehead. Getting right in Charlie's face, Hurts stated viciously through grinding teeth, "Now, you listen to me, and you listen good. I don't take orders from no man. I don't even take orders from God. So, why would I ever take orders from a piece of shit like you?!" Shaking Charlie hard, Hurts continued, "Do you hear me, Satan?!"

"Jim!" Tom cried. "What are you doing to Charlie?!"

Letting go of Charlie and rising, Hurts holstered his weapon. He turned and faced Tom. Feeling embarrassed, Hurts said, feigning laughter, "Oh, I was just practicing my quick-draw. You know me, Tom. I'm always prepared."

"Yeah," Tom replied doubtfully.

***

By 3:00 PM, Amanda, Tom, and Lill were so antsy, they couldn't stand just sitting around anymore doing nothing. Lill promptly announced, "I'm carving those three pumpkins that I bought!"

"Great!" Amanda said eagerly. "I'll help."

"Me, too," Tom said. "I'll get the pumpkins from the porch, and you and Amanda spread newspaper out on the table."

Tom left the kitchen and headed for the front door, eyeing Hurts who was fast asleep on the couch.

Amanda did the best job of carving a pumpkin—very ominous looking. Lill did a good job, as well. But, Tom's left something to be desired. The eyes of the pumpkin were just two round holes, and the mouth was nothing more than a horizontal five-inch hole.

The day dragged on.

They ate supper at four-thirty. As always, it was delicious—meatloaf, ears of corn with melted butter, a tossed salad, and green beans. For dessert, Lill had purchased four apple tarts, which she had served with a dollop of whipped cream and a dollop of vanilla ice-cream—and coffee, lots of cups of coffee.

At 6:00 PM, Lill turned on the front porch light for the little Trick-or-Treaters to come—and they did.

Amanda helped Lill dish out candy to all the little dressed-up goblins who came.

Lill had purchased four large bags of candy, but so many children came that it wasn't nearly enough. But, Lill and Amanda had found it to be great fun.

At ten-after-eight, the hordes of children who had come seemed to suddenly dwindle down to no one else coming. Reluctantly, and with sadness, Lill turned off the front porch light.

Like it had been during the day, the night dragged on.

They all watched a silly Halloween movie on TV called *Ernest Scared Stupid*. During the watching of that movie, Hurts said, "I guess we'll leave at 11:30."

The night dragged on and on.

It seemed like the night would never end—that their individual waiting, agonizing over it, would never stop, but it finally did.

11:30 finally came.

As they had for the last three days, they stood at the hallway closet by the front door. As always, Tom first handed Hurts a sword, then he handed Amanda one. Then he handed both of them one of those full-length black topcoats. He got himself the remaining sword, strapped it on, and then put on the remaining topcoat.

They were now all dressed and ready to leave. Lill had her purse and Amanda did, too.

Tom was the last to exit the front door.

Before Tom left, he turned back around and looked about the living room. As he looked, he told himself that if his mother and he were never to return here again, he hoped that whoever would buy this house would love it as much as he loved it. From where Tom was standing, he could see into the kitchen. In his mind's eye, he saw all of his family at the kitchen table. He saw his mom—young again, defiant, self-assured, and full of life. He saw his dad—alive again, young, authoritative, talkative and a face that had in it much pride for his family. He saw both of his two older sisters,

Mary and Eve, and he saw his older brother, James, who had been killed while riding his bike when he had been only ten years old.

Yes, it had been a good house and a great home.

Tom closed the door and locked it behind him.

253

Chapter Thirty-Three

The Old Cathedral is one of the oldest buildings in downtown St. Louis. It is over one hundred and eighty years old. Designated as the oldest Roman Catholic church in St. Louis, it has survived cholera, fire, early migration, plagues, urban development, and social and political unrest. It sits on a hill just east of the Market Street exit of Highway 55, overlooking or standing sentinel over the grounds of the historic Gateway Arch and, of course, over the banks of the mighty, muddy waters of the Mississippi River.

It's a deceptive building. Viewing it from the outside, it seems small, but once inside, it's cavernous and grand.

The outside structure of it is white stone, with tall, narrow, arched, wooden-framed tinted windows with Biblical depictions on them. Above the Romanesque stone columns of the entrance to the church, on the face of the portico, are the words written in Latin: DEO UNI ET TRINO. A loose translation of this is: Rejoice in God; one God; one Trinity. The steeple of the church is simple looking, but inspiring: a single triangular-shaped stone structure, reaching for heaven, with a gold-plated cross capping its top.

The church runs north and south.

As Hurts parked in the small parking lot of the church, he saw the long, sparkling white limousine they had used parked in the parking lot. Hurts told himself that Williams must already be here. He also told himself that Williams must have used that limousine to come to the church with his four remaining soldiers. He knew that Williams drove a fancy, expensive dark-blue BMW.

Tom, seeing that limousine, became angry—remembering the indignity of having to wear that damn monkey suit, that chauffeur's uniform.

They exited the car and headed for the three cement steps that led to the enormously tall, ornate, dark-stained double wooden doors to the entrance to the vestibule of the church.

After entering the vestibule of the church, Hurts opened and held one of the four wooden doors open to the entrance of the nave of the church.

It was awesome inside the church—breathtakingly beautiful. It was like stepping into another dimension of time and space—a spiritual dimension! A religious dimension! The arched ceiling with Biblical fresco paintings upon it; the sides of the church lined with marble columns; gold waist-high metal stands with rows of frosted-white glass containers with lit candles in them, whiffs of white smoke emanating from them, and the fragrant smell of wax burning; full-size statues of Jesus, of Mary, of Joseph; hanging chandeliers; marble floor; two long rows of high-gloss wooden benches; and following down the aisle of those two rows of benches lay the one-step to the waist-high dark-stained wooden parapet that guarded the altar.

The altar of white stone. The top of it covered with a white cloth and two tall burning candles at both ends in gold-plated candle holders.

Overlooking the altar was a man-size statue of Jesus, in agony, badly beaten, blood pouring from his wounded body and head, hanging on the cross. Dying for our sins, freely given salvation to us all.

As Hurts passed through the door, he saw Mr. Williams' four soldiers standing guard at the doors. They, too, were all wearing the full-length black topcoats.

Hurts then saw Mr. Williams. He was facing the altar, kneeling in one of the rows of pews about halfway down from the altar, on the east side of the church.

They walked down to him.

"Hey, Williams," Hurts said after they had reached him.

Mr. Williams opened his eyes, made the sign of the cross, stood up, left the pew, turned and greeted them.

Mr. Williams, as always, was impeccably dressed, wearing a dark gray suit with a matching tie. Over this suit, he also had on a full-length black topcoat.

"Although I didn't want to involve you in this, Amanda—and you, too, Mrs. Mayor," Mr. Williams stated, "I'm glad you are both here."

Lill, Tom, Amanda, and Hurts all sat down in the pew behind the one that Mr. Williams had been in.

He then returned to the pew that he had been in and sat down, too. He sat with the upper-half of his body turned so that he could face them.

"So, what's your plan, Williams?" Hurts asked.

"I know that you're a man who always has a plan," Mr. Williams said, "but, honestly, my only plan is to prevent Satan from getting to that altar and impregnating that girl, Eve, on the thirteenth stroke of the thirteenth hour."

"Well, then, to be honest with you, Williams," Hurts replied. "Sometimes a good ass-kicking—I mean, a good fight," Hurts stated quickly, remembering where he was, "is the only plan you got."

Mr. Williams looked at the Rolex wristwatch on his right arm. It was exactly twelve o'clock.

One hour until the thirteenth hour, and if any of them had thought that the day had dragged on and on, it was nothing compared to how that last hour dragged on and on.

It was nail-bitingly long.

Mr. Williams kept looking at his wristwatch, and as each minute passed agonizingly slow, the tension on his usually hard-to-read, calm, always-in-control face deepened to the point in which one could almost read what he was thinking and was inwardly saying, which was, "Come on, Satan. Where are you?! Come on! Where are ….?"

Then, at exactly three minutes to the thirteenth hour, the two middle doors to the entrance to the nave of the church swung open.

All eyes turned to those doors.

In perfect formation, in lines of two, marched in twelve men, all dressed in full-length black topcoats and all wearing sunglasses. They stopped about seven feet from where Mr. Williams, Hurts, Amanda, Tom, and his mother were sitting.

Mr. Williams' four soldiers started to draw their swords, but Mr. Williams raised up his right hand, indicating for them to wait.

From the two doors, now stood the figure of a man. He was also wearing a full-length black topcoat, but this topcoat had a hood to it. The hood was pulled over the person's head, obscuring his face. This gave a bone-chilling, ominous aura to the man—that, and the fact that, slumped over the left shoulder of the man was the seemingly dead, or unconscious, body of a young girl. The girl's body was wrapped in a white blanket.

Mr. Williams rose from the pew. He stepped out of it, and then he stepped two pews towards the twelve men. Hurts, Amanda, Tom, and his mother rose, stepped out of the pew, and stood behind Mr. Williams.

Mr. Williams first removed a blue cloth from the right pocket of the topcoat. Holding it with his left hand, he removed the cross from the inner pocket of the topcoat and held the bottom portion of the cross, wrapped in that blue cloth, in his left hand. With his right hand, he withdrew his sword from its scabbard.

Hurts, Amanda, and Tom removed their crosses and swords. Lill held up her purse by its long strap, ready to fight.

"Well, this is it," Hurts said to Amanda.

"No, it's not, Uncle Jim," she replied knowingly. "No, it's not."

Hurts didn't know what Amanda meant by that, but there wasn't any time to ask her. He dismissed it.

"Attack!" Mr. Williams shouted. "Attack!"

The twelve demons drew their swords, and the fight began.

Actually, it wasn't that bad of a fight. It didn't last long, only a few seconds.

Mr. Williams' team won.

Mr. Williams had been correct when he had told Hurts that many demons don't have the strength of vampires, and that they definitely don't have the speed of vampires.

With the help of Mr. Williams, and with the help of Mr. Williams' four remaining soldiers, as well as Hurts, Amanda, and Tom who fought a demon, this gave Mr. Williams and his soldiers the time they needed to sever the heads of the demons.

The bodies and the heads of the demons lay strewn upon the high-glossed marble floor of the church; blood poured from their decapitated heads and bodies.

The only foe who remained alive was the hooded being who was still standing at the two open doors at the entrance to the nave. He was still holding the seemingly lifeless girl over his left shoulder.

With cross and sword still in hand, Mr. Williams began to approach the man, slowly and cautiously. Hurts and the others followed him.

Mr. Williams felt good, though. He had stopped Satan. All that remained to do was to cut the head off of the old man whose body and mind Satan now possessed. Then this nightmare—this threat of the beginning of the end, the apocalypse, Armageddon, would be over.

Coming abreast of the man, Mr. Williams placed his sword in his left hand, holding on to both the cross and the sword with his left hand. With his right hand, he reached out and pulled the hood from the person's head.

Mr. Williams was shocked and devastated!

It was not the old man. It was a demon wearing sunglasses.

Looking at Williams, in a low-sounding voice that seemed to come deep from within his body he said, "Are you Mr. Hurts?"

Hurts stepped forward and said, "I'm Hurts."

"I have a message for you," he replied.

"What?" Hurts asked.

The demon removed the girl wrapped in the blanket from his shoulder. Holding her limp body with his hands under her armpits, he extended his arms out to Hurts, giving him the girl, and saying, "Checkmate."

Mr. Williams severed the demon's head from his body.

Mr. Williams and Hurts looked at the face of the girl. It was Eve.

Hurts asked one of Mr. Williams' soldiers to take her.

Mr. Williams was in a daze, confused.

"Is that little girl alright, Williams?" Hurts asked.

"What?" Mr. Williams responded, not really hearing Hurts. "Oh, she's still under Satan's spell. I don't know—" He stopped speaking. Then he exploded with fiery anger. "I-I don't know anything! … I don't understand! Where's Satan?! … He had the girl, Eve, the Chosen One. Here's the church—the altar of stone! … Where is he?! … I don't understand! I don't!"

No one could give him an answer.

Hurts looked about the church. Then his gaze landed on one of those gold stands with the rows of tall frost-white glass containers with lit candles in them. The flame of the candle burning could be seen in each of them. White smoke rose from each of them, and the fragrance of wax and wick burning, a bit pungent, but at the same time, pleasant to the nose— and Hurts remembered!

Hurts was in the fifth-grade. It was lunchtime, and Hurts was sitting at a table with four other boys, eating lunch. Hurts took a box of matches from his shirt pocket. He removed a match from the box and struck the head of the wooden match against the rough side of the box. The match lit. Then he felt a hand on his shoulder. He turned and looked up. It was a teacher. Hurts knew he was in trouble. The teacher was a young man who fancied himself to be a scientist. Instead of reprimanding Hurts, the young man bent over, leaned into the table, blew the match out, and said, "Hmm. Smell it, James. Phosphorus. Sulfur." He snatched the box of matches from Hurts' other hand, turned, and walked away.

Shaking his head and giving a sardonic grunt, Hurt said, "Williams, Williams, Williams … You were right. Satan has played us like a fiddle since day one. This girl, Eve," he said, pointing to Eve in the arms of that soldier, "was never the Chosen One. The Chosen One has always been Phosphorus. The name, Williams—the name: Phosphorus. Sulfur! His unholy fragrance—and it was never about this church, or any other church for that matter. It was all about his origins, and his 'origins' had to do with where this all began—when he had first possessed the body and mind of that old man as a child. Alexian Brothers Hospital … The exorcism that took place there. That's why he sent that meteor to destroy the hospital—to give birth, or rebirth, to his church. And that stone altar? … Well, it's a-a large rock, or a boulder, or a chunk of slab from the destroyed building … And a stone altar of pure—what? A stone altar of pure GOLD! That's why he nicked the leprechauns' gold! To make a stone altar of pure gold … He's played us, Williams," Hurts continued. "He's played us. This here was all a trick. That's why he recruited twelve more demons … No, not here. The remaining demons, Satan, and Phosphorus are all at where this all began—Alexian Brothers Hospital."

Mr. Williams looked down at the wristwatch on his right arm—his expensive silver-plated Rolex wristwatch. It was eleven seconds until the thirteenth stroke of the thirteenth hour.

In the throes of utter despair, with his head bowed, too ashamed to even look someone in the eye, Mr. Williams said, "I have failed, Jim. I have failed."

"No, you haven't!" Hurts screamed at him viciously. "That's why you hired me!" Nodding his head and grinning from ear to ear, Hurts said, "I have a plan … Can you see to it that Eve is safe?"

Mr. Williams motioned for the soldier who was holding Eve to come to him. The soldier did. Mr. Williams said something to him, and he left the church carrying Eve in his arms.

"Okay," Mr. Williams said to Hurts.

"Listen to me, all of you," Hurts stated. "Draw your swords and be prepared to fight again. Now, this is very important. Repeat after me: Blah-blah-blah … Come on, say it! Blah-blah-blah."

They all began saying it.

"That's it … Keep repeating it. Think of nothing else … Keep saying it."

Hurts then looked straight forward, and he shouted three times, fast, "O'Malley! O'Malley! O'Malley!"

The church was full of leprechauns, and O'Malley stood before Hurts, saying, "Aye."

"Do you want your gold back?!" Hurts cried, looking down at him.

"Me gold! Me gold!" O'Malley cheered, jumping up and down.

"Save it, O'Malley," Hurts barked at him. "Can you transport all of us immediately to where Alexian Brothers Hospital once stood?!"

"Aye," he replied.

"Then that's the first of my three wishes. Do it! Now!"

"Granted!" O'Malley shouted—and they all disappeared.

Chapter Thirty-Four

In a flash, they all reappeared. They were still saying: Blah-blah-blah.

They were in the middle of a pit that was one block long and one block wide. The burnt ground was black, rough, and hilly. Rocks, boulders, and remnants of the destroyed building were strewn everywhere. It was hot, and smoke rose from the destroyed ground. The fetid smell of sulfur was almost unbearable to breathe. It was like—being in hell.

They were facing west, and about ten yards away from where they were all standing, stood the eleven remaining demons, all them wearing those full-length black topcoats and sunglasses. They, too, had been facing west. In front of them was a grand-size slab of white stone, which was six-feet-long, six-feet-wide, and six-feet-high. Its height, though, was reduced by being solidly embedded in the ground. Topping it was an inch-thick sheet of melted pure gold, the leprechauns' gold. Upon the top of it, lay the unconscious, or in a trance, naked body of a young girl. Her hair was red and curly, and her face adorned with freckles. It was Phosphorus.

Standing behind the slab of stone, or the altar, looking down upon the girl, was an old man. He, too, was wearing a full-length black topcoat. He was dressed as he had been when Lill had first encountered him at that basketball game: A Herringbone jacket and dark-colored dress pants. The only item different on him was the tie. He was now sporting a red polka dot bowtie, which gave him somewhat of a comical look.

Because they were all still saying blah-blah-blah when they reappeared, and because O'Malley was jumping up and down shouting gleefully, "Me gold! Me gold! HE-Heeeeee! Me gold!" the demons all spun around to see who was making this noise, and the old man, Satan, raised his head and looked in that direction, too.

Satan's eyes fell first upon Hurts—and the look upon Satan's face when saw Hurts standing there with sword and cross in hand was of total, total shock!

Hurts had tricked him! He knew it, and Hurts knew it, and the knowledge of having done that to Satan just tickled Hurts pink.

Hurts smiled and gave a wave with the blade of his sword to Satan.

Satan was infuriated. He stepped to the south-end of the slab of stone. He drew his sword. The demons drew their swords, too. Just as Mr. Williams had shouted "Attack!" back at the church, Satan did the same.

The battle began.

Zoom—Mr. Williams made a beeline to Satan.

As it had been at the church, the battle didn't last long. In fact, it was over in two minutes.

With the help of Mr. Williams' three soldiers, and now with the help of the leprechauns—who jumped on the demons, biting, scratching, and pulling their pants down, and with Lill hitting them over the head with her purse—the victory was theirs from the start.

Hurts was so proud of Amanda. She fought valiantly and skillfully. She crossed blades with one of the demons twice, and then she spun around a full 360-degrees and severed the head of the demon.

Mr. Williams, sadly, was having more difficulty with fighting Satan.

Hurts, Amanda, Tom, Lill, Mr. Williams' three soldiers, and the leprechauns all watched as the battle continued on between Mr. Williams and Satan.

Back and forth they fought; advancing, stepping back; blades crossing and clanging; lunging and parrying. Then, Mr. Williams tripped on a rock. He fell to his knees. He thrust both his arms and hands forward to steady his balance. In his left hand, wrapped in that blue cloth, he held the cross, and in his right hand he held his sword.

Satan took advantage of Mr. Williams' fall. First, he cut off Mr. Williams left hand at the wrist, and then he cut off his right hand.

Mr. Williams, bleeding profusely from his wrists, slowly rose to his feet. Satan stood before him. Satan raised his sword. Mr. Williams knew that he had lost. He stood at attention. He was stoic. He would die with honor. He saw Satan's blade begin its horizontal swing on the left side of his neck. Mr. Williams closed his eyes and prepared himself for death. Then he heard the clang of two swords crossing. He opened his eyes. The blade of Satan's sword was only an inch from the left side of his neck. He turned his head a bit and followed the length of the sword, towards the tip of it. About four inches from the tip of Satan's sword was another sword. Mr. Williams' eyes now followed that sword. The hand that held that sword was Hurts'.

"Step away, Williams," Hurts stated.

Mr. Williams did.

Lowering his sword, Hurts said with a smile, "Now, you dance with Hurts."

Satan laughed, a laugh of derision. "You?!" he stated. "You?! A mere mortal?! Do you actually believe you can defeat me?!"

"Yes," Hurts replied simply.

"How?" he asked.

"O'Malley!" Hurts shouted.

"Aye?" O'Malley replied.

"For my second wish, I want the skill, the agility, and the strength of the finest swordsman on the planet."

"Granted!" O'Malley cried.

Still looking at Satan, Hurts said, "And just for the hell of it, my third wish is to have the intelligence of Einstein."

"Granted!" O'Malley cried again.

Raising his sword, Hurts said, "Shall we?"

Hurts took a fencing position. He turned to his right side. He moved his right leg forward. He squatted at the knees. He raised his left arm behind him. In his left hand he held the cross that Mr. Williams had given him. He bent his left arm at the elbow. Stomping the ground with his right foot, Hurts said, "En Guarde! ... Hey!" he shouted, shocked. "I speak French!"

The battle began.

Advance, parry; step back; advance, parry, advance-lunge, parry, step back; circle-parry—trapping the opponent's sword with a circular motion of your sword—corps-a-corps; their bodies smacked into each other— parry; step back; advance ...

It was a sight to behold!

The battle ensued like that for five full minutes. It was like watching a fight scene from Robin Hood or from, for a more contemporary audience, The *Game of Thrones*.

In the end, Hurts was victorious. Some would say that Hurts, from the very beginning of the fight, was simply toying with Satan. For his last move, Hurts lunged forward, circled Satan's sword three times with his sword, gave a sharp flick of his wrist, and Satan's sword went flying out of his hand.

Hurts stood straight up, brought his sword up to his face, brought the sword down, and then he bowed to Satan. This, of course, was done out of proper protocol of the fight.

Satan was, again, stunned. He could not believe that he, Satan, Prince of Darkness, had been beaten by a mere mortal.

Hurts raised his sword again. Leveling it horizontally, he brought it to the left side of the old man's neck. As Mr. Williams had done, Satan closed his eyes. Hurts moved the blade of the sword far back for maximum swing. He was just about to release his swing when he stopped, saying,

"Oh, by the way, Satan." Satan opened his eyes again and looked at Hurts. "I have a message for you."

"What message?" Satan replied.

"Checkmate. You lose!" Hurts said—and he let the sword fly.

The severed head of the old man hit the ground with a dull, smacking sound. It bounced twice and then rolled away. The headless body of the old man stumbled back, then stood still, and then the body began shaking violently. A red mist began emanating from the neck. As this red mist emerged from the neck, it took human form, except this human form had wings. When this human form had completely emerged from the headless body, the wings spread, and it was gone.

The headless body plummeted backwards to the ground.

The smoke that rose from the ground stopped. The air no longer smelt of sulfur. The air now felt and smelt fresh and inviting. The night sky sparkled with diamonds of stars. Tomorrow would be the beginning of a new month, the beginning of a new day—for all.

"Help me!! … Mom?! Dad?! Where are you?! … Help me! Help …." The cries were heard coming from the stone slab. It was Phosphorus.

With his hands reattached now, Mr. Williams zoomed over to her. He quickly removed his topcoat and covered her naked body with it.

She was sitting up, still crying and screaming uncontrollably.

"… I want to go home! … Who are you?! … Don't hurt—"

Holding her by her arms, Mr. Williams said, "You're safe, child. You're safe. I'm taking you home. You—"

"Can I go now?!" she pleaded. "I want my Mom and—"

"Yes, child," Mr. Williams said. "I'm taking you home. Rest child … Look into my eyes, Phosphorus. Look into my eyes … That's it … Deeper. Deeper … Yes, you're getting sleepy, Phosphorus. So sleepy." Phosphorus began closing her eyes. "That's it, my child. You're getting so sleepy … Sleep. Sleep. Sleep."

Phosphorus closed her eyes. Mr. Williams kissed her on her forehead. Then, gently placing his right hand behind the back of her neck, he lowered her back down onto the slab of stone. The slab of stone, now minus its sheet of pure gold. The gold was gone, and so was O'Malley and the other leprechauns.

Mr. Williams walked back to Hurts.

"Well, Hurts," Mr. Williams said cheerfully. "You saved the day again."

"I get the job done," Hurts replied with a wink.

Lill, looking up into the night sky, said with marvel joy, "Look at all of those stars. Hundreds and hundreds of them. Beautiful."

"Actually, Lill," Hurts began. "There are billions and billions of stars—and stars are actually suns. Suns, as with our sun, with planets revolving around them. Now, light travels at 183-thousand miles per second. So, when one gazes into the—" Hurts stopped speaking. Shocked, he said, "Did that just come out of me?!"

They all began laughing uproariously.

"You idiot," Tom said to Hurts through his laughter. "Your last wish was to have the intelligence of Einstein."

"Oh, well," Hurts replied with a shrug of his shoulders. "Knowledge is good to have."

"Yes, but what about your riches—about being the richest man on earth?" Tom asked.

"Well, I-I used up all of my wishes!" Hurts cried. "Oh, no! No! No, no, no, no! … What have I done?! Noooooooooooooo!" Hurts raised his hands to heaven and screamed, "O'Malley! You-you-you—Damn leprechauns!"

From the night sky, they heard O'Malley's reply. "Me gold! Me gold! … Hee-Heeeeeeeeeeeeeeeee!"

A VERY HAPPY HALLOWEEN

The Author

Author of private investigator mysteries, humorous occult fiction, fantasy adventure fiction, and short stories.

After many years of being a "struggling" actor in LA, Alan turned to writing.

"My writing has always been for entertainment--to put a smile on someone's face who might be having a bad day. I write, mostly, light-horror and murder/mystery. I like these two genres because of the freedom they give me to explore man's inner emotions, feelings and emotions--but it must always have humor! We must always laugh; mostly at ourselves. I have had MS for serval years now; I know physical and mental pain; so I need much laughter to endure it. Hopefully, my novels do just that--give you much laughter."

ACKNOWLEDGMENT

Thank you, Erika M Szabo,
Without your professionalism, her kindness, and her unfailing knowledge
of publishing, formatting, and book-cover design—this novel would not
have been possible.
Thank you, Tricia Drammeh,
For your thorough and professional editing.

Books by the Author

Contents